the LAST TRAIN from PARIS

STACY COHEN

GREENLEAF
BOOK GROUP PRESS

Published by Greenleaf Book Group Press
Austin, TX
www.greenleafbookgroup.com

For ordering information or special discounts for bulk purchases, please contact Greenleaf Book Group LLC at PO Box 91869, Austin, TX 78709, 512.891.6100.

Cover design by Greenleaf Book Group LLC

Publisher's Cataloging-in-Publication Data
(Prepared by The Donohue Group, Inc.)

Cohen, Stacy
    The Last Train from Paris / Stacy Cohen. -- 1st ed.

    p. ; cm.

    ISBN: 978-1-929774-52-4

1. Jewish artists--France--Paris--Fiction. 2. World War, 1939-1945--France--Paris--Fiction. 3. France--History--German occupation, 1940-1945--Fiction. 4. Paris (France)--Social life and customs--20th century--Fiction. 5. Historical fiction. I. Title.

PS3603.O3467 L37 2009
813/.6   2009925201

Part of the Tree Neutral™ program, which offsets the number of trees consumed in the production and printing of this book by taking proactive steps, such as planting trees in direct proportion to the number of trees used: www.treeneutral.com

TreeNeutral

Printed in the United States of America on acid-free paper
12 11 10 09   10 9 8 7 6 5 4 3 2 1
First Edition

To my husband, the love of my life, for being my inspiration

CHAPTER I

J EAN-LUC BEAUCHAMP WATCHED the jeep rumble up rue Blomet and
stop ten meters in front of him. Soldiers in mouse-brown uniforms
scanned the area, trying to look important, while the driver held a brief
conversation with an officer patrolling the street. Jean-Luc pulled his tweed
coat tighter around him and hoped to disappear. He had no choice but to
keep walking. German eyes glossed over him, probably not even noticing
the color of his hair or the painting tucked under his arm, but giving him
just enough attention to make him feel uncomfortable.

The German soldiers had become a familiar sight in Paris, infesting
the streets, their guttural language defiling the air. *Cockroaches*, Jean-Luc
thought as a young *Boche* soldier, barely more than a boy, caught him staring. Quickly turning his eyes to the street, Jean-Luc tucked his chin into
his green scarf and tried not to pick up his pace.

The sputtering resumed and soon faded into the distance.

Jean-Luc unclenched his fists in his pockets. He never would have
believed that a mere six weeks of fighting would end in the surrender of his
beloved Paris, nor would he have believed Paris would still be occupied four
years later. Ration lines were inconvenient, but he understood the need for

them. Curfews were an annoyance he could live with. But Nazis marching down the Champs-Élysées? Flying their flag atop La Tour Eiffel? Dictating the sort of art to be created? They treated Paris—*Paris*—as an inferior territory of the Third Reich. It made his blood boil.

But he was an artist, not a soldier. He couldn't do anything about the Boches running his city. Most of the time, he could ignore all signs of their presence. He couldn't see their flag on La Tour Eiffel from his Montparnasse studio; when he was near the monument, he didn't look up. While soldiers frequented his usual haunts, foreigners had always been drawn to Le Café d'Anton, the Louvre, and the Galerie Pierre; he was used to tuning out their languages and minding his own business.

"Bonjour, Jean-Luc," sang a voice sweet as honey. A pretty young girl wiggled her fingers at him as she walked down rue Blomet toward him, a paper bag on her hip.

"Bonjour, Sophie! Where are you off to?"

"Home. Maman sent me to get rations. The lines are so long, I only just finished." She tilted her head to the side and looked up at Jean-Luc through her thick lashes. "Luckily, it's a lovely morning."

"That's because you stepped into the sun. It won't be nearly as lovely once you go inside. Come to the café with me. I'm meeting Paul."

Sophie shook her head. "I'm sorry, Jean-Luc, I have to get back to Maman. Perhaps some other time."

She placed her fingers on Jean-Luc's arm, stood on tiptoe, kissed each of his cheeks, and walked away with a sway to her hips. Jean-Luc clasped his free hand to his heart and staggered backward.

"I will mourn the loss of such a beautiful morning," he called.

Sophie giggled and turned to wave. "Au revoir, Jean-Luc!"

As Jean-Luc rounded the corner of rue Blomet and rue Petal, Le Café d'Anton came into view. While not as large or posh as some of the others in Montparnasse, Jean-Luc preferred this café above them all. It was a small, busy establishment with cracked plaster walls painted pale gold to make them look as if they were wallpapered in parchment. Jean-Luc had known the owner, Pierre Anton, nearly all of his life. Monsieur Anton hung only local artists' paintings on those walls—which meant his café had once been decorated with treasures by Max Jacob, André Masson, Joan Miró, and other members of the now-scattered Rue Blomet Group—and sold them only to French buyers. Despite having to make thin coffee and limit his chef's use of sugar, Monsieur Anton managed to keep his café distinctly Parisian and his mostly French clientele happy.

It was still far too cold to enjoy a meal outside. The outdoor tables stood empty and unadorned. Through the large front window Jean-Luc could see Paul LeChoix and Christophe Martin sipping their coffees and checking their watches. Jean-Luc checked his own watch.

Nine thirty. Not bad.

Jean-Luc entered the café and was disappointed to see so few paintings. Many of the more distinguished artists had left Paris, so the walls showed only a few works by local amateurs—Michel LeCompte, Hélène Dunat, Jean-Luc Beauchamp, Claude Lévy—and one small Miró, which Monsieur Anton refused to sell. The Germans had goose-stepped all over creativity in Paris, stomping it out until it was as scarce as sugar.

Paul grinned as he saw Jean-Luc approaching. "Only an hour late, Jean-Luc? What did you do? Wrap up your latest conquest in your bedsheets and toss her out the window?"

Jean-Luc laughed as he took off his coat and scarf. "No, I woke up alone this morning. I simply deserved a *grasse matinée*."

Paul raised an eyebrow. "You do realize you sleep in every morning, don't you?"

"I deserve it every day, then."

Christophe placed his coffee cup on the table and leaned back in his chair, a bemused smile upon his lips. "No wonder you never finish a painting."

Jean-Luc smirked and presented the painting under his arm to Paul and Christophe. "Painting takes a little longer than snapping a photograph, my friend."

Christophe took the painting in his hands. He wrinkled his nose, looked from Jean-Luc to the painting, then back to Jean-Luc again. "It seems a little . . . off balance. It has no focus. Has Miró seen it yet?"

Jean-Luc had the good fortune of being Joan Miró's friend and, for half of the year, neighbor. Though he wasn't an official student of the great artist, Jean-Luc had spent countless hours in Miró's studio discussing technique and assisting him with some of his projects.

"No," Jean-Luc answered. "Not yet. I planned on giving it to Monsieur Anton and showing Joan later."

"So how many titles does this one have?" Paul asked.

Jean-Luc forced a laugh. Taking criticism from Miró was one thing—Miró's work had been featured at the Galerie Pierre and he was a recognized and accomplished artist. Paul, on the other hand, was a student who worked part-time as a store clerk and dabbled a little in sculpting. His crack was especially painful for hitting so close to home.

Jean-Luc had a tendency to name his paintings for women—as Paul well knew. When Jean-Luc began this particular piece, he had originally christened it *Mademoiselle Colette*. Not long after, he changed the title to *Mademoiselle Brigitte*, then to *Mademoiselle Odette*, *Mademoiselle Christiane*, and *Mademoiselle Adèle*. He finally settled on *Mademoiselle*.

"At least you finished one." Christophe handed the painting to Paul. "You haven't in a long time."

"I know. Now that I have, though, I'm flooded with ideas. I'm sure I could have another completed in a month or so."

"Were you up all night finishing it?" Paul asked.

"Well," Jean-Luc winked, "first I entertained Mademoiselle Nicole Devereux, but she insisted on going home to her mother before curfew, so I began to paint."

Paul groaned in envy. "Nicole Devereux? Did you see her—"

"So that's the real reason you're so slow," Christophe interrupted with a laugh. "Too many muses, not enough canvas. You need to settle down and choose one."

Jean-Luc laughed and held up his arms in exaggerated protest. "If I can't choose a title for a piece, how am I going to choose one muse?"

"You don't get much prettier than Nicole Devereux," Paul said.

A cocky half-grin spread across Jean-Luc's lips. "But if I choose Nicole Devereux, it would deprive me of receiving any inspiration from Sophie LeChoix."

The joke earned him a playful punch in the arm.

"Stay away from my sister, Beauchamp."

"That reminds me," Jean-Luc said as he rubbed his arm, "are we boxing tomorrow?"

"No. I'm working tomorrow."

"So am I."

"Ugh, the two of you and your jobs. No wonder these café walls are nearly bare."

"We can't all be professional artists. We have to work to live," Christophe said.

"I'm not recognized and I manage, don't I?"

Paul sighed. "You turn on your charm to get everything you need. I don't have that kind of skill."

"And you, Christophe? What's your excuse?" Jean-Luc asked.

"My wife would kill me," Christophe said.

"Yet another reason not to choose one muse."

Christophe laughed. "Well, I don't think anyone else will be able to go boxing either."

"Whatever happened to Claude Lévy?" asked Jean-Luc. "He hasn't been boxing in a while."

Outside a jeep drove slowly by the café. While most of the café patrons did not notice it, Paul, Jean-Luc, and Christophe, who could see clearly through the window, ceased their conversation until the car was out of sight. Paul didn't answer Jean-Luc's question. Instead, he began to mutter into his thin coffee.

"*C'est des conneries,*" he swore. "Parading around our city, pretending they belong here. I ought to join the Resistance and show them a thing or two."

"Calm down, Paul."

"Calm down? When these swine walk our streets and make our laws?"

"Jean-Luc," a hearty voice called out. Never more grateful for a distraction, Jean-Luc turned to see Pierre Anton weaving his way toward them. "You're earlier than usual today."

"Bonjour, Monsieur." Jean-Luc stood up to greet Monsieur Anton, leaving Paul to grumble to his coffee. He snatched up his painting and, with a flourish, presented it to the café owner. "I've brought you a gift."

Taking the flawed painting in his hands, Monsieur Anton's face broke into a wide smile. "Ah! Jean-Luc, it is a masterpiece. Thank you." He leaned toward Jean-Luc and lowered his voice. "I take it that this is my form of payment for today and all of last week?"

"Why, Monsieur, you are too kind. What a generous offer."

Paul rolled his eyes, but Monsieur Anton laughed and gave Jean-Luc an affectionate pat on the shoulder. "I suppose I could always make you wash dishes for me. Croque-madame and café au lait coming up." Painting in hand, Monsieur Anton walked away, calling for his wife. "Celeste! Where is the hammer?"

Paul shook his head. "Another free meal. I need your luck."

Jean-Luc tossed his auburn waves out of his eyes. "No, you simply need to present Monsieur Anton with a masterpiece."

"You know your paintings are only displayed here because Monsieur Anton has known you since you were small," Paul said.

"And he thinks everything is a masterpiece. He is a kind man, but he wouldn't know art if it danced on his head," Christophe added.

"And he knows that those paintings are probably the only form of payment he will ever get from you," Paul finished, sending a ripple of laughter through the table and out to others nearby. Jean-Luc chuckled along with them.

Christophe rose from his seat and placed a few francs on the table.

"Where are you going?" Jean-Luc asked.

"Home. Dominique expected me ten minutes ago."

"Already?"

"You were an hour late." Christophe placed his hat on his head and nodded to Paul and Jean-Luc. "I'll let you know about boxing next week."

"Au revoir, Christophe."

Christophe made his way out of the café just as Monsieur Anton returned with the croque-madame. The café owner pointed at the far wall by the kitchen door, where Jean-Luc's painting had been placed, and set off to take care of some customers walking in the front door. Jean-Luc sipped his café au lait, noting that barely any steamed milk colored the watery coffee. Rations, curfews, and the irregular operation of the métro were the most inconvenient parts of the war.

At least this café is not overrun by Germans. The thought had barely formed in his mind when Jean-Luc heard Monsieur Anton speak in a forced cheerful tone.

"Good morning, Messieurs."

A rough accent scratched at the air. Jean-Luc looked over at Paul, who was scowling once again and muttering under his breath.

"Boches! Go back to the whores who bore you!"

"Shut it, Paul," whispered Jean-Luc.

Paul continued to grumble insults as five Nazi soldiers stalked around the café, rejecting every table they passed. Their crisp uniforms clashed horribly with the parchment-like walls, and their erect military posture destroyed the comfortable, casual atmosphere. People sat up straighter, laughter ceased, and any conversations that had not halted were carried on in lower volumes. The soldiers had transformed Le Café d'Anton into a place in which Jean-Luc would rather not be. Each heavy footfall made his teeth clench, but he sat in silence, munching on his meager meal.

The tallest among them—and clearly the highest-ranking—led the way past table after table until he paused and took a step back to examine Jean-Luc's painting.

"What is this monstrosity?" he boomed in heavily accented French. He pulled Jean-Luc's painting off the wall, tilted it from side to side, and brutally mocked it in German, sending a ripple of laughter among his fellow officers.

"Did the owner let his dog play with paint and canvas?" he asked in French.

He pulled a knife from his belt and held it over the canvas. Jean-Luc let out a moan. The soldier's head snapped in his direction. He locked eyes with Jean-Luc and began slashing the painting to shreds. Each shriek of torn canvas cut through Jean-Luc as if he, himself, were being mauled.

The work he had been so proud of, despite its faults, was mangled beyond repair. If that weren't insult enough, the soldier threw the remains to the ground and, with a few stomps of his heavy boot, smashed the stretcher frame to splinters.

Deafening silence fell upon the café. Change jingled in Paul's pockets as he shifted uncomfortably in his seat. The entire café could hear him mutter, "Good thing we have the Germans here to show us how French art should look. Fashion and art are certainly not our forte."

The Nazi's grin vanished. Hands behind his back and flanked by the other four soldiers, he slowly made his way toward the table. He stopped behind Paul's chair and barked an order. "Up!"

Paul froze. Eyes wide, he stared up at the figure towering over him.

"Oberst Lorenz gave you an order." One of the other soldiers gripped Paul's dark hair. "He said, 'Up!'"

He jerked Paul to his feet and twisted him around to face the Oberst, while another officer helped restrain Paul's arms. Horrified dark eyes met icy blue as Lorenz gripped Paul's chin and examined his face.

"Death thanks you for your gift, *Schweinehund*."

Paul struggled to defend himself, but the two soldiers held him firmly. Lorenz's left fist pushed into Paul's gut. As Paul doubled over, the Oberst's right fist thrust upward, making contact with Paul's jaw. Blood dribbled down the corner of Paul's mouth, and he spat out a tooth. Two tables away, Madame Jaudon and her sister rose from their seats and left the café. Slowly and quietly, others followed their lead.

Lorenz lifted Paul's head by his hair and slapped his cheeks playfully.

"Your manners need improving, French pig."

Lorenz delivered punch after punch to Paul's face and body. Helpless, Paul twisted in the soldiers' arms, struggling to break free, but he only succeeded in exposing himself to more devastating blows.

Jean-Luc tensed and took a deep breath. He wanted to leap to his feet, but his body felt too heavy. He couldn't move. *There's nothing I can do*, he thought. *Sometimes it's best not to intervene.*

Paul cried out each time a fist made contact. Blood streamed from his nose, mouth, and forehead, and both his eyes had swollen shut. Lorenz laughed as the other soldiers joined in, hitting Paul with their rifle butts.

Jean-Luc looked from Paul, to the table, to Paul, and then back to the table. He and Paul had known each other for almost ten years. Paul had been with him when his father had died. Paul had helped him move into his studio on rue Blomet. They had drunk together to toast the start of nine new years. It was Paul he had wept with when the German army marched into Paris, Paul he had complained to, Paul he had joked with moments before . . .

Do something, he told himself. *Don't just sit here.*

Jean-Luc winced as he heard a bone crack. He lifted his cup to his lips and drank. The café au lait burned his tongue and the back of his throat as he gulped it down.

They may leave him alive. They'd definitely kill us both if I jumped in. My God, will they ever stop?

He wanted desperately to leave but could not do so without asking the Germans to step aside so he could get by. Paul had stopped crying out. From the corner of his eye, Jean-Luc could see that he had stopped struggling as well.

Coward! Help him!

The two soldiers threw Paul to the ground and joined in, kicking him and beating him with their rifles until Oberst Lorenz held up his hand. Jean-Luc choked down the rest of his croque-madame.

They would have beaten us both—killed us both . . . but at least I would have done something.

Lorenz barked out an order in German. Two of the officers pulled Paul's limp figure from the floor and dragged him out of the café.

I would've died in the process. There's nothing I could have done.

"We require your table."

It took Jean-Luc a moment to realize that Lorenz was speaking to him. He looked up, hypnotized by the cold blue eyes.

"Do I have to repeat myself?" Lorenz asked, cracking his knuckles.

Jean-Luc stood up and put on his coat and scarf. Nodding to the Germans, he gathered up the remains of his *Mademoiselle* and made his way toward the exit, trying not to step on the bloody smears on the floor.

CHAPTER 2

J EAN-LUC LEFT THE CAFÉ in a daze. He looked around, trying to regain his bearings. In the distance on his right, he thought he saw the Nazis dragging Paul's limp form. He chose to go left.

"Where are you off to, Jean-Luc?" came a calm voice. The Catalan accent pulled Jean-Luc from his trance, and he turned to see Joan Miró walking toward the café's entrance. "I was on my way to remind you that you have an appointment with me in twenty minutes. I had a feeling you would be here."

Jean-Luc didn't answer. He looked down at his mangled painting. Miró frowned and took a step closer.

"What happened?"

Jean-Luc looked over at the café window. The three German officers could be seen through the glass, laughing as they gestured, reenacting Paul's beating.

"They . . . Paul . . . he said something to them—"

Miró closed his eyes and nodded. "I see. Follow me, Jean-Luc."

Jean-Luc was barely aware of the ground beneath his feet as he followed his mentor back to rue Blomet and into their apartment building.

"Was that a painting of yours?" Miró pointed to the fragments in Jean-Luc's arms.

Jean-Luc nodded. "He destroyed it . . . then he beat Paul."

"We'll see what we can piece together. In the meantime, tell me about your painting, Jean-Luc. What was your intention? What were you trying to convey?"

Jean-Luc shuffled into the apartment building behind Miró, but he did not answer. He never wanted to think about his *Mademoiselle* again. He wasn't even sure why he had collected its remains—habit, he supposed. A habit of seeing what could be reused.

Hands stuffed in his pockets and chin tucked into his scarf, he looked down at his feet. He had failed as a friend, failed as a Frenchman, and failed as an artist, all in one swoop.

Miró placed a hand on Jean-Luc's shoulder. "I understand you are grieving, but there is nothing you could have done. Come," he said as he climbed the steps to the second floor. "Work will at least distract you."

Jean-Luc lingered at the bottom of the staircase and leaned on the banister. He was worthless, useless—a coward who had bowed to a German when his friend was in need.

"Do you wish to discuss your art, or not?"

"Do you think he's dead?"

Miró paused just before he reached the landing but did not turn around. "If he's not, he will be before long."

"I did nothing. I just sat there and—"

"And there was nothing you could have done." Miró turned. "Any move on your part would have resulted in your own death. Dwelling on it is pointless."

"I should have died at his side."

"And what would that have accomplished? Believe me, Jean-Luc, when I was a young man, there were many times I did not act when I felt I should have. We must all put aside our personal struggles when it is time to work. You are an artist. Your job is to paint. Do you wish to improve?"

Jean-Luc nodded.

"Then come."

Jean-Luc followed Miró up the stairs to Miró's studio.

Furnished with only a sofa, a stool, and an easel, the apartment was, as usual, immaculate. Not a speck of dust soiled the room; even the myriad of art supplies, paint, and finished projects was arranged in a neat and orderly fashion. Near one of the windows, the easel displayed a work-in-progress, but all materials were neatly placed on the small table next to it. Every paintbrush was clean and placed bristles-up in an empty tin can on the table, alongside a palette, specifically arranged tubes of paint, and a phonograph. A homemade brazier made from a large flowerpot sat near the second window, with some heavy paint-stained rags folded neatly next to it.

An aluminum tub filled with soapy water was tucked into a corner next to a white porcelain sink. Above the tub, several clothespins were clipped to a thin rope strung from the adjacent walls.

Miró took his coat off, sat down on the sofa, and gestured to Jean-Luc to do the same. Jean-Luc slumped down next to him. Resting his elbows on his knees, he buried his face in his hands and sobbed.

Paul was dead—or as good as dead. How would Jean-Luc ever break the news to Paul's mother? To Sophie? How could he look any of them in the face knowing that he'd sat sipping café au lait while Paul was helplessly beaten by the Boches?

"Jean-Luc," Miró began, "you can't blame yourself for this."

"I'm a coward. I should have done something."

"Done what? They would have killed you—and maybe even a few other innocents who just happened to be sitting near you."

Jean-Luc gripped his long auburn hair. "At least I would have made the effort. Paul would have."

"You forget that Paul never joined the Resistance, no matter how much he talked about it. It was too dangerous for him. If the roles had been reversed, he would have done the same thing. Men are heroes only when their efforts accomplish something."

Jean-Luc took a deep breath, letting the distinct smells of soap, paint, and turpentine course through him. When he exhaled, guilt eased its grip on his heart. With each breath, his tension ebbed.

Miró was right. He would not have done Paul any favors by stepping in. It would only have made the situation worse for everyone in the café—including Monsieur Anton. He couldn't blame himself for what the Germans had done. They were the enemy. They were the ones to blame.

"Joan?"

"Hm?"

"Thank you."

Miró granted him a slight smile. "You're welcome. Now, let's try to piece together your painting."

The two of them placed the torn canvas and broken framing on Miró's floor and pieced together the fragments as best they could. When they were finished, only a triangular section in the upper right-hand corner was unaccounted for.

Miró carefully assumed his usual examining posture: chin lifted, head cocked slightly back and to the right. He dropped his left shoulder and pursed his lips, making the wrinkles on his forehead and between his eyes more prominent. Jean-Luc waited in silence for his response.

Nearly five minutes went by. Contempt and praise usually came quickly to Miró, unless a piece really drew him in. It was criticism that had to be carefully weighed, selected, and worded. If he began his analysis by pointing out flaws, chances were he was nitpicking. If he began with a compliment—as he usually did with Jean-Luc's paintings—unless he found absolutely nothing wrong, a long stream of criticism would follow.

"This is the one you started just before Christmas?" Miró flicked his eyes toward Jean-Luc.

Jean-Luc nodded and sat down on the edge of the couch. Would it be a compliment, or a correction?

"It's an improvement over your last one. It looks like you selected the background first before you began to paint this time, but the painting still lacks identity. It seems like the work of several different artists, none of them Jean-Luc. Over here it looks like a Matisse, down here it looks as if Max Jacob and I were fighting for the canvas. You can't rehash. You need to express yourself, not me or Max Jacob or anyone else."

Jean-Luc leaned over Miró's shoulder. Miró carefully tore the piece apart, somehow managing to leave Jean-Luc humbled but not crushed.

"This has a few holes. It doesn't look balanced, see? Something is missing here."

"If I had extended this curve, would that have been better?"

"Hmm . . . that might have thrown off the proportions over on the left. Another object altogether would have been best."

"What about the colors?"

"I like your choice of warm colors in the center, then the blend outward to cooler tones—at least, I like it over here. Everywhere else, it seems too bright. Was that your intention, or was it serendipity?"

"A bit of both."

"How so?"

"I noticed the warmer colors fading to cooler ones in one section and liked it, so I tried to change the rest of the painting."

"The result?"

"It looked awkward everywhere else, but I still liked the effect where it was originally."

"Try to apply colors like notes that shape music. Repetition is fine when it works for the piece, but sometimes, it is better to change the key or the rhythm. Always select your colors carefully. One note can change the feel of a symphony, so one color can completely alter the meaning of your art."

Miró went to the sink and began to wash his hands thoroughly. Once he was finished, Jean-Luc followed suit. No one, not even Miró himself, was permitted to touch even a paintbrush in Miró's studio before going through this ritual, even if he had washed only moments before. After both had scrubbed their hands clean, Miró made his way over to the easel and carefully removed his unfinished painting. Unlike Jean-Luc, who preferred stretched canvas, Miró liked to experiment with other mediums.

"It still amazes me that you work only on paper," Jean-Luc said.

"I don't. It's just been awhile since I've worked on anything else. Paper is light. It's easier to travel with." Miró grabbed another sheet of paper and placed it on the easel. "It's not washed or prepared, but this is just an experiment. I want you to start one for me. Choose your colors."

"Now?"

"What better time?"

Jean-Luc looked down at his attire and examined his fingernails. "Could we maybe do this tomorrow? I'll get paint all over my clothes and hands."

"So go change your clothes. I'll wait."

"It would still be on my hands, though."

Miró raised an eyebrow. "Wash them in turpentine."

"I'd smell of turpentine all night."

Miró sat down on his stool and waited.

Jean-Luc looked at his fingernails. "I was hoping to finish what I started with Nicole—"

"Ah. I see. More pressing matters." Miró removed the large sheet of paper from the easel and replaced it with his own painting.

"Joan, I—"

"No need." Miró held up his hand. "Only you can decide what is most important to you."

"Love is important," Jean-Luc protested.

"Love," Miró intoned, "is the most important thing of all."

"Then why do you sound so disappointed? If love is—"

"Love is, yes. Not lovemaking. As I said, only you can decide which is more important to you."

Jean-Luc could not meet Miró's eyes. He stared at the pristine floor, feeling like a failure all over again. He knew how callous his words had sounded and he was ashamed, but after Paul's death, everything seemed so fleeting. Life seemed even shorter than before, and he longed to feel the warmth and comfort of a woman's arms. Nicole, he knew, was the type who would hold him and stroke his hair, as if her slim frame could protect him from all the woes of the world. Under Miró's gaze, however, Jean-Luc no longer felt longing; he felt embarrassment. He did not love Nicole. Miró was right.

"Here," Miró said after a few minutes of silence. He handed Jean-Luc a few sheets of the large paper. "Help me prepare these, then. Wash them and hang them. When they're damp, scrape them, and then let them dry thoroughly."

Truth be told, Jean-Luc was not eager to work elbow-deep in soapy water and end up smelling like dirty laundry. He realized, however, that Miró's patience was wearing thin. While Miró selected music to play on the phonograph, Jean-Luc rolled up his sleeves. Nicole Devereux would have to wait for some other time.

Miró sat at his easel, selecting brushstrokes and colors to the sound of Mozart. Jean-Luc watched his every move. Once each sheet of paper was clothespinned to the rope above the tub, Jean-Luc approached his mentor.

"The colors seem too dark," he observed.

"Gouache always dries a little lighter."

"I've never worked with gouache. Only oils."

"Perhaps you should try something else."

"You think that will help give my work more meaning?"

"A painting arises from brushstrokes as a poem arises from words. The meaning comes later. It's identity that you have to give. Others may inspire you, but you can't try to mimeograph their work."

Miró continued the lecture while Jean-Luc waited for the paper to be dry enough to scrape. Before long, Miró had cleared a space on the table for a fresh sheet of paper and Jean-Luc was experimenting with colors. He was still reluctant to get his hands dirty, so Miró did most of the mixing. Once the paper Jean-Luc had washed was ready, he set to scraping it. Miró went back to his own painting, lost in the music that flowed from the phonograph.

"By the way," Miró said, "Henri Matisse is in town."

"Matisse?"

Miró nodded. "I ran into him yesterday. He's obtained permission to come to Paris so he can paint the backdrop for a ballet. But he's recovering from surgery and is in so much pain that it took him much longer than expected to prime the canvas."

"Will he be able to finish the backdrop?"

"He will, but he needs an assistant. I told him you were the man for the job."

Jean-Luc scraped the paper absentmindedly as he considered Miró's news. To meet Matisse and learn from him was one thing; a steady, time-consuming job was another. Painting or not, it would hinder his ability to drop everything if inspiration hit him.

"It's not a permanent position, but it's something. Besides, it's an excellent opportunity to study under someone else," Miró continued. "You start tonight. I told Matisse you'd be there by four."

"Where?"

"L'Académie Nationale de Musique—Théâtre de l'Opéra."

Jean-Luc nodded. The opera house was one of most beautiful structures in Paris—a work of art in itself, conveniently located near the Louvre. If he decided to skip work at the last minute, at least the trip would not be a complete waste.

"Would you—"

"Yes, I will lend you some money for the métro. Just be sure you leave early enough, in case the trains aren't running."

Hours floated by. Surrounded by Miró's work, Jean-Luc drifted in a dream that included neither the Germans nor Paul. He allowed himself to laugh and joke as he scraped paper, experimented with colors, and discussed art theory with his mentor.

Before long, Jean-Luc's stomach made a slow, gurgling demand, but he knew better than to interrupt a painting lesson with Miró for food, of all things. Cooking and eating would make a mess. Miró could not work unless his studio was impeccably clean.

Without warning, the door swung open. A short, stout woman in a blue dress appeared in the doorway, carrying little bundles of twigs tied with thin string.

"I have a gift for you, *mon enfant*."

Miró turned his head toward the door with a bemused smile. Paulette Cordier, the landlady, insisted on calling all of her tenants her "children," including Miró. Though she was only four years his senior, she pampered him with all the rest, picking up his rations for him, mending his clothes, scolding him if he didn't eat right. Miró was much like her eldest son, who was expected to be an example to the rest of the children.

No one, however, held her favor quite like her youngest "son."

"Bonjour, Madame." Madame Cordier looked left and spotted Jean-Luc standing by the tub, sleeves rolled up to his elbows, scraping paper. She beamed at him.

"Starting a new painting?" she asked as she made her way over to the brazier.

Coal was so carefully rationed that the winters were nearly unbearable. Try as she might, Madame Cordier could scavenge only so much coal to heat her rooms. Her children, like most other tenants in Paris, had taken to building braziers with pipes that filtered the smoke out the windows. They would burn anything—leaves, twigs, any scrap of wood they could find. Madame Cordier would go out to the parks every morning after getting rations to gather whatever she could find for her enfants, determined to be a proper landlady and a good "mother."

"No, this is for Joan."

Putting a bundle of twigs down next to the brazier, she clucked her tongue. "Joan! Making the poor boy slave for you."

"Without pay, either," Miró answered.

"Or lunch," Jean-Luc added.

Madame Cordier dropped the three other bundles in her arms and crossed her arms under her massive bosom. She gave Miró a reproachful glance and said, "Clean up those paintbrushes right now, Monsieur Miró. I will not have you starving my poor boy to death."

Miró laughed. "Oui, Madame."

"But Madame," Jean-Luc pretended to whine. "I was enjoying my art lesson."

Madame Cordier held up her finger against his protests, "No, Jean-Luc. You will help Monsieur Miró clean up, then go to your own room."

"Oui, Madame."

Madame Cordier bent to gather up her bundles of twigs. Jean-Luc was instantly at her side, piling them in her arms.

"Yours is already in your room, dearest."

"Merci, Madame. Are you sure I can't help you deliver them?"

She stood on tiptoe and kissed both of Jean-Luc's cheeks. "You're a good boy, Jean-Luc. But I can manage. Help clean up, and then I'll bring some lunch to your room. Joan, have you eaten anything?"

"Not yet, but I will. I promise."

"Good man." Madame Cordier kissed Miró's cheeks, kissed Jean-Luc again, and left the room.

Miró stood up from his easel. After stretching out his back, he gathered his paintbrushes for cleaning. "Leave the paper clothespinned. I'll finish it later."

"I can finish it later," Jean-Luc offered. "I can come by after lunch and—"

"You will be working later, remember?"

"Oh, yes. Of course."

Miró began cleaning his paintbrushes, then lifted his head. "*Maladita!*" he swore. "I forgot to give Madame the rent money."

Jean-Luc laughed, "She won't mind if it's a little late."

"I like to give it to her on time. I'm already two days late."

"Well, she hasn't been around much lately. Besides, you know she'll stop by later to make sure you've eaten."

CHAPTER 3

JEAN-LUC'S STUDIO MADE a stark contrast to Miró's. The rooms were nearly identical in size, though Jean-Luc's seemed infinitely smaller. Like Miró, Jean-Luc had an easel set up near one window and a brazier near the other, but the rest of the room was entirely different. A table, similar to the one in Miró's room, stood against the wall next to the easel's window, but a chair was pushed up against it and its contents were anything but neatly arranged. Multicolored paint splotches dotted the floor, trailing from the easel to the table and back again, staining the floorboards and some rumpled clothes that had fallen nearby.

On either side of the pathway the floor was covered with clothing, dirty dishes, rags, old tubes of paint, and discarded, unfinished projects. Madame Cordier had cleared a little area in front of the brazier for her gift of twigs. The dishes that had been there were now in the sink, which was splattered with red, yellow, blue, and green.

The cleanest thing in the room, a full-length mirror, stood in the corner near an unmade bed fit for two. Sitting on that bed, naked and slightly annoyed, was Jean-Luc, his chiseled muscles reflecting in the glass.

His hands were covered in paint. A line of green showed under his fingernails. Washing in turpentine would be no use—not when he had to go to work and paint again. He preferred paint under his fingernails to going to meet the great Matisse smelling like that.

At least his clothes were clean. He had stripped them off and examined them carefully as soon as he stepped into his own room. Of course, Miró's studio floor now had a spot that Miró wasn't happy about, but it would clean up, and Madame Cordier would not be angry. If Jean-Luc had let the paint spill onto his lap, it would have ruined his trousers.

The question remained as to what he would wear to the Théâtre de l'Opéra. First impressions were important. Ruining perfectly good clothes, however, was sacrilege. With the Germans around, it wasn't as if he could get new clothes, even if he had the money to buy them. True, he would be painting, but he liked his appearance to be perfect, particularly when meeting someone of great importance or beauty. The opera house would undoubtedly have both, since the ballerinas were sure to be rehearsing.

After rummaging through his closet and sifting through the clothes strewn across the bed, scattered over the floor, and draped over the mirror and the easel, he finally found the pair of trousers he was looking for, wadded up in a ball under a chair. Brown, a little tattered, and splattered with blue paint on the left leg, they wouldn't be ruined by a little extra paint.

For a moment, he debated putting them on at all. Work. He loathed the word. He wasn't sure which was the worse offense: work that took time away from painting, or turning painting into work. Painting should be creativity. It should come on a whim. It shouldn't be forced.

Then again, he wouldn't be working for just anyone. He would be working for the great Matisse! To know Miró was an honor; to work with and learn from yet another great artist was a rare opportunity.

But how could he go to work for Matisse, today of all days? Paul was dead. Jean-Luc would never again joke with him about courting his sister, never toast the start of another new year with him, never visit the Louvre with him again.

I will be too distracted, Jean-Luc thought. *My heart will not be in my work at all. How can I make such a terrible first impression?*

Jean-Luc felt a stinging behind his nose and eyes as the lump in his throat threatened to form tears. He could not go to Matisse like this. No, he wasn't going to paint for work. It wasn't right. It wouldn't help his art, either. He would visit the Louvre instead. A visit to the Louvre would provide sufficient distraction, honor Paul's memory, and inspire him for his next work.

He pulled on the trousers and looked down at the splatters. The blue paint seemed to stand out more against the faded brown of the material now that he was wearing the pants. He decided they would have to do, and just as he was buttoning them up, the door opened. Madame Cordier walked in with a steaming bowl of soup and a chunk of bread on an engraved silver tray— the one treasure she refused to sell for more coal.

Shaking her head and clucking her tongue, she looked about the room. "A mess, as usual," she scolded. "Hold this, dear." She handed Jean-Luc the silver tray while she cleared paint-encrusted brushes, clothes, some dirty dishes, and an empty wine bottle off the small table opposite the bed.

Jean-Luc glanced down at the silver tray and read, for the thousandth time, the words engraved in curly script at the top center:

Paulette Jardin
et
François Cordier
le 12 juin
mille neuf-cent dix

Hidden beneath the soup bowl were two doves in flight, carrying a ribbon they had formed into a heart.

The tray had been a wedding gift from Madame Cordier's parents. Monsieur Cordier had always loved the tray, so his wife had served every meal on it, setting the plates, bowls, and glasses around the inscription so he would always be able to see their names and their wedding date.

When Monsieur Cordier went off to fight in the Great War, Madame Cordier took over running the apartment building. Determined to make her husband proud, she set herself to the task with a firm yet gentle hand. When he came home on leave, he was shaken, shell-shocked, and distant.

Sometimes he refused to get out of bed, so she would bring him meals on that very tray. He said it always calmed him to see their names written together, reminded of the happiest day of his life. It seemed to be the only thing that would make him smile.

On their five-year anniversary, Monsieur Cordier was killed in action. Madame Cordier had been so distraught at the news that she lost her footing and tumbled down a flight of stairs. Three months pregnant, she had suffered a mild concussion, a broken arm, and a miscarriage. All that she had left of her husband were the apartment building and the tray. She refused to give up either one and poured all of her efforts into her tenants, thinking of them as the children she and Monsieur Cordier should have had.

The first time she had told Jean-Luc the story was the night the German army marched into Paris. Jean-Luc had returned home to find her throwing anything within arm's reach against her wall, sobbing with rage. No one in Paris hated the Germans more than Madame Cordier.

"Much better," Madame Cordier said once a place was cleared on the table. "Go on. Sit down and eat."

Jean-Luc carried the tray over to the table and sat down. The soup was thin, but it was nice and hot. While he ate, she walked around his room, picking up dirty clothes here and there, clucking about one thing or another.

"Tsk, tsk, Jean-Luc. Such a messy boy. What would you do without your Madame to take care of you?"

She gathered all of his clothes and began sorting them into piles, muttering to herself all the while.

"Dirty . . . dirty . . . needs mending . . . painting clothes . . . Jean-Luc, what is this?"

Jean-Luc turned with a mouthful of bread and saw Madame Cordier holding up a pair of women's undergarments, one eyebrow raised. Jean-Luc swallowed. He stared at her for a moment. The corners of her mouth twitched.

She laughed. "Oh, who can blame you? You are a handsome boy—as handsome as my François was. Your eyes are just the same shade—green like sea glass. Oh, but he wasn't nearly so tall, and he . . . he was b-blonde."

Madame Cordier paused and dabbed her eyes on one of Jean-Luc's dirty shirts. She finished separating his laundry and went to the sink to wash his dishes.

"Jean-Luc?" she said after a moment. Her voice was timid. "I heard about Paul. Are you all right?"

Jean-Luc lowered his eyes. "I should have helped him."

Madame Cordier dried her hands, abandoned the dishes for a moment, and wrapped her arms around him. She kissed the top of his head.

"No, no, my sweet Jean-Luc. No one could have done anything. Don't blame yourself."

Somehow, those words meant more coming from Madame Cordier than from Miró. She cradled him for a moment longer and then went back to cleaning the dishes.

"Do you . . . that is, have you sold a painting recently?"

"This morning I brought a finished one to the café, but some Boche destroyed it. Just before he destroyed Paul."

"I . . . well, I only ask because . . . because the rent . . . it was due two days ago."

"Oh, yes. Joan has it for you. He feels terrible that it's late, but he hasn't seen you in a few days."

"Oh, I know. Not a problem, but—"

"I told him you wouldn't be angry, but that's Joan for you."

"Jean-Luc, what about you?"

"Oh, Madame, my painting was destroyed today. I was counting on the money from it. Couldn't you overlook the rent this month?"

"I would, my pet, but . . . well . . . it's just . . . I do need the money."

"You can have my tobacco rations. Would that help? You know I don't smoke, so you could trade them for—Madame?"

Elbow-deep in dishwater, Madame Cordier was sobbing. Jean-Luc dropped the last bit of bread into the soup and rushed to her side.

"Madame? What's wrong?"

"Oh, Jean-Luc," she wailed. "I don't want to pressure you, but the economy isn't what it used to be. The ration coupons aren't enough. You know

I wouldn't ask for it if I didn't truly need it—I know you're studying very hard to be a great painter, but I don't know what to do. I could lose this building or worse—be forced to let it out to the Germans. The thought of those monsters living in my house, sleeping in my rooms! Any one of them may have killed my François."

A Boche, sleeping in his studio? The very thought made Jean-Luc sick. But nothing, absolutely nothing, broke Jean-Luc's heart more than seeing Madame Cordier cry. In the nine years that he had been her tenant, she had cared for him like her own son, cheered him when he was down, and encouraged him to continue with his painting. She had even introduced him to Miró.

Anyone or anything that made Madame cry deserved to die slowly and painfully. Try as he might to remind himself that the Germans were the ultimate cause of Madame Cordier's pain, he could not ignore the fact that his inability to pay the rent was the immediate reason for her tears.

His nose tingled. A lump of self-hatred rose in his throat. He was hurting Madame.

"Madame," he croaked, "don't cry. Please don't cry."

Madame Cordier wiped her eyes on her sleeve and took several deep breaths.

"Shh. I'll make things right, Madame. I promise."

"Your tobacco rations are not enough. I can't ask you to give up more."

"Joan has set me up with a job. I start tonight. I don't know if I'll be paid each night or at the end of the week, but I will have the money for you soon."

"A job? You will work a job?"

Jean-Luc nodded.

"Washing dishes at the café?"

"No. Joan has talked to Matisse. I will be his assistant temporarily."

Madame Cordier cracked a teary smile. She dried her soapy hands on a towel and patted Jean-Luc's cheek. "Such a good boy. You make me so proud. What time do you start?"

"Four."

"Well then, you'd best finish up your lunch and get a shirt on." She walked over to her separated laundry piles and pulled out a white shirt with a dash of paint on the collar. "Here. Wear this one. You'll look clean and presentable for a first impression, but because of the stain on the collar, you won't have to be afraid of getting it dirtier." She tossed the shirt to Jean-Luc.

"Merci, Madame."

She watched him put the shirt on. "Such a handsome boy. If you had a steady job, I'd marry you off to my niece in Avignon."

"Would she ever live in Paris?"

"No, I'm afraid she prefers the south."

"Then it could never be. What would I do without my Madame?"

Madame Cordier laughed.

"Besides," Jean-Luc continued, "I'm sure she's far too good for me."

"Don't be silly. You're a good boy. Now, eat. I won't have you going to work hungry."

"Oui, Madame."

CHAPTER 4

DRESSED, FED, WITH FINGERNAILS as clean as they were going to get without turpentine, Jean-Luc pulled on his coat and scarf and headed out the door into the late afternoon light. Frosty air slapped his cheek. He stuffed his hands into his pockets and tucked his chin into his scarf. It would be another cold night.

Smoke was already trailing out of kitchen windows, staining the front of the buildings with soot from the burning leaves, twigs, and, quite possibly, broken-up pieces of furniture. He would have to light a fire in his own brazier that night, and he knew it would take seemingly forever to heat up the room.

He hoped the métro was running. Otherwise he'd never make it to the opera house by four. Miró had warned him to leave early, but he'd wanted to make sure he was presentable and had lost track of time. He had changed his clothes three more times before taking Madame Cordier's advice on the shirt and switching to another pair of trousers that wasn't so obviously stained—just a little on the bottom.

Jean-Luc turned down rue Copreaux with a heavy heart. He was not looking forward to using his creative energy working for someone else, even if it was Matisse. He shuddered at the thought—or perhaps it was the chill. With every step, the temperature seemed to drop. He turned left onto rue de Vaugirard with his elbows tucked to his side, trying to pull in as much warmth as he could.

The Volontaires station came into view, and Jean-Luc cursed the power shortages. The station had been closed for some time, and he would have to walk further down to get to Pasteur station.

Cars bearing German officers drove by. Soldiers patrolled the streets, and red, white, and black swastika flags of the Third Reich hung from windows. Jean-Luc stared resolutely at his feet. He didn't want to look at any of it.

He continued down rue de Vaugirard, past the Pasteur Institute. As he reached Boulevard Pasteur, he slowed his pace to admire the cast-iron Art Nouveau of the Pasteur station.

Elegant curves arched up above the entrance, framing a sign with "Métropolitain" written in fancy black letters. From either side of the arch, two posts curled up into budded lamps. Modern, yet aesthetics were never removed from the list of priorities. This was Paris.

Jean-Luc descended the stairs to the station and made his way to the ticket booth to ask if the underground was in operation.

"Oui, Monsieur. The train should be here in five minutes. One ticket?"

Jean-Luc nodded and paid for his ticket with the money Miró had lent him.

"Merci. The last train is scheduled at nine."

Through the turnstile, Jean-Luc found a small crowd on the platform of the cylindrical station, waiting in the dim, yellowish light. Two elderly men sat on a bench below a mosaic spelling out "Pasteur" in white block letters amid a rectangle of blue tile. They argued over an upcoming football match, betting on the outcome. Over to the left, three middle-aged women in feathered hats were swapping sugar-substitution tips. Not far from them, a young mother stood with one little girl on her hip, another attached to her hand, and a little boy standing less than a meter away from her. She scolded the boy for staring at the soldiers pacing up and down either side of the tracks. Caught, the boy turned to stare at a young couple kissing, made a face, and then stared at Jean-Luc. Jean-Luc smiled and waved to him. The boy stuck out his tongue and turned away.

Jean-Luc turned to find someone else staring at him: a pretty girl around twenty, standing with her grandmother. Jean-Luc caught her eye and winked. She beamed at him, but her grandmother followed her gaze to Jean-Luc and pulled the girl to the far end of the platform.

Ten minutes dragged by. Jean-Luc shivered. Even sheltered from the wind, the station was very cold. The occasional gust from the tunnels was enough to send a shiver down anyone's spine.

Fifteen minutes. The tip-swapping women had moved on to coffee. One used dried apples, another chestnuts, while the third insisted that lupine seeds were the best way to go. Jean-Luc winced.

No wonder coffee tastes so horrible these days. I wonder what Madame Cordier uses? Hers isn't too bad.

After twenty minutes had passed, the train pulled up. Jean-Luc would be late, but only by a little. But was it wise to show up late to work on the first day? He could pretend to forget that he was supposed to start that day and show up the next evening, but that would make an awful impression on Matisse as well. Surely the great artist would understand if Jean-Luc was a little late. The métro was irregular at best. Getting anywhere on time was nearly impossible.

Few seats were available, so Jean-Luc grasped a strap in front of the arguing old men. The debate was still going strong, and the bet was now up to five cigarettes. A little further down the car was the young mother. Her son caught sight of Jean-Luc and stuck his tongue out again, but the elder of the two girls saw it this time and tattled on him.

After three stops, the tip-swappers and the kissing couple got off. More people piled in, and the standing room disappeared. By the time the train pulled up to Concord station, Jean-Luc had to shoulder his way through the crowd to exit the car. Hurrying alongside the young mother and her children, he barely made his connecting train on Line 1. Two stops and Jean-Luc arrived exactly where he wanted to be: Palais Royal—Musée du Louvre. He was late after all. Matisse probably wouldn't even accept his help at this point.

Deciding to go to the museum instead, Jean-Luc walked with a lighter step as he ascended the stairs to the street. He was nearly to the top when something small shoved his leg aside. He circled his arms about, trying to keep his balance on the stairs. With one quick twist of his body, he threw his weight forward and managed to emerge from the mouth of the station unscathed.

"François! Come back here! What is the matter with you?" Balancing the baby on her hip, the young mother grabbed her son by the wrist while her smug-looking older daughter looked on. She dragged the boy over to Jean-Luc, apologized, and made her son do the same.

"Not a problem. Just children being children," Jean-Luc said, dusting himself off.

"Yes. This one's quite a handful. Come on, François. *Grand-père* is waiting. I'm sorry again, Monsieur."

"Told you not to run off," the older girl said.

"Shut up, Marie."

"Quiet, both of you! François, behave yourself. And Marie, it's not your place to scold him," the mother snapped. She dragged her children off in the direction of the Louvre. Jean-Luc would have followed, but instead he glanced over toward the Théâtre de l'Opéra.

François. The boy's name was François.

An image of a tearful Madame Cordier burst into Jean-Luc's head. His heart ached. He had promised her he would have the money. While Jean-Luc had broken many promises in his life—mostly to himself and to young women he had seduced—he had never broken one to Madame Cordier. Late or not, he had to go to work.

The opera house was glorious on the outside, bathed in golden evening light. The colonnades, the archways, the friezes, the gilded roof statues—everything about the structure was perfect Neo-Baroque elegance. Nothing, however, compared to the splendor of the inside.

The golden sheen of the opulent marble and onyx staircase made Jean-Luc feel as if he should step lightly, lest he spoil the ambiance. Trying not to breathe too loud, he slowly made his way up the steps, careful not to let his unworthy, paint-stained hands tarnish the marble banister. He glanced down at the Venetian mosaics in the lobby, wishing the staircase had not drawn him away so quickly.

All about him were sculpted, painted, and architectural works of art that had no other place but within the walls of the Paris Opera. He stared up and out, his mouth agape and his eyes wide. Lost in his reverie, Jean-Luc made a series of wrong turns and somehow ended up in the main foyer.

It was enormous, with high archways separated by columns topped with elaborate gilded statues. Heavy red velvet curtains decorated every opening, and chandeliers dripped from the ceiling, casting their candlelight on magnificent paintings covering the ceiling and part of the walls. Jean-Luc frowned silently, cursing the war. The frequent power outages and the shortage of resources had reversed progress. He wondered how much damage the soot from the hundreds of candles would do to the paintings.

Not knowing where he was supposed to go and not in a hurry to find out, Jean-Luc wandered around the Théâtre de l'Opéra for nearly an hour, staring up at the chandeliers and craning his neck to study the paintings and the statuary.

How can anyone concentrate on an opera or ballet, or even bother going into the theatre, with all this unearthly beauty to distract them?

But he was going to help paint something that would be displayed here. Finally, a chance for recognition. He had to find the workshop where he and Matisse would paint the backdrop. He imagined himself with Matisse, standing before an enormous canvas, discussing the color scheme and desired brushstrokes, artist to artist. It was, after all, a great opportunity to work beside such talent. Perhaps Matisse would see something more in his work than Miró had.

The next thing he knew, someone slammed into him with a resounding "Oof!" Something heavy made contact with his right temple. He stumbled but managed to stay on his feet. Once he had fully regained his balance, he turned to see a woman bent over, picking up a toe shoe, rubbing her nose. The other shoe lay two meters to Jean-Luc's left. One glance at the shoes made Jean-Luc absently rub his temple. They were a lot heavier than they looked.

"Are you all right?" he asked, picking up the other shoe. The woman grumbled something that Jean-Luc couldn't understand, then glanced up at him and flushed. She smiled faintly, not meeting his eyes. He handed her the shoe. She glanced up at him again and straightened her posture.

At first, Jean-Luc had a hard time believing that this girl could possibly be a ballerina. She had thick, dark hair, eyebrows to match, and though she was trim and fit, and looked lovely in her polka-dot dress and black coat, her broad upper body and thick calves would have looked awkward in a costume. Her body was better suited for playing football than for dancing. She stood up with the grace of her trade, however, and Jean-Luc cast his doubts aside.

"I'm fine," she answered. Her voice was faintly accented, just enough to mark her as a foreigner—Russian, from the sound of it. "Thank you. I'm sorry. I just—I didn't see you. I was in a hurry and—"

"You speak French beautifully. Did you have a private tutor?"

She flushed again. "No. I've lived here for ten years with my family. When I arrived, I didn't speak a word."

"You have a lovely accent."

"Good thing I learned the language, then." She reached up to tuck a stray strand of her hair behind her ear. Once she was sure that her appearance was acceptable, she extended her hand. "I'm Anya. Anya Maximovna."

"Jean-Luc Beauchamp." Jean-Luc took her hand and brushed it with his lips. "Mademoiselle, would you be so kind as to help me find my way? I'm supposed to assist Henri Matisse in painting the backdrop for the ballet."

"You poor thing," Anya said. "He's the most foul, ill-tempered man I've ever met."

"Would you be able to show me to his workshop? I'm afraid the métro was running late, and so am I."

"Tell me about it," she said. "Now I'm late, too. Just barely, mind you, but the ballet mistress is still going to have my hide."

"You could just tell me where to go if you don't have time," Jean-Luc said.

Anya smiled. Her small but perfectly straight teeth had a slightly gray-ish tinge. She looked up at him with her chocolate eyes and batted her long lashes.

"What sort of person would I be if I didn't help you out?" she said, taking his hand. "Besides, he refused to set up shop anywhere but right on stage. Madame Fournier was furious."

"Who?"

"The ballet mistress," Anya explained. "Follow me, but quickly." She dragged Jean-Luc by the hand and led him down corridors and back stairways.

When they reached the stage entrance, Anya tried to sneak in without being noticed. But as soon as she opened the door, she stood face-to-face with a stern-faced woman in a black dress. One look at this imposing woman told Jean-Luc that this was the feared Madame Fournier.

"You're late. Again."

"The métro was late—"

"And I told all of you to leave early as if the trains would not come at all," the ballet mistress snapped.

"I'm afraid this is all my fault."

The ballet mistress looked at Jean-Luc, noticing him for the first time.

"And who are you?"

"Monsieur Matisse's assistant. I was lost and accidentally bumped into her—sent her flying, really. She was dizzy, so I had her sit for a moment, then I asked her to show me how to get here."

The ballet mistress frowned but dismissed Anya without punishment. Anya gave Jean-Luc a smile and then went off to change. Madame Fournier looked at Jean-Luc.

"As you can see, that madman insists on painting the backdrop on my stage—*during* rehearsal. See if you can talk some sense into him."

"I'll try, Madame."

The ballet mistress had already walked off. Jean-Luc shrugged. At least Anya didn't get into any trouble. She was a sweet girl. And though she was an awkward-looking ballerina, she was still very pretty. He glanced over in the direction that she had scampered and saw, instead, the most beautiful creature he had ever seen.

Graceful, blond, and perfect, she was a porcelain doll in a white costume. Her arms glided through the air as she spun on her delicate toes. The curve of her shoulder, the arch of her back, and the expression painted on her ivory face complemented the elegant surroundings, and not a strand of her sunbeam hair fell loose from the bun it was tied into as she twirled about. She was a work of art worthy of the Théâtre de l'Opéra.

Anya scuttled back into view and joined the beautiful girl. While they stretched, the two girls smiled at each other, chatting in Russian. Drawn by the aura of Anya's friend, Jean-Luc took two steps toward them.

Suddenly he heard a gruff voice shouting, "You! Are you my assistant?" Jean-Luc glanced far backstage, where a large canvas was secured against the wall. An old man with a white beard and round spectacles was making his way down a ladder, one hand clasped to his side.

"Henri Matisse," Jean-Luc breathed.

"About time," Matisse grumbled. He limped over to a cushioned chair that had been brought out just for him and eased himself into it with a wince. "Well, come over here, boy. Don't take all day."

Jean-Luc hurried to the artist's side, ready for words of wisdom, but Matisse squinted at him, looking him over.

"Those clothes are going to get stained with paint. You're going to ruin them."

"They're already stained. See?"

Jean-Luc pointed out the splotches on his collar and on his pants, but Matisse only grumbled, "What a waste." He handed Jean-Luc a pencil. "I finished priming already, and if it's not dry by now, it never will be. Here. I'll dictate what you draw. Every angle, every curve, will be precisely how I want it. Not a line will go anywhere if I don't tell you to put it there, understood? I'll watch your every move until I trust you. Then I can help you out and we can get more done."

"What is the ballet?"

"It doesn't matter," Matisse snapped. "I will tell you what to draw."

"But I'm not a bad artist, Monsieur—"

"So I hear. But Miró tells me your head, your heart, and your loins are elsewhere when you work. You need two of those for great art, and the third comes attached to the rest. Now get up that ladder and begin where I left off."

Jean-Luc leapt to his feet and climbed the ladder with the agility of a cat. Holding his balance, he peeked over his shoulder to see if the pretty ballerina had seen him, but she had her back to him and was concentrating on her own art. To his chagrin, Jean-Luc saw a handful of German officers seated in the audience, watching the rehearsal. Two more looked on from a vantage point offstage. Their very presence set the room off balance.

A sharp pain stung Jean-Luc's ankle, and he nearly toppled off the ladder. He looked down and saw Matisse standing at the base, one hand clutched to his side, the other holding a long, thin paintbrush.

"Stop gawking and start working," he barked.

Grateful that the ballerina hadn't been watching, Jean-Luc turned back to the canvas and penciled exactly what he was instructed to draw over the primed canvas.

Every few minutes, Matisse would criticize the angle he took, where he began a line, or how wide a curve was. When Jean-Luc repositioned the pencil, Matisse complained that he would butcher the backdrop if he didn't keep a steady hand. Jean-Luc was getting frustrated. How could Matisse even see the faint pencil marks from where he stood?

Before the first hour was up, Anya wandered up to him and giggled. "I saw you almost fall."

Jean-Luc laughed. "I seem to be doing that a lot today."

"Are you even getting anything done?" She squinted up at the canvas. "I can't see anything."

"Pencil first, my dear. Then we paint."

"I still can't see anything," Anya said. "But I guess it's better than smelling that awful paint. Must be horrible having to smell that all the time."

"I love the smell of fresh paint," Jean-Luc said.

"Talk, talk, talk!" Matisse shouted, waddling over toward them. "You have wasted enough time. Young lady, please go back to your ballet mistress. Jean-Luc, get back to work."

Anya scampered back toward the main stage, glancing over her shoulder. She reached her fair friend, nudged her, and then jerked her head in Jean-Luc's direction. For a split second, the beautiful creature looked up at him. Jean-Luc's heart leapt. He wondered what her name was.

He leaned against the ladder and watched her dance for a while. She looked so beautiful, so focused. Somewhere, far in the distance, Matisse called his name.

"Jean-Luc! Come down here."

Jean-Luc climbed down the ladder and walked over to Matisse's chair. Matisse held out his hand.

"Give me my pencil. You're useless. Get out!"

That was the last thing he had expected. Sacked? Within the first hour?

"What?"

"You heard me. You are as useful as a hand brake on a canoe."

Crushed, Jean-Luc looked up at the backdrop. The way the light hit the canvas, he could easily see the faint pencil markings. He had made decent progress and couldn't tell the difference between his sketching and Matisse's, except in the place he had been working on while chatting with Anya. For the first time, he felt confident in his work.

"Monsieur, please—"

"You have wasted enough of my time. Good-bye."

"I'm sorry. Please. I'll work harder."

The Germans standing offstage were snickering at them. So were most of the dancers. Jean-Luc felt his face get hot, but he couldn't just leave. What if Miró was right? What if he needed a different teacher to push him to improve his work?

"Work harder? You need to work in the first place."

"I'm so sorry, Monsieur. I—"

"My pencil."

Jean-Luc imagined a Boche sitting on his bed in his studio, while a tearful Madame Cordier picked up the beast's laundry from off the floor. He would have to wash dishes to fulfill his promise.

"I'll concentrate. Please—"

"You'll only concentrate on chatting up the ballerinas."

He imagined someone else's work draping the stage on opening night.

"I need this job. I need—"

"You need the money? I'm sure someone else will give you a job. My pencil, please."

Jean-Luc needed this opportunity. He had to have his work displayed in this grandest of all art galleries. He *had* to.

"I need to become a great painter!"

Matisse studied him for a moment. Jean-Luc had never felt more desperate in his life. He stared into Matisse's face, searching for some compassion.

"You want to become a great painter? Cut out your tongue," Matisse huffed. "Now get back to work."

"Thank you, Monsieur Matisse. Thank you."

Without hesitation, Jean-Luc hurried up the ladder and began to take Matisse's orders on fixing the flaws in his work. Gruff laughter came from the direction of the soldiers standing offstage. The sound haunted Jean-Luc and made his stomach turn, but he would not risk his second chance— especially not for a German.

Besides, it couldn't be. Not here.

He built walls around his concentration, determined to block out any interruptions the same way he blocked out reminders of the Nazi occupation. He couldn't afford to upset Matisse again.

After an uneventful hour, he began to relax. Anya did not approach him again, but Jean-Luc began to steal a few quick glances at her pretty friend whenever he turned to clarify an instruction from Matisse.

Another hour streamed by. Jean-Luc, learning how to interpret Matisse's commands, felt his confidence return. He hadn't been smacked with the paintbrush in nearly ten minutes. He felt at home in front of a canvas. Ideas for his own art were forming in the back of his mind, just out of reach. He could almost touch them—and when he could, he would plant them on canvas and become a recognized artist like Matisse and Miró.

German words spoken by a woman with a French accent broke his concentration. Hearing them from soldiers was irritating enough, but those horrible sounds rolling off a Parisian tongue made the hair on the back of his neck stand on end. Jean-Luc's head snapped over in the direction of the offensive voice; the ballet mistress was carrying on a conversation with a soldier who had left his place offstage to examine the dancers up close. To Jean-Luc's horror, it was none other than the brute from the café—Oberst Lorenz.

Jean-Luc forced his attention back to the canvas, praying that he wasn't recognized.

What was that Boche doing here? What right did a man who ruined art have to walk within the walls of one of the greatest architectural masterpieces in all of Paris? What right did he have to be in Paris at all?

Jean-Luc gritted his teeth. He hated the Germans with every fiber of his being: for destroying his friend, for making a mockery of his city, for making Madame Cordier cry. He would have loved to shove his pencil right up the despicable man's—

Whap!

Matisse had smacked his ankle with a paintbrush again.

"What are you doing? Don't press so hard with the pencil. You only need a faint line. Concentrate!"

"Sorry, Monsieur Matisse."

Jean-Luc took a deep breath and, with a gentler hand, continued to sketch. The ballet mistress had switched back to French and was actually apologizing for her poor German. Another deep breath. At least she was speaking French again. Jean-Luc rebuilt his walls.

Eventually, Matisse told Jean-Luc to climb down the ladder and move it over a bit. While Matisse gave him back-and-forth orders on where, exactly, to place the ladder, Jean-Luc looked around for the porcelain ballerina. He couldn't find her, but Lorenz stood out like an infected wound, weaving in and out of the dancers as they rehearsed, nodding in approval or raising his chin in disdain. Jean-Luc scowled.

Parading about, leering at dancers half his age . . . it's disgusting!

"There—no. Back half a step. There," Matisse said. "Perfect. Now, go up about halfway."

With the ladder in the right place, Jean-Luc tucked the pencil behind his ear and began to climb. Two steps up, he spotted Anya and her friend practicing offstage where the soldiers had stood. He climbed a little slower.

His porcelain ballerina was radiant. A vision in white, her entire body seemed to glow. Every lift of her leg was controlled, was graceful, and parted the air slowly. She never stooped; she bowed. She never stood; she unfolded and blossomed.

Next to this perfection, Anya appeared even more awkward. Any beauty she had was lost in her friend's shadow. Her talent and obvious hard work were no match for the ease of the angel beside her.

Anya looked up at Jean-Luc and beamed. She continued to dance, exaggerating her moves a little more, but she only succeeded in making herself seem more out of place. She looked over at her friend then back up at Jean-Luc. Rather than continuing to mimic the other girl's steps, she began to perform more elaborate moves. She leapt from one toe to the other, grandly throwing her body a meter to her left. She thrust her foot out to the side, keeping her upper body perfectly poised.

Her leap had brought her too close to her friend. In the middle of the blond angel's pirouette, up swung Anya's foot. It made contact with the ballerina's leg, just under the knee. The porcelain girl teetered for a moment, then, with a twist and barely a sound, collapsed on the stage.

Anya spun around with a gasp and dropped to her knees beside her friend.

"Natasha!"

CHAPTER 5

"**N**ATASHA, DARLING, ARE you all right? I had no idea we were
so close."

Natasha curled up into a sitting position, fully intending
to rise to her feet and continue rehearsing. As she tried to push herself to
her feet, a bolt of pain shot through her. With a little trill, she fell to the
floor again, grasping her right ankle.

"You're hurt," Anya cried. "Oh, I didn't mean to! I didn't!" Distraught,
her eyes welled up with tears. She began to ramble in Russian. "I'm so
sorry! It was an accident! I didn't mean to really hurt you. I didn't see you.
I . . . I . . . I didn't know you were that close. Do you need a doctor? Somebody get a doctor! Is it broken?"

"I'm fine," Natasha reassured her in their native language.

"You're injured! Somebody please get a doctor."

"I'm all right."

"No, you're not. Why isn't anyone getting a doctor? Can't they see you're
hurt?"

"They can't understand you," Natasha hissed. "Don't make a fuss."

But it was too late. Voices all around were muttering her name, whispering words like "broken" and "fractured," and transforming "ankle" into "leg" in the same breath.

A shadow fell over her.

Perfect. The ballet mistress.

Natasha lifted her head, ready to take whatever criticism came her way.

It was not the ballet mistress who hovered over her. One of the German officers—an Oberst, Madame Fournier had said at the start of rehearsal—looked down on her, as a cat might look upon a trapped mouse.

"What has happened here?"

He spoke in even tones, his voice loud enough for his companions in the audience to hear every word. Natasha felt cold but refused to show any emotion. Men liked to see fear.

"I fell, Herr Oberst," Natasha answered.

No edge to her voice. No humble apology.

"Fell," he said. "Tell me, little ballerina, are you clumsy? Stupid? Or are you a weak, worthless doll, pretending to be a dancer?"

Anya pleaded with the officer. "Oh, please, Herr Oberst, I accidentally bumped into—"

Oberst Lorenz only raised his voice. "Do you have weak ankles?"

Natasha met his eyes.

"No." Her voice held no aggression, no meekness; she simply answered the question.

"Were you knocked off balance?"

"Yes." No explanations. No apologies. They were a useless waste of time, the ballet mistress said. Corrections were what mattered. Take the criticism and correct the behavior. That was the only way to improve.

"If someone knocks you off balance it is your own fault for not avoiding the situation. You should be aware of your surroundings at all times." He lifted his chin and peered down his nose at Natasha. "I expect better from someone who thinks herself worthy of performing before an audience that may someday include the Führer himself."

Natasha said nothing. The Nazi looked down at her curiously, with something close to amusement forming behind his eyes.

"You are not in France any longer. This is now a territory of the Third Reich. If you're lucky, your great-great-grandchildren will be German. Standards are higher. See that you meet them."

He turned on his heel and walked away, his heavy boots thumping on the stage floor. Natasha tested her ankle by applying pressure to it where she sat.

"Is it broken? Will you be all right?" Anya asked.

It hurt, but it was certainly not broken. Sprained, maybe. Twisted only, she hoped. Opening night was a month away.

"Let me take a look at that for you, Mademoiselle."

Natasha's head snapped up and she found herself face-to-face with the painter's assistant. She had not even heard him approach.

"No, thank you. I'm all right."

"All the same, I think it's best if I have a look."

Natasha glanced back at the painter, who was shaking with rage and glowering at his assistant, who was now lifting her ankle in his hands. Though his touch was gentle, she jerked her leg away.

"He's only trying to help," Anya said in Russian.

"But I have no need of his attentions," Natasha replied. She turned back to the painter's assistant and switched to French. "I'm fine. Thank you, Monsieur."

"Natasha, don't be so cold," Anya said. "He practically leapt off the ladder when you fell. A man so kind and brave at least deserves gratitude."

"Forgive my rudeness, Monsieur." Natasha extended her leg toward the painter's assistant. He smiled at her. She did not smile back.

"Anya Maximovna!" the ballet mistress called. With a tiny shriek, Anya popped up and scurried toward the front of the stage.

The painter's assistant drew Natasha's eyes to his and flashed a smile. "I hope she's not in trouble. That woman is frightening."

"Madame Fournier is strict but fair."

"I'm Jean-Luc."

"Natasha."

He stared at her a long moment, as if waiting for her to say something else. He certainly was a handsome creature, with long auburn waves in his hair, a chiseled jaw, and green eyes. But handsome, Natasha decided, was all that he was. Just a flirt.

"Let's have a look at your ankle then, shall we?"

"Are you a doctor, Monsieur Jean-Luc?"

"No. I am a painter." He executed a flowery bow.

"Then how would you know how to treat injuries?"

"Ah, well, here's the trick," he said. "As a boy I was always running around, getting into trouble—as all boys do—and I paid attention when Papa would test my ankles and wrists for injuries."

"Was he a doctor?"

"No. He was a soldier turned janitor, but he had learned a lot from my mother, who was a nurse in the Great War."

"And my ankle?"

Jean-Luc's eyes twinkled. "Beautiful."

"Its condition, Monsieur."

Jean-Luc's face fell a little.

Good, Natasha thought.

"Well?" Madame Fournier swept up beside them. "Is it broken?"

"No, Madame. Merely twisted. If she stays off it for the rest of the night, she should be dancing by tomorrow."

The lights flickered, then winked out. Groans and sighs of relief came from the ballerinas. Madame Fournier clucked her tongue. The candles and oil lamps reserved for such occasions did not cast enough light for either the dancers or the painters to continue their work.

Madame Fournier clapped her hands. The dancers fell silent.

"We will resume this tomorrow. I want everyone here an hour earlier—that includes you, Anya. Natasha, rest your ankle. If it's not healed by tomorrow, we'll find a replacement for your solo."

She turned and glided away, leaving Natasha on the floor with the painter's assistant. After a moment, Anya skittered up to them and knelt beside her.

"Everything all right?"

"Yes," Jean-Luc answered. "She'll be just fine."

"Well enough to come to the café with us?"

"No," Natasha said. "I can't risk it. I'm going home and heading straight to bed."

"That's too bad," Anya said, a little too sadly. She turned to Jean-Luc and batted her eyelashes at him. "Would you like to join us, Jean-Luc?"

"Thank you, but I want to make sure Natasha gets home safely. Next time?"

Natasha blanched. *Walk her home? No. Absolutely not.*

"Oh." Anya's voice softened. "All right. Next time." She walked away, shoulders slumped.

"Go to the café," Natasha insisted. "I want to rest a little before walking home, anyway."

"Perfect. I have to help Matisse clean up, and I'm sure he'll want to discuss a few things with me."

"I only want to rest for a few minutes—"

"But you also need to change," he pointed out. "Don't worry. I won't be too long."

Natasha was worried. She didn't want him to walk her home. Worry gave way to fear, and fear gave way to panic. He wouldn't be deterred. What if he had something else in mind?

What if he . . . ?

She shuddered at the thought.

"Please, Monsieur Jean-Luc, go to the café. I don't want to keep you from a good time."

Jean-Luc let out a warm, pleasant laugh. He leaned forward but kept a healthy distance between them.

"To tell you the truth, I wouldn't be able to go anywhere tonight. Every centime I earn is for my landlady. The economy isn't what it used to be. I promised her that all my wages from this job would go to her."

He was either a brilliant liar or the most sincere man Natasha had ever met.

"You seem very fond of her."

"She's like a mother to me. She raised me—almost. Practically. That is, she practically raised me."

Natasha raised an eyebrow. Well, he definitely wasn't a brilliant liar.

Jean-Luc laughed. "All right, so I've only known her since she became my landlady, but she is like a mother to me. Nagging, overbearing, and comforting all in the same breath. And I hate to see her cry."

"Why would she?"

"Her husband died in the Great War." He looked around for a moment, to make sure no one was in earshot, and then whispered, "She can't bear the thought of having to let rooms out to Germans. Especially now."

"I see. And you offered to help her out of financial trouble?"

"In a matter of speaking," Jean-Luc said. "I'm a poor artist trying to make my way. Madame Cordier will usually turn the other way when I don't have enough for the rent, but she desperately needs it this time, so here I am."

Natasha's defenses melted. He could have easily lied to her—not that he was a particularly gifted liar, but he had had the opportunity. Instead, he had chosen to tell her the somewhat embarrassing truth.

An honest man . . .

"Still here, are you?" Matisse said. "Thought you might have flitted off with the ballerinas."

Jean-Luc stood up.

"I won't be long."

Before she realized what she was saying, Natasha blurted out, "Take your time. I'll wait."

She watched Jean-Luc as he followed Matisse to the backdrop. Even in the dim candlelight, shadows seemed to move away from him. She smiled, stood, and began to limp toward the dressing room.

Monique, a lagging member of the group going to the café, was hurrying to button her blouse. She called to the other girls to wait. Anya was nowhere in sight.

She always did dress quickly, Natasha thought. *She's probably long gone by now.*

Humming to herself, she undressed, pausing to critique her posture in the mirror. She studied her reflection for a moment and unnecessarily smoothed her pale yellow hair.

His eyes were hypnotic, green, and deep.

She pulled on her skirt and blouse. She wished she had stockings, but material was scarce. She had no money to waste on frivolities. She grabbed her handbag and ruffled through its contents: a few francs, rouge, a compact mirror, keys, and a comb. She debated combing out her hair but decided against it. She would take care of it when she got home. She slipped on her high-heel shoes, winced, and thought better of it.

And his touch—it was so light. His hands had felt like silk wrapped around her ankle.

Shoes in hand, Natasha limped back to the stage, then sat down and waited for Jean-Luc. She began to rotate her ankle to stretch it out, all the while staring in his direction. Matisse was standing halfway up the ladder, nearly kissing the canvas. Jean-Luc stood below him, fidgeting anxiously. He glanced over his shoulder and winked at her, then turned his attention back up to the expert painter. Despite herself, Natasha blushed.

He was definitely a flirt—he probably had plenty of experience in the bedroom, and Natasha had no doubt that he'd broken his fair share of hearts—but something in his eyes told her he had never been intentionally cruel.

She yanked her gaze away from him and leaned over her leg, pretending to concentrate on stretching out her ankle. What was she thinking? She knew nothing about this man. Letting him walk her home? He had such an impressive physique. He could easily overpower her and take whatever he wanted.

And if he finds that what he wants has already been taken, then what will he do?

She looked around the theatre. The German soldiers had left with the rest of the dancers to go to cafés, parties, nightclubs, or bed. Even the ballet mistress had left. Jean-Luc, Matisse, an elderly night janitor, and Natasha were the only ones who remained.

She wished Anya hadn't left so quickly. She could have come up with some excuse. She wished he'd stop stealing glances her way. Then she would be able to slip out without his noticing.

*   *   *

Jean-Luc stole a glance over his shoulder while Matisse climbed the ladder to examine his assistant's pencil markings. She was dressed and ready, waiting for him. He winked at her and for a moment—just a moment—he thought he saw a tinge of pink on her cheeks.

He forced his attention back to Matisse. This was important.

Matisse grunted a few times, but whether with approval, disappointment, or pain from his side, Jean-Luc couldn't tell. He squinted at Jean-Luc's sketching, his nose almost touching the canvas. After a few more grunts, he proceeded to pick apart Jean-Luc's work. He complained of a line here, a slightly off angle there, too much detail here, heavy pencil lines there. When he came to places Jean-Luc had given less than full attention, he let out a stream of vitriol, berating Jean-Luc until his side ached. Winded, he had to take a short break. After a few minutes, he was back on the ladder, nitpicking again.

"Ha!" he burst out. "Oof." He clutched his side again. "I knew you were pressing too hard. I could tell by your posture."

"Monsieur?"

"I'm going blind, son. Miró didn't tell you? No, of course he wouldn't. I asked him not to. I asked him not to tell anyone."

"But . . . the light by your chair! It was perfect. How could you see the—?"

"I'm not blind, yet. And I've always been near-sighted. For a while, I just had to squint. Then my eyes got tired and all I could see was your silhouette. Don't look at me like that, boy. I can see enough of you to box your ears."

"But why would you let me—?"

"Miró said you're a good artist—most of the time—and that's all I need. I just need to make sure you pay attention. Your sketching is fairly good, but keep in mind we don't need the detail in pencil. That's for the paint. We don't have time for detail. It took me far too long to prime this thing."

"Why aren't we working in a workshop?"

"Because we'll need all the time we can get. Unless things pick up, we'll be working until opening morning. If it's already here, it doesn't have to be moved too far." Matisse reached the bottom of the ladder and leaned against it for support. "Besides," he added, "I like to hear the ballet mistress complain."

Jean-Luc grinned. Matisse returned to his chair.

"There are places in your sketching that I could have hired one of those German oafs to draw."

"Perhaps if I knew what I was drawing—"

"It doesn't matter *what* you are drawing. You don't pay attention."

"Pardon me, Messieurs," the old janitor said, "but will you be finished soon?"

"Soon," answered Matisse. He turned back to Jean-Luc. "Come on. Help me straighten up. Then you can go home."

Jean-Luc hesitated. "Umm, Monsieur? I wondered . . . when will I be paid?"

Matisse tapped his chin with the paintbrush he had used to whack Jean-Luc's ankles. After a moment's thought, he reached into his pocket and pulled out a few francs.

"I should make you wait until next week, to make sure you'll be back. However . . ." He glanced over at Natasha then handed the money to Jean-Luc. "I have other insurance."

*   *   *

Though her face was a mask of serenity, Natasha was frantic. What was she still doing here? Her ankle was feeling a little better. She could limp home by herself. It would take a while, but she could do it. Why hadn't she begged Anya to stay? Why hadn't she just said she was going to the café?

Natasha watched Jean-Luc bid Matisse farewell. She swallowed. He was walking her way, beaming at her.

"Shall we?" he prompted.

Natasha nodded, slipped her shoes on, and carefully rose to her feet, keeping her weight on her left leg. She started to take a step when she felt something against the back of her knees. She shrieked and fell backward, only to feel a gentle pressure on the small of her back. Instead of falling, she was rising up, cradled in Jean-Luc's arms.

"Your ankle needs rest."

"This really isn't necessary—"

"It's my pleasure."

"It's too far. I live in the nineteenth arrondissement."

"You're light. I barely notice your weight."

"No, really—"

"I insist," he said. "I wouldn't want you to lose your solo."

Natasha fell silent. She sat stiff in his arms, refusing to put her arms around his neck. Instead, she gripped her handbag and toe shoes in her lap. He held her chest-high with hardly any effort at all. Natasha could not help but notice the way the candlelight danced on his face, or how he smelled of soap and fresh paint. She took a deep breath. Then another. He was looking straight into her eyes.

She pulled her gaze to her lap and began to rearrange her handbag and toe shoes so they sat comfortably. Jean-Luc waited for her to situate herself, then carried her out of the theatre, down the majestic staircase and out onto the chilly streets of central Paris.

"Thank you, Monsieur Jean-Luc," she said, her breath sending translucent streams into the frigid night air.

"Just Jean-Luc will do . . . Natasha."

CHAPTER 6

J EAN-LUC WOULD HAVE TAKEN the long way to the nineteenth arrondissement to prolong the time he spent with Natasha, but she was shaking.
She was stiff in his arms, and he couldn't seem to draw her eyes to his.
She had glanced at him once, for a fraction of a breath. Terror had washed
over her face, and the next instant, she had regained her composure.

"How long have you lived in France?" Jean-Luc asked.

"Ten years."

"Just like Anya. Did you know each other in Russia, or did you meet in
Paris?"

"I came here with Anya's family."

"Your parents are still in Russia?"

"My parents are dead."

Compassion flooded through Jean-Luc's veins. He fought the urge to
pull Natasha close to him and softened his voice.

"I'm so sorry."

At last, she looked at him. She searched his face for a moment and then
looked back at her lap.

"My parents are dead, too," Jean-Luc continued. "My mother died in childbirth, so Papa raised me by himself, with the help of a few neighbors and friends. He worked in the Louvre as a janitor." He let out a bittersweet laugh. "He used to bring me there when I was a boy. After the museum closed, he would pin my drawings to the wall in the supply closet so I could say that my art was hanging in the Louvre."

"And that's when you decided to be a painter?"

"It's an inherited passion. Papa could have worked in a factory for much higher wages, but he wanted to be around art."

"Did he paint, too?"

Jean-Luc laughed again. "Oh, no. He just appreciated it. He said that all types of art needed a good audience—and that was him."

"What about your mother?"

Jean-Luc shrugged. "I don't know too much about her; only what Papa told me. She had a sketchbook, but I've never seen her drawings. When she died, Papa tore them out and burned them in a drunken fit."

"Why would he do that?"

"To try to forget his pain. They fell in love because of art. They had known each other for nearly all their lives, but she had never liked him much until they bumped into each other at the Galerie nationale du Jeu de Paume. They spent the entire day together and were married six weeks later. Neighbors said that he was never the same after my mother died, but I had never known him any other way."

Natasha was still looking up at him.

"How did he die?" she whispered.

"Cancer of the liver."

"I'm so sorry." Natasha turned her eyes back to her lap.

"It's all right. He said he lived a good life."

Jean-Luc had told the tale of his father's death many times, but he still had to blink back tears. He walked on, searching his brain for some way to strike up a lighthearted conversation. It was Natasha who broke the silence.

"Tell me more about your landlady. Did she know your father?"

"No. When he died, I couldn't afford the rent on our apartment, so I sold most of our things and started looking for a place to stay. One day while I was out looking, I saw Joan Miró, Max Jacob, and André Masson coming out of the same building. I stood with my jaw hanging to the ground, unable to speak. A woman followed them out, scolding them for skipping breakfast. Every last one of them went back inside to eat before going about their business."

"Madame Cordier?" she asked. She no longer felt stiff in his arms.

"Of course. When she saw me standing there, she poked my ribs, said that I was too skinny, and pulled me inside to eat with the Rue Blomet Group. After I had stuck my elbow in the butter and knocked over a glass of wine, I finally was able to tell her that I was looking for an apartment. She had a studio available, and I have lived there ever since."

"She sounds very sweet. I'd love to meet—"

Natasha stopped and looked back at her lap. She was starting to stiffen again.

"She takes some getting used to, but she's wonderful."

"Getting used to?"

"The first week I moved in, she walked in on me naked four times. Once I tried to dive over my bed so she wouldn't see. I ended up hitting my head on the wall and knocking myself out. I woke up with a headache, still naked, with Madame Cordier hovering over me. She scolded me for jumping around in the apartment and told me to go outside if I wanted to play sport—and to wear a sweater because it was getting chilly."

Natasha laughed. The sound was like a thousand tiny bells ringing in Jean-Luc's ears. At last she was beginning to relax.

*　*　*

Natasha felt like she was floating. Jean-Luc had not once shifted her weight around in his arms. He kept his hands in appropriate places, and when he looked at her, he sought only her eyes.

She listened to his stories of Madame Cordier, laughing every time the brazen woman barged in at an inappropriate moment.

"I imagine Anya will be something like that one day," Jean-Luc said.

Natasha shook her head. She could definitely see Anya barging in on a naked man without a qualm, but she couldn't picture her gathering chestnuts and twigs in the park for her tenants.

"No," she said. "Not Anya."

"Are you two very close?"

"Sisters in every way except blood. Our mothers had been friends as children, too, so we were raised together. When my father died, my mother and I moved in with Anya's family."

"Were your mothers dancers as well?"

"My mother was. Anya's mother worked in a factory." Natasha's smile faltered. She turned her head away and looked up at the stars. Her vision blurred, but no tears fell. "I suppose I've inherited my passion as well."

Natasha never talked about her mother—ever. *What was she doing? Why was she telling this man anything about her past?*

Jean-Luc was looking at her. From the corner of her eye, she saw him follow her gaze up to the stars. Her arms were around his neck. *When had that happened?*

"When I told Madame Cordier about my father, she told me, 'The ones we love who pass on are up there, in the stars, doing what they love best.' She said to picture my mother and father walking hand and hand in Heaven, looking at art together. If you look hard enough, I'm sure you could see your mother dancing."

And how did he always know what to say? Natasha looked back at Jean-Luc.

"Thank you," she said.

He was so close. Natasha's pulse quickened. He was leaning in.

At the last second, he stretched his neck and kissed her forehead. Natasha closed her eyes and braced herself for his lips to travel down her cheeks to her throat, but Jean-Luc did nothing of the sort. When she opened her eyes, he was still walking in the right direction, smiling at her. She smiled back.

"So tell me, Natasha, what would you do in the stars?"

Natasha blinked. "I suppose—" She paused and looked up at the stars again. Her father, she imagined, would be watching her mother dance— perhaps she would be dancing as well. He used to love watching the two of them dance together . . . but Natasha was no longer the little girl who used to dance to brighten up her father's day. She tried to think of what her current favorite pastime could be, but she could only imagine being lifted again into Jean-Luc's strong arms. She felt her cheeks getting hot again. "I'm not really sure. I will have to think about that. What about you? Looking at art? Painting?"

Jean-Luc chuckled. "I always thought so . . . but right now, I feel like I'm already up there."

Natasha looked away, fighting the smile that threatened to spread across her lips. Was he trying to make her at ease with him so he could take advantage of the situation? But he seemed so genuine . . . and he hadn't tried anything thus far.

Why am I letting him get under my skin?

He was still staring at her. She cleared her throat. "What did Madame Cordier say that her husband is doing in the stars?"

"She says what he liked best requires her, so he'll just have to wait."

Natasha laughed. "So what's he doing in the meantime?"

"Watching over her, giving her strength to take on whatever comes her way."

Natasha thought for a moment and looked back up at the stars. The knot in her stomach unraveled and she leaned her head against his chest. He was so warm.

In the distance, they heard shrieks and laughter echoing.

"Sounds like a pair of lovers," Jean-Luc said.

"We shouldn't interrupt them. Turn left down the next street. It's a much longer walk, but at least we won't embarrass anyone."

Jean-Luc nodded. "Are you warm enough?"

"Yes," Natasha answered, listening to the steady rhythm of his heart. "I'm very comfortable."

*   *   *

Anya's knuckles were white from gripping her handbag and her toe shoes. She walked home with furious, large steps, paying no mind to her posture or how oafish she looked. She had been humiliated when Jean-Luc had brushed her off for Natasha. After she had bragged to Monique and Hélène and Svetlana and all the other dancers that Matisse's handsome assistant was going to come out with *her*, she just couldn't bring herself to go to the café and face their teasing.

She was used to men fawning over Natasha, but Jean-Luc had noticed her first. That had never happened before. Anya had gotten her hopes up. Tears stung her cheeks and she angrily swiped them away. She told herself not to care. She always told herself not to care.

It was freezing. Her hands and face were numb. Her feet were beginning to hurt, too. For the millionth time that night, she wished she had stockings. And thinner calves. And narrower shoulders. And lighter hair.

Anya let her breath float up into the night air. She loved Natasha. She really did. But Natasha had everything—talent, beauty, and the attention of every man who walked by.

When is it my turn? Anya thought, kicking a pebble.

She rounded the street corner and spotted the shadows of three soldiers further down the road. She stopped in her tracks and brushed any excess tears from her eyes. She liked to look her best for men in uniform. She touched up her appearance as best she could, then, careful to take smaller steps, continued toward the soldiers, swaying her hips as she walked. Though they spoke in German, Anya could tell they were drunk.

When she stepped into the moonlight, their eyes moved up and down her body as they joked and nudged each other. She smiled and winked at them, and then continued past, exaggerating the sway in her hips.

Hands grasped her waist, and Anya found herself backpedaling toward the group.

"What's your hurry, Fräulein?" one of them asked.

Anya turned to face the three soldiers. To her delight, all three were young and good-looking. The one who had grabbed her still had his hands on her waist and was stroking the curve of her hip. She tossed her head and batted her eyelashes.

"Oh, just heading home."

"From where?"

He had a lustful gleam in his eye.

"The Théâtre de l'Opéra."

"A long walk," he said, stepping toward her and slipping his hand around to the small of her back. "A long, cold walk."

She tilted her head to one side and puffed out her bosom so it touched the soldier's chest. It was the one thing she had that Natasha didn't.

He pressed his hips up against hers. "Let me keep you warm." His hand slid down and he squeezed her bottom. She shrieked and squirmed away, taking hold of his hand.

"Naughty boy."

He guided her toward him again. "It's another hour until curfew."

"I suppose I could stay awhile—if you keep me entertained."

"Or you could keep us entertained," one of the other soldiers said, lifting the bottom of her dress with his rifle. She slapped her dress down and stepped out of the way.

"I can think of something that will keep us occupied," the soldier who had grabbed her said, pulling her arm around his neck and sliding his hand down her sleeve.

Anya looked up at him with a mischievous glint. "But for an hour? Are you sure?"

He pressed himself against her again, grabbing her bottom with one hand and the back of her neck with the other. He planted a wet, sloppy kiss on her mouth. He tasted like brandy. She gave a muffled grunt and batted his chest a few times. He pressed harder against her, pulling her head into the kiss, not letting her go.

When he pulled away, Anya had to gasp for breath. He laughed. One of the others said something in German. He gave her bottom another squeeze.

"An hour or more."

Anya gave him a shaky smile. She wiggled out of his grasp and straightened her coat. Perhaps it was best if she went home.

"More than an hour? Then I don't have the time, since curfew's in less than that. Maybe some other time. Good night." She turned to walk away, but a hand gripped her wrist and yanked her arm back so hard she thought it would break.

"I'll walk you back, Fräulein. To my room."

"No. No, thank you. I have to get home."

He reached down her coat and fondled her breast with an icy hand. She tried to wriggle out of his grasp, but he gripped her tighter. His hands explored, while his fellows pinched her.

"Stop—don't—no—please," she said. "Stop it!"

He kissed her again. She bit his tongue. He jumped back in surprise and glared at her. He swiped the back of his hand across her face. She cried out and struggled to break free, but the other two soldiers descended on her, forcing her up against the wall of an abandoned bookstore.

Her handbag and toe shoes flew far out of reach. The soldier who had grabbed her gripped her jaw in his hands and rubbed his groin. He slapped her again and then said something in German that she did not understand. Laughing, the other two forced her to the ground. She screamed and kicked, thrashing her body around, trying to hold them off.

In the distance, she heard laughter. Hope rose within her. Someone was coming. She opened her mouth to shout for help, but a hand muffled her cry.

"Shh. There's no need to scream, Fräulein. I haven't begun yet." The soldier who had slapped her took a knife from his boot and held it to her throat. Slowly, he took his hand away from her mouth.

"Please," she whispered between sobs. "No."

The three of them hovered over her. She could smell the brandy on their breath. Their laughter rumbled in her ears, getting louder and louder by the second. They unbuttoned her coat and ripped the top of her dress, grabbing, squeezing. She slammed her eyes shut, silently calling out to the people whose voices she had heard.

Please, hurry.

The soldier unbuckled his belt.

Help me!

He reached up her dress. Hope drained away.

No one was coming. She must have imagined the voices.

Tears streamed down her cheeks. His hands gripped her undergarments.

"Was ist hier denn los?"

CHAPTER 7

"WHAT'S THE MATTER here?"
As he stepped out of his jeep, Oberst Heinrich
Lorenz watched his soldiers scramble to their feet. Hans
Kremmler's belt was unbuckled. All three of them smelled like brandy and
cigarettes.

Lorenz's eyes blazed. Away from their posts, smoking and drinking—
while in uniform! He looked down at the girl on the ground. She had
pulled her coat back around her and was retreating back up against the
wall. It was hard to tell in the dark, but at first glance, she didn't appear to
be Jewish. At least they hadn't stooped to that level of shame.

"Your uniform, Kremmler."

Kremmler nearly dropped his rifle. He attended to his belt and then
stood at attention. Lorenz studied the three of them, searching for a suit-
able punishment.

If alcohol and cigarettes were what they wanted, alcohol and cigarettes
were what they would get. They would drink and smoke until they were
sick, then they would drink and smoke some more. Then they would read
pamphlets on smoking aloud to him. If they vomited once while speaking

the Führer's words, then they would drink and smoke again and again until they got it right.

His boot knocked something aside. A ballerina's toe shoe lay at his feet. He scanned the area. The other was lying next to a handbag a few meters away. He took another look at the girl on the ground. She had curled up into a ball against the wall. She stared at him, terrified, as he walked toward her. He leaned over her. She pushed back against the wall. Placing one finger under her chin, he lifted her face to the light.

No. It was not the fair, delicate ballerina who had surprised him earlier. She did look familiar, though.

Ah, yes. The loud one who knocked over the delicate ballerina.

Lorenz turned to his soldiers. "Kremmler! Muller! Lichtman!" he bellowed. "Report to me first thing tomorrow morning, understood?"

With a final order, the three of them dispersed, heading back to their respective posts and away from Lorenz and the ballerina. Lorenz circled around her and nudged her with the tip of his boot.

"They are gone now. You can get up."

She looked up at him, as if waiting for him to take back his words, then stood. She continued watching him as she gathered up her shoes and her handbag. The top of her dress was torn, showing off the curve of her breast.

"Thank you, Herr Oberst," she said. She looked around, then back at him. Lorenz returned her stare. "They won't come back, will they?" she asked.

"I gave them an order."

She didn't move. She just stared at him, pleading with her eyes.

He decided to give her what she wanted. "You should not walk alone. Allow me to take you."

She smiled and took his arm. He gestured to his jeep.

"I . . . I didn't even hear it pull up," she said.

Lorenz opened the door for her. "You were probably too frightened to notice. Where do you live?" he asked.

"Rue Compans."

Lorenz started up the engine. Anya looked around, as if she was searching for someone she knew. Lorenz drove off. She sat tall in her seat, tilting her chin up. A smug smile spread across her lips. She scooted closer to him.

"I'm Anya."

"Yes. I know," he said. Remembering the ballet mistress's words, he added, "Anya Maximovna. I saw you at your rehearsal today."

"I can't thank you enough for stopping those men." She stroked his arm. "I don't know how to repay you. I can get you tickets to the ballet if you like."

"I already have tickets."

She inched closer.

"I'm sure I can get you better seats."

Lorenz laughed. "There are no better seats than the ones I have."

"Oh. Then I will have to repay you some other way." She stopped stroking his arm. "It's up here on the right."

He pulled the jeep to the side of the road and turned off the engine. Anya looked up at the apartment building, then back at him.

"Well, thank you again, Herr Oberst."

Lorenz studied her for a moment. *Why shouldn't I have a prize tonight?* he thought.

Even if Anya wasn't the fair one, she was pretty enough. He was her hero now. She would give him anything, let him do anything. He just had to be sure that he didn't pollute himself.

His trained eye checked her features for any of the telltale signs. Her nose, her eyelids, her ears, all looked acceptable. She was neither bow-legged, nor did she walk like she was flatfooted. He sniffed the air. No unpleasantly sweet odor; she didn't smell like a Jew.

Satisfied, he got out and opened her door for her. "I was thinking of going to a nightclub. I will wait, if you would like to go in and freshen up."

* * *

Anya tossed her clothes on the floor the instant she entered the apartment. She scrambled to the room she and Natasha shared and rummaged through the closet, looking for something to wear. Not for the first time, she wished that she and Natasha were the same size. Natasha had a lovely red crepe dress that would have been perfect.

She looked over at the bed to see if Natasha was sleeping, but Natasha wasn't there. Anya sniffed and turned her nose up in the air.

"I'm not going out, Anya, I'm just going home and going to bed," Anya mimicked. "Lying little sneak."

She pulled out Natasha's red crepe dress and tried to squeeze into it, but she couldn't pull the zipper up more than halfway. In the end, she had to rummage through the mending pile to dig up her own floral print swing dress. The hem was falling apart. She would have to pin it for tonight.

After washing her face and combing her hair, she dabbed a little of her mother's perfume on her wrists and dashed some rouge on her cheeks— more than her mother would have approved of, but her parents worked nights, and she and Natasha would be out the door and headed to rehearsal before her parents came home. Anya looked at her reflection in the mirror. Something else was missing. She grabbed one of Natasha's hats off the top of the dresser and put it on her head.

Natasha would never know it was gone, Anya thought. Off with Jean-Luc, lying to me, saying she was going to go home. Probably having a grand old time while I was being attacked.

Anya took a deep breath and grabbed her handbag off the bed. If she hadn't been attacked, she wouldn't be heading out to a nightclub at that very moment—with none other than Oberst Lorenz. When Lorenz gave an order, men jumped to follow it. He had power behind his words. Let Natasha have the handsome painter who nearly fell off his ladder and who nearly lost his job on his first day. She would rather have the man who controlled the city.

*   *   *

As Jean-Luc and Natasha rounded the corner to rue Compans, they heard the distinct rumble of a jeep fading into the distance. Natasha tensed.

"What is it?" Jean-Luc asked.

She shook her head. "Nothing. They just make me uneasy."

"Don't worry. They're gone."

"For now. Oh, that's it on the left. See?"

Jean-Luc nodded. "I would walk you up, but I don't want to disturb anyone."

"That's all right. You'll have to hurry home to make curfew anyway."

"Well, I doubt I'll make curfew, but I will hurry. I promise."

He let her down gently in front of the door. She slid to the ground, keeping her hands on his arms while she tested her weight on her ankle. The pain was almost gone.

"Thank you, Jean-Luc."

"It was my pleasure. I wouldn't want you to lose your solo," he said. "By the way, what ballet are you performing?"

"*Le Chevalier et la Demoiselle*," she answered. "Monsieur Matisse didn't tell you?"

"No," he said. "He refused to, actually."

"Then don't tell him I told you."

"Fair enough."

"Well, I suppose I will see you tomorrow, then. Good night."

"Natasha?"

Her heart fluttered in her chest. "Yes?"

"I . . . I would like to show you the Louvre sometime."

She smiled. "I would like that."

"When?"

"Tuesday?"

"Tuesday it is."

Natasha looked up at Jean-Luc. Would he try to kiss her? No one was home. He could still seize her and no one would be around to stop him.

He took a step back. He lifted her hand to his lips and kissed it.

"Good night, Natasha."

He took eight steps backward, waved, and turned around, whistling as he disappeared down the dark street.

Natasha caressed the skin on the back of her hand, feeling a little prick of disappointment. She entered the apartment building and floated up the steps to the Maximovs' two-bedroom apartment.

Barely noticing the disheveled mending pile or the polka-dot dress strewn across the floor of the doorway to the room she and Anya shared, Natasha was drawn to the window. She looked out into the night, searching for Jean-Luc in the shadows. He was already gone, on his way back to Montparnasse and his own bed.

She lit a candle on the bedside table and sat down on the bed, feeling strangely giddy. She felt frightened and safe. The memory of his lips on her hand and her forehead blazed to the surface, sending a thrill down her spine. Smiling, she closed her eyes and hugged her arms as she imagined what those lips would feel like against hers—soft, gentle, but filled with passion. She let out a sigh and opened her eyes. She could still see her breath in front of her, but she felt warm inside.

"Jean-Luc," she whispered.

She went about her nightly routine. Once she was entirely ready for bed, she went over to the dresser, opened the top drawer, and pulled out a set of nested matryoshka dolls with her name painted on the bottom of the outmost doll. She kissed the top of the outer doll's head, replaced it in the drawer, then blew out the candle and crawled under the blankets.

She felt as if her head had just touched the pillow when a thud and a giggle pulled her back from her dreams. She opened her eyes to see Anya leaning against the dresser. Natasha sat up in bed, trying to get a better look at her.

"Anya?" she whispered.

"Oh, good," Anya slurred. "You are awake." She snorted as she tried to stifle a giggle.

Natasha slipped out of bed and lit the candle. Anya's hair was disheveled beneath one of Natasha's hats. The hem of her dress was uneven, and the zipper was at least halfway down. Her bosom was all but hanging out of the top.

"Are you all right? What happened to you?"

Anya let out a loud, shrill laugh. "Shh," she added in a stage whisper, pursing her lips together to keep a straight face. She teetered and then slapped her hand on the dresser to keep her balance. "Shh!"

Natasha rushed over to her to get a better look. Anya reeked of spirits. Her makeup was smeared, but as far as Natasha could see, it was not from crying. Her face was not bruised.

"It's past curfew," Anya said.

"Come on, let's get you to bed. We have an early rehearsal tomorrow."

"It's past curfew," Anya repeated. "I was out dancing." She tapped Natasha's forehead with her finger. "You weren't out dancing."

"Stop that." Natasha pulled Anya's finger away.

"But you weren't."

"No, I was sleeping."

Anya struggled with her zipper. "It's caught," she said.

"Here, let me help you."

"With Jean-Luc?"

"What?"

"Were you sleeping with Jean-Luc?"

"Anya, do you see Jean-Luc anywhere?"

The zipper unstuck, she helped Anya change into a nightgown.

"Did you go to his apartment? Hypocrite. I bet he looks fantastic with his clothes off."

Natasha blushed. Anya had just pulled her from a dream where she might've found that out.

"I wouldn't know. He just walked me home."

"Don't believe you. Doesn't matter. I went dancing. You didn't. And it's after curfew."

"You're lucky you didn't get caught." Careful to avoid the nightstand and the candle, Natasha guided Anya to bed.

Anya giggled again. "That's where you're wrong," she sang. "It's all right that I'm out after curfew. I was with Heinrich."

Natasha stopped. "Heinrich?"

"Yes. Heinrich. He was wonderful."

"A German."

"Not just any German," Anya beamed. "But the Oberst that was at rehearsal today. Natasha, men jump to obey his every command. He can get people to do things with just a turn of his head."

"Fear will do that."

Anya rolled her eyes. "You're just jealous."

"Jealous?"

"Yes. For once, you're jealous of me because I have a powerful man and all you have is a poor painter's assistant."

"Anya, you're drunk. You need to get some sleep."

"Was Jean-Luc good to you tonight? Did he please you, too, or was he selfish?"

Natasha tensed. She did not like talking about this.

"He just walked me home. That's all."

"Then why do you glow whenever I say his name? Jean-Luc . . . Jean-Luc . . . Jean-Luc!"

"Anya, shh. You'll wake the neighbors."

"Admit it," Anya said. "You're jealous because Heinrich took me out to a nightclub, and then back to his room—at the Hotel Meurice, I might add—and you were stuck with a cold walk and a quick roll in a dirty apartment."

Natasha paled. "You went back to his room?"

"Yes. And he's taking me out tomorrow."

"Anya, you can't get this drunk tomorrow. You didn't say anything about—"

"I didn't tell him anything!" Anya said. "You can't be happy for me. All you care about is yourself. Oh, and don't worry, even drunk I would never tell him your precious secret. Believe it or not, we did not talk about you in bed."

She pulled the blankets up to her chin and turned away. Natasha touched her shoulder, but Anya jerked it away.

"Anya?"

No answer.

"Anya, please."

Still no answer. Natasha blew out the candle and slipped back into bed. Hopefully, Anya would come to her senses by morning.

"Good night, Anya."

* * *

The first thing Jean-Luc noticed when he returned to his studio was how warm the room was. The brazier had already been lit and its orange glow gave him just enough light to see a plump figure peering out the other window.

"Madame?"

Madame Cordier turned sharply, clutching her heart.

"Oh, Jean-Luc," she breathed. "I was . . . I was worried. It's past curfew."

"I know, but someone needed my help."

"One of the ballerinas?"

Jean-Luc nodded. "How did you know?"

Madame Cordier laughed. "I know you, pet. So that means you went to work? How did it go?"

Jean-Luc pulled out the money Matisse had given him and handed almost all of it to Madame Cordier.

"I would give you everything, but I need money for a métro ticket tomorrow."

Tears welled up in Madame's eyes. She patted his cheek. "You're such a good boy, Jean-Luc."

"Anything for my Madame. What are you doing up so late?"

Madame Cordier glanced toward the window. "You were late. I was worried."

Jean-Luc frowned at the brazier. Grateful as he was to have a warm room, he hoped she didn't do that every time he was late.

"Don't worry about me. I'll be fine. I usually don't stay out past curfew unless I don't plan on coming home that night."

Madame nodded, but her brow was still creased with worry.

"Madame? What's troubling you?"

"Get some sleep, Jean-Luc. You have another big day tomorrow at work."

Jean-Luc knew better than to argue when Madame Cordier gave an order that involved eating or sleeping.

"Oui, Madame. Good night."

She pulled his head down to her, kissed him between the eyes, and then crossed the room to the door.

"Sweet dreams, Jean-Luc."

CHAPTER 8

THE NEXT FEW DAYS were unreal. Every day, Jean-Luc went into work earlier and earlier. He and Matisse discussed the task at hand for a few minutes, and then Jean-Luc got to work. One or two Germans were always in the audience, watching, but not Lorenz. He must have been busy with something else. Jean-Luc was grateful.

Jean-Luc was impressed with his newfound ability to concentrate, though Matisse quickly learned to get his ankle-slapping paintbrush ready whenever Natasha practiced her solo.

After work, Jean-Luc and Matisse had discussions about art in general, sometimes for an hour or more. However long they went on, Natasha sat at the edge of the stage, waiting for Jean-Luc.

Every evening, Jean-Luc walked her home, secretly hoping that the métro was not running so they would have more time together. She would hold his hand the entire time, and then he would kiss her good night.

He added a kiss every night. First her hand. Then her hand and her forehead. Then her hand, her forehead, and her cheek.

On Monday night, the métro was running. Silently cursing his luck, he began heading toward the entrance when he felt a tug on his hand. Natasha had stopped in her tracks.

"Something wrong?"

She smiled and shook her head. "Why don't we walk?"

Jean-Luc gave a sweeping bow. "As you wish, Mademoiselle."

Though the air was still cold, it was warmer than it had been, with no biting wind. Hand-in-hand they strolled, lost in conversation, finalizing their museum plans for the following morning. To test his limits, Jean-Luc brought her hand to his lips every time he felt the urge to, and Natasha didn't seem to mind.

All too soon they stood in front of the Maximovs' apartment building, bidding one another good night. Jean-Luc kissed Natasha's hand, her forehead, then her cheek, letting his lips hover over her skin for a moment. He kissed her cheek again, closer to the jawline, then pulled away to look at her face. In her eyes was the longing he had hoped for.

Cupping her face in his paint-stained hands, he bent down and kissed her mouth. Slow and sweet, Jean-Luc lingered. When he broke away, she was standing with her lips still parted slightly, her eyes closed, and her chin still tilted upward.

Never before had Jean-Luc's heart pounded so hard. Every ounce of blood in him would explode out of his skin if he didn't reach out to her again, pull her to him, and kiss her in a way that would make time stand still. He had to restrain himself; he didn't want to frighten her.

Natasha licked her lips and opened her eyes. Without hesitation, she reached up and put her arms around his neck.

Jean-Luc descended upon her once again, holding her to him until he felt the familiar jerk of her muscles tightening.

He eased away. "Good night."

"Good night," Natasha breathed.

Jean-Luc pecked her lips, took his usual eight steps backward, and then turned toward Montparnasse to dream of painted lips and the sweet taste of Natasha's kiss.

* * *

As soon as the morning light crept into Jean-Luc's studio, his eyes shot open. He rolled over onto his back and pushed himself up on his elbows. Adrenaline coursed through him so fast, he did not know where to begin.

Tuesday. It was Tuesday at last.

He and Natasha had planned to meet just outside the entrance to the Palais Royal métro station at nine. They would spend the entire day at the Louvre. Then, if she gave her consent, he would take her to meet Madame Cordier and Miró.

Jean-Luc sat up and looked around his room. Clothes and art supplies still covered the tables and floor. Two dirty cups rested in the sink, along with paint-encrusted brushes. A stack of folded shirts lay by the door.

Those weren't there last night, he thought, eyeing the shirts. *Madame must already be out waiting in line.*

Jean-Luc climbed out of bed, then proceeded to wash the cups in the sink. He moved on to straightening his table, picking clothes up off the floor, and making his bed. He wanted his room to be somewhat present-able for Natasha, just in case she consented to meet Miró and Madame.

Once his room was in decent order, he bathed, dressed, and after a quick glance in the mirror, was out the door. He couldn't be late.

His coat unbuttoned and his scarf hanging loose around his neck, Jean-Luc made his way to the Pasteur station. The journey from one stop to the next became longer and longer as it brought Jean-Luc closer to Natasha. He changed lines at Concorde and, in a matter of two stops, was where he needed to be.

He followed the crowd up the steps to the mouth of the station. As he neared the entrance and the cluster of coats and hats dispersed, Natasha's slender figure came into view.

Her golden hair fell in loose waves to her shoulders, and her coat was unbuttoned, revealing a blue dress with a white collar. She was fidgeting with the strap of her handbag again, standing on tiptoe to peer through the flood of people emerging from the mouth of the station. She spotted Jean-Luc only seconds before he swooped down and kissed her.

The pair walked arm-in-arm down rue Rivoli, following the wall of the museum.

"There is so much I want to show you," Jean-Luc said. "Have you ever been to the Louvre?"

Natasha shook her head. "I've mostly concerned myself with dancing."

Jean-Luc leapt in front of her. Walking backward and gesturing wildly, he said, "Never? You've lived in Paris for ten years and you've never been to the Louvre?"

"No."

"You're in for a treat. We can start with Matisse's *Odalisque*. And Monet's *Charing Cross Bridge*. I wish I could show you the *Mona Lisa*, but it has been moved."

"Show me everything," Natasha said, taking his hand.

Jean-Luc laughed. "That, ma chérie, would take months, possibly years." He pulled her over to a small side door and kissed her. "But I am willing if you are."

Natasha smiled and tried to continue walking, but Jean-Luc held her back. He kissed her again. She laughed. "I thought we were going to the Louvre."

"We are," Jean-Luc answered. He reached into his pocket and produced a key. "This is an employee entrance. And this," he wiggled the key between his fingers, "was my father's."

Jean-Luc turned the key, creaked the door open, and led Natasha inside.

"Haven't seen you here in a while, Jean-Luc."

Natasha jumped at the deep voice. A stout man lumbered into view. He had a round face and a bald head, red and creased with wrinkles. Gray straggled through his full brown beard, threatening to take over. His broad shoulders hunched, he carried a mop in one massive paw and a bucket in the other.

"Bonjour, Monsieur LeMiel," Jean-Luc said, leading Natasha in. "Allow me to introduce Natasha Karsavina. Natasha, this is Jacques LeMiel."

"Pleased to meet you."

"Likewise, Mademoiselle."

"Monsieur LeMiel was a good friend of my father's."

"The man cheated at cards," grunted Monsieur LeMiel. He lifted his mop and bucket. "Better get back to work." He excused himself and disappeared inside a broom closet.

"He keeps a few bottles in there," Jean-Luc whispered.

He led Natasha up to the third floor of the Richelieu wing and down toward the room where Matisse's *Odalisque* was kept. Along the way, he pointed out various paintings to Natasha, pausing only for a few seconds before continuing on to their goal.

He gestured toward the *Odalisque* as they entered the room and described Matisse's processes, how he used layers of paint to create a sense of motion. Natasha leaned toward the painting, then back into Jean-Luc's arms.

"Do you like it?"

"She looks . . . familiar. It doesn't look at all like the scenery."

"That's because the scenery is not his own work. There are restrictions, but he has made his mark."

Natasha nodded. "I'm sure you've made your own mark as well."

"Well, to keep everything consistent, I've been trying to emulate Matisse, though he says that's a mistake. He says that if I can't liberate myself from the influence of past generations, then I'm digging my own grave—I shouldn't just paint something in a particular style; I should paint the emotion it produces in me."

Footsteps echoed in the hall just outside the room. German voices scratched Jean-Luc's ears. Natasha tensed in his arms.

"Can't the Boches stay away for just one day?" Jean-Luc could ignore their voices and stay out of their way—pretend they were only foreign tourists—but they made Natasha uncomfortable.

One of them entered the room, slowly making his way around to study the paintings.

"German beasts—rot in Hell," Jean-Luc muttered.

"Jean-Luc, please," Natasha said. "What if they speak French?"

"They wouldn't if they could, disgusting Boches. They don't belong here."

"Please, Jean-Luc." Natasha hugged his arms. "Let's just have a nice time. We'll go to a different museum. The Galerie nationale du Jeu de Paume. Isn't that where your parents met? We'll go there. Please?"

The desperation in her voice brought forth the same shame Jean-Luc had felt when he made Madame Cordier cry. He took a few deep breaths and tucked all thoughts of the Germans into a corner of his mind.

"I'm sorry." He turned her around to face him.

"It's all right. Let's just try to have a nice time. To the Galerie nationale du Jeu de Paume?"

"No," Jean-Luc said. "I'm all right. Germans will be there, too. I'll watch my temper and my language—if Madame Cordier had heard me say any of those things, she'd skin me alive."

Natasha smiled. "All right. We'll stay here."

"But if you like," Jean-Luc said, "we can go to the Galerie nationale du Jeu de Paume next week. I think you would like Degas. He has some marvelous paintings of dancers."

She stood on her toes and kissed him. "Next week, then."

Jean-Luc took her hand and led her out of the room to continue their tour of the Louvre. They passed many Germans along the way, including many officers with French women on their arms. Jean-Luc gritted his teeth.

"I thought there would be more paintings here," Natasha said.

Jean-Luc wrinkled his brow. "There usually are. I suppose . . . well, they must have been moved. Maybe they're finally getting some new art. It's been a while, with the war and all." He shrugged. "That room has the Monet I was telling you about. Come on."

At the doorway, Jean-Luc stopped dead. No paintings remained in the room. Jean-Luc stared at the empty spaces.

It couldn't be.

He spun around. The empty spaces glared back at him. His stomach churned. He remembered the sparse hallways—and the German in the room with Matisse's *Odalisque.*

"Maybe they've all been moved—for safekeeping," Natasha said.

Jean-Luc wanted to believe that the paintings had only been moved. He wanted to think that everything was as it was before, but he had to know.

He led Natasha back down the hallway. Every empty peg called out to him.

They had infiltrated the city. They had set curfews. They had starved and exploited the French people. They made Natasha worry—the Germans were the plague of the world. Were they stealing art as well?

"Do you want to leave?" Natasha asked.

Jean-Luc nodded. "I just have to see something first."

Jean-Luc and Natasha returned to the room where he had begun her tour. Empty pegs jutted out from the wall where the *Odalisque* had once been. Every painting in the room was gone.

Jean-Luc let go of Natasha's hand and gripped his hair, staggering around the room. The art—France's art—was being plundered without so much as an argument.

He turned toward Natasha, who was covering her mouth with both of her hands. Her eyes were wide and her face was chalk white. She whispered something in Russian.

"Wastes of life," Jean-Luc said through his gritted teeth. "Horrible, despicable, German filth!" His voice grew louder. "German pigs!" He ran to the hallway, shouting as loud as he could. "Go back to the whores who gave birth to you! Bastards! Robbers!" Every word he had ever held inside his head echoed in the halls of the Louvre. Tears streamed down his face, and his entire body shook. He couldn't feel Natasha's touch on his arm or hear her voice. His rage had consumed him, and he wanted nothing more than to lash out at those who insulted and mocked his city.

"Jean-Luc!" Natasha placed her hands on his chest. He paused and blinked down at her. She looked up at him with glistening eyes. "Please," she whispered.

Jean-Luc nodded and pulled her to him. "I'm sorry. It's just—I'm so sorry, Natasha. It's just, they've come here and—"

"I know," Natasha said. "I know."

"Let's go," he said, taking her hand and leading her to the stairs. "Let's get away from these German pigs. I'll take you to meet—"

"Halt!"

Jean-Luc's head whipped around to see a German soldier running their way, rifle in hand. Natasha gasped. Jean-Luc turned to see another one charging at them from the other direction.

Pulling Natasha along behind him, Jean-Luc ran down the steps. Heavy boots thundered after them. Commands rang out in French and German, ordering them to stop where they were. Jean-Luc knew better. Paul's beating would seem like a friendly boxing match compared to the punishment for Jean-Luc's tirade.

Natasha shrieked and froze in her tracks. He chanced a look back up the stairs. One of the soldiers was taking aim with his rifle.

Jean-Luc swept Natasha in front of him. "Go! Go!"

Natasha ran. Jean-Luc followed, stealing glances up, bracing himself for the bullet. The other soldier caught up with the first and shouted something in German. He knocked the barrel of the gun aside and gestured around him. Their boots pounded the steps once again.

Natasha reached the second floor and started toward the steps to the ground floor. Jean-Luc seized her wrist and pulled her in the other direction.

"Where are you going? We need to get out of here," Natasha said.

"Trust me."

He rounded the corner and skidded to a halt. Another soldier stood in their path, examining a sculpture. He looked up at Jean-Luc and Natasha. Shouts from the other officers echoed behind them. Before the third soldier could react, Jean-Luc pushed past him and dashed down another staircase to the ground floor.

"This way," Jean-Luc said, leading Natasha off to the right. Greek statuary blurred by as Jean-Luc followed his memories, trying to find a way out. He remembered a lot of the employee passageways, but not all of them would bring him out of the museum. He preferred paintings to sculpture and had spent most of his time on the upper floors. The ground floor, particularly the Denon wing, was the least familiar.

"Here!" He pulled Natasha over to a closed door. He drew his father's key from his pocket and inserted it in the keyhole. Praying that the locks hadn't been changed, he turned the key.

The bolt clicked back and Jean-Luc threw the door open, urging Natasha in first. The Germans appeared just as Natasha entered the doorway. Jean-Luc ducked inside and slammed the door behind him. He fumbled at the lock with shaking hands. When he found it, he snapped the bolt in place, then hurried Natasha along the dimly lit passage. The soldiers banged on the door behind them. Jean-Luc picked up their pace.

They soon came upon a winding staircase, leading only down. Jean-Luc's heart sank. It wasn't an exit, as he had hoped; it was a passage to the basement level. He remembered now—they were headed toward the vaults.

"Where are we going?" Natasha whispered.

"The basement. They'll figure it out soon enough. If we hide down here, we might be able to sneak out once things calm down a bit."

At the end of the passage was another door. Jean-Luc pulled back the dead bolt and peeked outside. No one was in sight. He and Natasha crept out into the open and looked around.

They were in the middle of a wide hallway that stretched down toward a staircase. Several steel vault doors, one of which stood slightly ajar, lined the brick walls.

"We'll hide until things calm down."

"What if they find us?" Natasha clung to his arm.

"I don't think they could find out where that door leads unless Monsieur LeMiel opens it for them. I doubt they'll be able to find him. He has an uncanny ability to avoid the Germans."

"What about somebody else who works here?"

"Don't worry. By the time they locate someone with a key, they'll think we're long gone. If they're stealing art, no one working in the museum will give them an accurate answer." He gestured toward the vault.

She looked up at him.

"I'll give you a tour," he said. "The paintings in there will keep us occupied. There are some that people haven't seen in nearly a century."

He kissed her. She relaxed a little and entered the vault. Jean-Luc followed, easing the door closed behind him. He wanted it to appear to be shut all the way without locking them inside. When Jean-Luc was satisfied, only a sliver of light cut into the darkness. Jean-Luc stepped out of its path and allowed his eyes to adjust.

Natasha stood with her hands over her mouth, her back unnaturally straight.

She turned to him. Jean-Luc clamped his eyes shut for a few seconds. When he opened them, he could see a little more clearly. Her face was full of pity.

He looked around and felt his heart rise to his throat, then drop to his stomach. He returned to the vault door and eased it open a little more, allowing in enough light to see into the far corners of the vault.

It was empty.

No wonder the vault had been open. Every painting, every piece of pottery, every sculpture that had been housed here was gone. Hundreds and thousands of years of history, of priceless creativity—it had been stolen. The Germans were raping Paris for everything she was worth.

A lump rose in Jean-Luc's throat. He spun around, trying to find something, somewhere. With a strangled cry, he dropped to his knees, sobbing on the cold stone floor.

He felt Natasha's hand on the back of his head. She knelt beside him, stroking his hair. He looked up at her. The dim bluish light on her face made her glow like the moon in the darkest of nights. She pursed her lips together and stood up, pulling gently on his arm.

Jean-Luc obeyed. He took a few shaky breaths.

Without art, the Louvre was just an old palace. Paris was just a city.

Everything remaining in the galleries upstairs was now vulnerable, like wounded soldiers in hospital beds. The vault was a graveyard. Only Natasha remained. She was the one work of art left.

Jean-Luc wrapped her in his arms and kissed her with the passion of a lifetime. When she tensed, he loosened his grip but never his intensity. He needed her.

Jean-Luc slipped her coat off her shoulders and moved his mouth down her jawline to kiss her throat. Tilting her head back, she let out a little moan and slid her hands up into his hair.

Caressing and kissing, they explored one another, discarding any clothing that blocked their way. Jean-Luc could hear his own heartbeat drumming in his ears. He loved her. He had never loved anyone like this. It was unfamiliar, but he knew it as sure as he knew his way home.

Pressed in his arms, she stood on tiptoe and whispered his name. Jean-Luc swept her up in his arms and gently placed her down on their discarded coats. He watched her face for the slightest sign of apprehension but found only desire. She eased back and guided him to her.

He moved slowly, drinking in her scent and savoring the taste of her skin. Nothing had ever felt more natural. She was radiant. She was compassionate. She inspired him. He loved her.

She arched her back and let out a long moan, then pulled him closer, her breath heavy in his ear.

"Natasha," Jean-Luc murmured into her neck. "My love . . ."

CHAPTER 9

I‌T TOOK NATASHA and Jean-Luc three tries to get dressed. The first time, Natasha had been pulling her dress over her head when Jean-Luc approached her and helped her take it off again. The second time, she was in her undergarments. The third time, Jean-Luc had only slowed the process by kissing her wrists and neck, running his hands along the curve of her waist.

"Do you think they've given up?" she asked as he pulled his shirt over his head.

Jean-Luc crept over to the narrow opening in the vault door and creaked it open. He poked his head out, looked around, and then turned back to Natasha.

"Hopefully, we won't run into them and find out."

Natasha nodded. "What do we do?" she asked.

"If they are still searching for us, I doubt they are looking in the museum. It's been a while." He grinned.

Natasha's face flushed, and she smiled despite herself.

He reached out his hand. "Come on. We'll sneak out, and then I'll take you to meet Madame Cordier. She should be home by now."

Walking as quickly and quietly as her heels would allow, Natasha allowed Jean-Luc to lead her out of the vault and into the wide hallway. To the right was the door that led back up the passageway. To their left, the hallway stretched down to a winding staircase. Jean-Luc tugged her hand, urging her toward the staircase. She followed him without thought back into the museum, casually strolling through the corridors, pausing to pretend to look at art every time they heard voices. Finally, Jean-Luc brought them back to the employee entrance and out into the open air.

Natasha breathed a sigh of relief. Jean-Luc squeezed her hand. Together, they set off toward Montparnasse.

*   *   *

As Jean-Luc and Natasha walked down rue Blomet, a thickset woman opened the door to an apartment building and smiled at Jean-Luc. "There you are, mon chou," she said, rushing up to kiss his cheeks.

Natasha beamed. Short and stout, the woman fussed about Jean-Luc like an overprotective mother. This had to be Madame Cordier. She was exactly as Natasha had pictured her.

"Madame," Jean-Luc said as he swept Natasha forward, "this is Natasha."

Madame Cordier smiled politely and kissed both of Natasha's cheeks. "Skinny as a nail," she said. "Come inside and I'll fix you something to eat. Jean-Luc, would you tell Monsieur Miró that he will also be joining us for dinner?"

"Of course, Madame." Jean-Luc opened the door to the building, and after allowing Natasha and Madame Cordier to enter, he disappeared up the stairs.

Madame Cordier took both of Natasha's hands and pulled her through a door with the number "1" painted above the peephole, into the tidy living room of a cozy apartment.

Two armchairs stood on either side of a radio, against the left wall. An old trunk, topped with a yellowed lace doily and several framed photographs, served as a coffee table. On the opposite wall stood a hutch, empty save for one silver tray.

"Have a seat, my dear. Would you like some coffee? Artificial, I'm afraid, but what isn't, these days?" Her voice held a touch of bitterness.

Natasha sat down in one of the armchairs and ran her hands over her dress and hair.

"No need to fidget, dear. You look fine."

Natasha froze and blushed. "Thank you."

"I could give you a few tips, if you like."

"Madame?"

Madame Cordier clucked her tongue. "Fashion, ma petite, fashion. Paris may be overrun with Boche filth, but her citizens are still French. For example, you could put paste on your legs to make it look like you are wearing stockings—and have a friend draw a seam up the back so it looks real. Large flaws can be hidden, but details are everything. So. Coffee?"

"Yes, please."

Madame Cordier excused herself to the kitchen, leaving Natasha to look around the living room.

It reminded her of her old home, back in Russia, before her father died. She leaned forward to look at the photographs on the coffee table. There were several group shots of men standing in front of the building, including one with Jean-Luc standing next to an older man, watching him paint. A military photo showed a man with oversize ears, and a very old wedding photo showed a thin, pretty woman with the same gangly man.

The man looked different somehow. She picked up the wedding photo and studied his face. He was awkward, to say the least, but he was smiling so brightly in the photograph that he looked every bit as attractive as Jean-Luc.

"He was very handsome when he smiled," said Madame Cordier. She appeared in the kitchen doorway, carrying the silver tray from the hutch with four cups of coffee. Natasha stood to help her, but Madame Cordier clucked her tongue. "No, dear, I've got it. Would you mind moving my photographs to the hutch? They really belong there. I just like to look at happy times when I sit here."

"You have so many," Natasha said as she moved the photographs so Madame Cordier could place the tray on the coffee table.

Madame Cordier handed her a cup. "I've known a lot of artists. One of them was bound to take photographs."

"Thank you," Natasha said, accepting the coffee cup.

"I'd offer you cream and sugar, but the Boches have it all," Madame Cordier said as she nestled down into the other armchair with a little grunt. "Well, my dear, let me have a look at you."

Natasha put down her cup and looked over at her hostess's kind face. She tried not to pull her eyes away while Madame Cordier studied her, as if she were selecting fruit at a market. "Lovely. So tell me, Natasha, what do you think of my Jean-Luc?"

Natasha blinked.

"He's very sweet and charming," she said. "He—" Her thoughts drifted to his touch, his kiss, and the feeling of his weight upon her as they made love in the vault of the Louvre. Her face grew hot again, and she picked up her coffee cup. "He . . . he makes me smile—forget every sad memory."

Madame Cordier nodded. "Jean-Luc does have that effect on people, doesn't he? He's a good boy with a big heart. Be careful not to break it, now."

Before Natasha could say anything more, a knock came at the door. Madame Cordier stood up.

"That'll be Jean-Luc and Joan now. Answer that for me, will you? I'm going to start making lunch."

"Do you have enough? Rations, I mean. I wouldn't want you to waste them. I can eat at home—"

"Nonsense," Madame Cordier sniffed. "I have some relatives in the country. New laws permit food packages into Paris. Now answer the door while I make lunch."

Natasha opened the door. Sure enough, Jean-Luc stood there with an older version of the painter from Madame Cordier's photograph.

"This must be Natasha," the older man said. "Very nice to meet you." He took her hand and kissed it.

"Natasha, this is Joan Miró, my good friend and an accomplished artist—you would love his work."

"It is not polite to keep ladies waiting, Monsieur Miró," Madame Cordier's voice called from the kitchen.

"My apologies, Madame," Miró said with a bemused smile. "But I don't like to leave a mess when I'm painting."

"I tried to get him to hurry, Madame," Jean-Luc said.

Natasha laughed. "There's coffee on the table for you two."

Jean-Luc and Miró sat down in the armchairs, while Natasha knelt on the floor beside Jean-Luc.

"Any word from your wife, Joan?" Jean-Luc asked.

"Yes. Pilar and my little Maria have asked me to join them in Palma de Mallorca sooner than planned this year."

"But they know you always stay in Paris until May."

"They know, but they also didn't want me to come to Paris this year at all—or last year, or the year before that, for that matter. But my inspiration comes from France, and I want to stay as long as I can so I don't fall into another crisis."

"Your 'crisis' still produced wonderful art, Joan. You even had your own show at the Galerie Pierre. What I wouldn't give for such recognition."

"I prefer my *Constellations* to my savage paintings."

"So what will you do?"

"I'll try to stay until May, but I promised Pilar I would return early if I felt it was too dangerous. Either way, I doubt I'll be back next year."

Jean-Luc put on a little pout. Natasha pressed her lips together to keep from giggling. She wondered if he even knew he had done it.

Miró and Jean-Luc started on the subject of painting mediums. Natasha leaned her head against Jean-Luc's leg and let her mind wander. Looking around Madame Cordier's apartment again, she spied the photographs on the hutch and imagined herself and Jean-Luc in the wedding photo.

She blinked in surprise. She had only met him a few days before. Why was she thinking of such things?

She looked up at Jean-Luc. He was talking to Miró with the same serious set of the jaw he used when he talked to Matisse. She imagined him wrinkled and gray, the mentor instead of the student, offering advice and listening with that same adorably serious look. She allowed herself the fantasy; it could be her own little secret.

It was nice to daydream. She had never before imagined anything in her life beyond securing a prima ballerina role, and that thought had always come along with the pressure of succeeding before her youth ran out. Now she saw a future beyond ballet.

She smiled at the thought of Jean-Luc bouncing a toddler in his lap while she set the table for dinner, her belly round with child. She pictured herself a few years older, sitting against Jean-Luc's knee like this while he talked with other artists. She imagined the two of them sitting in armchairs, listening to the radio and drinking real coffee with cream and sugar after having eaten a hearty dinner unrestricted by rations.

Jean-Luc leaned toward Miró and confessed his outburst in the Louvre. He told Miró about the soldiers chasing them, but to Natasha's relief, left out the vault.

"The Galerie Pierre has also been looted," Miró said. "Along with several private collections. A man I know is missing, and so is his Picasso. I doubt they are in the same place."

"I haven't seen Claude Lévy in a long time. His family had several beautiful paintings—including a Cézanne."

Miró nodded. "Madame Lévy, if I am not mistaken, also bought one of my paintings at the Galerie Pierre."

"I wonder if they've been robbed, too."

Miró took a sip of his coffee. "If you haven't seen your friend in a while, I'm sure that's the least of his concerns. I don't think it's any coincidence that my friend and the Lévys both happen to be Jewish."

"What do you mean?" Jean-Luc asked.

Though Miró answered, Natasha could recite the restrictions in her head. "New laws govern the Jews now. They must wear yellow badges identifying themselves; they are not permitted to change their residence or hold certain jobs, they have an earlier curfew, and they are not permitted on the ration lines until late morning."

"But by that time, isn't everything nearly gone?"

"Exactly."

Jean-Luc stared at Miró for a moment. "Where do you think your friend is?"

"I've heard rumors that political prisoners are all taken to Germany to work."

"That's enough talk about Germany," Madame Cordier said from the doorway to the kitchen, shaking a wooden spoon in their direction. "I hear enough about the Boches all day and night. Come and eat lunch and we'll talk about lighter things."

"Yes, Madame," Miró and Jean-Luc said.

Natasha laughed. She allowed Jean-Luc to help her up and followed him to the kitchen, feeling at home for the first time in twelve years.

CHAPTER 10

A COLD DRAFT PULLED Natasha from a comfortable sleep. She shivered and opened her eyes. Candlelight flickered off the walls. Had she left one burning? But the walls were a different color, the furniture was arranged in an unfamiliar way, and Anya was not snoring—in fact, Anya was not even in the room.

Jerked awake by the realization that she was not at home, Natasha sat upright. Jean-Luc looked up from his easel and smiled. Relief washed over her.

"Hello," he whispered, resting his paintbrush on the ledge of the easel. "Couldn't sleep?"

Natasha shook her head. "No. I was sleeping very well, actually . . . just a little chill."

"Oh." Jean-Luc stood up, gathered a few shirts from the floor, and proceeded to stuff them in the cracks of the windows. "This room is sometimes drafty in the winter." He walked over to the door and grabbed a folded shirt from a pile by the door. "Here." He handed the shirt to Natasha. "This will help keep you warm."

Under the blankets, she was still naked. She did not feel embarrassed in the slightest. She felt relaxed, as if Jean-Luc's bed were the most natural place to be.

"Thank you," she said. He watched her slip the shirt over her head, then leaned over and kissed her. Warmth flooded Natasha, and she pulled him to her, inviting him to return to bed.

Is this me? she thought. *But everything feels so right.*

Jean-Luc needed little coaxing. Natasha gasped when his hands caressed her leg.

"Your hands are like ice," she whispered, giggling.

"Well then, my love, it is your job to thaw them out." He kissed her ear. Natasha whimpered and surrendered to his touch.

They made love again, heat rising with every second. When they finished, both were pleasantly warm and relaxed.

Natasha rested her head against Jean-Luc's chest, letting her fingers brush over the skin and muscles of his stomach. "I think I have an answer for you—to your question about what I would do in the stars."

"Oh?"

"Promise not to laugh?"

"I would never."

"On warm summer nights when there's a nice breeze blowing in through the window, I like to let my hair down and brush it in the wind while I dance. If . . . if I couldn't be with you, then I think that is what I would be doing." She laced her fingers through his. "Silly, I know."

"No," said Jean-Luc, kissing her hand. "Not silly at all."

"What were you painting? I've never seen your work before."

"I wish it was my own work, but it's not. I wanted you to see Monet's use of color in *Charing Cross Bridge*, so I sat down, intending to paint it for you."

"You can paint a replica from memory?"

Jean-Luc nodded. "I've always had a talent for it. That was how I started painting—making copies of the works of art I had memorized when my father worked at the Louvre."

"Did you sell your replicas to tourists before the Germans came?"

"Sometimes, but not very often. I want to be a serious, accomplished painter. I could have probably made a decent living painting replicas, but I preferred to challenge myself. My own work gives me a little trouble, but I truly want to earn a reputation as a real artist."

"I know what you mean," Natasha said. "It's the same with me and dancing."

"How so?"

"A few years back, I had an opportunity to leave France and dance in Denmark. It was better pay, and it was hinted that I would become the prima ballerina assoluta in no time. But I opted to stay in Paris. I told everyone that it was because Anya's family is here, and they are all I have, but truthfully, it was because of the prestige. I'd rather be just another dancer in Paris, trying to make my way to the top."

"Challenging yourself to see if you have what it takes," Jean-Luc said.

Natasha nodded.

Jean-Luc kissed her forehead. "I'm glad you stayed in Paris."

"So am I. May I see the painting?" Natasha slipped out of bed and walked over to the easel. The coloring was not nearly as bright as Jean-Luc had described.

"This doesn't look like the style you described for Monet."

"Oh . . . well, I started to paint the Monet, but instead, I painted Eugène Delacroix's *The Barque of Dante*."

"Why? Are the styles similar?"

Jean-Luc laughed. "Oh, no."

"Why go from Monet to this, then?" Natasha asked. She crawled back into bed and put her feet on Jean-Luc to warm them.

"*The Barque of Dante* is more than one hundred years old. It is a piece of France's history. If the Germans are stealing art they consider to be inferior, they're probably stealing the older, more valuable paintings as well. I'm not sure what I can do, but if I can trick them into taking a replica instead, then the art would be safe. I just . . . I don't know how I would do it. I can't very well switch the paintings. The curator would think I'm trying to steal the real one."

"Perhaps Monsieur LeMiel can help you."

Jean-Luc shook his head. "He takes his work very seriously. I'm not sure if he would consent to such a thing."

"Monsieur Miró always seems to know what to do. Maybe he can figure something out."

Jean-Luc looked at Natasha and smiled. "You inspire me in so many ways. I feel like a better man with you."

Natasha laced her hand with his and kissed each of his fingertips. She closed her eyes and listened to the steady rhythm of Jean-Luc's breathing until she fell asleep, safe and warm in his arms.

CHAPTER 11

"ANYA? ANYA, WAKE UP. We have rehearsal."

Anya pulled the blanket over her head. She felt as if she had just fallen asleep. She couldn't understand why Heinrich didn't let her stay with him at the Hotel Meurice. It wasn't as if anyone checked on—or cared about—what the officers did in the privacy of their rooms.

"Anya, come on. We'll both be late if you don't get up," Natasha said, pulling the blanket from her.

Anya groaned and sat up in bed. She had a funny taste in her mouth but only a slight headache. She looked back at her pillow, sighed, and then stood up. Natasha was already dressed and ready.

"How is it you are so fresh at this hour?" Anya said.

"I went to bed early last night."

Anya rubbed the fogginess out of her eyes. "No, you didn't. You weren't even here when I got home last—oh!" She smirked. "Where were you, little Natasha?"

Natasha blushed and Anya snickered.

"With Jean-Luc, of course," Anya said. "Tell me, does he use a thick paintbrush?"

"Anya!"

"That's a no. How disappointing."

"No!"

"That's a yes!"

Natasha's blush deepened. "I'm not going to discuss that with you. It's private."

"At least tell me about his performance."

Natasha laughed and tossed Anya's clothes at her. "Get dressed. We'll be late."

Anya rolled her eyes. "Yes, Mother."

Anya hounded Natasha for details all morning, not letting up until they entered the dressing room at the Théâtre de l'Opéra. Natasha gave her only the boring version. She went on and on about how sweet Jean-Luc was, how he made her so happy, and how nice his friends and landlady were.

"Madame Cordier really is wonderful. Though it was a little awkward when she woke me up this morning. I was . . . well, I wasn't decent." Natasha opened her locker.

"Did you and Jean-Luc have another go after she left?"

Natasha raised an eyebrow and didn't answer.

"So why did you come home this morning? Why not go straight to rehearsal?" Anya asked.

"Somebody had to make sure you were awake. Besides, I needed my toe shoes. I wasn't planning on spending the night. It just . . . happened. I really have to discipline myself. I haven't practiced at home in a long time."

"How long has this been 'just happening'?"

"This is the first night I've stayed there."

"That doesn't answer my question."

"No," Natasha said. "It doesn't."

Anya stuck out her tongue. "Mule."

"Oh, I meant to tell you," Natasha said, unbuttoning her blouse. "Madame Cordier showed me how to use paste to make it look like you're wearing stockings. After rehearsal, I can show you."

Anya grinned. "Thanks, but I won't need it. Heinrich bought me a new dancing dress and a pair of real stockings. I saw a pearl necklace the other day and hinted to him that I liked it, so I think he may buy it for me, too."

Natasha frowned.

Anya's anger rose again. "Will you stop? Can't you be happy for me, for once?" She pulled off her dress and threw it into her locker.

Natasha gave a horrified shriek. Anya, along with the other girls in the dressing room, jumped.

"What? What's wrong?" Anya snapped.

The other dancers were staring at them, and Svetlana was muttering translations to the French girls.

"What is that on your leg?" Natasha asked.

Anya looked down to her lap. "I don't see anything."

"Right there, on the back of your thigh!"

Anya thought for a moment. "Oh, that." She stuck her bottom out, showing off a fresh bite mark high up on her leg. "If you don't tell me your details, why should I tell you mine?"

Natasha was still frowning. "Has he been beating you?"

Anya rolled her eyes. "Calm down, Natasha. He's not beating me. He's just very aggressive in the bedroom. I like it."

Natasha looked her over.

Looking for a breakdown? Well, you're not going to get one, Anya thought, staring right back. She had never felt so important, so wanted. Heinrich took her to all the exclusive parties, kept her out way past curfew, brought her to expensive cafés for every meal, and had bought her a dress and stockings. Natasha would have to learn sooner or later that Heinrich was not the monster she thought he was.

"I'm sorry. If you're happy, then I'm happy for you," Natasha said.

Giving Natasha a quick hug, Anya said, "He's coming to rehearsal to see me today. I'll introduce you afterward. You'll see that he's different."

Natasha nodded. The other girls were no longer staring. They had finished getting dressed and, one by one, were heading out to the stage.

"Listen, Natasha," Anya said. "I haven't told him anything, and I won't. He wouldn't care anyway."

Natasha nodded again. She looked around the dressing room. "We're the last ones in here. We'd better hurry."

The ballet mistress gave Anya and Natasha disapproving looks for being the last two on stage, but she had nothing to say about it and began rehearsal. Anya's headache was gradually fading. After the first hour of rehearsal, she felt much better, but there was still no sign of Heinrich Lorenz. Heavy with disappointment, her timing was slightly off, which earned a good tongue-lashing from Madame Fournier.

After going over the same scene twelve times—the first nine of which were imperfect, due to Anya's mistakes—Madame Fournier allowed most of the dancers to take a break while Natasha performed her solo.

"Monsieur Matisse," the ballet mistress called, "you will need your paintbrush for your assistant now."

The other ballerinas giggled, but Natasha didn't even flinch. Anya admired that. When Natasha danced, she was completely focused. No outside source could make her blush or laugh.

Or cry, thought Anya.

When they had first come to France from Russia, Natasha would not speak unless it was about dance class or a new ballet. It had taken three years before Anya could convince Natasha to come out from behind the walls she had built for herself. Even after that, Anya had awoken in the middle of the night and found Natasha practicing by the light of a single candle, the same stony look on her face.

Anya shuddered. Natasha built her walls high and thick. She had a lot to block out.

* * *

Anya had been thirteen years old when she first woke up to the sound of someone crying. Quietly as she could, she crept out of her bedroom and made her way toward the kitchen, careful to avoid the floorboards that creaked. Once she was close enough to recognize the voice, she froze. It was Natasha's mother.

"Hush . . . hush . . ." Anya's mother soothed. "What happened?"

Natasha's mother tried to stop sobbing but nearly choked. She moaned something inaudible, but Anya's mother couldn't understand her either.

"Larissa, calm down. Take a deep breath and tell me what happened."

"He—he came—to—to—the ballet," Natasha's mother wailed.

"He?"

"Beria. Lavrenti Beria."

Anya recognized the name. He was a Party secretary—or something like that; someone very important in the government. *Why was Natasha's mother upset? Had she performed badly in front of him?*

"A-after the ballet, his bodyguard approached me," Natasha's mother continued.

Anya's mother let out a little gasp.

"He said that Beria was inviting me for dinner. He's a member of the Party. How could I refuse? I ate dinner with him, and I told him I was married. He seemed pleased to know. Then I felt so tired. My head was so heavy and the next thing I knew, I was—I—I was—he was on top of me and I—I—" Natasha's mother broke down again.

"What am I going to do, Galina? He expects me tomorrow. He said he would kill my family if I didn't go to him."

"Have you told Maxim?" Anya's mother asked.

"No. How can I tell him? He'll be so angry, and he may get himself killed."

"You have to tell him—for Natasha's sake. He can shield her from the truth."

Anya heard a chair scoot back from the table. Sure her mother had heard her, she dashed back to her room.

Every night for the next two weeks, Anya woke to the sound of Natasha's mother sobbing. Natasha's father's voice joined the discussions eventually, as did Anya's father's. There were hushed conversations about leaving Russia—an idea that Anya's father was against.

"If we leave, he'll follow you and kill all of us. We can't put our children in such danger."

So much was said and so little was done that Anya soon learned to ignore the crying and go right back to sleep.

One night, Anya's mother woke her up as she guided Natasha into Anya's bedroom.

"Keep her company. She can't be alone," Anya's mother said. She closed the door and went back to talk with the adults.

Anya looked over at Natasha. Her face was whiter than snow, and though her eyes were wide open, it was as if she saw nothing in front of her. She was shaking from head to toe.

"Natasha?"

No response.

"Natasha?" Anya touched her friend's arm. Still no response.

She guided Natasha to her bed and sat her down. Leaning over her, Anya cupped Natasha's face and tilted her chin up.

"Natasha. Look at me."

Natasha blinked a few times and focused her eyes on Anya.

"What happened?" Anya whispered.

Natasha threw her arms around Anya and cried until her face was hot and red and her breath grew short. She coughed and sputtered and cried some more. Anya stroked her friend's hair and made her mother's soothing noises until Natasha fell asleep. In the morning, Anya's mother told her what had happened.

Beria had seen Natasha and told her mother to bring her to his house. Natasha's mother had refused, so one of Beria's bodyguards had killed Natasha's father—right in front of Natasha. Natasha's mother had come home to a silent daughter standing in a pool of blood, staring down at her father's corpse.

The next evening, Natasha and her mother moved in with Anya's family. For weeks, Natasha's mother dreaded her continued trips to Beria's residence. She often came home covered in bruises, and she hardly ever touched her food. Anya overheard her mother saying to her father that if Natasha's mother didn't start eating again, Beria would tire of her and go after Natasha full force.

Sure enough, two days later, Natasha's mother came home and took Natasha back out with her. They didn't return until after midnight.

Anya awoke to find Natasha staring at her in bed.

"There were six of us," Natasha whispered.

Anya sat up in bed and made room for Natasha. Natasha sat down stiffly. When Anya moved to hug her, she flinched and backed away.

"There were six of us," she repeated. "He said we were going to play the flower game."

Anya listened as Natasha told her all about the appalling game. Beria had made the girls strip, leaving only their shoes on. He forced them to get down on their hands and knees, their foreheads touching. He paced around them, wearing only his bathrobe, selecting the girl he would drag to his bed. He had chosen Natasha.

After that, Natasha's mother began to sell every valuable she owned on the black market to raise money for a move. Beria called her to him nearly every night. He soon demanded that she bring Natasha again. Helpless, Larissa Karsavina agreed.

When Natasha learned what her mother had promised, she retreated to icy silence and refused to look her mother in the face.

"I told him I'd bring you next week," Natasha's mother said. "I love you, Natasha. Don't forget that."

When Larissa Karsavina left for Beria's the following night, Anya saw her hand Galina Maximovna a stack of papers.

"Tonight."

Anya's mother shook her head. "What is this?"

"Forged traveling papers. Leave tonight."

Anya's mother nodded. "All right. As soon as you get home, we'll be out the door."

"No," Larissa said. "Leave without me."

"Don't be ridiculous. We'll wait for you."

"No. You can't."

"I don't want to move," Anya said.

Her mother ignored her. "We'll wait for you," she insisted.

"No. If his toy is missing, he'll know. He'll find us. If you leave without me, he'll only suspect when Natasha doesn't show. By then, you'll be gone."

"So we will move quickly—when you get home tonight."

"No!" Natasha's mother shouted. "You will leave without me tonight, or so help me, I will kill myself here and now!"

"Larissa—"

"Galina, I cannot do that to my daughter again!"

Anya's mother was silent. She and Natasha's mother stared at each other for a long while.

"Anya." Anya's mother did not look at her. Her voice shook and her eyes glistened with tears. "Go to your room and pack."

"No. I'm not moving," Anya protested.

"Do as I say, Anya."

Anya folded her arms across her chest and didn't move. "I'm not going anywhere."

"Go to your room, Anya!"

"No!"

Anya's mother brought the palm of her hand across her daughter's face, leaving a stinging red handprint, and a ringing in Anya's ear.

"Unruly child! You do as I say right now!"

Anya stared defiantly at her mother for a moment. When Galina Maximovna brought her hand up a second time, Anya turned and marched toward her room, tears sliding down her stinging cheek. She turned back toward the door and saw her mother and Larissa Karsavina embrace before Larissa ran out the door. That was the last any of them saw of her.

Natasha had remained in Anya's room. She had refused to speak to her mother and had never said good-bye.

*   *   *

Natasha performed an *entrechat-quatre*, her willowy body in perfect position. Anya looked on in envy. Natasha's performance was perfect, as usual. Her pale body seemed to glow as she floated across the stage, finishing in a slow, sweeping bow.

The familiar slap of Matisse's paintbrush on Jean-Luc's ankle marked the end of the solo, but this time, it wasn't alone. Slow, heavy claps resounded through the theatre, applauding Natasha's performance. Anya looked out into the audience and saw Heinrich Lorenz walking toward the stage. She beamed. He was here at last. She puffed out her chest and pranced across the stage to greet him. Now it would be Natasha's turn to envy her.

"I'm so glad you came, Heinrich," she said. "Let me—"

Heinrich walked right past her. He did not even spare her a glance.

Anya stood, frozen, feeling more embarrassed than she had the night Jean-Luc had refused to come to the café. She didn't need to turn around. She already knew that he was approaching Natasha.

CHAPTER 12

"A VERY MOVING PERFORMANCE, Fräulein."
The voice made Natasha's entire body grow cold. She looked up. Anya's German officer removed his hat.

"Thank you," Natasha said. She stood up and began to make her way over to the ballet mistress to receive her criticism, but the German side-stepped to block her path.

"Your ankle is better?"

"Yes." Natasha glanced over at Anya, who still stood in the middle of the stage, her arms at her side and her shoulders hunched, facing the other way.

"I am Oberst Heinrich Lorenz."

"Natasha Karsavina."

Lorenz reached out, took her hand, and kissed it. A hollow shock shot up Natasha's arm and down into her heart. Her eyes flickered to Jean-Luc, who was now concentrating on his painting.

"Walk with me, Natasha."

"I am working. The ballet mistress—"

Lorenz turned toward Madame Fournier and said something in German. She nodded.

"Take a break, Natasha."

Lorenz offered his arm, and Natasha took it hesitantly. She found herself being led out of the theatre, her insides screaming for help. She looked back over her shoulder. Anya was watching them leave.

"You impress me, Natasha," Lorenz said, once they were in the main foyer. "Not many people do that."

"Thank you," she said, keeping her voice even.

"Join me for dinner tonight."

It was not a request. Natasha's thoughts flitted to Jean-Luc. She wanted him to sweep her up in his arms and save her from this dragon, but he was still in the theatre.

"Something wrong, Fräulein? Are you married?"

She couldn't tell Lorenz about Jean-Luc. Men like Lorenz and Beria wouldn't hesitate to kill such obstacles.

"No."

"Dinner, then."

Natasha nodded.

"Good. Right after rehearsal. I will wait in the audience."

Lorenz motioned back toward the theatre. He walked Natasha back to the stage, said something to the ballet mistress in German, and then took his seat in the audience.

Rehearsal had never flown by so fast. Natasha felt all the color drain from her face when the ballet mistress clapped her hands and ordered the girls to change. Natasha dragged her feet on the way to the dressing room.

"Natasha, are you all right?" Svetlana asked as Natasha opened her locker. "You look a little pale."

"She's fine," Anya snapped. "Just feeling sorry for herself. Must be so hard being pretty and desirable."

Anya slammed her locker and, not even bothering to put on her brand-new stockings, stormed out of the dressing room. Svetlana watched Anya leave, gave Natasha a sympathetic look, and went about her business.

Natasha was the last to emerge from the dressing room. As soon as she stepped through the doorway, she found herself face-to-face with Oberst Lorenz.

"Ready?"

Natasha glanced ahead at the other ballerinas, who were giggling and gossiping in a group as they walked past Matisse and Jean-Luc. Lorenz took her hand and kissed it again. She fought the impulse to jerk her hand away and allowed Lorenz to lead her out of the Théâtre de l'Opéra. Jean-Luc was still absorbed in his discussion with Matisse.

"Have you ever been to the Drouant?"

Natasha shook her head. The Drouant restaurant was far too expensive.

"You will tonight."

*   *   *

Natasha fidgeted with the straps of her handbag as the waiter pulled her chair out. She felt out of place and underdressed, and she wanted nothing more than to run screaming back to Jean-Luc.

German officers sat at every table. Some were with other soldiers in black uniforms, some were with fellow officers, and others were with pretty girls in fancy dresses and fur coats.

Men in black uniforms walked past. Lorenz stood erect and saluted them.

"Heil Hitler!"

"Heil Hitler," they responded, and continued to their own table.

"SS," Lorenz explained. "They are handpicked by the Führer and are given the most crucial tasks."

The waiter began speaking in German. Lorenz answered, and the waiter walked away without even sparing Natasha a glance.

"I must admit," Lorenz said, returning to his accented French, "you have intrigued me since I first met you. You seem intensely dedicated to your dancing."

"I am," Natasha answered. "I hope to be a prima ballerina one day."

"An admirable goal. With your talent, I'm surprised you aren't already. If you like, I can ensure that you become one."

Natasha swallowed. She didn't want to know how he planned to do that. "Thank you, Herr Oberst—"

"Heinrich," he corrected.

"Heinrich," she said. "Thank you, but I'd prefer to earn it. The ballet itself is more important than my ambition. I must be the best for the role and not have anyone influence decisions."

She regretted her words instantly; surely he would be insulted. Natasha looked up at Lorenz and found a smile.

"You are a German at heart, Fräulein. You're a hard worker who puts the whole before herself. I like that." Natasha stared at him in silence. She clenched her hands in her lap to keep them from shaking.

"We are similar, you and I," Lorenz continued. "We both are willing to start at the bottom and work our own way to our goals."

Natasha nodded and looked down at her napkin. She could feel his eyes upon her.

"You are very surprising, Natasha."

"Thank you."

He reached across the table and placed two fingers on her chin, lifting her face to look at his. "Surprising and exceptionally beautiful."

The waiter returned with their first course—a puff pastry filled with vegetables—and two glasses of water. Natasha licked her lips.

"I had him bring water, but you may order whatever you like—wine, brandy, schnapps—anything you wish."

Natasha seldom drank anything save a little watered-down wine with dinner; she preferred to keep her head clear. Having no desire to repeat Anya's embarrassing drunken antics—and not trusting Lorenz at all—she declined.

"Do you smoke?" Lorenz asked.

"No."

Lorenz looked at her a moment, then nodded. "Neither do I. It's unhealthy. The Führer doesn't smoke or drink at all."

"I do have some wine now and then," Natasha said. "But not often."

"Well, not everyone has the strength and will of the Führer. I, too, have had a bottle or two of schnapps on the battlefield—no one could deny a man a nip after a day of fighting. However, I am proud to say, I have not consumed spirits since the day we marched into Paris."

"Oh?"

"Not once. What about you? Why don't you drink?"

"Ballet," she said. "I practice at home and like to keep a clear head."

"Again, your dedication." He lifted his glass of water in a toast to her. Natasha thanked him again. After she finished her first course, she sat with her hands folded in her lap, listening to the sounds of forks and knives dinging against the plates amid conversations in German.

"You're very quiet, Natasha. You're not having a good time? The food is not good?"

Natasha looked up at him. He was staring at her, those cold blue eyes boring into her. "I—I just don't know what to talk about. I don't want to bore you. Most of my life revolves around the ballet."

"Your parents must be proud."

Natasha hesitated. *Don't be so quiet. Don't anger him.*

"My parents died back in Russia. I moved here with Anya's family."

Lorenz frowned. Natasha's heart raced. *I shouldn't have mentioned Anya.*

"I'm sorry to hear of your loss. Have you ever gone back to visit their graves?"

"I'm never going back to Russia."

"You have no love for your own country?"

"It is not my country. It is run by twisted, corrupt people."

"Good. You're not a Communist. They're almost as bad as the Jews." Lorenz smiled again, sending a shiver down Natasha's spine. He let out a heavy laugh. "Don't look so pale, Natasha. I could tell right away you weren't a Communist. I know their ways. I have a good eye for spotting their habits."

Natasha forced a smile.

"You're trained to recognize them?"

"Of course. How to recognize a Communist, a spy, a Jew—all the enemies of the Third Reich. I think my skills would be put to better use in the SS, though."

"Why is that?"

"They're the ones working to solve the Jewish problem."

Natasha swallowed. "And you wish to join their ranks?"

"I would be willing to start at the bottom—anything to be part of such an elite group."

"Do you think you'll be selected?"

"I have a few connections, but like you, I would rather be chosen for my own talent, rather than who I know."

The second course replaced the first. Natasha struggled to keep the conversation light: the recent harsh winters, ballets she had performed in, operas she had seen. Lorenz, however, wanted to know about her past—who she was. Natasha told him a few stories about her early childhood, turning each of his questions around to take the focus away from her. But this only encouraged Lorenz.

By the time the third course arrived, Lorenz had moved his chair around to her side of the table. As the waiter placed the two plates in front of them, Lorenz put his arm around her shoulders.

Natasha's insides screamed in protest, but her body only stiffened. She stared at the plate of meat. She hadn't tasted meat—real meat—in so long. The sight of it made her mouth water, but her stomach churned as Lorenz caressed her shoulder. He leaned toward her and placed a finger on her cheek.

"So beautiful . . . so delicate."

His face was getting closer. Natasha trembled from head to toe.

He chuckled. "So natural on stage, but so shy up close." He eased away but kept his arm around her. "Perhaps not here."

As she feasted on real meat, real cheese, and a dessert with real sugar, Natasha wished she was in Madame Cordier's kitchen, eating meager portions of thin soup and stale bread and drinking black artificial coffee. She wanted the evening to be over, to forget everything about Heinrich Lorenz.

At last, dinner was over and they exited the restaurant. More than ready to go home, Natasha relaxed. Lorenz, however, drove to the Hotel Meurice.

"Come inside," he said. "I have a gift for you."

"Thank you, but I really couldn't accept—"

"Of course you can. Come." He opened the door for her and offered his arm. Hesitantly, she took it and followed him into the hotel.

More Germans were here than had been in the Drouant. Uniformed soldiers marched through the hallways, saluting superiors or parading around giggling French girls too drunk to stand.

Someone screamed. Shouts in German followed. Makeup smeared, blouse unbuttoned, and hat askew, a woman ran down the steps and smack into Lorenz, elbowing Natasha in the chest and knocking her aside. The woman scrambled to run past them, but in one sweeping motion, Lorenz grabbed her by the throat and pulled her back to face him.

"Please . . . no . . . I'm not. I swear. I swear," she sobbed.

A bare-chested German came running into view, holding up his unfastened trousers. He took a look at Lorenz, smiled, saluted, and slowed his pace.

After a brief conversation in German with the soldier, Lorenz turned back to face the woman, tightening his grip on her throat.

"Asking so many questions . . . perhaps you can answer ours about the Resistance."

"No . . . I'm not—I was just curious."

"Liar! And a terrible spy." He narrowed his eyes and jerked her head closer. Her face was red. She was trying to pry Lorenz's hand from her throat to no avail. What little breath she had came in short, wheezing gasps.

Lorenz looked at her ears and hair, and then sniffed the air around the woman. He glared at the soldier and said something in German. Natasha recognized one word: "Jude."

With his free hand he slapped the shirtless soldier, and then backing away as if she had the plague, Lorenz shoved her toward his comrade. The shirtless soldier gave the woman a look of disgust and then dragged her out of the hotel by her hair.

"No! Please! No!" The woman's cries faded away.

Lorenz turned back to Natasha. "Are you all right?"

Natasha nodded. Lorenz offered his arm and led Natasha up the stairs to his suite.

His room was warm. There was no smoky smell of burned leaves and twigs, and no homemade brazier in sight. Expensive furniture was neatly arranged over an Oriental rug. The windows were framed by heavy curtains tied with tasseled gold rope. Paintings adorned every wall. Above a marble fireplace was Matisse's *Odalisque*.

Natasha released Lorenz's arm and stepped over to the fireplace to stare up at the painting. Within seconds, she felt Lorenz's heavy hands on her shoulders. She tensed.

"You like it? It is a Matisse. Though not good art by the Führer's standards, we all have our guilty pleasures."

Natasha nodded.

"That was why I first went to the opera house. I had heard Matisse was doing the backdrop and wanted to watch him work. Imagine my disappointment when I learned that his assistant was going to do most of the work."

Natasha's heart clenched. Was Lorenz angry with Jean-Luc?

"No matter," Lorenz murmured in her ear. "I have found something else to be passionate about."

He took her coat and steered her toward the opulent couch.

"Please, sit," he said, taking her handbag and placing it on an end table.

Natasha did as he commanded. He disappeared for a moment, and then reappeared with a long string of pearls strung through his fingers.

"Something to wear around your pretty neck."

"Herr Ob—Heinrich. I really couldn't—"

"They are yours." He opened her handbag and dropped the pearls inside.

"Thank you." Natasha looked down at her feet, feeling helpless. Lorenz sat beside her on the couch and tilted her face toward his. Taking her by the waist and twisting her body around, he leaned in.

She didn't want this. She wanted to be with Jean-Luc in his messy little studio. She wanted to be wakened by Madame Cordier's voice. She wanted to shove Lorenz away with all her might—but she knew the price of resistance. She couldn't bear to see Anya in a pool of her own blood—or Jean-Luc, if Lorenz ever found out about him.

Natasha closed her eyes.

Lorenz kissed her, sliding his hand from her waist, down her leg, and up again to her bottom. He pulled her to him, pressing his hips against hers. She tried to imagine Jean-Luc in his place, but everything—the smell, the taste, and the feel of Lorenz—was all wrong. Lorenz was not as rough as Anya had said he was, but he did not have the light touch of an artist's hands.

Lorenz's mouth was at her throat almost instantly, his hands groping wherever they pleased. He ripped her blouse open and reached up her skirt. He sat up, working quickly to unfasten his belt.

No, she silently pleaded. *Jean-Luc—help!*

She tensed, no longer able to imagine even a glimmer of her sweet, gentle Jean-Luc. She felt a lump forming in her throat and threw all her effort into fighting back the tears. She couldn't stop herself from shaking.

Lorenz stopped and looked down at her. She stared back up at him, her eyes wide, and her heart racing.

"Schatzi, you're trembling." He leaned over her again and kissed her, then sat up. "I should have known." He chuckled and refastened his belt. "It's all right, meine Liebling." He leaned over her again, kissing any exposed flesh and pushing up her skirt so he could stroke her thigh.

Natasha was still shaking. Lorenz kissed his way up to her neck. Then, nibbling on her ear, he murmured, "A beautiful virgin like you is worth waiting for."

Though Lorenz did not press her to go to bed with him, he continued to kiss and fondle her. Curfew came and went. Eventually, Natasha found an opportunity to point out the time.

"I must be getting home. I—I have rehearsal."

Lorenz gave her bottom one last squeeze before sitting up and allowing her to straighten her skirt and button what she could of her blouse. Only three buttons remained after Lorenz had torn it open. It was a good thing she had her coat.

* * *

Too angry to feel tired, Anya stared out her bedroom window, a blanket wrapped around her shoulders, waiting for any sign of Natasha. She scowled as she rubbed her cold hands together, her breath forming misty clouds in front of her.

Natasha just couldn't allow her this one thing. No. She had to snatch Jean-Luc away when her back was turned and then steal Heinrich right out from under her. She would pretend to be so innocent, too, just to lure these men to her side, to make them worship her.

So what if Natasha was prettier, more talented, and more graceful, with a better figure and delicate features? What right did that give her to step on a friend's toes?

Heinrich's jeep pulled up. Anya fumed as she watched Heinrich open the car door and pull Natasha into a long kiss, his hands groping Natasha the way they should have been groping her. He then released Natasha and watched her disappear inside the apartment.

With a grunt of frustration, Anya sat on the bed, tossing the blanket aside and wiping angry tears from her eyes. She heard the jeep rumble away. In a matter of moments, the door opened and Natasha stepped into the room. Her shoulders were slumped; she took sluggish steps.

Anya folded her arms over her chest. "Drunk, are you? Serves you right if you're sick. Did you have a good time with Heinrich? Was it worth hurting me like that?"

Natasha looked up. Her expression was blank, and her eyes were round and miserable.

"You couldn't let me have this? Just once?" Anya continued. "No, of course not. You're too selfish for that. Heaven forbid plain, boring Anya get a little attention over perfect Natasha."

Natasha took a few steps and stood over Anya just long enough for Anya to see the glistening tears in her eyes. Anya paused and unfolded her arms. Natasha didn't smell like alcohol. Anya's tone changed from anger to concern. "Natasha—"

Natasha dropped her handbag, its contents spilling all over the floor. She fell to her knees, sobbing in Anya's lap.

"I didn't want him," she wailed. "I don't want him. I want Jean-Luc. I don't want him, Anya. I don't."

"Then why did you go with him?"

"I was frightened. He could kill you—kill me—kill your parents or Jean-Luc. Just like Beria. He had the same look in his eyes . . ."

"He didn't force you, did he?"

"No," Natasha sobbed. "But he only stopped because he thinks I'm a virgin. What if he just takes what he wants and finds out I'm not? What if he—oh, no! What if he finds out I'm—I'm a—he'll kill me, Anya!"

Natasha rambled broken words between sobs. Anya could barely understand the mix of French and Russian as Natasha spilled her every fear.

"Shh . . . hush, Natasha, hush." Anya stroked her hair. "He was taken by your beauty. You're prettier than anyone I've ever known—but men like him need a woman with more meat. He's rough in bed. He needs a woman who likes it." She urged Natasha to lift her head. "Shh . . . calm down. You would never do the things he likes—I'm better suited to him." Anya wiped Natasha's tears from her cheeks.

"I don't want him, Anya. I never did, I swear."

Anya nodded. "I believe you. He probably went after you to make me jealous—he's a man. He has needs. My monthly curse just ended yesterday—he was probably frustrated. I'll go to him tomorrow—remind him why he chose me to begin with. I'll win him back and he won't bother you anymore."

Natasha clung to Anya, sobbing apologies and thanks. Anya made soothing noises, just as she had when Natasha's father was killed. Out of the corner of her eye, she glimpsed a string of pearls lying among the contents of Natasha's handbag.

"Don't worry," she whispered. "I'll win him back."

CHAPTER 13

L ORENZ DID NOT come to rehearsal the next day, much to Natasha's relief. Jean-Luc didn't question her disappearance the previous evening, either. He had been so lost in conversation with Matisse that he hadn't noticed the time, and he had barely made it home before curfew. He assumed that Natasha hadn't wanted to risk waiting for him.

Natasha didn't bother to correct him. She stayed with Jean-Luc that night and urged him to touch and kiss her all over, trying to erase the feeling of Lorenz's hands and mouth.

When Natasha arrived home the following morning, Anya was already awake.

"Good morning," she sang when Natasha entered the room. "I have good news for you." She unbuttoned her blouse and showed Natasha a large purple bite mark on her breast, then moved her dark hair aside to reveal another one on her neck. "I went to his room last night wearing nothing under my coat," she said. "Heinrich couldn't get enough of me. See? I told you he really wanted me."

Natasha wrapped her arms around her friend. "Thank you," she said, her eyes misting.

"So where is Jean-Luc?"

"Painting with Miró. I thought you and I could go for a walk and catch up on things. It's been so long since we've had a day for just the two of us."

"Sure. Only I have to be back by three. I want to show up at Heinrich's again. Last night was wonderful."

Natasha changed her clothes and headed out the door with Anya. No sooner had they walked out of the building than Lorenz's jeep rounded the corner. Anya opened her coat and adjusted her bosom to show more cleavage when she saw him approaching. "I may not be able to go for that walk after all," she said.

Lorenz pulled to a stop in front of the girls and got out of the car.

"Good morning, Natasha." He wrapped his arms around Natasha and gave her a long kiss. He did not even look at Anya.

"Good morning," Natasha mumbled.

"Come. I will take you to breakfast." He went over to the passenger's door and opened it for her. Natasha reached for Anya's hand, but Anya yanked it away and stormed back inside.

Natasha looked back at Lorenz, feeling small and helpless all over again. She stepped forward and allowed Lorenz to help her into the car.

Anya wouldn't speak to her when she came home that night.

Lorenz soon developed the habit of showing up wherever Natasha was. He surprised her after work, when she arrived at home, or when she waited in the ration lines. Natasha began jumping at every movement she perceived from the corner of her eye—particularly when she spoke to Jean-Luc.

Natasha began to avoid Jean-Luc unless she was absolutely certain Lorenz was busy doing something else. She stopped waiting for Jean-Luc after rehearsal, making excuses for her early departure, and she began to hint that she might not be able to go to Le Café d'Anton as often as they had before. She could not bring herself to tell Jean-Luc about Lorenz.

Two days later, Anya put on her new dress and stockings, applied liberal amounts of rouge, and announced that she was going to try again with Lorenz.

While Anya tried to win Lorenz back a second time, Natasha went to Le Café d'Anton with Jean-Luc. At the first sight of German soldiers, Natasha begged Jean-Luc to cut the date short, saying she was afraid the soldiers would recognize them from the Louvre. They returned to Jean-Luc's studio, where they spent the entire day and night in each other's arms.

"How is your painting coming along?" Natasha murmured as she and Jean-Luc lay in bed. Ever since Lorenz began to chase her, she hated to sleep when she was with Jean-Luc. She wanted to savor every moment, remembering the feel of his touch.

"Hm?" Jean-Luc's eyes opened slowly, then drooped shut.

"Your painting—the replica. How far along are you?"

"I'm al . . . almo . . . ," Jean-Luc yawned. He pulled Natasha closer to him and kissed her forehead. "Almost finished."

"Then what will you do?"

"I took your advice and talked to Miró. He said he'd . . ."

Natasha nudged him. "He'd what?"

Jean-Luc yawned again. "He . . . said he'd see what he can do."

"Do you think he knows anyone who can help?"

"Hm?"

Natasha smiled and brushed a lock of hair away from Jean-Luc's eyes. She brushed her lips over his.

"Never mind. Get some sleep."

"I love you," Jean-Luc mumbled. Seconds later, he was fast asleep. Natasha watched him breathing for a few minutes before her own eyelids became very heavy.

She nestled her head just under his chin and whispered, "I love you, too."

Sleep found her quickly, and morning came all too soon.

* * *

As time went by, finding opportunities to see Jean-Luc became increasingly difficult for Natasha. All of Anya's efforts to regain Lorenz's affections failed, and Lorenz's surprise visits to Natasha occurred more frequently. He took her to restaurants, cafés, nightclubs, and exclusive parties. He showered her with expensive gifts, taking new liberties with each one. Decorative ivory combs, a mink stole, dresses, stockings, jewelry. He took off all of her clothing and most of his, his mouth and hands caressing, probing—but he always stopped before things could get too far.

Natasha hadn't seen Jean-Luc outside of work for three days. Once again, she found herself in Lorenz's arms, wishing for Jean-Luc while Lorenz kissed and caressed her.

Lorenz pressed himself up against her naked body and whispered words of love in her ear. He was almost fully clothed, but he would not be for long. She had grown so used to their routine that she felt numb when he touched her.

She wasn't sure she could deter him this time. When she had entered his hotel room, wearing a new dress he had bought her, he had ripped it off, tearing the precious fabric to shreds, and carried her off to his bed.

She played her part, kissing back when his mouth was on hers, moaning in appropriate places. She had stopped trying to imagine Jean-Luc in Lorenz's place, worried that she would call out his name and get them both killed.

Lorenz stripped off the rest of his clothing. Natasha stiffened. Her eyes grew wide, and she began to shake.

Lorenz kissed her throat. "Tonight, my love."

"Please," she whispered. "I—"

"I can't wait any longer. I want you so."

"Heinrich, please . . ."

He sat up and narrowed his eyes. "Why won't you have me?"

"I—I'm not ready."

He studied her for a minute. "Has someone taken what should have been mine?"

Natasha began to sob. She couldn't tell him about Jean-Luc, and she didn't want to tell him about Beria—she hadn't even told the man she loved about that.

Lorenz gripped her shoulders and pulled her to him. "Is another man eating from my plate?"

"No." Natasha swallowed. Tears dripped out of the corners of her eyes, down her temples and into her hair. He would take what he wanted eventually—and know she wasn't a virgin. She had to tell him something. "I was—when I was—the reason we left Russia—"

She took a deep breath and told the story she had kept locked inside for ten years. She wasn't sure if it was easier or more difficult to tell it in French, rather than Russian. The only time she had told the whole story was when she confessed everything to Anya. She still had to pause every now and then to regain her composure, and she could not look Lorenz in the face at all. He reached for her hand, and she flinched. "He . . . he paced around us three times, then he grabbed me by my ankle and dragged me off to his bed." Natasha kept her eyes in her lap, silent tears pouring down her face. She could still hear his voice: *Scream for me. Call my name. Tell me you like it—or I will kill you.*

Lorenz looked at her. She turned away. She didn't want to look at him. She wanted to look at Jean-Luc.

Lorenz's rough hands touched her cheek and turned her head back to face him. "Schatzi, have no fear. This is something you want. Don't be afraid to take it."

He kissed her. Tears spilled out of Natasha's eyes. He would not let her get away.

He rolled on top of her and took what he wanted. Though not as gentle as Jean-Luc had been, he never hurt her. He pulled her to him, moaning in German. Whenever he would start to get rough, she could feel him forcing himself to slow his pace.

Natasha cried the whole time.

When Lorenz finished, he remained on top of her. He wiped away her tears, and she struggled to smile.

"You see, my little treasure, there is no shame in getting what you want.

"You wanted that, didn't you, my little flower petal?

"Did you enjoy that?" he asked, kissing her breast.

"Tell me you liked me inside you."

Natasha swallowed the lump in her throat. "Yes." She felt sick.

"I have a gift for you." He rolled off of her and reached over to the nightstand. After fumbling through the drawer, he produced a gold ring set with a large emerald.

She accepted the gift without protest and thanked him. He pulled her close.

"It wasn't easy to tell me about Beria, was it?"

Natasha shook her head.

"It's better that I know. I was worried it was another man." He laughed, sending a chill up Natasha's spine. "If there was another man, I'd kill him."

Natasha said nothing. She examined the ring he had given her. Engraved on the inside of the gold band were the initials J. S.

"Pretty, isn't it?"

"Oh—yes." She slipped the ring on her finger. It was a little too large.

"I saw it and thought of you."

Natasha gave Lorenz a weak smile and started to get up. He pulled her back into bed. "No, my love. You will stay here with me." He ran his hands over her body. "Will you have me in the morning?"

Natasha felt cold. "Yes."

He ran a finger down her cheek. He was so large—he could easily strangle her with one hand. "You love me."

Natasha's lip trembled.

Tell me you want me again. Tell me you want me every night—or I will kill you.

"Yes."

CHAPTER 14

"WHY DID YOU CHOOSE this particular color here, Jean-Luc?"

Jean-Luc jumped. He had been so lost in his painting, he hadn't even noticed Miró pacing behind him. He blinked and looked at his watch. It had been hours since he had moved his easel into Miró's studio. He was due to meet Natasha for lunch at Le Café d'Anton in twenty minutes.

Miró assumed his critiquing posture. "I'm not fond of your color choice here. It seems too loud for the rest of the piece. What do you plan to do with it to make it work?"

Jean-Luc flexed his stiff fingers. "I was just painting what I feel."

"As I thought. Something is troubling you, then," Miró said. "It's shown in your style over the last few days."

Jean-Luc braced himself. "And?"

Miró patted Jean-Luc's shoulder. "It's no better, no worse. It's still your own—it just conveys a different emotion. You have to incorporate all of these feelings in a way that works with the piece. Let your emotions form the idea, but your mind and hands must remain detached in order to execute it. It is not about what you feel at any given moment. Paint what you feel about the object you are trying to portray."

Jean-Luc nodded, stretching out his back. "That replica I was telling you about is finished. You said you know someone on the black market who can help?"

"Don't change the subject. What's troubling you?" Miró asked.

"It's Natasha," Jean-Luc said as he gathered up his dirty paintbrushes for cleaning.

Miró wrinkled his brow. "Last night, when she was here, you two seemed so happy."

Jean-Luc shook his head. "She's wonderful—I think I would have proposed to her already if I had the money or the means. It's just . . . she's been acting strange lately."

"How so?"

"She's been very distant—very jumpy. She doesn't want me to hold her hand in public anymore or even talk to her much when we're at the Théâtre de l'Opéra."

"Don't get too offended, Jean-Luc. She's working. Maybe the ballet mistress said something to her—or Matisse might have." Miró smiled. "I hear you're quite distracted when she dances."

Jean-Luc shook his head. "I wasn't too concerned at first, but then yesterday, we were walking along the Seine, talking—it was the first time I'd seen her in days—and every time I moved to kiss her, she moved away. She kept looking around, as if someone were following her, and she—well, she had these combs in her hair."

"Combs?"

"They looked expensive. I'd never seen them before."

Miró laughed. "I never thought I'd see the day when Jean-Luc Beauchamp became paranoid with jealousy. Relax. They may be a family heirloom."

"I suppose," Jean-Luc said. "It's just . . . she's never mentioned them before."

"Did you ask her about them?"

"No."

"Then don't jump to conclusions. If you're so concerned, ask her, but don't accuse her. You must trust each other." Miró placed a hand on Jean-Luc's shoulder. "Believe me, she loves you. I could see it in her eyes."

Jean-Luc nodded, but he could not shake his uneasy feeling. Natasha had said that Anya's family had struggled to pay for ballet lessons and were still trying to pay off a few accumulated debts. How could she afford such an expensive treasure?

"So you've finished *The Barque of Dante*?"

"Yes."

"If you don't mind, I'll go into your room while you're gone and take a look, though I'm not really concerned. You've always been gifted at replicas."

"Thank you."

"I'll arrange to have it picked up tonight."

"But what will he do? He can't just sell it as the original if the original is in the Louvre."

"I don't know. I'm not involved. I just know someone who knows someone. But he assures me he'll be able to save the original with this one," said Miró.

Jean-Luc finished cleaning up. After bidding Miró a quick farewell, he changed his shirt and headed for the café. Natasha was waiting for him inside Le Café d'Anton, at a cozy little table tucked away in the back of the café, out of sight from most of the other patrons. Her entire face lit up as Jean-Luc approached.

Joan's right. It's nothing. I'm being ridiculous.

When Jean-Luc reached the table, he bent to kiss her. She leaned back, took a quick look around, and then granted him a quick peck. Disappointed, but trying to shake things off, Jean-Luc took off his coat with a little shiver.

She laughed. "Your nose is so red."

"It's colder today than I expected."

"You should have worn your scarf."

Jean-Luc winked. "As long as you don't tell Madame, I'll be fine."

"I could keep you warm later," she said, blushing and biting her bottom lip.

"Don't tempt me, my love. I have to go into work later. We have a little more than a week until opening night, and Matisse and I hope to finish the scenery tonight."

"Maybe we should skip lunch." She reached across the table and placed her hand on top of Jean-Luc's. A large emerald ring adorned her middle finger. "I've missed you."

Jean-Luc stared down at her hand. He opened his mouth to ask her about the ring but couldn't find the words. Natasha pulled her hand away and tucked it into her lap.

Jean-Luc cleared his throat. "I finished that painting—you know, the Delacroix?"

"Oh? What are you going to do with it?"

Jean-Luc leaned toward her and whispered, "I'm just going to give it to Miró. He said he knows someone who knows someone."

"And how will he protect the original?" Natasha whispered back.

Jean-Luc shrugged. "I don't know. He didn't tell Miró either. I suppose that's a secret only members of the Resistance are allowed to know. I just hope this person doesn't steal the original and keep it for himself."

"You would rather a Frenchman have it than a German."

"In a way. But I would have little respect for any Frenchman who would steal a piece of history. Are you excited about next Saturday?"

Natasha nodded.

"Nervous?" he asked.

"Not really. Dancing calms me more than anything—even with a large audience."

"I'm a little nervous."

"You?"

Jean-Luc nodded. "Opening night will be the first time my art will be displayed as more than just an amateur painting in a café one of my father's friends owns. It will be a test—am I good enough to become a real artist like Miró or Matisse or Cézanne? Or am I just another local dreamer? I don't know what I'll do if I fail."

Natasha smiled. "You're brilliant, Jean-Luc. Everyone will love your work."

Jean-Luc felt his pride swell. Even if the entire world condemned his art, as long as Natasha liked his painting, he would be content.

"You think so?"

"Trust me."

Trust her. He wanted to—no, he did. He trusted her with all of his soul. The ring might be borrowed from Anya's mother—and the combs. He was just jumping at shadows.

"So when you sign autographs, will you write your name in Russian characters?" Jean-Luc asked.

"Autographs? Don't get too excited, Jean-Luc. I have a solo, but I'm not the lead."

"Well, I would ask for your autograph."

Natasha laughed. "Would you?"

"Of course. I wouldn't be able to read the name, but I'd want it anyway."

"Then here, let me show you."

Natasha stood up and walked over to stand beside Jean-Luc. She placed her hand over his and extended his finger forward. Guiding his hand, she traced the letters of her name on the tablecloth. "See?"

Jean-Luc looked up at her. The hollow of her throat was calling to his lips. "Maybe you're right. We should skip lunch."

Natasha beamed. Jean-Luc stood up to help her into her coat. She buttoned it up, then took a mink stole from one of the wall pegs and draped it over her shoulders.

"Ready?" she asked.

Jean-Luc didn't move. Madame Lévy had a fur just like that one; she used to brag about how much it had cost.

"Natasha?" His knees shook. "Where did you get that stole?"

Natasha blanched. "Oh . . . I've—I've always had it."

Jean-Luc frowned. "When we first met, it was even colder than it is today—why didn't you wear it then?"

Natasha took a step back.

"You wore ivory hair combs yesterday—and now you're wearing that ring."

Natasha backed up against the wall. Her eyes were wide and glistening with tears. Jean-Luc slowly walked toward her, his brow creased with worry.

"Tell me what's happening, my love." He reached out to hold her. "Whatever it—"

"No!" Natasha jerked herself away and pushed past Jean-Luc. "I can't do this anymore." Sobbing, with all the other café patrons staring at her, she tore through the crowd and disappeared out the door.

Jean-Luc slumped back in his chair and buried his head in his hands. Nicolas, the headwaiter, approached him after a while. "Would you like anything, Jean-Luc?"

Jean-Luc pulled out a few francs from his pocket. "A bottle of wine, Nicolas."

*   *   *

Jean-Luc spent the entire afternoon at the café. One bottle of artificial wine turned into four as lunch turned to dinner and day gave way to night. He drank and stared at the empty walls, ignoring everyone except when he ordered another bottle. He had stopped using a glass hours ago.

"Nicolas—more wine," he called, taking a last swig.

Without warning, the bottle was wrenched away from his grasp. Wine spilled out of his mouth and down his chin, staining his shirt. Annoyed, he jerked his head up. The room swayed for a moment before he could focus.

Celeste Anton stood over him, one fist on her hip and the other holding the bottle aloft.

"Pay your bill and go home, Jean-Luc."

"No. 'Nother bottle."

"I said, 'Pay your bill and go home.'"

"I've 'nough fonother." He pulled out money and handed it to Madame Anton. "Here. Brinme 'noer—nother." He struggled for control of his heavy tongue. "Bring . . . me . . . another."

"If you want to drink yourself to death the way your father did, be my guest—but you will not do it in my husband's café. Now out. Before I tell Paulette Cordier what a wreck you are."

Jean-Luc scowled at her. He made a rude gesture, vaguely realizing that he would pay for it later, then scooted his chair back and stood up.

He didn't remember the room being so tilted. It tipped over to the left so far that he had to lean to his right to keep his balance—and he fell right into one of the tables. Thankfully, no one was sitting there. No one was sitting anywhere.

Madame Anton grabbed his arm and helped him up, pulling and pushing him from side to side whenever the room tilted. He made it to the door without falling again.

"Nicolas, grab his coat," Madame Anton said.

Jean-Luc felt heavy fabric across his shoulders and shrugged it off. It was draped over him again. With an angry grunt, he threw whatever it was to the floor. It was too warm.

His head was fuzzy. Where was he again? Ah yes. The café.

He lifted his hand and asked Nicolas for another bottle of wine, but Nicolas didn't move. He'd take his business elsewhere. Was it curfew yet? He looked at his watch, trying to remember how to read it. After a few seconds, he gave up and decided to listen to the conversation Madame Anton was having with Nicolas.

"What about his coat?" Nicolas was saying.

"Just bring it with you. I'll tell Paulette all about this when she gets here. That'll teach him."

Jean-Luc watched Nicolas's head blur into a nod. A gust of cold air slammed into Jean-Luc's face as soon as Madame Anton opened the door. *This is much better.*

With Nicolas holding him by the arm, pushing and pulling him whichever way Paris tilted, Jean-Luc made his way down the street back toward rue Blomet. Little flurries of snow floated down from the heavens and disappeared on Jean-Luc's skin. He stopped in his tracks and looked straight up, following a snowflake down until it faded away on the pavement. He bent over, trying to see if it was still there. Nicolas grabbed his waist and yanked him upright. The world flipped upside-down and spun about, and Jean-Luc did not like the sensation at all. He fell to his knees and vomited in the street.

* * *

Jean-Luc almost wished he was still too drunk to guess the size of the hangover that awaited him the next morning. By the time he and Nicolas arrived at 45 rue Blomet, his head was already starting to ache. The world would not stop swaying, and his stomach felt like a glass bowl filled with liquid. As long as that liquid remained still, he was fine, but every step disrupted it, and he barely held back an empty heave. Sober enough to know what was going on but not enough to walk straight, Jean-Luc still needed Nicolas to help him up the stairs.

"I'm sorry, Nicolas."

"Don't worry about it," said Nicolas. His voice suggested otherwise. "Get some rest."

Leaving Jean-Luc to figure out how to open the door to his studio, Nicolas went back down the stairs and out of the apartment building. Jean-Luc leaned against the wall and stared at the doorknob.

Without warning, the door opened. There, in a long brown coat, stood Anya.

"It was open," she said, taking Jean-Luc's arm and throwing it over her shoulder. "You look awful. Come on, let's get you inside." Supporting him as he stumbled into the studio, she brought him over to the bed and handed him a glass of water. "Here, drink this—little sips now."

Jean-Luc just stared at the glass in his hand. Seeing Anya reminded him just why he was in this state to begin with. He put the water aside. A hangover was preferable to the heartache.

"Natasha told me that you noticed her gifts. Do you know where they came from?"

Jean-Luc shook his head.

"Heinrich Lorenz gave them to her. He's the Oberst who comes to rehearsal sometimes."

Jean-Luc clenched his fists. *Paul's murderer.*

"You should stay away from her—for your own good. Heinrich has told her that he would kill any other man." Anya sat down next to him on the bed and began to unbutton her coat. "And I don't doubt that he would." She gently touched his cheek and turned his head toward her. "She's not stupid, you know. She would not have worn any of those expensive things if she hadn't wanted you to find out. It was her way of telling you to stay away from her. She really can be a coward."

Jean-Luc jerked his head away and said nothing. The room followed shortly after, and he regretted having moved so fast. He took a few labored breaths, trying to keep his stomach under control.

Anya waited until he was settled, then guided his gaze back toward her. "You're heartbroken, I know. So am I. Heinrich was mine, but he saw her and forgot all about me." She slipped her coat off her shoulders; she wore nothing underneath.

Jean-Luc looked up at her face. Anya stood up and let her coat slide to the floor. She kissed his forehead, flaunting her bosom in front of Jean-Luc's face. "You wanted me once, before you saw Natasha. I wanted you, too. We could find comfort in each other." She leaned forward to kiss him, but Jean-Luc placed his hands on her shoulders, stopping her.

Anya opened her eyes. Jean-Luc stood up, fought off the dizziness, then pulled the blanket off his bed and wrapped it around Anya.

"You're a beautiful woman, Anya. You have a spirit in you that will make some man very happy one day—but that man is not me."

Tears welled up in Anya's eyes. She pulled the blanket around her and sat down on the bed. Curling up where she sat, she muttered a little in Russian, then looked back at Jean-Luc.

"I can't help that she's prettier than I am. I can't help that I don't dance as well as she does. It's just the way I am."

"I know. I'm sorry. But it's not just her looks. It's the way she makes me feel. She is my muse."

"What is so wrong with me, Jean-Luc? Why won't you take me as a second choice? She's too afraid of him to leave him. Take me in her place. I can cook. I have good hips. I can bear you a lot of children. You can imagine her in my place, call her name—and over time, maybe you'll grow to love me."

"I'm sorry. I can only love Natasha."

"I shouldn't be surprised," Anya said, her voice cracking and tears pouring down her cheeks. "Why would anyone choose me? You would even rather be alone than love me."

Jean-Luc put an arm around her and hugged her. "Someone will grow to love you, Anya. But I won't lie to you and pretend I could. It wouldn't be fair."

Anya wiped her eyes and took a few staggered breaths. Without looking at Jean-Luc, she reached for her coat. Jean-Luc checked his watch. His head was pounding full force, but he was sober enough to remember how to tell time. Curfew was in ten minutes.

Jean-Luc grabbed Anya's arm. "You'll never get home in time." He picked up one of his clean shirts and handed it to her. "Here. You can sleep in the bed and I'll take the floor."

Anya shook her head but did not meet Jean-Luc's eyes. Her face was a deep scarlet. "No. I . . . I have to get home."

"I insist."

Jean-Luc turned around while Anya got dressed. With a rolled-up shirt as a pillow and his coat as a blanket, he curled up on the floor. It wasn't long before Anya drew long, even breaths and began to snore.

Between the pain in his head, his queasy stomach, and thoughts of Natasha and Lorenz, Jean-Luc had a hard time getting to sleep. As the predawn light crept through his window, he vaguely registered that his copy of *The Barque of Dante* was gone. Without giving the painting a second thought, he drifted off into tormented dreams.

Lorenz. Of all men, it had to be Lorenz.

*   *   *

When Anya awoke, she had no idea where she was. She sat up with a tiny gasp and looked around her. She was in a studio—a small, messy studio. A man with a tweed coat draped over him was curled up on the floor.

Jean-Luc. Now she remembered.

She looked down at him for a moment, enjoying the way the sunlight changed the color of his hair. He certainly was handsome—much better looking than Heinrich, anyway—and loyal. Too drunk to remember his name, with a naked woman in front of him, and he *still* only thought of Natasha.

Anya felt her face get hot. He hadn't even gawked at her. At least when Heinrich pushed her away, he'd tell her bosom to leave and sometimes give her a little grope. Jean-Luc hadn't even been tempted. He probably thought of her as a cheap whore—when it was his perfect little *Natasha* who had gone behind both of their backs.

Anya couldn't face him, not after such rejection.

She eased out of the bed, cringing at the creaking floorboards. Jean-Luc rolled over but didn't wake up. Throwing her coat on over Jean-Luc's clothes, she crept out the door and down the steps. She was almost out of the building when the door flew open and a stout woman almost plowed into her.

"Oh!" the woman cried. She staggered back, clutching her heart. Anya wanted to push past her and hurry on her way, but the woman was blocking the door.

"Are you all right?" Anya asked.

"Just a little fright, dear." The woman blinked at her. "But you're Russian—are you Natasha's friend?"

Anya tossed her head and puffed out her chest. "No." An idea struck her: she may not have bedded with Jean-Luc, but this nosy woman didn't have to know that. "Please tell Jean-Luc I will return his clothes whenever I can."

The woman narrowed her eyes but nodded. Anya pushed past her. With any luck, the woman would report back to Natasha. *Then* the little thief would see how it felt to have a man snatched away.

CHAPTER 15

"RISE AND SHINE, mon chou."
Madame Cordier's voice was followed by the sound of window shades being rolled up. Jean-Luc squeezed his eyes shut, but the light still made his head pound. He rolled over and pulled his blanket over his face—that was a mistake. Taking forced, even breaths, he fought the queasiness and waited for his stomach to calm down.

He needed a drink. A drink had worked the past three days—it had taken him a while before he could keep anything down, but it took away the shakes and a little of his headache. A few bottles would dull the pain in his heart for another day.

"Wake up, Jean-Luc. You've slept enough in the past three days."

The blanket was ripped off him. He was cold and shirtless, and that relentless light would not stop boring into his brain. "Madame," he said, "I don't feel well."

"I would imagine not," she said as she gathered up bottle after bottle of artificial wine—both empty and full. "You drank enough, too."

Jean-Luc groaned and threw the pillow over his head. "Madame, I'm so ill. Please."

"You have work today. Monsieur Matisse came by to see Joan earlier. He said the ballet opens on Saturday and your backdrop is not yet complete. Monsieur Matisse says that one more day of work should do it."

"I can't go back, Madame. Not ever."

Madame Cordier sat on the edge of Jean-Luc's bed, the bottles clinking in her arms. "Jean-Luc, listen to me. I have never forced you to go to a job. I have begged you for rent money only once in all the time you have lived here. You are an artist. Artists should not be bound by the same rules as the rest of us. I have tried to do my part to make that possible for you. But I will not allow you to toss away what you've always wanted. You will finish what you started, my dear, or I will drag you by your ear down to the opera house—and you will thank me for it one day."

Jean-Luc eased the pillow off his head and looked at Madame Cordier. She was staring back at him, a determined glint in her eye. Jean-Luc sat up and put one hand to his head and the other to his stomach.

"That's better," said Madame Cordier.

"Madame, please close the shades."

"No. Now stay in bed while I get rid of these bottles. I'll be right back with some breakfast for you."

Madame Cordier disappeared, leaving Jean-Luc to his pounding head and unsettled stomach. She returned with her silver tray in her hands and Miró in tow.

"Good morning, Jean-Luc," Miró said. "Matisse tells me you haven't been at work for some time."

Jean-Luc groaned. Work had never mattered to him before. Why should it matter now?

Madame Cordier set the tray on Jean-Luc's lap. The smell of the food made him want to retch over the side of the bed.

"Only bread and broth, I'm afraid, but I doubt you could handle much more. So tell me, who was that young Russian lady who spent the night here a few nights back?"

"That was Anya. She's Natasha's friend."

"She said she didn't know Natasha."

"That's odd. Natasha lives with her."

"Eat. I didn't put it in front of you so you could look at it." Madame Cordier crossed her arms.

Jean-Luc gathered a spoonful of the steaming broth and blew on it. He slurped the broth off the spoon. His tongue, throat, and stomach all screamed at him to spit it out, but he forced it down and took another spoonful.

"Why was she wearing your clothes?"

"Who?"

"That Russian girl—Anya."

Jean-Luc took a tentative bite of bread. His clothes?

"Oh. That. She came here wearing nothing but her coat—but I didn't, Madame. I told her I couldn't."

Why was he defending himself? He had never had to explain anything about any of the girls he had actually brought home.

"Tell me what happened. Why are you doing this to yourself?"

"You confronted Natasha about the hair combs?" Miró asked.

Jean-Luc nodded.

"And?"

"She ran off. Then Anya came and told me they were gifts from her new lover—that German pig who killed Paul."

Madame Cordier inclined her head. "Can you really trust that Anya? She lied and said she didn't know Natasha."

"Anya came here because Natasha is now with her German."

"So that Anya is a liar and a collaborating whore."

"It doesn't change that Natasha pushed me away—she has a fur and some expensive jewelry now. Anya's story makes sense."

Miró nodded. "I saw Natasha walking with a German officer two nights ago," he said. "She looked thoroughly miserable—terrified, in fact."

Jean-Luc looked down at his spoon and said nothing. He stirred his broth.

Miró placed a hand on Jean-Luc's shoulder. "Eat up. Matisse expects you at the opera house in a few hours. If you are going to finish that backdrop today, I suggest you get there on time."

Jean-Luc took another bite of his bread but didn't look up. Even if Natasha had become Lorenz's lover out of fear, that didn't change anything. She still wouldn't be his, as long as that filthy Boche lived.

"Your job with Matisse is almost finished?" Madame Cordier asked.

"Yes." Jean-Luc looked up at her. She had a peculiar expression on her face. "Madame? Are you all right?"

Madame Cordier closed the door and moved closer to Jean-Luc. "You should get a steady job for the time being, selling your paintings on the side. Save your money—no more cafés or wine. You will need it if you're going to elope with Natasha."

Jean-Luc's heart sank. "It's a lovely thought, Madame, but Natasha won't have me."

"Oh, yes she will. You trust me on that."

"Even if she would, the Germans are everywhere. I couldn't get out of Paris, let alone France—and where would I go?"

"Sweden—until the war is over. I have some friends who can help you."

"Thank you, Madame, but I don't see how your friends could do anything."

"Have faith in the Resistance, Jean-Luc. We have limited resources but heart beyond all measure."

CHAPTER 16

J EAN-LUC'S MOUTH HUNG open. Half-chewed bread dropped down into his broth.

"Close your mouth, dear. It's very unbecoming." Madame Cordier tapped his chin. "Think about it, and let me know." She turned toward the door, then stopped. "Oh, yes. I almost forgot." She gave Jean-Luc a kiss on the cheek then cracked the palm of her hand across his face. "Do not ever let me hear again that you were rude to Celeste Anton." She kissed his other cheek, gathered up some of his vomit-encrusted clothes, and left the room, closing the door behind her.

Jean-Luc rubbed his stinging cheek and looked up at Miró. "Did you know?"

"I had a feeling, but I didn't find out until a few months ago. I accidentally walked in on a meeting she was having in your studio." He laughed. "You were staying with one of your girls."

Jean-Luc shook his head. "I can't believe it. Madame?"

"You shouldn't be that surprised."

"But . . . sweet Madame? Sabotage?"

"She's mostly involved with the organization—though she does forge ration coupons and documents to raise money for the black market. She's not a bad artist herself."

"How long has she been involved?"

"From the beginning. She helped form her group."

Jean-Luc shook his head. "I never thought . . . not for one second."

Miró looked around the studio. "You've been painting over the last few days. Do you remember coming into my studio and dragging your easel back?"

"No. I remember wondering when I had done that, but then I drank some more and didn't care."

"You've improved a lot," Miró said, "but you've fallen back into your old habits. Your own voice has vanished." He gestured at the painting on the easel. "This looks like something you showed me when we first met."

"I've lost my muse."

"A muse never leaves you. She may change her influence, but she will never fade and never die." Miró sat down on the edge of the bed. "So. Are you going to try to elope with Natasha?"

"I've known her for a month."

"Only a few days ago, you told me you would have proposed already if you had the money. Are you willing to do what it takes to make her your bride?"

"I don't think she'll have me."

Miró studied Jean-Luc for a moment. He grabbed the tray from Jean-Luc's lap and placed it on the table. "You're not eating anyway. Come with me."

"Where?"

"To my studio."

Jean-Luc eased himself out of bed. His hands shook, his head pounded, and he felt weak. Taking small steps and leaning on the wall for support, he followed Miró to his studio. As soon as they entered, Jean-Luc went over to the couch and eased himself onto it.

"I want to show you something," Miró said. He walked to a corner of the room.

Jean-Luc closed his eyes and leaned back. He didn't want to think about Natasha. It hurt too much.

"Here."

Jean-Luc opened his eyes. Miró held a completed painting before him. Jean-Luc felt himself being pulled into the piece. His mind floated through a dream world of stars and colors. The piece had something else, too—a warmth, a comfort, an allure.

"Natasha," Jean-Luc whispered.

"I call it *Woman with the Fair Armpit Dressing Her Hair by the Light of the Stars*."

"It's beautiful, Joan."

"When Natasha looked at you, this was the look in her eyes." Miró held up his painting. "She doesn't believe a life with you is possible—because it's too good to be true. You must prove her wrong. Fight for love. Believe me, it is worth any cost."

He brought the painting back over to a corner, where a large satchel and a long cylindrical tube were sitting. Miró rolled the painting back up and placed it in the cylinder.

For the first time, Jean-Luc noticed how sparse the room was. Paint and paper were no longer on the table next to the phonograph, and no brushes were in sight. Everything that belonged to Miró, save for the phonograph, had been packed up.

As if reading his thoughts, Miró said, "I will be leaving earlier than expected. I didn't even bother applying for permission to cross the border—I wouldn't get it. Madame Cordier said that some of her spies overheard a conversation about me."

"What about you?"

"It's not safe for me here. My art is not up to German standards, but apparently a secret admirer of my work wants my paintings for his private collection. I don't want to wait around for him to steal my art and decide that my death would bring the value up."

"How will you get out?"

"Madame's connections, of course."

"When?"

"I'm not sure, yet. When I do leave, I won't tell you, just in case." He went over to his closet and pulled out a bottle of real wine. "If you don't tell Madame, I won't. I'll give you one glass—to take away your shakes and to toast our farewell."

Jean-Luc stared at Miró. After a long while, he nodded.

Miró poured the wine and lifted his glass. "To art, and the end of this god-awful war."

"And a safe journey home."

They drained their glasses. The wine was sweet—a 1902 Bordeaux. Jean-Luc licked his lips. Miró studied Jean-Luc with the same analytical expression he used when critiquing a painting. After a moment, he went back to his closet and pulled out another bottle of the same vintage and handed it to Jean-Luc.

"Here. A farewell gift. Save it for your wedding night."

*　*　*

Jean-Luc did not even look at the ballerinas as he walked across the stage to where Matisse stood on the ladder.

"Hmph! Nice of you to show up." Matisse hobbled down the ladder and over to his chair. "Had a fit, did we?"

"I'm sorry, Monsieur."

"Apologies don't make good art." He handed Jean-Luc a paintbrush. "Get back to work. I want to finish this today."

Jean-Luc went up the ladder and took a deep breath. Natasha was there, in the same room. How could he get her alone and ask her to elope with him? His hands shook. Was she watching? Was that swine coming to pick her up today? Had he hurt her? Had she bedded with him?

Jean-Luc took a deep breath. Time to work. He cleared his mind as best he could. Once he was able to look at the canvas with a calm, detached mind-set, he began to paint.

Hours flew by. Before the rehearsal was over, Jean-Luc had finished the backdrop. He climbed down the ladder to admire his work.

He had turned the landscape Matisse had created into a painted tapestry. He puffed out his chest in pride.

"Well done," Matisse said. He handed Jean-Luc the remainder of his payment, along with a few ration coupons and tickets to opening night. "The seats aren't the best, but at least you'll see the dancers performing in front of your backdrop."

"What about you?"

"I'm going back to the south. My paperwork expires tomorrow. Good luck, Jean-Luc. You're a fine artist. I hope my children will one day hang your paintings next to mine."

Matisse nodded to Jean-Luc and hobbled off the stage. Jean-Luc looked up again. It really was a work of art.

For the first time all night, Jean-Luc risked a glance at the ballerinas. Lorenz was there, talking to Natasha. His hands were on her waist. Natasha did not smile, nor did she lean into him. Her entire body was stiff.

Hope rose within Jean-Luc. Without a second thought, he ran out of the opera house, praying that the métro was running. He needed to get to Le Café d'Anton as soon as possible.

CHAPTER 17

LORENZ PULLED UP to the Maximovs' apartment and opened the car door for Natasha.

"I'm sorry, Schatzi," he said. "I can't have you stay tonight. I have duties to attend to—and the SS is here. I want to impress them."

Natasha nodded. She almost didn't believe it—a night without Lorenz.

"I will see you tomorrow. Come by before your dress rehearsal and I will make it up to you." He pulled her into a deep kiss. "Good night, my love." He grabbed her chin and looked into her eyes. "Tell me."

"I love you." The lie still brought a foul taste to her mouth.

Lorenz kissed her again, slipping his hands underneath her new fur coat to grope and fondle her. Finally, he returned to his jeep and drove away. Natasha shuddered and went inside.

She hated herself. She could still see the look on Jean-Luc's face when he noticed her ring and fur. She did not want to imagine the hurt look he must have had when Anya told him about Lorenz.

A tear slid down her cheek. *I should have let him kill me.*

She opened the door to the apartment and made her way to the room she and Anya shared. Candlelight shone through the cracks of the door.

When Natasha opened it, she found Anya standing in front of the vanity mirror. She was wearing one of Natasha's dresses, its back zipper only halfway up and her chest almost falling out of the bodice. The string of pearls Lorenz had given Natasha was around Anya's neck, the stole was draped across her shoulders, and J. S.'s ring was snug on her finger.

Anya looked up and saw Natasha through the mirror.

"Just trying to remember what it feels like," Anya said, applying some rouge. "Oh, by the way, if you see Jean-Luc—"

"You know I can't talk to Jean-Luc."

"Well, if you do see him, tell him I have his clothes. They're clean."

A lump formed in Natasha's throat. "Why do you have his clothes?"

Anya just smiled.

"You're lying."

"You took Heinrich. Why shouldn't I take Jean-Luc?"

"You're lying!" Natasha shouted. She pulled off her fur coat and tossed it at Anya's feet. She yanked at the necklace she wore, snapping the chain, and threw the remains at Anya. "You want Lorenz? You can have him! Take him! You want the jewelry? The furs?" She pulled off all of her rings and threw them at Anya, too. "Take them! Take them all! You can have him touching you in the middle of the night, making your skin crawl! You can have all his gifts, and you can wonder which Jew this ring belonged to, which Jew once owned that fur. You can wonder where they are and what he did to them!" Natasha collapsed to the floor. Head in her hands, she curled up into a ball and cried.

Anya looked down at her. She took off the pearls, the stole, and with some difficulty, the ring. She knelt down beside Natasha and tried to help her up.

Natasha threw her off. "Don't touch me."

"Natasha—"

"Don't."

Natasha stood up and wiped her eyes. Without looking at Anya, she went about getting ready for bed.

"Natasha, please talk to me."

Natasha crawled into bed. Tears welled up in her eyes. Anya had to be lying. Jean-Luc wouldn't. *Would he?* Natasha wrapped the blanket closer around her. Staring at the wall, she wished with all her heart that she would die in her sleep.

*   *   *

Natasha was pulled from a dream by the feeling of breath on her face. Her eyes snapped open. A man's shadow hovered over her in the darkness. She tried to scream, but the sound was muffled by a hand over her mouth. It was then that the scent of paint hit her.

"Shh. Natasha, it's all right."

Natasha's heart soared. Slowly, Jean-Luc pulled his hand away from her mouth and kissed her.

The familiar taste and feel of his kiss pulled her in. She wrapped her arms around him and breathed in his scent, never wanting to let him go. When he pulled away, he kept his face close.

"I'm dreaming," she whispered.

Jean-Luc shook his head. "No."

"How did you get in here?"

"The window."

"Did you wake Anya?"

Jean-Luc chuckled. "She seems to sleep through anything."

Natasha looked over at Anya's bed. She had pulled her blanket over her head and hadn't moved. Anya could never sit still when she was awake. She had to be asleep now, and for once, she wasn't snoring.

Natasha looked back at Jean-Luc, still not willing to believe he was really there. "But . . . why did—?"

"Natasha, I need to know something. I need you to tell me the absolute truth, no matter how much you think it will hurt me. Promise me."

Natasha hesitated, then said, "I promise."

"Do you love me?"

"Yes." She paused. *The absolute truth.* "But Lorenz will kill—"

"I know about Lorenz. It doesn't matter. All I need to know is that you love me." He brushed a strand of hair behind her ear. "I love you, Natasha—more than anything. I can't give you jewels or furs, but I will never hurt you, and I will never leave you, so long as I live. If you will have me, I will marry you and take you away from France—away from the Germans and Lorenz."

Natasha's heart pounded. "Yes," she said.

Jean-Luc kissed her again. "Monsieur Anton gave me a job washing dishes at his café. I'm going to work as often as I can until I save up enough money to get us to Sweden."

"Lorenz will kill us both if he finds out. I'll have to keep seeing him."

"I understand."

"I can sell his gifts when we get to Sweden—get a place to live and buy you art supplies."

Jean-Luc smiled. "I have to get going."

"Jean-Luc? Anya said she . . . she . . ."

"No. She tried, but I couldn't. Don't be too hard on her. She's having a hard time living in your shadow."

Natasha pulled on his arm. "Please stay with me tonight?"

"I can't. It's almost morning. When are you supposed to see Lorenz again?"

"Tomorrow—well, today, just before dress rehearsal."

"Can you come to see me early in the morning?"

Natasha nodded. "Tell me again that I'm not dreaming."

Jean-Luc caressed her cheek. "You're not dreaming, my love. I'll see you in the morning."

Jean-Luc left through the window and down the fire escape. Natasha watched him as he disappeared into the darkness, then went over to her dresser and lit a candle. She pulled out her nested dolls and kissed the outermost doll's head. After saying a heartfelt prayer for the former owners of all Lorenz's gifts, she blew out the candle and went back to bed.

She was going to marry Jean-Luc. He was going to take her away from France and make her his bride. She would cook for him, take care of him, and bear him children, just like she had imagined. The thought should have calmed her, but her stomach twisted into a knot.

Her menses were already three days late. What if she were pregnant? If she was, whose child was it? Would Jean-Luc accept a child that wasn't his? What if they couldn't flee Paris until after the baby was born? What would Lorenz do if the child had auburn hair and green eyes?

What if the child looks like my father?

Natasha went cold at the thought. She looked over at the vanity, where J. S.'s ring caught the dim predawn light. She went over to the vanity to study the ring.

What would Lorenz do if he knew he had taken this from one Jew, only to give it to another?

She needed someone to talk to about this. She needed someone to tell her she was worrying too much; that if she relaxed, her menses would come.

"Anya?"

No response.

"Anya, wake up. I need to talk to you."

Still no response. Natasha took the few steps to Anya's bed and tried to shake her awake but found only pillows and blankets. Anya was gone.

CHAPTER 18

ANYA STOOD IN the early morning light, looking up at the Hotel Meurice, muttering to herself.

"You can do this. You can."

She checked her reflection in her compact mirror. She needed rouge but didn't have any; she had used the last of it for her botched seduction of Jean-Luc. She pinched her cheeks. That would have to do.

She closed the mirror and replaced it in her handbag.

"You can do this, Anya. You can. He loves you—really. She's just an infatuation." She took a deep breath and nodded. Unbuttoning the top two buttons of her blouse, she adjusted her bosom one last time and marched into the hotel.

She made awkward eye contact with one of the officers she had dined with when Heinrich was all hers. He looked down at her unbuttoned blouse and smirked. Anya jerked her head forward and stuck her nose in the air.

From the corner of her eye, she saw other soldiers nudging each other and nodding in her direction. She heard snickering and caught a few jokes at her expense but she continued walking toward the staircase. When she reached the door to Heinrich's room, she checked herself over again and knocked on the door.

"You're early today, Schatzi," Heinrich said as he opened the door wearing only a towel. He stepped back when he saw Anya.

Anya froze for a second, then she puffed out her chest and strode past him into the hotel room. "May I come in?"

"I told you not to come back here. I am expecting someone."

"Natasha, you mean?" Anya said, sliding her coat off her shoulders and tossing it on the couch. "She was still sleeping when I left. Apparently you wore her out last night." She smiled and walked toward him. "I remember nights when I was so exhausted I thought I could sleep for days. You really were marvelous."

Anya lifted her hand to touch the muscles on his chest, but Heinrich grabbed her wrist and shoved her away.

"You are not welcome here. Leave."

Anya rubbed her sore wrist. Bruises would show later.

"Natasha is still sleeping. I could keep you company until then." Anya began to take off her blouse. "You can do whatever you like to me. I'm sure Natasha doesn't let you—"

"Enough!" Heinrich brought his hand across the side of her head, knocking her over.

Ears ringing and face red, Anya stood up and forced a laugh. "See? I'm better for you. You can hit me. You can pull my hair and be rough. Natasha would never stand for—"

Heinrich grabbed her by both of her wrists, threw her against the door, and spat in her face. "I have no need for a whore like you. Get out." He let go of her and backed away, crossing his arms over his chest.

Anya wiped her forehead and looked up at him. In his eyes was the loathing he usually reserved for Communists, Jews, and other "undesirables." It was a look that she would never have received from him if it weren't for Natasha.

"I see," Anya said. "She is your treasure now, is she? Anything and everything for her, right? Of course. That's how it's always been. Spoiled little

Natasha. My family has done everything for her. There wasn't a thing I had that I wouldn't gladly share—except one. And she had to take it from me."

"Don't blame her for your shortcomings."

Anya gave a mirthless laugh. "*My* shortcomings? Ha! Look at your Natasha. She could never give you what you want. You like to be rough in bed, but you chose someone so delicate, she would probably snap in two if you had her the way you've had me. You want at least six good, strong German children, but you would rather have a woman with hips so narrow, she'd probably lose the first one and be barren from then on. You look away from those things, don't you? Just like you look away from my strengths. I'm a better cook. I have larger breasts. I laugh. I smile. I am much better suited to you . . . but that doesn't count, does it?"

"You are nothing next to her."

Tears spilled down Anya's cheeks. "Oh, yes. Perfect Natasha. What have I done wrong?" She paced back and forth, her arms flailing about. "We have the same upbringing, yet you see her as so much more sophisticated. We eat the same meals, yet my frame is so much larger and heavier than hers. We both dance—we've had the same lessons—yet she is so much better than I am. We drink the same water, but her teeth are whiter. I'm not pretty enough for you—too dark, too thick, too clumsy. She is everything, isn't she? You don't even try to see past her façade. She plays the fragile role so well. Drew you right in, didn't it? All you see is a delicate doll. I'm so horrible compared to pretty little Natasha. What is so wrong with me that a man who hates Jews would choose one over m—"

Anya clapped her hand over her mouth, but it was too late. Heinrich relaxed the crease in his brow and unfolded his arms. He placed the palms of his hands against the door over Anya's shoulders. Anya flinched.

"A Jew?"

His expression was unreadable, but Anya felt cold from looking into his eyes. Then, to her surprise, he kissed her. When he broke away, he cupped the back of her neck with one hand and fondled her breast with the other.

"Natasha is a Jew, you say?" he asked, nibbling on her ear.

Anya sighed with pleasure. She had known he was different. Heinrich wouldn't be angry that Natasha was Jewish—he just wouldn't want her anymore. "Yes," Anya whispered.

The hand on her breast moved to her leg. He pressed himself up against her. "An Aryan and a Jew—that is forbidden. You know this, right?"

Anya nodded and let out a little moan.

"Who else knows?"

"No one—only my family. We never told anyone when we moved here."

"Good," he said, his voice deep and seductive in her ear. "I would hate for anyone to find out."

Anya wrapped her arms around his neck. *I told her he was different. I told her she was worried over nothing—he just doesn't want her anymore. He wants me again. I knew he loved me . . .*

Heinrich chuckled, then tweaked her breast and grabbed her by the throat. Anya's hands flew up to his, trying to pry them loose. He squeezed. Anya tried to draw in breath, but the air wasn't there anymore. She flailed her legs around, but he pressed her body against the door and lifted her so that her toes barely touched the floor.

"I would rather keep her secret."

Anya managed to pull in a thin, whistling breath. Heinrich tightened his grip. She could feel the blood pounding behind her eyes. Black spots clouded her vision, thickening at the edges, and closing in. She tried to call out for help but could only mouth the words. Her head felt heavy, and she was having trouble finding the strength to reach up and pull at his hand. She gave one last feeble effort and then the last of her vision faded into darkness.

*   *   *

Lorenz held Anya up against his door for a full minute after she stopped twitching. He then eased her to the floor and snapped her neck, just to be sure that the whore was dead.

A Jew. She had to have been lying—but Anya was not one to make up stories in a rant. That was usually when her truth came out. He had learned that much from Natasha.

Natasha is a Jew—an unregistered, illegal, sneaky, underhanded Jew. Lorenz ground his teeth. He looked down at Anya's body and slammed his heel against her lifeless face. Blood trickled out of her mouth, and her neck twisted at an odd angle.

How could his beautiful, delicate Natasha be Jewish? How could he have missed the signs? Had she worn perfume to cover the sickly sweet Jew smell? Had the Jew smell rubbed off on him?

He went into the bathroom and scrubbed his hands until they were red, then he splashed water on his face and looked up into the mirror. If anyone found out, he would be ruined—he would never be able to join the SS.

He took another shower with scalding hot water, scrubbing himself until he was sure no trace of a Jew scent survived. Throwing on a bathrobe, he went back out to Anya's body and gave it another kick, dislocating the jaw and staining the carpet with more blood. The Jew-housing bitch deserved to die. He only wished he had sent her off to Drancy first—let her be of use to the SS and pay for her crime.

Lorenz paced around the couch for an hour. His soft, beautiful Natasha, the epitome of Aryan beauty, was a Jewess—a lying, sneaky, manipulative Jewess. Had she been laughing at him the whole time? He tried to remember the expression on her face when he had told her how gifted he was at picking out a Jew. Had she been smirking?

How could Natasha possibly be a Jew? Anya had to have been lying. Natasha was hardly slothful, and she did not look at all like a Jew. She didn't have the thick protruding lips, or the Jewish Six nose, or dark, rough hair—she was beautiful. Perfect.

Perfect, Lorenz thought. *Not anymore.*

That was the worst. Natasha had been perfect—the kind of woman he would have been proud to take back home to Germany to be the perfect wife and raise perfect Aryan children. Now, she was flawed.

He sat down on the couch and looked at his hands. They were shaking. He rubbed them together, his temper rising. What poison had the Jewess fed him that had made him lose control? Wasn't it bad enough that the Jews were trying to destroy Germany from the inside out? They also had to destroy German men, one by one?

Lorenz glanced at the mantle clock. Natasha was due to arrive in ten minutes. She was never late.

I should gouge her eyes out with a hot poker for making a fool of me, Lorenz thought.

He could not kill Natasha himself. She had wound herself too tightly around his heart for his own good. He could turn her over to the SS—but then he would lose face. He could say that she was a Resistance spy, but even then he would be mocked for not catching on sooner. His career would be ruined.

He looked down at Anya's body. That little whore had caused him more trouble than she was worth. She had ruined everything. It was better when he hadn't known the truth.

He leaned over and picked up the telephone on the end table. No one could ever find out about this.

"Kremmler," he said into the receiver, "I want to see you in my room in twenty minutes."

CHAPTER 19

NATASHA'S HEART WAS POUNDING when she entered the lobby of the Hotel Meurice. *What if Lorenz noticed how happy she was? What if he discovered her plan?*

She smoothed her hair for the hundredth time that morning. If she were going to marry Jean-Luc, she would have to play her part for a little longer. Uneasiness would arouse more suspicion than a smile.

Natasha made her way across the lobby to the stairs. A few officers nodded to her and then averted their eyes. Lorenz did not like it when anyone stared at his treasure for too long.

She reached the door to Lorenz's room and fished around in her handbag for the key he had given her. From inside, she heard the thump of a fist against the wall.

Was she late? The clock in the lobby had said she still had almost ten minutes. But she couldn't take any chances. She knew she shouldn't have stayed those extra few minutes with Jean-Luc in his studio, but it felt so good to be back in his arms again. Was she glowing? Would Lorenz ask where she had been?

No more stalling. Don't get him angry. Just let him have his way and then go to rehearsal. You're going to marry Jean-Luc. The more gifts Lorenz gives you, the more you will have to sell when you get to Sweden.

She ran her hand over her hair one last time and opened the door. Lorenz was sitting on the couch, the phone to his ear. Natasha forced a smile and started to walk toward him, but her foot nudged against something heavy on the floor. She looked down and froze. Lying in a crumpled heap, with crusted blood all over her face, was Anya.

"Close the door, Natasha," Lorenz said. He then continued his conversation in German.

Natasha did as she was told. Too shocked and horrified for tears, Natasha could only stand with her back against the door, staring down at Anya's body. Anya's eyes were open and rolled back into her head. Red marks blistered her neck, and her head was twisted into an awful, unnatural position.

No, Natasha thought. For a moment, she was thirteen again, staring down at her father's body, the blood spreading under her shoes.

Tell your mother that this is the price for her insubordination.

The sound of the phone being hung up pulled Natasha back to the present. Without even looking down at Anya's body, Lorenz shifted his weight on the couch so he could look over at Natasha.

"You have put us in a very precarious position, my love," he said.

Natasha's throat went dry. She glanced down at Anya's body then back up to Lorenz. *Had Anya told him about Jean-Luc?*

"Do not pretend with me, Natasha." He stood up and slowly walked over to her. "Were you laughing at me? Were you?"

Natasha cowered back against the door. She fumbled for the doorknob, but Lorenz pulled her away from the door and bolted it.

"Sit down," he said, gesturing to the couch. Natasha looked down at Anya's body and didn't move.

"It is your own fault." His voice was still low and calm. "You have made us all vulnerable, and as a result, your whore of a friend is dead. Now sit."

Natasha crept over to the couch, her eyes darting from Lorenz to Anya to the door. As she sat down, Lorenz stepped in front of her, blocking her path and view of the door. He stared down at her, tilting his head and sniffing the air. He studied her profile. Was he searching for bite marks? The scent of a man? She hoped Jean-Luc's paint smell did not linger on her.

"A Jewess with no features. Interesting."

Natasha felt as if all of her blood was rushing down to her toes. She looked up at Lorenz, wide-eyed.

"Tell me, Natasha. Who knows this secret? The ballet mistress? Some of the other dancers?"

Natasha could not speak. She could not blink or pull her eyes away from Lorenz's. Lorenz grabbed her by the shoulders and shook her. "Who knows?" he shouted. His face was red, and a vein throbbed on his forehead.

Her throat dry and her voice barely a whisper, Natasha managed to stammer, "N-no one."

"No one?"

Natasha shook her head. "Anya. That's it."

"Only Anya? No one else?"

Natasha shook her head. "No. No one else."

"Wouldn't her family know?"

"N-no. My family hid it in Russia as well. I only confided to Anya later."

Lorenz released Natasha's shoulders and paced back and forth in front of her, blocking, then revealing, the view of Anya's dead body.

"It appears, my love, that there are choices to be made." He adjusted his bathrobe. "I could kill you now." He opened a drawer and pulled out a revolver. Natasha shrank back, trembling. "It would be a shame to kill something so beautiful, though. Perhaps I could just have my way with you as I like it—and kill you as I finish?" He pointed the revolver at her.

Natasha clamped her eyes shut and waited for the blast, but none came. She opened her eyes to discover that Lorenz had lowered the gun and was now looking at her with an amused expression.

"Or perhaps, I could arrange passage for you out of Paris—out of France."

Natasha sat up straight, her heart pounding in hope. *Had Anya been right? Did this man have a gentle side?*

Lorenz laughed, squashing Natasha's optimism. Natasha sank back into the couch.

"Germany?" she asked.

"Of course not Germany," Lorenz said. "Do you think we want Jews there? We're looking to get *rid* of your filthy race."

Lorenz looked over at Anya's body with a wild grin. "Have you ever heard of Auschwitz, Natasha?" He did not wait for her to answer. "Of course you haven't—it is not a secret told lightly. But I know your secret, so perhaps you should know mine.

"I could put you on a train with, oh, maybe a hundred other Jews in a cattle car—where you belong—and take you away to Auschwitz." Lorenz turned back to Natasha and leaned over her. "There, you will see the answer to the Jewish Question." He caressed her arm. "I have seen it. My friends in the SS have taken me there. It is what made me want to join their ranks. There, the Jews finally pay for their crimes against Germany.

"And you, deceitful little Natasha, would have an advantage—my gift to you. You would not be burdened by false hope." Lorenz ran his fingers through her hair and whispered in her ear, telling her what she could expect at Auschwitz. He told her all about a selection process—work or death.

Natasha drew a gasp and tried to stand. Lorenz put his hands on her shoulders and held her down. "Shh . . . have no fear, Natasha. You're rather frail, but a closer look would reveal the strength from dancing. There is a good chance you could be selected for work. Work, after all," he let out a grim chuckle, "makes you free."

He held her down and told her more horror stories about dysentery, typhus, and the "Gestapo kitchens"—torture chambers he promised to send her to first, before shipping her off to Auschwitz. "They might be interested to see how a Jewess managed to be born without any of the telltale features."

He's lying, Natasha thought. *He has to be exaggerating. No one could be this cruel . . . no one.*

"I trust you will be a good girl and not give the SS a hard time. I would hate to hear from a friend that he had to beat you."

The stories became worse. Standing for roll call for hours in the snow; eating out of bowls that had been used as chamber pots. Anyone who attempted to escape was rewarded not with a quick death but with a slow punishment of torture and starvation.

All the while, Lorenz spoke with a loving caress in his voice. Natasha would have shuddered if she had not been numb. She could not move. She could not blink. She stared at Anya's corpse on the carpet, envying her fate.

Large teardrops spilled out of Natasha's wide eyes. It couldn't be true.

Lorenz paused and placed his hand on her throat. "Or," he said, "I could just break your pretty neck." He did not squeeze. "Hmm? Should I do that instead?"

Natasha stared up into his eyes. *Please. Just kill me. Anything but that place. Anything.*

He looked down at her and something in his face softened. "Damn you," he said, shoving her down on the couch.

He paced around the room, walking around Anya's body as if it were a piece of furniture. He ran his hands through his hair, and then he turned sharply back to Natasha.

"Do you love me?"

Natasha did not hesitate in the lie. "Yes," she said.

"No one else knows?" he asked again.

"No one," Natasha whispered.

"You lying Jew!" he spat.

Natasha flinched and braced herself for a blow, but a knock at the door saved her. Lorenz looked from Natasha to Anya's body, then back to Natasha. He called out something in German and the door opened.

A soldier entered and then stopped at the sight of Anya's dead body. When he realized Lorenz was glaring at him, he saluted.

They had a brief conversation in German. Lorenz gestured to Natasha, then down to Anya's body. The soldier's eyes widened. Lorenz lifted his chin, the way he always did when he gave a command. The soldier nodded, saluted, glanced over at Natasha, and left.

"You are indebted to me, Natasha. And I expect gratitude."

Indebted? He can't mean—

"I have told Kremmler that you discovered that Anya was a Communist, and that she and her parents were involved in an anti-German plot."

"Anya's parents. No!"

"You have lied to me. That filth," he gestured to Anya's body, "already told me that her family knew. Why did you lie to me, Natasha?"

"I . . . I thought you meant anyone outside the family."

"And did you think I would not silence her family? Are you not grateful that I have saved your secret? I commended you for your courage to come forward."

Natasha could not believe her ears. He would not send her to that horrible place?

"So quiet, Natasha. I said, 'Are you not grateful?'"

"I—" Natasha could hardly form a sentence. "I am grateful. Thank you," she said.

Lorenz would not look at her. "You are not to go back to that apartment. Everything you need is here. You will come here directly after rehearsal tonight, after your performance tomorrow night, and every night after that—until I tire of you and report you as a traitor and a Jew."

Natasha nodded. Lorenz untied his robe.

"Into the bedroom. Now."

CHAPTER 20

THE THOUGHT OF MARRYING Jean-Luc was the only thing preventing Natasha from sobbing as she lay wrapped in Lorenz's arms. She could hear the little mantle clock chiming twelve times. Dress rehearsal started in two hours. From the Hotel Meurice it was not a very long walk to the opera house; Natasha doubted Lorenz would let her leave so early.

He had his way with her whenever he was ready, getting more intense each time. He still did not strike her, but he was no longer gentle, and he expected her to moan and cry out his name. Each time, Natasha felt a little piece of her soul being torn away. She had to get out.

"Heinrich?"

"Hmm?" Lorenz's hand moved to cup her breast.

"My toe shoes—they're at home."

His eyes narrowed. "This is your home now. You will call it as such."

"I'm sorry. I—my—they're at Anya's. May I go get them?"

"I have already told Kremmler about your toe shoes. When he returns, he will bring them."

Natasha nodded. Lorenz began to kiss her neck. "Should I make you answer the door as you are when he arrives?"

Natasha stiffened. Lorenz had not let her get dressed since he had first ordered her clothes off.

"Please, Heinrich. Don't."

"Why not?"

"I—I am only for your eyes—my love."

"You are only for me because I say you are. If I tell you to answer the door, you will answer the door."

"Please," she said. "I don't want any other man to see me."

As if on cue, someone pounded on the door.

"There's Kremmler now."

"Please—"

Lorenz laughed, giving her breast one last squeeze. "Natasha, I would rip the eyes out of any man who dared to look at your body." He stood up and threw on the bathrobe that he had dropped to the floor so many hours ago. "Wait here for me."

Natasha pulled the sheet up around her and stared at the wall. *I'm going to marry Jean-Luc. I have to play my part.*

She could hear Lorenz speaking German. Laughter. More words. The sound of something dragging on the floor. "Heil Hitler!" Then the door clicked shut.

Lorenz returned carrying two pairs of toe shoes: hers and Anya's. They were the same size; though Anya's feet were slightly larger, she had been determined to squeeze into the smaller size shoe, which often had a terrible effect on her performance.

"Kremmler wasn't sure which pair was yours. Now you have two." Lorenz dropped the shoes and his robe to the floor and pulled the sheet away from Natasha. "No hiding, my love. I will be ready soon enough."

"Is she—is Anya—?"

"No. Kremmler took her body away."

"Will there be a funeral?"

Lorenz laughed. "No. Of course not." He crawled into bed with her and stroked her hair.

"Per . . . perhaps I should go to rehearsal early. We open tomorrow, and we will have to redo the choreography—"

"And no one else will be so early. There will be no point." He sat up and glared at her. "Why so eager to leave, Natasha? You don't want to be here with me?"

Hating herself, Natasha rolled onto her side and kissed Lorenz's chest. Moving her lips up to his neck, she closed her eyes and imagined Jean-Luc.

"Of course I want to stay," she said, sliding her leg up around his. "I just want the ballet to be worthy of a German audience. I wanted to help the ballet mistress reorganize."

Lorenz pulled her face to his and kissed her hard. "Soon, then, my love. But not yet," he said and seized her again.

He tossed her about on the bed, roughly grabbing her wrists and groping her flesh as if trying to pull it off. He moved his mouth from hers, to her throat, to her shoulder, and back to her mouth, as if trying to devour her. He nibbled and bit, but not enough to cause any pain or leave any marks. His breath came in quick gasps that escalated into moans as he pressed into her.

Eyes closed, Natasha tried to picture the last time she and Jean-Luc had made love. But it was hard to ignore the rough hands, the hairy chest, and the German-accented voice that called her name.

"Tell me, my love . . . tell me you're mine."

I am going to marry Jean-Luc. I am going to marry Jean-Luc.

"I'm yours . . . I'm yours."

Lorenz grabbed her wrists and pushed her against the headboard.

"It's illegal and unnatural . . . but oh, Natasha, my love . . . It will be our secret."

He slowed his pace but held onto her wrists and pinned them over her head. She clamped her eyes shut and began to exaggerate her grunts. *Jean-Luc. Think of Jean-Luc.*

"Natasha . . ."

"J—" Natasha's eyes snapped open, and she immediately turned her blunder into a long, feigned moan.

The act was convincing enough for Lorenz. He increased his pace again and soon after collapsed on top of her. Bathed in sweat and panting heavily, he kissed her roughly, then ordered her into the shower.

"I want to watch you bathe."

*   *   *

Finally permitted to get dressed, Natasha gathered up her clothes. She felt disgusted with herself. She had never invited Lorenz before.

I had to, she told herself. *He was getting suspicious. It was the only way to distract him.*

She pulled on her skirt and blouse, trying to ignore her rumbling stomach. She hadn't eaten anything since breakfast and wouldn't have time to stop at a café. It was going to be a very long night of rehearsal, too.

"Heinrich?" she said as she pulled her hair into a bun. "I don't want you to worry—but it will probably be a very long rehearsal, with . . . with all of the changes we will have to make."

Lorenz laughed. Natasha shivered.

"I know." He smacked her bottom. "Go on. Off to rehearsal. When you are finished, come back here immediately, understand?"

Natasha nodded. "Of course."

Lorenz pulled her into a long kiss good-bye, then escorted her to the door. A few bloodstains remained where Anya's body had been. Natasha was glad she hadn't eaten.

Another kiss. Another squeeze.

"Tell me."

The lie: "I love you."

At last, Natasha was able to slip into the hallway. Lorenz closed the door behind her.

Down the hall. Down the staircase. Across the lobby. *Don't look at any of them*, Natasha told herself. She tried to hold herself as she usually did, but before she had reached the hotel entrance, she could feel her eyes burning with tears. *Hold back, Natasha. Don't let them see you.*

Before she could stop herself, she picked up her pace and nearly ran out the door. Tears spilled down her cheeks as she ran toward the Théâtre de l'Opéra. Anya, the only friend she had known for so long, the person she had cried to, the one who had whispered soothing words when everything came crashing down in her life, was dead.

And it's all my fault.

Now Anya's family was paying the price for Natasha's failure to register as a Jew when the law was first passed. After everything they had done for her, this was how she repaid them?

What have I done? God, what have I done?

When Natasha reached the opera house, her eyes, cheeks, nose, and ears were red, and she was in desperate need of a handkerchief. She tore through the building, calling out Madame Fournier's name, praying that the ballet mistress was there as early as she always claimed she was.

"Madame Fournier!" Natasha called as she entered the theatre. Her own echo answered her. She spun around, dizzy and nauseous, only to be met with the finished backdrop, hanging in its rightful place.

It was a beautiful landscape, painted to look like a tapestry and accented with all of the colors that Jean-Luc had always favored on her. She fell to her knees in front of the masterpiece. It was beautiful: a work of art made just for her; a gift from the man she loved—the man she wanted to be with.

She couldn't bear to see Jean-Luc lying dead on Lorenz's floor. Three lives had already been destroyed because of her. She could not add his to the list.

"I'm sorry," she whispered between sobs. "I'm so sorry."

"Natasha?"

Madame Fournier placed a hand on Natasha's shoulder. Natasha jumped and stared up at her for a moment, then broke down and began sobbing at the ballet mistress's feet.

"What happened?" Madame Fournier asked. "What's wrong?"

Natasha choked on her sobs, trying to form words. Where could she begin? Her face was hot and every breath brought a tight pain in her chest.

"Natasha, calm down."

Madame Fournier clapped her hands. The sound echoed throughout the theatre, reminding Natasha where she was and what she was. She had a job to do. Grief was no excuse for a poor performance.

After a few deep breaths, Natasha was able to speak.

"Anya is dead. We need to adjust the choreography."

Madame Fournier jerked her hand away. "What? How—?"

"Anya is dead," Natasha repeated, lifting her head to meet the ballet mistress's eyes. "We need to adjust the choreography."

Pale, with her hand pressed to her mouth, Madame Fournier looked around the theatre, blinked several times, and nodded.

"Get dressed, Natasha. I will need you to help me."

Natasha wiped her eyes and glanced at the backdrop—the little piece of Jean-Luc towering over her. She summoned the strength to stand. Her knees felt weak, and though her stomach gurgled in hunger, she had never had less of an appetite. Without a word, she turned and took one last look at the backdrop. Feeling a surge of courage, Natasha walked offstage toward the dressing room. Jean-Luc would rescue her.

*　*　*

It was nearly curfew when Madame Fournier clapped her hands and gave everyone permission to leave. She yawned, waved her hand, and gave explicit instructions for everyone to arrive early the following morning for another run-through before the ballet opened that night.

Every one of Natasha's limbs was heavy with exhaustion. Her body begged for sleep, though she knew Lorenz would demand otherwise when she returned. Dread in every step, she changed and shuffled out of the opera house.

It was a warmer night than she had expected. The sliver of moon shining overhead provided little light to walk by, but Natasha didn't mind. For once, she wanted the City of Lights to be dark, so she could hide her tears.

"Natasha?" a familiar voice whispered from the shadows.

Heart soaring and sinking at the same time, Natasha stopped and pretended to adjust her shoe. "What are you doing here? It's not safe. I'll come see you when I can."

She tried to walk away, but Jean-Luc reached out and grabbed her hand. He stepped into the light. "One kiss?"

Trying to swallow the lump in her throat, Natasha looked away. "I have to go to him. Please let me go. We can't be seen."

Jean-Luc leaned close. "Lorenz isn't here. I just saw him walking to the Hotel Meurice—"

"We can't be seen by any German." Natasha tried to pull away. "Lorenz—"

"Lorenz doesn't scare me," Jean-Luc said.

"He should."

"Well, he doesn't."

"You don't know what he's capable of."

"But I do. He killed Paul, remember?" Jean-Luc touched her cheek to turn her face toward his, then pulled his hand away and rubbed his fingers together. "What happened?"

"Nothing—"

"You're crying."

"I'm all right. It's just been a long day."

"What did he do to you?"

"The same thing he always does."

"Did he hurt you?"

"No—"

"If he hurt you I'll—"

"No! Jean-Luc, please stay away from him. He's dangerous."

Jean-Luc wiped the tears from her cheeks and pulled her into the shadows. "I've missed you, my love."

He kissed her. Natasha felt warm, comfortable, and strong again. The world could crumble around her as long as she had Jean-Luc. In an instant, the feeling vanished, and the image of Jean-Luc lying dead on Lorenz's floor flashed into her mind. She pulled herself away.

"Are you out of your mind? What if someone sees you?"

"Natasha—"

"Go, Jean-Luc. Wait for me to send word to you."

Natasha spun on her heel and marched off toward the Hotel Meurice. He could have ruined everything! What was he thinking? Had he breathed in too much paint? How could he be so careless?

She was still in view of the opera house when she almost collided with a solid frame in a German uniform.

"Herr Kremmler," Natasha said, "I'm sorry. I didn't see you."

"Who was that man?"

Natasha's heart dropped to her stomach. "What man?"

"The man you were talking to. Who is he?"

What did he see? What did he hear?

"A nuisance."

"Then why talk to him?"

Her voice faltered. "He was looking for A . . . Anya."

Kremmler arched an eyebrow at her. "I am here to escort you home."

Natasha could feel all the color drain from her face. Once again, she was grateful for the darkness. "Thank you."

CHAPTER 21

K REMMLER DIDN'T SAY a word to her the entire way to Lorenz's hotel room. He walked half a step in front of her, occasionally giving her a sidelong glance. Heartbeat thundering in her ears, Natasha fought to keep her features smooth. Had he seen Jean-Luc kiss her? He wouldn't tell her if he had, but he would tell Lorenz—right away.

Think, Natasha, think, she told herself. *You need to think of an excuse.*

She tried to come up with questions Lorenz was likely to ask and rehearsed her answers in her head. She could not hesitate in her answers when the time came.

What if Lorenz had Jean-Luc followed and discovered he was painting replicas for the Resistance? He would be killed. So would Miró. So would Miró's contact.

Over and over she repeated the lies in her head, imagining different inflections in her voice, trying to guess which sounded the most believable. She could only hope her exhaustion had not clouded her judgment.

In the hotel lobby, Natasha turned to Kremmler and gave him a small smile. "Thank you again, Herr Kremmler. I'm sorry I wasn't very talkative. I had a very long rehearsal."

Kremmler nodded, but he did not go to his own room. He followed Natasha up the stairs and down the hall to Lorenz's door. Before knocking, Natasha looked up at him. He gave her a smug smile and gestured toward the door. She knocked.

Lorenz answered the door fully dressed this time, in uniform. He said something in German to Kremmler. Kremmler saluted and said something back—undoubtedly relaying whatever it was he saw.

Her German was still awful—she had no desire to learn the language—but she did catch a few words: *Natasha, painter, shadows*. At the very least, Kremmler had seen Jean-Luc. She listened, trying to keep her expression as natural as possible.

Kremmler spoke without hand gestures or body language, not once acknowledging Natasha's presence. Lorenz looked her way a few times, but his expression didn't change. Natasha looked at him with what she hoped was mild curiosity. Lorenz said something else to Kremmler, then dismissed him and opened the door, allowing Natasha to enter.

"Hopefully, after tomorrow night, I'll have more time to brush up on my German," Natasha said as she took off her coat. "I'm tired of not knowing what's going on." She stood on her toes and leaned forward for Lorenz's usual greeting kiss. His lips were limp against hers.

"Heinrich? Are you all right, my love?"

"Who is he, Natasha?"

She knew he would ask that. It was best not to play dumb here. "I told Kremmler that he was a nuisance looking for Anya."

"Kremmler says he grabbed you."

Natasha felt sick. "He should have also told you I pushed him away."

"Why would he grab you in the first place? Kremmler says you didn't scream."

"Because I knew who he was. He's just a harmless flirt who went after every ballerina at the opera house."

"How would he know every ballerina?" Lorenz spoke very quietly and hovered over her, his eyes narrowed.

Natasha backed against the wall. *Stick to your story. Just keep repeating yourself.*

"He was Matisse's assistant—just a no-talent annoyance. He wanted to know where Anya was. He saw you and me together and thought he would have a chance with Anya, now that you had chosen someone else."

Lorenz grabbed her by the chin and pulled her face close to his. "Don't lie to me! I have seen him look at you while you dance. I have seen the two of you speak at rehearsal. Has he had a taste of what is mine?"

"No!"

"Your whore of a friend was walking alone when I met her. You had your sore ankle that day. Why wasn't she helping you home? Were you with him?"

She had not expected this. Her fright would give everything away. She had to twist the truth. An outward lie would ruin everything. "I—"

Lorenz shook her. "Where were you?"

"I was with him, but not like that! He's a flirt—I was ... amused by him at first, so I went to a café with him. He annoyed me, so I left. Then I met you—my love. He is nothing to me. I hadn't met you yet. I didn't know. He's a no-talent, lazy buffoon. He's harmless."

"Why are you so concerned, then?"

"B ... because I don't want any more death. Please, Heinrich, I love you and only you."

The lie tasted worse than ever. Lorenz's eyes bored into her own. After a few seconds, he loosened his grip but kept his stony expression.

"You are never to see him again," he said.

Natasha nodded. "I don't want to. He's an idiot. But I can't help it if he approaches me."

"Then from now on, you will have an escort wherever you go to protect you from him. If he talks to you again, I will kill him."

Natasha wanted to scream and cry and throw herself from the top of the Eiffel Tower. She was not going to Sweden. She was not going to marry Jean-Luc.

"Into the bedroom, Natasha. Now."

Natasha felt as if her feet each weighed ten kilograms. Each step toward the bedroom took twice the effort of the last. She was surprised she was able to stay awake as Lorenz seized her with such wild force that she felt she would be split in two.

When he finished, he ordered her to bathe and then finally allowed her to go to sleep. Though she was exhausted physically and emotionally, sleep would not claim her. She lay in the dark on soft pillows, covered in warm blankets, her eyes closed and her heart racing.

She would live out her life as Lorenz's whore, however long that might be. Who knew when he would tire of her and send her off to that awful place?

Lorenz threw a heavy arm around her. She swallowed the lump in her throat. *The ballet opens tomorrow*, she thought. *I have to concentrate on my work. I can't think about that torture now.*

She dozed lightly for a few hours, but the heavy sleep that should have been upon her never came. Lorenz snored away at her side, louder than Anya had ever managed.

She could not believe her friend was gone—and she was sleeping next to her murderer. All the blankets in the world could not warm her after that thought.

Natasha's head spun. She thought of her childhood and the times she and Anya had spent together in Russia, laughing and playing. She thought of the countless rehearsals she and Anya had been through together and the nights when she had cried in Anya's lap.

Natasha's nose tingled. *No. Don't cry. You'll wake him.*

Lorenz stirred a little and rolled over, pulling his arm off her. Natasha opened her eyes and looked at Lorenz. In the dark, she could barely make out his features, but even in sleep his jaw was set and his brow was wrinkled. In less than a minute, he was snoring again.

Her stomach was turning over. Her mind was plagued with thoughts of people being forced to stand for hours in the snow, starved and with no water, suffering from typhus and dysentery. Had Lorenz been lying? Surely they couldn't be rounding up the Jews and shipping them off to be tortured and starved to death.

But something about the loving caress that had been in Lorenz's voice told her that every word he had spoken was true.

Natasha felt the bile rise in her throat. She scrambled out of bed and ran to the lavatory to vomit.

She felt dizzy. She was so tired, but she could not sleep. She leaned over the toilet, holding her hair back from her face, tears streaming uncontrollably down her cheeks.

The death camps. Anya's body. Lorenz's threat to kill Jean-Luc. It was too much. And her menses still had not come. She heaved again.

"Natasha?"

She had woken Lorenz.

"In here," Natasha managed. She wiped her eyes, trying to hide her tears as best she could. Lorenz stood in the doorway and looked down on her, his arms folded across his chest.

"What's wrong?"

"I—nothing. Just nerves."

"Nerves? But you said you do not get nervous when it comes to dancing."

"I've never performed in front of you before."

"There is something else. Tell me."

He stared at her, cold and unfeeling, as she heaved again. Unable to hold anything back, Natasha coughed and sobbed, dripping tears into the toilet.

"What is it?" Lorenz asked.

She couldn't speak. Every attempt ended in a stream of blubbering moans.

"I can't understand you. Tell me what is the matter." His voice held a touch of annoyance.

"Anya," Natasha croaked out. She broke into sobs once again. It was as if someone had reached into her chest and was squeezing and twisting her heart.

"I see," said Lorenz. "Don't waste your tears on that lying whore. You have a big day tomorrow." He turned and walked back to the bedroom.

Natasha tried to cry as quietly as she could. She heaved a few more times before she was calm enough to sit with her head against the cool porcelain. Tears dangling from her jawline, she stared at the floor for a long time.

At long last she stood up, rinsed her mouth out, and splashed water on her face. She considered putting on her toe shoes and losing herself in the dance but thought better of it. If Lorenz woke up and found her disobeying him, there was no telling what he might do.

CHAPTER 22

NATASHA AWOKE TO THE HOLLOW GURGLE of her stomach. She wasn't hungry, but she knew she would need to eat if she was going to have the strength to perform that night. Lorenz grunted next to her, stretched, and opened his eyes. He caressed her side and kissed her shoulder. Without a word, he pulled her to him and rolled on top of her. When he finished, he held her for a few minutes before patting her buttocks.

"Time to get out of bed. We're going to a café before I walk you to the opera house. You have to eat something."

Natasha nodded and sat up, feeling dizzy all over again. The smell of Lorenz's sweat made her stomach clench. She fought back the nausea. It was opening night; she had to perform.

She went about getting dressed, humming the ballet's music to herself, going over the dances in her head, taking into account the adjustments that had been made the previous night. Her concentration, usually impossible to break, kept faltering when she thought of dancing in front of the backdrop that Jean-Luc had painted.

Jean-Luc would be there that night. So would Lorenz. Jean-Luc would approach her after the ballet, despite her warnings. If Lorenz saw him . . .

She hummed louder, trying to force her thoughts back to dancing. The lump in her throat hardened and she struggled to swallow it down.

"Come, Natasha," Lorenz said, holding the door open.

Like his little Russian spaniel, Natasha thought.

Lorenz did not say a word during the entire walk to the café, and Natasha was grateful. Toe shoes in hand, she continued to hum to keep her emotions well below the surface, but it took much more effort than usual. She hoped it would not be so difficult during the performance.

They reached the café just as a light drizzle began to dot the streets.

"An indoor table, then," Lorenz said.

He opened the door to the café and let her walk in before him. As soon as Natasha stepped into the warmer air and smelled the mixture of eggs, coffee, bread, and whatever else the patrons had ordered, the color drained from her face. The odor of eggs was so powerful that she nearly retched.

Lorenz asked for a table near a window. As the waiter led them past table after table, Natasha tried not to breathe in too deeply. *What was it that smelled so strong?* Quick-tempered Lorenz had not complained yet; perhaps he hadn't noticed it. *But how could he not?* The smell was so distracting that, for a moment, Natasha forgot the first few bars of the music that accompanied her solo.

The waiter pulled out her chair, and Natasha murmured thanks. Then Lorenz ordered for the both of them—thankfully, not eggs.

"You look pale. I thought you were calm before a performance."

"It's the smell. I wish it wasn't raining. I could use some fresh air."

"Smell? It smells like every other café in here."

Natasha shrugged. "Maybe it's just me. Probably nerves. I've never had them before."

"Why have them now?" Lorenz narrowed his eyes.

"I've never performed before a German audience. You say they have higher standards."

Lorenz grinned. "You will be brilliant, my love. Then, after your performance, we will have dinner, and I will congratulate you for hours in the bedroom."

"I look forward to it." She forced a smile. The waiter brought her a cup of coffee—a blend of real and artificial. She tried not to inhale.

For Natasha, breakfast seemed to take forever. She took tiny bites of her brioche and even smaller sips of her coffee. Lorenz watched her the entire time, as if making sure she ate and drank.

At long last, Natasha choked down the last of her brioche and took the final sip of her lukewarm coffee. Lorenz motioned for the bill. Once he had paid, Natasha all but rushed out the door.

In the fresh air, with the light rain on her face, Natasha's color returned almost immediately. Free from the odor of eggs and coffee, her stomach settled back into its knot.

Lorenz walked her all the way to the stage and back toward the dressing room. Some of the other ballerinas were already going over the revised dances. When they saw Natasha with Lorenz, they began to whisper to each other, shooting glances and suspicious looks her way. Natasha ignored them.

The entire theatre reeked of paint, but Madame Fournier was not complaining about it. *Maybe she's used to it by now*, Natasha thought.

The smell was such a comfort to her. It was like being wrapped in Jean-Luc's arms, assured that everything would be all right. Almost as soon as the thought popped into her head, Lorenz pulled her into a deep, passionate kiss.

"Tell me."

"I love you."

The whispers increased. Natasha didn't care. She had never been close to any of the other dancers. They were coworkers, not friends; competition for prima ballerina roles, not companions. They could think what they wanted.

"I will see you after the performance." Lorenz kissed her again and then left her so she could get changed.

Natasha sat on the bench in front of her locker and took her shoes off. She stared at the ribbons of her toe shoes. She did not want to undress again. She felt odd, queasy, and a little dazed. Every scent invaded her nose and twisted the knot in her stomach. More ballerinas came and went, deliberately avoiding eye contact with her, only to peek her way as they whispered.

Natasha still stared at her toe shoes. Anya, Jean-Luc, and Lorenz—the three faces floated around in her mind, echoing her memories back to her.

Spoiled little Natasha . . .

If you will have me, I will marry you . . .

If he talks to you again, I will kill him . . .

The invisible hand around her heart tightened its grip. She knew what she had to do, she just didn't know if she could go through with it.

Madame Fournier clapped her hands from the doorway to the dressing room.

"Ladies, let's go. I want to go through the changes with you once more before the audience begins to arrive."

Natasha took a deep, staggering breath and began to undress. Her thoughts could not interfere with her performance.

*   *   *

Lorenz took his seat in the front row, next to Generalleutnant Boineburg, the military governor of Paris. Boineburg settled into his seat, giving Lorenz a little nod.

"I understand you have had relations with one of the Russian ballerinas," Boineburg said. "I never would have thought you'd take a Communist to your bed."

Lorenz sat up straighter but did not let his expression or his voice show any disrespect. "Natasha? A Communist? No, she left Russia to be free of the Communists. She hates her home country and never wants to go back."

"Be careful you don't fall prey to a spy, Lorenz."

"I would never reveal secrets to her, even if she were German."

Lorenz and Boineburg stared at each other for a long while. A voice interrupted their silent battle.

"Heinrich! How are you? Excellent seats, aren't they? Oh. Hello, Herr Generalleutnant."

A man in a black uniform took the seat on the other side of Lorenz. Three more took the next few seats in the same row and peeked over at Boineburg with smug smiles. The corner of Lorenz's mouth twitched. Boineburg scowled for an instant then relaxed his features.

He never did have proper respect for the SS, Lorenz thought.

Lorenz greeted the men with the salute he had neglected to give the military governor. Boineburg scowled again.

The SS officer closest to Lorenz glanced over at Boineburg and granted him a practiced smile before turning back to Lorenz.

"No need to salute, Heinrich. This is a social affair. We wouldn't want you interrupting the ballet if more officers were to arrive a little late."

Lorenz laughed. He knew better than to deny the SS a salute.

"Herr Generalleutnant, have you met SS-Gruppenführer Werner Ostendorff? He is the youngest divisional commander in the SS."

Boineburg muttered greetings but did not salute.

"I could not help but overhear your comment to Heinrich about spies, Herr Generalleutnant. Surely, you must have been joking," Ostendorff said. "Heinrich is an exceptional soldier, isn't he, Herr Generalleutnant? He has a talent for recognizing spies and enemies of the Third Reich. Has he told you about the little test we gave him?"

Boineburg shook his head, his jaw set and his eyes cold.

"We brought him four prisoners and he had to pick out the Jew among them. We made a little wager. It was the first bet I had lost in ten years."

Lorenz remembered that day. It was when he had first seen Auschwitz. Ostendorff had placed a call to a friend in another division of the SS and arranged for Lorenz to be shown around the camps. When Lorenz arrived, Ostendorff ordered four women, naked and shivering in the mid-November air, to be brought before him. The women were all disgusting animals. All had their heads shaved and were so thin that they would have made Natasha look plump. They were filthy, hunched at the shoulders, and hobbling along. None had the protruding ears, the Jewish Six nose, the heavily lidded eyes, or the thick lips. All of their knees were knobby, and all of their feet were flat. When Lorenz tried to sniff the air around them for the Jewish scent, he had to fight not to stagger back. They all smelled as if they had rolled in their own waste and then tried to cover the stench with cologne that reeked of rotting corpses.

He noticed, however, that one was much dirtier and looked far more weary, as if she had been treated more severely than the others. Yet she did not have the dead-eyed look of someone who had been forcibly used. He pulled out his pistol and shot her in the head.

"There's your Jew," he had said, and then he shot the other three. "And they are enemies of the Third Reich. They may as well be Jews."

Ostendorff, of course, left out the details of the test. Auschwitz was none of Boineburg's concern—especially if the rumors were true and the Führer was already looking to replace him.

"I'm sure he could pick out a spy from a crowd," Ostendorff continued. "Wouldn't you agree, Herr Generalleutnant?"

Boineburg grunted in agreement then quickly turned to his left and struck up a conversation with the young French girl he had brought as his date.

"The nerve of that man," Ostendorff mumbled. "To suggest that you would reveal secrets to spies when the Resistance united and blossomed under his command."

"If not for Klaus Barbie, I doubt that that pest Moulin would ever have been taken care of," Lorenz said quietly.

Ostendorff nodded. "He was making things more difficult here, especially with the news from the front."

Lorenz squared his shoulders. He threw his support behind the Führer's every decision, never doubing Hitler's judgment, and believed in everything he said. Adolf Hitler had told him—and all Germans—that they would win this war and that the Third Reich would rival the Roman Empire in the history books. News from the front said that they were losing the war, but to speak of such morale-destroying topics was taboo.

"Intelligence knows the enemy is planning an invasion of some sorts. We don't know when, but we don't think it will be too much longer." Ostendorff peeked across Lorenz's body to make sure Boineburg was still engaged in conversation with the pretty French girl. "If that happens, talk will turn to action, and this half-wit will no longer be in charge."

"Do they have anyone in mind?"

Ostendorff caught Lorenz's tone and chuckled. "I'm not sure, Heinrich. Though I know where my recommendation would lie."

Lorenz grinned. He would love to see the look on Boineburg's face when he walked into Boineburg's office, flanked by the SS, ready to replace him. For a moment, he almost wished the Allies would invade.

The orchestra began to tune up, so Lorenz and Ostendorff removed their hats and turned their attention to the heavy velvet curtain. The theatre fell silent, and the overture began.

Lorenz stole a glance at Ostendorff. The man rivaled him in the ability to spot a Jew. He had met Natasha before, but only briefly, and Lorenz knew better than to think that Ostendorff trusted his judgment as much as he claimed to. Ostendorff hated Boineburg and would do anything to make him look like a fool. Though he and Lorenz were on friendly terms, Lorenz knew it was more of a business relationship. Werner Ostendorff thought only of his career and was entirely dedicated to his task of solving the Jewish Question and bringing glory to the Führer and the Third Reich. Now that Boineburg had suggested that Lorenz's feelings for Natasha had clouded his judgment, Ostendorff would be watching her for some sign that she was an enemy of Germany. He wouldn't find anything Communist about her, but would he see through her beauty to her Jewishness?

The overture ended and the curtain opened. Lorenz clenched his fists and forced his eyes back to the stage. Frozen in position, the dancers remained still until the applause died down and the orchestra began again. Then, one by one, they came alive. A dark-haired ballerina moved first, performing a short but precise routine. After three beats on a drum, the music repeated, a little louder this time, and another dancer joined the first, their bodies in perfect time with one another.

The heavy drumming came again and Natasha leapt into life. Dressed in a green so pale it was almost white, she was a vision of Aryan beauty. She moved in exact time with the other dancers, like a marching soldier. Each dancer's leg was raised to the same height and hit the stage at the exact time the timpani sounded. It was uniform, structured, and disciplined.

Lorenz felt his heart pound in time with the beat of the timpani drum. From the corner of his eye, he saw Ostendorff nodding, exchanging glances with the SS officer to his right. Lorenz smiled. No one would guess that underneath Natasha's fair exterior was an unregistered Jew.

He should have denounced her, he knew. But she had woven her way so deeply into his heart that he could not hand her over to be eliminated.

It was a shame that she could never be more than his mistress. He had wanted to bring her back to Germany, make her his wife, and raise strong German children with her, children with good values and in high standing with the Hitler Youth. Now, if she became pregnant, a doctor would have to be called in. If she was too scarred from the operation, he would be able to discard her, denounce her. She would then be shipped off to Auschwitz, and Lorenz would have the answer to his own Jewish Question.

* * *

Toward the back of the theatre, away from the sea of black and mouse-brown uniforms, Jean-Luc watched Natasha move across the stage. His breath caught with each pirouette and plié. Every position of her leg, every sweep of her arm, was deliberate and graceful, like brushstrokes in the air.

She was artist, muse, and masterpiece all in one, perfect and radiant in front of the backdrop. Jean-Luc felt a surge of pride. The backdrop was by far his greatest accomplishment as an artist, and Natasha completed the piece. The discipline he had learned from Matisse and Miró, coupled with his inspiration from Natasha, had helped bring out that greatness in his own work.

That's my wife, Jean-Luc thought as he watched her complete the cycle of movements. The timpani pounded three more times, and the entire company joined in.

His wife. Just thinking the words made his skin tingle. Though she was technically his fiancée, Jean-Luc had thought of her as his wife the instant she had accepted his proposal.

He imagined them in Sweden, living simply but comfortably, hiding from the war and everything that went along with it. He would paint her nude form when she was heavy with child. He would make her laugh, and they would live out their days in perpetual bliss.

His seat was so far back he couldn't see the look of serenity Natasha usually wore while dancing, but he had watched her at rehearsal so often he could picture it in his mind. He leaned forward, watching Natasha glide across the stage in perfect time with the music and the other dancers. He took his eyes off her only when she disappeared backstage.

With Natasha hidden from view, the prima ballerina assoluta no longer had any competition for the spotlight. She moved with graceful precision, and Jean-Luc found himself appreciating her talent for the very first time. He had never really paid much attention to the other dancers—or, for that matter, to the dances that did not include Natasha. Those were the times he had found it easiest to concentrate on his painting.

The tempo picked up, and the other ballerinas—save Natasha, who was changing for her solo—joined the prima ballerina assoluta on stage. Jean-Luc watched them glide in unison, impressed by their abilities. He had assumed that Natasha was naturally more graceful than everyone else and that her solo had been won before she had auditioned for it. Now he realized the competition she had been up against, and his pride swelled further.

With a twinge of guilt, he remembered that Anya was in this scene. He had made silent assumptions about her talent and half-hearted effort, but if she was a part of this marvelous execution of choreography, he had been dead wrong. He scanned the ballerinas, trying to pick her out, but he was too far away to see their faces clearly. He was sure the dark-haired girl near the front was the one named Monique.

Ah! There she is . . . no. That can't be her. The frame is too small and the hair is a shade too light, he thought.

The music slowed and the ballerinas parted to reveal Natasha, dressed in a pale blue costume that Jean-Luc knew would make her eyes sparkle. The orchestra held a grand pause while the audience rewarded the dancers with a round of polite applause. The noise settled down, and for a half note, the opera house was absolutely silent. Poised and unwavering, Natasha stood in the spotlight, a vision of perfection. Jean-Luc forgot all about Anya. A single flute began a slow, mournful tune and Natasha began to move.

*   *   *

Natasha lifted her leg and curled it out behind her as she let herself get lost in the music. She did not look at the audience. Instead, she kept her gaze slightly elevated and stared off into space, imagining herself on a stage in the deserted Galerie nationale du Jeu de Paume, Degas' painted ballerinas coming to life and joining her in every step.

Together, Natasha and Degas' visions danced as the music built to a crescendo. Their audience was composed of ghosts: her mother and father, Anya, Anya's parents, Monsieur Cordier, and a couple who looked just as she had envisioned Jean-Luc's parents to be. She danced her heart out for them, leaping and twirling across her stage.

Then, slowly, the music began to wind down. One by one, the ghosts floated back to the stars to continue doing what they loved best. Degas' dancers leapt back to their paintings and froze in their places. The Galerie nationale du Jeu de Paume faded away, and Natasha was once again onstage in the Théâtre de l'Opéra, performing for a German audience. She swept down into the final position of her solo, wishing she, too, could freeze into the painting behind her, a part of Jean-Luc's art forever.

Thunderous applause erupted, and Natasha realized that her cheeks were wet with tears. She wondered how much of that applause was Lorenz's influence and how much was genuine. But then she was pulled back into her trance as the music resumed and the other ballerinas flitted onstage.

Knowing what she must do made concentrating on the ballet increasingly difficult as the first act ended and the second began. Natasha dreaded the end of the ballet. All she could do was pour every ounce of her soul into her art and hope that Jean-Luc, wherever he was in the back of the theatre, knew that it was for him.

She refused to look at the audience, not wanting to make any sort of eye contact with Lorenz. She knew where he was sitting; he had told her a number of times. She could feel his eyes upon her, undressing her, planning the rest of the evening. It made her skin crawl.

Natasha's final scene came to an end; the rest of the ballet was dedicated to the two leads. Natasha watched from the side of the stage, wishing for time to stand still.

The music ended on one long note. The lead dancers froze in their positions and the curtain closed. Applause thundered, and Natasha felt the pressure of tears in her eyes.

The curtain opened. The leads took their bows, then reached out to either side of the stage for the rest of the dancers to join them.

The applause grew louder as Natasha stepped onstage. She scanned the far reaches of the standing ovation, searching for Jean-Luc, but she couldn't find him. She looked down to the front row, where Lorenz sat between a black-uniformed SS officer and the military governor of Paris. Lorenz nudged the SS officer and nodded in her direction.

The cold eyes regarded her for a long while. Natasha forced herself to smile at Lorenz and bat her eyelashes at him. She then dipped into another bow.

The curtain closed before the dancers, shutting the audience from view. Monique and a few of the other dancers embraced in celebration of a successful opening night. Even the experienced prima ballerina beamed with pride. Madame Fournier congratulated them all, then clapped her hands three times to silence them.

"Wonderful. Now get changed, and I will see you here tomorrow afternoon."

Everyone hurried to the dressing room, eager to go out and celebrate with friends, husbands, and lovers. Natasha shuffled along behind.

She changed slowly and then sat on the bench in front of her locker, staring at the toe shoes in her lap until she was the only one left in the dressing room. She could hear a commotion just outside the door. Reporters were probably bombarding the prima ballerina assoluta with questions.

Just three weeks ago, she had wanted nothing more than to be a part of that buzzing crowd: to stand with Anya, hoping the reporters shot a question their way; to laugh and wonder if their names would appear in the newspaper as they made their way to a café for a celebratory meal. Now she wished it would all disappear so she could slip out into the night and disappear herself.

She stood up. Perhaps the crowd would conceal her from Jean-Luc so she wouldn't put him in danger. He would be there, she knew. So would Lorenz.

As soon as she opened the door to the dressing room, a camera flashed in her face, and bouquets were thrust in her arms.

"There she is!"

"Natasha Karsavina!"

"Was this your first solo role?"

"What are your thoughts on your performance?"

"How long have you been dancing?"

"Can we expect to see more of you?"

Frozen, Natasha stared wide-eyed at the group of reporters. Almost as many crowded around her as surrounded the prima ballerina assoluta.

Natasha glanced around. Standing near the backdrop was Lorenz, grinning at her. She looked up at the backdrop behind him.

I'm sorry, Jean-Luc. I'm so sorry.

"Natasha! How long have you been in France?"

Natasha looked at the reporter. "Ten years," she replied.

Reporters fired more questions, and she tried to answer them as best she could. Between questions, she caught Lorenz smiling at her. Was this his doing, or had she earned the attention herself? Surely he didn't have this much pull with the press.

"What was it like performing in the Théâtre de l'Opéra?"

"I am thrilled to be on this stage," Natasha said. "This building is an architectural work of art, swimming with masterpieces of every kind. To be part of one of those masterpieces is a great honor."

From the corner of her eye, she spotted the crowd being pushed apart. Jean-Luc was making his way to her, a broad smile on his face.

No, she thought. *Stay away! I can't see you!*

Jean-Luc pressed on. She knew that look in his eyes. He was going to approach her and give her a congratulatory hug, precautions be damned.

"However," Natasha continued, raising her voice so the entire crowd could hear her, "it is a shame we all had to perform in front of an amateur's painting."

"Amateur?" one reporter said. "I thought Matisse painted the backdrop."

"Matisse dictated it, but the actual work was by the hand of his assistant, who took forever to get it done and wasted his time leering at the dancers. He was a plague on our performance. I am embarrassed to have danced in front of his slipshod work."

Jean-Luc had stopped in his tracks. Natasha felt sick. The look on his face was one of utter devastation.

I had to do it, she told herself. *Lorenz would have killed him. It's better this way.*

She longed to shout out what she truly thought, to give Jean-Luc some sort of apologetic glance, but she had to make sure Jean-Luc never approached her again. Instead, she forced herself to cast Jean-Luc a smug smile as she turned away with her nose stuck in the air.

"I danced my heart out for our elite audience. Hopefully my performance has enabled them to overlook the horrendous scenery."

She batted her lashes at Lorenz. Reporters followed her gaze and began scribbling furiously on their notepads. Cameras flashed and even more questions were thrown her way. Natasha gripped the ribbons of her toe shoes to keep herself from crying.

It's for the best. Jean-Luc cannot die.

Over and over, Natasha repeated reassurances in her mind, but they did nothing to fill the hole in her heart. She had crushed the spirit she loved so much. She would never forgive herself.

CHAPTER 23

J EAN-LUC TORE THROUGH THE STREETS of the city, not even bothering to see if the métro was running. The look on Natasha's face when she had made eye contact with him while ripping his art to shreds was burned in his mind.

Shoving him away and proclaiming him a mindless flirt he understood, but upholding appearances with Lorenz did not require her to dismiss his art so heartlessly. No. She knew it would crush him. She knew such heavy criticism would break his heart. It had been deliberate.

Had she been toying with him, telling him she would be his wife? Had she wanted Lorenz all along?

He needed to drink her away, to drown her memory in that bottle of Bordeaux that was supposed to be for their wedding night. Tears pricked the corners of his eyes. Why had she accepted his proposal? Had he frightened her by showing up in her room that night? Or had she said yes just to mock him?

The smug smile, the look of adoration she cast Lorenz's way—it was clear to Jean-Luc that Natasha wanted nothing to do with him.

By the time Jean-Luc had walked all the way to Montparnasse, his hands, nose, and ears were red and numb, but he still had no desire to hurry home to the warmth of a lit brazier.

If I stay out here long enough, maybe my heart will become numb, too.

He couldn't get her out of his mind. Her smiles, the kisses, the love they had made, the life he had imagined with her . . .

His heart was torn apart and stomped on with high-heeled shoes. He had broken his fair share of hearts, but he had never done it so cruelly. He had never led a girl on the way she had done to him.

Try as he might, he could not hate her. That was the hardest part. Jean-Luc blamed Lorenz for everything Natasha had said. His mind flashed to the night Anya had tried to seduce him, and he was filled with overwhelming sympathy.

I should visit Anya and apologize, Jean-Luc thought. The image of the room Anya and Natasha shared popped into his mind, and his eyes filled with tears again. *Maybe in a few months . . .*

He couldn't visit Anya anytime soon. The memory of Natasha was far too painful and would be for some time. He didn't want to see anyone or anything that would remind him of her, nor did he want to run the risk of bumping into her. Plus, he didn't want to give Anya the wrong idea.

He told himself he didn't care what Natasha thought and that he *did* hate her for breaking his heart. It wasn't true.

He rounded the corner to rue Blomet and kept a steady pace toward his apartment building. Madame Cordier's window was dark; she was either asleep or at a meeting somewhere. Miró's windows faced the other side of the building, so he couldn't see whether there was light in either of them.

Praying that Madame Cordier wasn't holding one of her meetings in his studio, Jean-Luc entered the building and bumped right into Miró.

"Jean-Luc?"

"Yes."

The stairwell was dark, so Jean-Luc could make out only Miró's silhouette. He was carrying something under his arm, and his posture was rigid.

"Why are you back so early? I thought you would be with Natasha," Miró said.

Jean-Luc groaned at the sound of Natasha's name and buried his face in his hands.

"What happened? Is she all right?"

"She's fine," Jean-Luc said, failing to keep the bitterness from his voice.

Miró stood still for a minute, then his shadowed body shifted to peek over Jean-Luc's shoulder and into the night.

"Is the ballet over?"

Jean-Luc nodded.

"Walk with me." Miró grabbed Jean-Luc's forearm and urged him back out into the street. In the moonlight, Jean-Luc could see how gaunt and fearful his face was. He was dressed in layers and carrying his painting cylinders under his arm.

"Joan—"

"What happened with Natasha?"

"She is with her soldier." Jean-Luc stuffed his hands in his pocket.

"I thought you understood that she had to play her part."

"She played her part for me, not him." Jean-Luc took a deep breath and told Miró what Natasha had said to the reporters.

Miró shook his head as Jean-Luc repeated her words. "Perhaps . . . perhaps she was just playing her part."

"She wasn't."

"How do you know that?"

"You didn't see her face. She looked right at me and smiled as if I were getting what I deserved."

Miró said, "It doesn't seem right. I saw the way she looked at you. There was true feeling behind her eyes."

"But why attack my art? What would Lorenz care about that? The reporter didn't ask her about the scenery. She was trying to hurt me, Joan, and she knew just how to do it."

Miró and Jean-Luc turned a corner, and Miró picked up his pace.

"It doesn't add up," Miró said.

"She must have chosen that soldier—he can give her furs and jewelry and prestige. All I can give her is my heart." Jean-Luc wiped his eyes with the back of his hand. "But apparently that's as worthless as my art."

Miró held up his arm and stopped Jean-Luc in his tracks. He motioned for Jean-Luc to be silent and ducked into a narrow alleyway between two buildings. Heavy footsteps resounded on the cold pavement, and Jean-Luc held his breath. Was it curfew already? He checked his watch, but he couldn't decipher the time in the darkness of the shadows. He didn't think it had taken him that long to walk back to Montparnasse from the opera house, but then again, he wasn't sure. His head was cloudy.

Voices exchanged a few German words. The steps grew louder. Jean-Luc could see the forms of two soldiers patrolling the streets past the alley where he and Miró hid. Jean-Luc held his breath.

The voices and footsteps faded into the distance. Jean-Luc breathed again, but Miró still kept his hand up. Another few minutes went by. Then Miró motioned for Jean-Luc to remain silent and follow him out to the street. Jean-Luc glanced at his watch. It was another twenty minutes until curfew. Why all the secrecy? Was Miró going to one of Madame's Resistance meetings?

Miró rounded the first corner, and he and Jean-Luc weaved their way through the streets. After a few twists and turns, Jean-Luc risked a question.

"Where are we going?"

"We are going as far as the Pasteur Institute. Then you are going home."

"And you?"

"I am going home as well." Miró hugged the cylinders under his arm closer to his body. "Madame Cordier's spies have heard that I may be in danger. The message was jumbled, but I will not take any chances."

"How are you getting there?"

"Madame has arranged for me to sneak away on the last train from Paris to Bayonne."

Jean-Luc frowned. "It can't be that easy."

"She has forged traveling papers for me and arranged for a spy to be working as a conductor on the train. Once I'm in Bayonne, I will have a lot of walking to do."

"Why tonight?"

"Most of the higher-ranking officers were at the ballet. They will be celebrating by now, no doubt, leaving the other soldiers with no supervision. It will be easier to go unnoticed."

Jean-Luc nodded. "Your wife," Jean-Luc choked on the word, "will be happy to see you."

"And I will be relieved to see her."

Mentor and student walked side-by-side through the streets of Paris, the wooden soles of their shoes clunking on the pavement. Jean-Luc walked in silence, not knowing what to say. Miró was a treasured friend, and Jean-Luc did not want him in any danger, but he was saddened by Miró's sudden departure. Jean-Luc was torn between begging the man to stay and insisting that he go with him, to protect him.

Jean-Luc could do neither. Accompanying Miró would only put him in greater danger, and Jean-Luc could not ask Miró to stay in Paris—not when brutes like Lorenz walked the streets.

The Pasteur Institute came into view. Jean-Luc tried to slow their pace and savor their last moments together, but Miró only quickened his step. When they reached the building, he stopped and looked at Jean-Luc.

"I . . . I suppose this is good-bye," Jean-Luc said.

"Until the war is over."

"Natasha has chosen the German and said my art is rubbish," Jean-Luc said. "She told the entire press. I have no reason to live."

Miró touched Jean-Luc's shoulder. "You can't think that way. There has to be more to this. War does terrible things to people. It turns men into murderers and homes into battlefields. You have improved your art—"

"But I've lost my muse . . . she is dead to me."

Miró said, "You're heartbroken. You know Natasha best. If you say that she deliberately hurt you, I believe you, though I still think some other reason must be behind it all. Let Natasha the woman be dead to you if that is the only way you can cope, but let the muse live on.

"I'm very proud that you consider me your mentor. I think you are a very gifted artist—when your attention hasn't strayed to someone or something else. I hope you don't give up on painting."

"Anger and heartache are very distracting," Jean-Luc said.

"Harness that anger, then. If you cannot remain detached, find an outlet." Miró stared at Jean-Luc, forcing him to meet his eyes. "Madame Cordier," he said softly, "should be home in a bit. You should go and have a talk with her. She may need you."

They were silent for a moment. Jean-Luc regarded Miró for a long while, trying to burn the image of his friend into his mind.

"Safe journey, Joan."

"Thank you. I will see you when the war is over."

Jean-Luc and Miró embraced as brothers, and then Jean-Luc turned and began to walk toward rue Blomet.

"Jean-Luc?" Miró called.

Jean-Luc turned back.

"Sometimes, when circumstances are your enemy, you must fight for your heart."

Jean-Luc could only watch as Miró slipped into the shadows and disappeared. He looked up at the stars and imagined his parents looking down on him. What did they think of the world he lived in? What would his father have done if he had been alive when the Germans marched through Paris?

Madame Cordier must have thought the same thing the day the armistice was signed.

Jean-Luc walked home, keeping his eyes fixed on the stars, pondering Miró's advice. Should he join the Resistance? He had never fired a gun, and he didn't think he would be able to kill a man, even one such as Lorenz. He had no skills other than painting. Could he be of any use? More likely, he would only be in the way. Wasn't that why he hadn't already joined the Resistance?

Jean-Luc squared his shoulders and shook his head at the nothingness. If he were honest with himself, he hadn't joined the Resistance because he was afraid—afraid of dying, but also afraid of the Resistance interfering with his painting and flirting. He had hated the German presence in Paris, but he had never realized just how bad things were. If he would be of no use, Madame Cordier would tell him so and convince him to continue painting—but at least he would have offered his life to the cause.

He walked a little faster and then broke into a run. If a soldier spotted him, he could say he was trying to make it home before curfew. With any luck, Madame Cordier would already be there.

CHAPTER 24

THE WINDOWS TO MADAME CORDIER'S APARTMENT were still dark. Jean-Luc entered the building and stood at the foot of the stairs for a minute, looking back and forth from the stairs to her door.

He didn't want to wake her if she was asleep—she was usually up so early to wait for rations and gather whatever tidbits she could from the parks—but he had never been one for patience. He would never get to sleep if he didn't talk to her as soon as possible.

He quietly rapped on her door. No answer. He knocked a little louder. No answer.

She must be sleeping, he thought.

As Jean-Luc turned toward the stairs, the door to the building swung open and Madame Cordier slipped in. She took two steps in the dark and bumped into Jean-Luc. She wheezed and staggered back, hand clutched to her heart.

"Madame," Jean-Luc whispered.

"Oh! Jean-Luc," Madame Cordier said. "You gave me a fright, mon chou."

"I'm sorry."

"Not to worry, my dear. How was the ballet?" Madame Cordier reached into her handbag and pulled out the key to her apartment.

"I—the ballet was nice."

Key held just before the lock, Madame paused and looked at Jean-Luc. "Nice?" she repeated.

Jean-Luc shrugged.

"Come inside, dearest."

Jean-Luc followed Madame Cordier into her apartment. He knew the layout of the furniture so well, he didn't need any light to find his way to one of the armchairs by the radio. As he eased into the chair, he felt a pang. The last time he had sat there, Natasha had leaned against his knee.

Madame Cordier lit a candle and sat down in the other armchair. "Now," she said, "tell Madame all about it."

Jean-Luc related the evening's events. The story was just as painful a second time around.

"She told the press—it'll be in the papers tomorrow—that she thinks I'm a horrible artist."

Madame Cordier scoffed. "I wouldn't worry about that, my pet. If a collaborationist paper prints that your work is trash, then every true Frenchman will be banging down your door to buy a painting."

"I don't care about that, Madame. She dismissed my work. That backdrop was for her more than anything. It was my love for her . . . and she knew it."

"Hmm." Madame Cordier frowned. "She must have had her reasons."

Jean-Luc shook his head. "That's what Joan said. But you didn't see her face."

"You ran into Joan, did you?"

Jean-Luc nodded.

"That means he was running late. I hope he made it in time."

"We didn't have a lengthy good-bye. And I only came home a few minutes before you did."

"Well, that's somewhat of a relief."

"Who will move into his studio?"

Madame Cordier shifted in her chair. "I'm not sure. No one, for now. I haven't heard from Monsieur Gargallo, but Joan has paid the rent up until his usual time. I'm hoping to keep it a secret for a while. I don't want a Boche moving in."

The sculptor Pau Gargallo and Miró shared the studio, living in it at set times during the year. Although in previous years the two had religiously moved in and out, Jean-Luc had the feeling that Gargallo would not be back—at least not until the war was over.

"I can move a few of my things in for the time being, to make it look like someone lives there," Jean-Luc said.

"That would be nice, dear. But all you have to do is unpack Joan's things. I told him to take only what he absolutely needed."

"Madame?"

"Yes, my pet?"

"I—that is, when I told Joan about . . . about Natasha, he said that I should harness my anger and turn it into a more productive emotion."

"Your paintings will have a lot of red in them, I imagine."

"That's not what I mean. Madame, I would like to join you in the Resistance."

Silence.

In the candlelight, Jean-Luc could see Madame Cordier's entire body tense. She did not look at him.

"Madame?"

"Is this what you want?"

"Yes, Madame."

"No." She looked over at him, her face a cold mask that he had never seen before. Her eyes held no tenderness, and her voice held no affection. "I mean, is this what you *truly* want? Will you want it tomorrow? Or next week? Or in a month, if Natasha comes back to you? The Resistance is not a petty job, Jean-Luc. If you join, you have committed your life and your soul to fighting the Germans. *Nothing* is more important. Not art, not friendship . . . not love."

Jean-Luc found himself leaning away from Madame Cordier's hard gaze. An entirely different person sat across from him. For the first time, he could imagine Madame Cordier leading a Resistance group.

"I want the Germans to pay for ever setting foot in our city. I hate them, Madame. You know that."

"How deep does your hatred run? Would you be able to kill? You must be hard, strong, and above all, discreet. You must be willing and able to withstand torture or take your own life rather than be captured. German and Vichy spies are everywhere. Some of our best have been victims of betrayal."

"I can do it, Madame."

"Can you? If you are serious about this, you will think on it tonight. Think long and hard, Jean-Luc. This is no decision to be made in a fit of passion. If you still want this in the morning, I want you to meet Madame Françoise at Le Café d'Anton at eight-thirty. Understood?"

Jean-Luc stared at Madame Cordier. "How will I know Madame Françoise?"

"Monsieur Anton knows everyone in Montparnasse. He can point her out to you."

"Why shall I say I'm meeting her?"

"You're trading your daily bread for tobacco rations."

"But Monsieur Anton knows I do not smoke."

Madame Cordier held up her hand. "Do not question me. Listen carefully: you are trading your daily bread for tobacco rations."

Jean-Luc nodded.

"Good night, Jean-Luc. It is late." Madame Cordier stood up and walked toward the bedroom. "Snuff the candle before you leave."

Jean-Luc was too stunned to move. She did not kiss his cheeks. She did not call him "pet" or "dearest." She did not even look over her shoulder at him after walking toward her room. Where was his motherly, sweet Madame Cordier?

Licking his fingers, he pinched the candle's flame, leaving the room in complete darkness. He left the apartment in a daze, trying to imagine himself in the Resistance.

He wasn't exactly sure what he'd be doing, but since he was an artist, he had assumed he would be assigned to forging papers and the like. Madame Cordier had made it sound so much more dangerous.

He climbed the stairs and followed his feet into his studio, where he lay awake on his bed for a long time, staring into the darkness.

Could he withstand torture? How could anything be worse than the torture of losing Natasha? And though he had thought about throwing himself into the Seine just a few hours ago, he wondered if he could, indeed, take his own life.

I would never do anything to hurt Madame—and giving up information would get her killed. I would rather die than see her suffer.

He loved Madame as his mother; he could withstand torture and would be willing to give his life to avoid compromising her. But the question remained, could he kill? Most of these Germans were boys, barely old enough to grow hair on their chins. Mindless Boches or not, somewhere, back in Germany, they had mothers, sweethearts, and lives—lives, Jean-Luc reminded himself, that they had left behind to destroy everything his city stood for. Even so, Jean-Luc did not know if he could kill anyone.

Then there was Lorenz. Jean-Luc hated Lorenz with every fiber of his being; he wouldn't mourn Lorenz's death in the least. But could he be the one to kill him?

Jean-Luc rolled over and drifted off to an uneasy sleep, haunted by the image of Natasha's face. He woke up from nightmares several times during the night, all of which involved Lorenz and Natasha. Each nightmare became progressively more vivid—Jean-Luc could almost hear Natasha's laughter as she compared him unfavorably to Lorenz.

He awoke with a start, sweat dripping off his brow and tears clinging to his lashes. Early morning light spread across his bed, and he could hear the wooden soles of women, already on their way to the ration lines, clopping on the street.

The indecision was still eating away at the back of his mind. Could he kill Lorenz—or anyone for that matter?

I will have to, Jean-Luc thought. *I will do whatever it takes to get these Germans out of my city. If I have to kill, so be it.*

After a quick wash, Jean-Luc threw on some paint-stained clothes, grabbed the piece of bread Madame Cordier had left for his breakfast, and left.

He arrived at the café fifteen minutes early. Celeste Anton was outside, shaking the bread crumbs off a tablecloth. She tilted her head at him.

"Jean-Luc? I didn't think you were working until this evening."

"I'm meeting someone here, Madame Anton."

"Oh? Your Russian ballerina?"

The reference to Natasha brought a horrible feeling to the pit of Jean-Luc's stomach. "No," he said. "Actually, maybe you can help me. Do you know Madame Françoise?"

Celeste Anton froze. She glared at Jean-Luc from the corner of her eye.

"I can't say that I do." She gave the tablecloth one last shake, then spread it over one of the outdoor tables and went inside.

Jean-Luc followed her. "Is Monsieur Anton here? Madame Cordier said that he would be able to point her out to me."

Celeste did not look back at him. "Are you tired of your ballerina, then?"

"I . . . no." He was unable to keep the despair out of his voice.

"Well, then, why are you here?"

"I'm here to trade my . . . er . . . daily bread for tobacco rations," he whispered.

He expected Celeste Anton to ask when he had started smoking. He expected her to comment on his poor timing to pick up such a habit. He expected her to cluck her tongue and lecture him on the vice. Instead, she spun around to face him.

"What time are you supposed to be here?"

"Eight-thirty."

"You're early," she said. The contempt in her voice made it sound as if he were late.

"Yes, I—"

"We can't afford to pay you for twice your hours, Jean-Luc," she said in a loud voice.

"But I—"

"I'm glad to see you're not late, but hours early? You can't be serious."

Jean-Luc blinked at her.

She sighed. "Follow me. I'm sure we can find something for you to do in the kitchen for today—but just for today, mind you."

Celeste Anton led the way back to the kitchen, nodding to the staff and motioning for Jean-Luc to follow her.

"I know you're eager to work, Jean-Luc, and I'm very happy you finally are, but unless you want to work for free, I suggest you come in only when you are scheduled."

"Yes, Madame," Jean-Luc said.

"Just for today, I have a job for you. Dry storage is a mess. I want you to dust and organize it for me." She pulled out her key to the storage closet, where she kept the canned goods locked up, in case any of the hungry employees were tempted to steal a few extra rations. She unlocked the door and pulled on the string to click on the lightbulb overhead. She gestured inside to the pristine floor and the perfectly arranged shelves. "As you can see, it's a mess in here. I'm going to lock you in—you know I don't trust anyone in here. Straighten it out and I will check on you in a few hours."

She walked into the closet, reached behind a can of pectin, and pulled. The shelf-lined wall swung back on hinges, revealing a narrow staircase leading down into a basement that Jean-Luc had not known existed.

"Jean-Luc? Don't ever be early again. Only on time. And next time, come to the back door."

Celeste Anton squeezed her way around Jean-Luc and closed the door to the storage closet, shutting him in. Jean-Luc heard the lock click into place as he stared at the false wall. Feeling very insecure, he swung the door open all the way. He could see the dim glow of a light coming from wherever the steps led. Taking a deep breath, he entered the passageway.

He heard hushed voices—voices that were silenced when he reached a step that creaked. Jean-Luc paused, and then slowly continued down, following the light until he came upon a small musty room. As he dipped his head below a low beam to peer into the room, he reached the last step. Without warning, someone grabbed him from behind.

The attacker pinned Jean-Luc's arms to his side and pushed his face against the wall. Cold steel was at his throat and a voice hissed in his ear.

"Who sent you?"

"Let him go, Monsieur Philippe," said a familiar voice. "This is the boy I was telling you all about." The stranger loosened his grip on Jean-Luc, and the blade fell away from his throat. Slowly, Jean-Luc spun around to see Madame Cordier. "You're early."

"I'm sorry."

"Never mind. Shall we continue?"

She gestured toward the center of the room, where a moth-eaten carpet lay on the floor, with an old wobbly table from the café in the center. Around it, a dozen or so people sat on crates or leaned against the walls. They were all staring at Jean-Luc. He quickly averted his eyes.

The man who had grabbed him—a tall, sandy-haired man probably in his early forties—took his place beside Madame Cordier and eyed Jean-Luc suspiciously.

Jean-Luc found a section of the wall to lean on and took a look around. A mimeograph stood in the corner, next to a small desk covered in papers. Empty wine racks were scattered here and there, and a single lightbulb swayed on a cord from the ceiling. Though the room smelled like mothballs and mold, and the damp air sent a chill to Jean-Luc's bones, there wasn't a single cobweb or any layers of dust. It looked as though Celeste Anton had done her best to make the room presentable, but she had lacked the resources to do anything beyond a basic cleaning.

"As I was saying," Madame Cordier said, "I have received a message from Rouen. The Boches have been punishing innocent people for sabotage carried out by Resistance groups. The Germans are trying to change public opinion through fear, so I feel we must triple our efforts to protect the innocent."

"There is no way we can do that, Madame Françoise," Monsieur Philippe said.

Jean-Luc wrinkled his forehead. *Madame Françoise?*

"We are already stretched thin," Monsieur Philippe continued. "We are only a small group, and we have our own lives to worry about."

"That's exactly why we should help," Madame Cordier said. "We are a small group, but we are part of the Resistance nonetheless. We take ultimate orders from de Gaulle's men, but in the meantime, we set our own agenda. And our agenda should be to protect the innocent."

"While protecting Paris's history and culture," said a thin, homely woman sitting on a crate near Madame Cordier. "And spying on the Boches, and sabotaging phone and rail lines, and smuggling goods, and hiding people . . . the list goes on, Madame Françoise. We don't have the means to protect everyone."

"I don't want the citizens of Paris to suffer any more than they have," Madame Cordier said. "Our job is to do whatever we can."

"But we can't do anything," said Monsieur Philippe. "The citizens of Paris should know that what we do is for the preservation of France and for the French people. Anyone who does not understand that is a collaborating swine."

"Not everyone who isn't in the Resistance is a collaborator," said a third, familiar voice. Jean-Luc turned to see Christophe Martin, with whom he used to box every week, leaning against the wall. "My wife is pregnant. She doesn't know anything about my involvement in this. She hates the Germans, but she is first and foremost concerned for our unborn child. And what about Sophie? She blamed herself when her parents were murdered—that was why she killed herself."

"Sophie?" Monsieur Philippe said.

"Mademoiselle Alice—her real name was Sophie LeChoix. In death, let us remember her by her real name."

Jean-Luc felt his heart clench. *Paul LeChoix's sister, Sophie? Dead? And her parents?* How long had he kept a blind eye to everything going on around him?

"I understand that your wife is not a collaborator, Monsieur Alain," said the homely woman. "But what do you propose we do to protect innocent people? We can't warn everyone of our plans. The Germans would be more likely to find out. I sympathize with the innocents, but I can't see any way of protecting them, short of giving the Germans exactly what they want."

The group talked in circles for a few minutes. In the end, Madame Cordier held up her hand. "Very well. We're wasting time and getting nowhere. We can't give up—not now, not ever. But at least we know to be prepared and to guard our loved ones very carefully. Moving on to the next topic: the Lévys. Madame Dominique?"

"I brought them food, one of our newspapers, and a few books yesterday," the homely woman said. "Claude saw the bit about Sophie's death in the paper—apparently he knew her. But when I told him about the rumors of an Allied invasion, he seemed to be in better spirits."

Jean-Luc could hardly believe his ears. *Claude Lévy?*

"Be careful not to overfeed them from the rumor pot. We don't know if the rumors are true, when it will happen, or if the Allies will succeed. What about Marie? Is she feeling better?" Madame Cordier said.

Madame Dominique nodded. "Yes. Her fever has broken, and she's itching to jump around and play. Most of the books I brought were children's stories to keep her occupied."

"Well, that's good anyway. I'll go next week."

Jean-Luc itched to ask Madame Cordier if he could come along, too, but every time he shifted his position against the wall, looks of contempt were shot his way.

"Moving on," Monsieur Philippe said. "Your friend made the last train, I hope?"

Madame Cordier nodded. "He should have. He wasn't home this morning."

"Good. I sent Messieurs Gerard and Maurice to take care of the rail line at dawn."

"Speaking of railways," a pretty young girl said as she stood up. Jean-Luc stared at her in surprise. She couldn't have been older than fifteen. "I have noticed a lot of German activity at the Austerlitz train station. I think we should send someone to sniff things out."

"There is always German activity at the train stations. Their supplies come in by train—that's why we sabotage the lines," a man with gray streaks in his black hair said.

The girl tilted up her head and looked down her nose at him. "Don't speak to me like that because you're older. I'm not stupid. But a lot of trains have been going in and out, and even the higher-ranking officers have complained about the lack of fuel. They say it all goes to the SS. I have never seen a soldier in the army go in there unless he was accompanied by a man in a black uniform."

"They *say* that, huh? And why should we believe you? You live at a brothel and speak fluent German. Tell me, have you whored yourself out to a Boche yet?"

"Monsieur Louis!" Madame Cordier said. "There will be none of that. We all have our disagreements, but we must cooperate. Fighting among ourselves is what *they* want."

The girl and Monsieur Louis glared at each other for a moment, and then she sat down. Monsieur Philippe looked at Madame Cordier. "We should send a small group to take a look. If they see anything, we could send a message to de Gaulle's people in London."

"I agree," said Madame Cordier.

"I'll go tonight after curfew to take a look," the girl said.

"Go with two others. Monsieur Raoul and—and Monsieur Beau," Madame Cordier finished, gesturing toward Jean-Luc.

Heads snapped in his direction.

"With all due respect, Madame Françoise," Christophe said, "I think it would be best to send a more trusted member on this mission. We can start this guy out forging papers."

Surprised that his friend would say such a thing, Jean-Luc crossed his arms over his chest. "If you think I would be more useful forging papers, then that's one thing, but if you're afraid I will betray you, then you are sorely mistaken."

Christophe stood up. "The question is, would you betray under torture? You have not been trained—"

"And neither were you, Monsieur Alain," the young girl said.

"None of us were," said Madame Dominique.

"My point is, we should be. But when we joined up, there was no way we could do that. Now we have the means to," Christophe said.

"What could he learn?" Monsieur Louis said. "Nothing without being out there, letting his instincts take over."

"Monsieur Beau is willing. He will go," Monsieur Philippe said.

The discussion was over. Christophe did not look pleased. The meeting continued. Monsieur Philippe talked about news and propaganda posters. Christophe was asked to write an article for the group's newspaper. Madame Cordier filled them in on what she had heard from BBC radio. Monsieur Philippe told everyone about another small group's infiltration and subsequent execution.

"I will contact you all and let you know where and when we will meet again," Madame Cordier said when the meeting had ended. "Monsieur Louis, Madame Hélène—you first."

Everyone stood up and helped move the crates and the wobbly table. Madame Cordier pulled the moth-eaten carpet aside, revealing a small trapdoor. The hinges were well oiled—they didn't squeak at all.

Monsieur Louis and a woman with stringy dark hair disappeared down the trapdoor. Madame Cordier closed it behind them, replaced the carpet, and waited.

Jean-Luc caught Christophe staring at him. They made eye contact; Christophe turned away. Jean-Luc walked over to him.

"I hate the Germans. You know that."

"But you have never been interested in such affairs before. Why now? It could be that they are holding something over your head. Sometimes I wasn't sure if you were infuriatingly oblivious or deliberately ignoring what was happening to Paris."

"I've been concentrating on my painting—"

"You've been concentrating on women, Monsieur Beau. Are the Germans threatening your latest love?"

Jean-Luc said, "That's hardly fair."

"I don't think you're a collaborator, but it wouldn't surprise me if you gave in to blackmail. I don't trust you."

"Monsieur Alain, Monsieur Raoul," said Madame Cordier.

With a final contemptuous glance, Christophe walked toward the trapdoor. He whispered something to Monsieur Raoul, a young man no older than twenty, who looked up at Jean-Luc before disappearing down the trapdoor.

"He's been exceptionally nervous since he found out his wife is pregnant," said a small voice beside Jean-Luc. He turned to see the homely Madame Dominique looking up at him. "Though with all the infiltrations, I can't say I blame anyone for being suspicious of every new member. We used to be a little family—but not anymore. It's too dangerous, you understand."

Madame Dominique walked away without another word. Just when Jean-Luc was about to follow her and continue their conversation, another voice stopped him.

"Tell me, have you ever been on a mission with another group, Monsieur Beau?"

Jean-Luc turned to see the young girl staring at him. He shook his head. She clucked her tongue. "I would have preferred someone with more experience," she said. "But if Madame Françoise thinks you're the best person for the job, then so be it." She tilted her head and looked him over. "Well, you're strong enough at least . . . I suppose I should explain the rules." She held up a finger. "First and foremost, never talk about what you know. If you see someone from the group out on the street, treat them as a stranger. If you knew him beforehand, try to avoid as much contact and association as possible. Pretend to have a falling out if you must. When you are on a mission and must interact, speak to one another in public as casual acquaintances. Second," she held up another finger, "if you do know someone, never refer to him by his real name here. Ever. Third," she held up three fingers, "if you are caught, try to take your own life rather than be taken alive. Not only will you be tortured and given a slow, painful death, but depending on how well you withstand the pain, you may also give up the rest of us and destroy all our efforts."

"What do I call you?" Jean-Luc asked.

"Mademoiselle Simone."

Jean-Luc nodded. "You seem so young."

She gave him the same indignant look she had given Monsieur Louis. Jean-Luc held up his hands in surrender.

"That's because I am young. But my age does not matter. My accomplishments do," she said.

"Mademoiselle Simone, Madame Dominique," said Madame Cordier.

"Where shall I meet you?" Jean-Luc asked.

"I'll find you."

With that, Mademoiselle Simone joined Madame Dominique and disappeared through the trapdoor.

"Monsieur Beau, I believe our hostess let you in through the other door?"

Jean-Luc looked up at Madame Cordier. She was so different from the woman who scolded him for not eating, who fussed about his health, and who kissed his cheeks. Her voice held no warmth. She didn't smile.

"Monsieur Beau," she narrowed her eyes. "I asked you a question."

"Yes, Madame . . . Françoise," said Jean-Luc. He, Madame Cordier, and Monsieur Philippe were all who remained in the room.

"Very well. Come, Monsieur Philippe," said Madame Cordier, holding open the trapdoor.

"You mean to leave him alone?"

"Of course. He can replace the carpet and the table after we leave."

"A new member—"

"When you brought Mademoiselle Simone, I did not question your judgment."

Monsieur Philippe deferred to Madame Cordier.

"Put the carpet back over the door and the table on the carpet, but be careful not to put it over the door. Then turn out the light and go back up the stairs."

"Yes, Monsieur."

With one last suspicious look, Monsieur Philippe followed Madame Cordier down the trapdoor. Left alone in the basement room, Jean-Luc did as he was told, then glanced around the room to make sure nothing looked disturbed. He piled the crates against the wall and then examined the room again. He pulled the cord that dangled from the lightbulb and felt his way to the stairs. He followed the dim light that crept through the cracks in the false wall, making his way back to the dry storage closet.

No sooner had he closed the door to the passageway than the closet door unlocked and Celeste Anton threw it open.

"Sorry I took so long, Jean-Luc. I forgot all about you, and then I saw Paulette Cordier walk by and remembered you were in here." She frowned. "Not much of a cleaning . . . oh, well. I suppose I'll do it right later. You still have a few hours until you have to work. Why don't you go home and fix yourself something to eat?"

Jean-Luc thanked Madame Anton and allowed her to show him out the back door. He walked home slowly, mulling over everything he had seen and heard at the meeting—a secret basement in his favorite café, Madame Cordier's cold demeanor, Sophie LeChoix's suicide, the too-young Mademoiselle Simone. So many surprises, too much to grasp . . . but at least his mind was off Natasha.

As her face flitted to his mind, Jean-Luc forced his thoughts back to Christophe's reaction. They had been good friends, boxed together, and talked about art. Jean-Luc could not help but feel a pang of resentment as he considered that no wedge would have been driven between them if Jean-Luc had remained oblivious and carefree.

It's the Germans, thought Jean-Luc. *They drive friends apart. Christophe is afraid. His wife is expecting a baby. You will have to prove yourself to him.*

Hating the thought of having to prove himself to a man who should be his friend, but determined to do it, Jean-Luc's mind turned to his mission that night. How would Mademoiselle Simone find him? Should he try to look for her around the Austerlitz train station? Go about his day as usual?

He would ask Madame Cordier what she thought was best. Perhaps Mademoiselle Simone had already discussed things with her.

When Jean-Luc reached his apartment building, he knocked on Madame Cordier's door. There was no answer. He retreated to his studio.

I suppose I'll just go about my day as usual—Mademoiselle Simone said she'd find me, after all.

He sat down at his easel and stared at a blank canvas. He tried to remember the lessons Matisse and Miró had taught him, to harness his feelings and paint with detached hands, but he felt empty. The blank canvas was fitting.

Jean-Luc's gaze moved from the canvas to his paint tubes, now neatly arranged on the table next to his easel. No single color popped out at him, except white.

Normally, he would have gone to talk to Miró, to get lost in the world of Miró's instruction and artwork—but Miró was gone, on his way back to Spain and his family. Only the empty studio remained.

Ah, yes, I told Madame Cordier I'd unpack his things, didn't I? I hope his door isn't locked.

Miró's door was not locked—it had not even been closed all the way. Jean-Luc pushed the door open and took a tentative step inside, half-expecting his mentor to be sitting at his easel, beckoning Jean-Luc to come in.

But Miró was not there. His easel stood in its usual place beside the window, and the studio was, as usual, immaculate, but no paintbrushes or paint tubes were arranged on the table beside the phonograph. No paper hung to dry. Only a small bundle of packed clothing and personal articles sat in a corner of the room, looking more like furniture than belongings.

Jean-Luc began to unpack the bundle. It didn't hold much: a frying pan, a few clothes, a blanket, two nearly empty tubes of paint, a small can of turpentine, a Mozart record, and a few ration coupons. Tucking the rations into his own pocket, Jean-Luc set up the room as he remembered it. Looking around, he frowned. Without a painting, or the beginnings of one, the room was empty. No one who knew anything about Miró would believe he still lived here.

Jean-Luc returned to his own studio and grabbed the blank canvas from his easel, a handful of paintbrushes, a clean palette, and a few tubes of his own paint, and took them to Miró's room. He set the canvas on the easel, put the Mozart record on the phonograph, and sat down on Miró's stool.

Listening to the grainy sound of the record, he thought about nothing. He only felt. His hands were not a part of his body but of someone else's. They mixed paint, dabbed some on a brush, and stroked the canvas with a loving, gentle touch, like a dancer gliding across a meadow without bending a blade of grass.

*   *   *

Jean-Luc looked up from the painting and stretched his back. How long ago had the record ended? He wasn't sure. He glanced down at his watch and jumped up from the stool. If he didn't hurry, he'd be late for work. Leaving the paint as it was, Jean-Luc hurried out of Miró's studio and down to the café.

He arrived only five minutes late. Pierre Anton greeted him at the front door, laughing and shaking his head.

"Same old Jean-Luc," he said. "Early when not needed, late when expected."

"Sorry, Monsieur."

"Well, go on. There are dishes to be done."

There was, indeed, a pile of dishes already waiting for him to wash. Jean-Luc rolled up his sleeves and dived into his work, the music of Mozart still floating through his head, thinking of the painting he had begun in Miró's studio.

Hours later, the café was not as busy. Jean-Luc leaned against the wall, waiting for more dishes. The café would not close for another hour.

"Jean-Luc?" Pierre Anton appeared in the kitchen. "Since we're not too busy, and since I'm already paying you for cleaning out the storage closet,

I'll do the dishes for the rest of the night. I'll pay you for the extra hour, but I have a favor to ask."

Jean-Luc nodded. "Of course, Monsieur."

Monsieur Anton handed him a quarter loaf of bread wrapped in brown paper. "My mother is very sick. Would you be so kind as to take her daily bread to her?"

Jean-Luc looked up at Monsieur Anton. Their eyes locked, and Jean-Luc nodded.

"Thank you," Monsieur Anton said. He scribbled something on a piece of paper. "Here's the address. You know how to get there?"

Jean-Luc forced himself to laugh. "I know how to get everywhere in Paris, Monsieur."

"Good. Now, off you go! And hurry home. The métro isn't running. By the time you get there, it will be almost curfew."

*   *   *

Jean-Luc stared up at the house and checked the address for the fifth time. It was the right place. When Jean-Luc had heard Monsieur Anton say "daily bread," he knew that this "favor" would lead him to his mission for the Resistance, but he never expected to be sent to a brothel.

"You going to stare at it all day? Or are you coming inside, darling?" a woman wearing no more than a slip called from a window two stories up.

"I . . . I think I have the wrong address," said Jean-Luc.

"They all do, dearie, they all do. Come on in and we'll show you how to get home."

Jean-Luc felt the color rise to his cheeks as he debated going inside. Monsieur Louis had said that Mademoiselle Simone lived in a brothel, but he couldn't have been serious. After all, he had accused her of speaking fluent German as well.

The door opened before he could knock, and Mademoiselle Simone stood in the doorway. She was fully dressed, showing no more skin than was decent. She looked out of place answering the door to a whorehouse.

"May I help you, Monsieur?" she asked. She looked up at him as if she had never seen him before.

"I . . . I'm not sure if I have the right address. I'm bringing bread to a friend's sick mother."

"Let me see the address."

Jean-Luc handed her the piece of paper Monsieur Anton had given him and waited to be invited in.

"You're on the wrong street, Monsieur. Go down the road, make your third left, then the second right." She handed the paper back to him.

Jean-Luc blinked a few times and rechecked the address.

"Good night, Monsieur," Mademoiselle Simone said. Without another word, she closed the door. Jean-Luc stared at the door for a moment, and then checked the address again. He backed away slowly, not sure what to think.

"I wouldn't get your hopes up," called the woman in the window. "Her legs are glued shut."

Jean-Luc ignored her and followed Mademoiselle Simone's directions down the road, taking the third left and then the second right. He found himself on another street lined with apartments and a few small shops. He paced up and down the street, checking the numbers on the buildings against the address Monsieur Anton had given him. There was no number 27. He retraced his steps, looking for the number again.

"Hello, Monsieur Beau," said a voice behind him. Jean-Luc turned to see the young man Christophe had whispered to at the meeting leaning against the darkened window of a pâtisserie—Monsieur Raoul.

"Monsieur Raoul, how are you?"

"Very well, thank you. What are you doing here?"

"Taking bread to a friend's sick mother."

"Ah."

"You?" asked Jean-Luc.

"Meeting my lover—ah, here she is."

Mademoiselle Simone's tiny frame was walking briskly toward them. When she reached them, she gave a curt nod.

"You stopped and stared long enough, Monsieur Beau. I wasn't sure if you were confused or playing your part too well."

"I was surprised. I thought Monsieur Louis was just being cruel—"

"Thanks to Monsieur Louis, now everyone knows I live there. And the only reason he knows is because he frequents the brothel when his wife annoys him. The rent is cheap, that's all you need to know."

"Do you speak German, too?"

"Yes, I do."

Jean-Luc involuntarily recoiled. She rolled her eyes.

"Not that it's any of your business, but my grandmother was a German who married a Frenchman. She raised me. My father was French and I am French. And though I speak the language, I have no loyalties to Germany. Do you have any other questions for me, Monsieur Beau? Shall we stay in front of this store for another hour so I can answer them?"

Stung, Jean-Luc remained silent. He liked Mademoiselle Simone less by the minute.

"Good," Monsieur Raoul said. "Let's go."

"Monsieur Beau, you walk a little behind us. Look at street signs, look at your address, and pretend you're still looking for it. Here." She and Monsieur Raoul took a step closer, creating a tight circle that shielded Mademoiselle's hands from view as she reached into her handbag and pulled out a small pistol. She handed it to Jean-Luc. "Keep it hidden."

Jean-Luc tucked the gun inside his coat, pretending to try to keep his hands warm. He could feel its weight pulling him to the earth, making it harder to move. A gun. Would he have to use it?

Mademoiselle Simone reached out to Monsieur Raoul's hand, and the two ran off ahead, ducking into shadows, then running down the streets. Jean-Luc followed behind them, close enough to see clearly where they were going, but far enough away that it didn't look like he was with them. He heard Mademoiselle Simone giggle and wondered if the two were really lovers.

The hot tingle of heartache washed over Jean-Luc as he remembered how he and Natasha had run through the streets, stealing kisses and whispering words of love. He shook his head and looked up at the street signs, then at building numbers. Natasha was gone. And he had a job to do.

*   *   *

As they neared Austerlitz station, Mademoiselle Simone and Monsieur Raoul ducked into an alleyway beside an old apartment building. Jean-Luc followed and saw that someone had conveniently left the ladder to the fire escape down. Mademoiselle Simone and Monsieur Raoul were waiting for him. Mademoiselle Simone motioned for quiet, and then she climbed the ladder.

Jean-Luc cringed at her every step. Though Mademoiselle Simone did not have a heavy step, he worried that the slightest sound would attract the Germans if something were, indeed, going on at the train station.

Monsieur Raoul went up after Simone. Keeping the gun tucked inside his coat, Jean-Luc followed. Jean-Luc felt disgusting holding the weapon.

If I have to kill, I will, he told himself.

He followed Mademoiselle Simone and Monsieur Raoul all the way up to the roof and took a look around. As far as Jean-Luc could see, the only lights came from the flicker of an occasional brazier candle. The power was out again.

The dark streets were as much an advantage to them as a disadvantage. They could hardly make out anyone walking by, let alone someone in a black uniform.

"There," whispered Monsieur Raoul, pointing down toward the entrance to the station. Jean-Luc strained his eyes and caught the slight movement of someone in black walking along the street. That someone was carrying something under his arm, but it was impossible to tell what it was.

It looks like a painting, Jean-Luc thought. He dismissed the possibility immediately. *Don't be stupid. Why would they bring paintings to a train station?*

The three of them sat in silence for a while, watching the soldiers in black go in and out of the station, all carrying things in. Everyone who walked out was empty-handed.

"We need to get closer," Mademoiselle Simone said. "I can't hear them."

"It'll have to be during the day. Even lovers and people taking bread to the sick can't be caught out past curfew," Monsieur Raoul said.

"It's strange," said Jean-Luc. "They carry things in—sometimes it looks like suitcases, other times it looks like paintings or boxes."

"Could be luggage," Monsieur Raoul said. "It's a train station, after all."

"But no trains are running," said Jean-Luc.

Mademoiselle Simone rubbed her arms. "It's getting chilly. Let's go. This is pointless. We can't see anything, and we can't hear anything. We'll try again another time."

She led the way back down the fire escape to the street. Feeling disappointed and relieved all at once, Jean-Luc followed her out of the alleyway. They ducked into dark corners as they made their way back toward the brothel to avoid the patrolling soldiers and collaborating police. So many SS officers were heading toward the station now that they often had to stay hidden until any Germans passed by.

Mademoiselle Simone led the way, darting around corners as if she knew exactly where each German was patrolling. Her memory must have failed her, however, for when she turned the corner to the street the brothel was on, she bumped right into a young soldier.

He seemed just as surprised as she was. He took two steps back and looked the group over. The moment's hesitation was all Jean-Luc needed. He pulled the gun from his coat and held it against the German's head.

"Don't move," he whispered, trying to prevent his voice from shaking.

Monsieur Raoul took the soldier's rifle and began checking the ammunition.

"Kill him," Mademoiselle Simone said to Jean-Luc. "He's seen all of us."

Jean-Luc looked from the German to Mademoiselle Simone and back to the German. He was so young—he did not even look eighteen.

"Kill him," Mademoiselle Simone snapped. "Before others come."

"The gunshot will attract others," Jean-Luc said.

"So leave the gun with me and wander around, pretending to look for your address. I'll take care of things. If you're searched, you won't have a weapon."

Jean-Luc's hands were clammy. The German peeked at him from the corner of his eye. This boy had a mother somewhere—a mother who would weep for him. What if that same mother had already lost her husband and other sons?

"Monsieur Beau." Mademoiselle Simone narrowed her eyes at him.

Jean-Luc shook all over. The gun rattled against the soldier's temple. How could he kill? Who was he to decide when a man's life should end?

In the next second, the soldier reacted to Jean-Luc's weakness. He ducked away from the gun and thrust his fist into Jean-Luc's stomach. Jean-Luc doubled over, only to meet the soldier's other fist with his jaw.

Jean-Luc saw stars for a moment and staggered where he stood. When he regained his balance and focused his eyes again, he saw the soldier lying on the ground, blood pouring from his throat. Mademoiselle Simone stood over him, wiping a knife clean on his uniform.

"Give me the gun," she said. Jean-Luc handed it to her. "Now go! Go!"

Without hesitation, Jean-Luc tore off into the night, running toward Montparnasse. Tears stung his eyes as he imagined a German woman—who looked mysteriously like Madame Cordier—weeping over the body of the dead soldier. He saw the cold, unfeeling look on Mademoiselle Simone's face as she wiped her knife on the boy's uniform.

Somehow, he managed to avoid every soldier out on patrol and soon found himself back in his studio, sitting on his bed, shaking from head to toe. Hot shame washed over him. He couldn't take someone's life, German or otherwise. Was he weak? Would Madame Cordier ask him to leave the Resistance? Would Mademoiselle Simone kill him to silence him?

He looked down at the bread Monsieur Anton had given him and thought of Claude Lévy and his little sister, Marie, in hiding, wherever they were.

Madame Dominique did not mention Monsieur or Madame Lévy. I wonder if they are alive—maybe it was *her fur Natasha was wearing.*

The thought of Natasha brought a lump to his throat. He fought it back down. He wanted to be angry with her, he wanted to hate her, but he couldn't.

Jean-Luc pulled his blanket over him and stared up at the ceiling until he fell into a sleep tormented by nightmares of Natasha, dead boys, and a weeping Madame Cordier.

*   *   *

"He almost destroyed the mission by being soft," Mademoiselle Simone said. "He showed mercy to a Boche, and I don't believe he is qualified or serious about taking care of the German problem in Paris."

Jean-Luc sat on one of Madame Cordier's armchairs, feeling the eyes of the entire Resistance group upon him. Madame Cordier had called him to her apartment a few hours earlier, only to reveal that Monsieur Raoul and Mademoiselle Simone had asked for a meeting to discuss Jean-Luc's behavior on his last mission. His cheeks were hot with shame, but he kept his shoulders squared as he listened to criticism thrown his way.

"It leaves the question: has he been placed here as a spy? Is he trying to protect someone else?" Christophe added.

"He's too soft for spy work. And too soft for what we do. We have no use for him," Monsieur Raoul said.

Voices chimed in, adding their opinions of Jean-Luc's hesitation in killing. Madame Dominique wondered if Christophe was right. Monsieur Philippe doubted that he was but thought Jean-Luc's pity could destroy them all. Monsieur Anton, who went by Monsieur Maurice, suggested that perhaps this was a game to Jean-Luc. Nobody trusted him.

Madame Cordier said nothing for a long while, then finally held up her hand and waited for silence.

"While I admit he has always been a lazy, distracted boy," she said, "he means well. Monsieur Alain, I assure you, Monsieur Beau is not trying to protect anyone who is being threatened by the Germans. And even if the Germans were threatening someone, he is not the sort who would cave in to blackmail. He would fancy himself the hero and get himself killed in the process, following his heart to the point of folly."

Jean-Luc felt his face get hotter. Hadn't he tried to free Natasha with patience? He hadn't attempted to take Lorenz head on. Why was Madame Cordier embarrassing him like this?

"But," Madame Cordier continued, "he would never cave in to the blackmail of a Boche or deliberately endanger any of us."

"How can you be so sure?" Christophe asked. "I knew him before and I don't trust him—especially because he has my real name to hang over my head."

Jean-Luc leapt to his feet. "How dare you, Monsieur Alain! I would never compromise you or anyone here. You, too, know *my* name. Did you forget? Fine, then! Do not call me 'Monsieur Beau.' My name is Jean-Luc Beauchamp. I am a painter, and I live in the studio upstairs from this very apartment. Is there anything else you think everyone should know? I hesitated because that Boche was only a boy. Who are you to play God with a life?"

"Who is anyone, Jean-Luc?" Madame Cordier said. "The point is, that boy would have killed you. Or he would have followed you and killed us all without a second thought. You put everyone in jeopardy without even thinking."

Jean-Luc turned to face the entire group. "If you all feel that you would be better off without me, if you feel I can't be trusted and that my knowledge would only hurt the Resistance, then kill me."

No one said anything. Mademoiselle Simone was the only one who met his eyes. He walked over to her. "Is there a pill I can take? Poison? Or would you rather murder me in cold blood?"

She looked away. "Don't be ridiculous."

"I believe," Madame Cordier said, "that Jean-Luc has made his point." She looked at him. "However, Jean-Luc. You did put us all in danger. You can't hesitate next time. For a while, perhaps I should pair you up with Monsieur Gerard. You can help him in his missions. He rarely has confrontations. Are we all agreed?"

There were a few grunts of approval. Mademoiselle Simone glared at Jean-Luc and then nodded her head once.

"Agreed," she said.

"Where is Monsieur Gerard?" Jean-Luc asked.

"Over here," said a gruff voice from the corner of the room. A man Jean-Luc had not seen stood up and lumbered into view. Jean-Luc tried to keep his face impassive as he looked at the red-faced Monsieur LeMiel.

"I normally work solo, but you're a painter. You'll appreciate what I'm trying to do."

"And what's that?"

"I save the treasures of our city—not all of the art missing from the museums was stolen by the Boches. Some is hidden for safekeeping."

CHAPTER 26

JEAN-LUC MET MONSIEUR LEMIEL at the Louvre the next morning. As he approached the museum, Jean-Luc felt his stomach twist. He had not been there since he and Natasha had gone together.

Jean-Luc swallowed the lump in his throat and, using his father's key, entered the Louvre through the same entrance he always used. Monsieur LeMiel was waiting. He grunted a greeting and then gestured for Jean-Luc to follow him into the storage closet.

The familiar room seemed to have gotten smaller. Jean-Luc's head almost touched the ceiling; the shelves he had been so proud of being able to reach were at his eye level. Pinned to the wall was a collection of old drawings on composition paper, with a child's untidy scrawl spelling out "Jean-Luc" in red crayon at the bottom of each page.

Monsieur LeMiel caught Jean-Luc staring at his old drawings.

"Simpler times, weren't they?"

Jean-Luc nodded.

"Come on. Let me show you something."

At the back of the storage closet was a little cubbyhole where Jean-Luc's father and Monsieur LeMiel used to keep several bottles of wine and a composition notebook, a few charcoal pencils, and a handful of broken crayons to keep young Jean-Luc occupied. It was now filled with empty frames and a few small paintings wrapped in old tattered blankets. The overpowering smell of mothballs caused Jean-Luc to take a step back.

Monsieur LeMiel closed the cubbyhole's door.

"Smells awful, doesn't it? But better that they smell like mothballs than to let the Boches get their hands on them. I usually store one or two here before I can get them out of their frames and transport them to a hiding place. I don't want to do too many at once, mind you. Just the ones that I think are about to be stolen. And I can't get them all, you understand."

"So the *Odalisque*—"

"No. I didn't get to that one in time." Monsieur LeMiel scowled. "Here's what I do: I go about, mopping my floors, changing my lightbulbs, and dusting the frames, and I watch to see which Germans are eyeing which paintings. Then, when the Germans leave—if I can—I steal the painting, keep it in the museum for a few days, and then bring it to a hiding place. I will replace every single one of them when we get these filthy Germans out of France—do you understand, Jean-Luc? You will not collect any of France's treasures. Only protect."

Jean-Luc was scandalized at the thought of keeping the art for his own. "Of course, Monsieur. I would never—I couldn't—"

"Don't look so shocked, boy. Believe me, it's tempting. Now, I want you to try to be here as often as possible, following the soldiers around, seeing which paintings they admire. Let me know when one seems in danger, and we'll try to get to it before they do—keep in mind, we can't take too many at once. Some will be stolen. We can only save so many."

Jean-Luc nodded.

"Do you have time now?"

"I have to work at four—"

"Good. You will be here until lunchtime. If you see that anything is in immediate danger, let me know before you leave." Monsieur LeMiel shooed Jean-Luc out of the storage closet. "Off you go, then. I have work to do."

Monsieur LeMiel grabbed his mop and locked the closet behind him. He walked past Jean-Luc as if he had not even seen him and shuffled toward the museum corridor. Jean-Luc followed, and then the two went their separate ways.

Jean-Luc, fighting every instinct, forced his feet toward the sound of voices speaking German in the Richelieu wing. It didn't take him long to find a group of soldiers, their rough speech echoing through the museum. They fell silent when Jean-Luc appeared.

Jean-Luc walked past them, trying to pretend they didn't exist. If he ignored the Boches, they usually didn't bother him. He paused to study a painting at the other end of the room, and though he caught the soldiers glancing at him every now and then, he did not spare them a glance.

The Germans resumed their conversation in low voices at first. After a while, they grew louder. Jean-Luc moved on to another painting in the same room. They became louder still until, once again, their voices could be heard from the floor below.

For the first time in his life, Jean-Luc wished he understood German.

He moved on, pretending to study another painting. The soldiers still stood around the same painting. Were they considering taking it for their own? Critiquing it? From the corner of his eye, Jean-Luc saw one of them make a crude gesture. The others laughed, and the volume of their conversation increased.

I'm wasting my time here . . . they're not even looking at the paintings.

Jean-Luc left the room, the German voices echoing behind him. He wandered around, trying to find more German voices, but the three he had left behind were so loud they drowned out any others nearby. He saw one officer parading about with a pretty French girl, but he decided not to follow them. He doubted the officer would steal anything while a French girl watched, collaborator or not.

Curiosity carried his feet up to the older French paintings to see whether *The Barque of Dante* was still there. His heart sank when he saw the empty pegs. Whoever Miró had known must not have gotten there in time.

There were giggles outside the room, and then the officer and his collaborating mistress entered.

"Oops," said the French girl. "We were here already."

She tried to turn the soldier around, but he held her arm. "One moment. I want to look at this one again."

The French girl giggled and leaned against the officer's arm. "You're never going to see anything new if you keep looking at the same paintings over and over. You looked at that painting of the girls at the piano for ages today."

Renoir, thought Jean-Luc.

"I just want to see this one again."

Don't watch him. Don't stare.

Jean-Luc walked away from the empty space where *The Barque of Dante* had hung and made his way out. As he passed the officer and the girl, he looked over his shoulder to see which painting they were admiring. He paled when he saw them approaching Anne-Louis Girodet de Roussy-Trioson's *The Sleep of Endymion*, a masterpiece more than one hundred years old.

He stood there with his jaw hanging slack, horrified at the hunger that the soldier's posture suggested.

The German turned and met Jean-Luc's eyes. Jean-Luc froze, no excuse coming to mind for his staring.

"She is beautiful, isn't she?" the German asked.

Slowly, Jean-Luc nodded.

The German squeezed the French girl's bottom. She squealed with delight.

"Franz!"

"Too bad for you. She prefers real men."

He sneered at Jean-Luc and then turned back to the painting. Appalled, Jean-Luc left the room and continued wandering his beloved museum.

I was too late to save the Delacroix . . . but I can still save that Renoir—and The Sleep of Endymion.

* * *

Jean-Luc fell into a routine. When he wasn't working at the café, he was at the Louvre. Either just before the museum closed or just after it opened in the morning, he would meet Monsieur LeMiel at the side entrance and tell him his observations; then the two would devise a way to get a popular painting out of harm's way.

Their efforts were rarely successful. It was difficult for Monsieur LeMiel to sneak away a painting and even more difficult for him to get to one before the Germans did. Jean-Luc was afraid that the older, more famous paintings would be stolen, and argued continually for them to be removed.

"This is still the Louvre, Jean-Luc. And it is still open to Parisians. We cannot take the more precious works unless someone looks eager to take them," Monsieur LeMiel whispered as he crouched in front of the cubbyhole, carefully removing a painting from its frame.

"But Monsieur—"

"The missing painting would be noticed, not just by Frenchmen, but by the Boches, too. They would wonder who took it and start asking questions, and then we would be doomed. I'm sorry, but *The Sleep of Endymion* will have to remain where it is. We must hope that the Germans will leave it on display for their fellows to observe."

"But they have been stealing more and more lately," Jean-Luc said. "Their army is not doing well in Russia, and you heard Madame Cor—er, Madame Françoise yesterday. Rumors are flying everywhere that the Allies are planning an invasion. They are losing the war and they know it!"

"Keep your voice down!" Monsieur LeMiel hissed. "Bad enough we're talking about this here. Wrong person hears you talk about them losing and you'll be arrested for 'anti-German activities.'"

"Sorry," Jean-Luc whispered. "But shouldn't we do all we can to preserve the art?"

"Without hurting our cause, yes. But arousing suspicions by making the older, more famous works disappear *will* hurt our cause."

Jean-Luc spun around, wanting to punch the wall, but thought better of it. He looked at the pinned-up drawings he had made as a child. They were crude replicas of all his favorite paintings, clumsily drawn, but very well done for a boy of only seven. Jean-Luc couldn't help but critique his work and think how much better he could do now—and an idea struck him.

"Monsieur . . . what if we replaced it with a replica?"

"And where would we get a good enough replica of *The Sleep of Endymion*?"

"I will paint it. You can switch them in the frame, keeping the original here, still in the Louvre. This way, if it gets stolen, there is no need to worry."

Monsieur LeMiel studied him for a moment and glanced up at the old drawings.

"I made a replica once before of *The Barque of Dante*. I was told it would be used to save the original," Jean-Luc said. "I know that whoever Miró gave it to was too late, but maybe you could get there in time."

"That was you, huh? Well, I've got news for you, boy. It did get there in time. Whatever Boche has that painting displays a Beauchamp, not a Delacroix."

Jean-Luc goggled at LeMiel. His painting had been hanging in the Louvre? A replica, true, but it had been passable enough to take the place of a Delacroix?

"And the original?" Jean-Luc asked.

"Safe in one of my hiding places. It will be replaced, I promise you, when the damned Boches leave our city." Monsieur LeMiel looked at Jean-Luc as if seeing him for the first time. "Your father always did say you had a talent." He glanced up at the drawings. "Will you be able to get enough materials?"

Jean-Luc nodded. "I should be."

"All right, boy. But paint quickly. We don't have much time."

*   *   *

Three candles next to the easel did not provide nearly enough light for Jean-Luc as he mixed colors and carefully copied *The Sleep of Endymion* from memory. For three weeks now, he had been going to the Louvre and staring at Anne-Louis Girodet de Roussy-Trioson's painting, committing every color and line to his memory, section by section. And while he worked at the café, he would think about the painting, how he would mix colors, where he would work the next day, and try to remember little details he did not want to miss.

When he came home, he painted until he could barely keep his eyes open, and then he memorized the replica to compare it with the original when he returned to the Louvre the following morning.

Jean-Luc stretched and pinched the inside corners of his eyes. He needed to buy more candles from the black market. If he kept this up, it could damage his sight, and he didn't know if he could bear life as a blind man.

He moved his hand from his eyes to massage the back of his neck and looked around the room. Hanging above his sink was a large sheet of paper that he had washed and prepared the way Miró had taught him, blank and begging to be caressed with his paintbrush. Jean-Luc looked at the replica for a long while.

I can't rush this. I'm almost done, he thought. *Another hour or two and it should be complete.*

Forcing his own work to the back of his mind, Jean-Luc focused on *The Sleep of Endymion*. He worked slowly, trying to remember every crack in the canvas, every speck of color, and every detail about the painting. The color was off for now, but when the paint dried, if his memory served him correctly, it would be so exact that the curator would have trouble telling the two paintings apart. It had to be.

A little over an hour later, Jean-Luc sat in front of his completed replica, exhausted but still inspired. He had completed another one. It was still strange to him that one of his paintings had passed for a masterpiece worthy of the Louvre. Either the curator was turning a blind eye to the disappearances or Jean-Luc's talent was greater than he had imagined. Daring to hope it was the latter, Jean-Luc shifted to his own work, striving to paint something from his heart that would one day hang in the galleries of his beloved city.

Putting the canvas aside, he pulled down the sheet of paper and, using clothespins, secured it to his easel. He sat back down on his stool and examined the grooves of the paper, trying to imagine and select colors.

The first color that came to his mind was a pale blue, like Natasha's costume for her solo in the ballet.

As he thought of her, a light breeze drifted in through the open window and ruffled his hair. Though it was quite warm for a May night, the breeze sent goose bumps running all over Jean-Luc's body.

He wondered how she was doing—she was undoubtedly still with her German soldier, feeling safer and more secure in the arms of a man in power. Jean-Luc tossed his head and wiped his eyes before the tears could fall. He would not think of her.

But it was too late. The memory of her consumed every corner of his mind. He found himself reliving their moment in the vault of the Louvre, their walks along the river, their nights in his studio. He was no longer sure if she had meant what she had said about his art, but one thing was certain: she had rejected him. By saying what she did, she had made it very clear to Jean-Luc that she never wanted to see or hear from him again.

He still couldn't hate her, but he didn't want the pain of seeing her, either. Whenever he thought he smelled her perfume or saw her walking, he diverted his eyes and moved in the other direction, forcing his thoughts to focus on something else.

Sitting in his studio, painting from his heart, he could not help but think of her. His hands, with a mind of their own, had already begun mixing paint to create a soft pink. Jean-Luc watched as his hands began to sweep the paper with long, heavy strokes. Detached but interested, Jean-Luc let his hands paint as his heart dictated while keeping his mind alert, ready to stop his hands if his heart began to take too much control.

The candles burned until they were barely more than wicks holding onto a flame. What was left of the wax was spread almost flat on the plate Jean-Luc had placed beneath them. Yet somehow, the light was improving. Jean-Luc looked up to find the entire room filled with a soft bluish light— dawn was approaching.

The door to his studio creaked open and Madame Cordier stepped in.

"Oh! Jean-Luc." She placed a bundle of his freshly laundered clothes by the door. "Mon chou, have you been up all night?"

Mon chou. She had not called him that since he joined the Resistance. Was he dreaming?

"Yes, Madame."

"You should get some sleep."

"I have to meet Monsieur—"

She closed the door. "Never mind that. I will tell him I put you to bed."

"Thank you, Madame, but I will meet him. I don't do much anyway, and I would like to earn the respect of the other members. I can't have excuses made for me."

Madame Cordier put her hands on her hips. "You can't very well go without sleep, either."

"For one night, I can. I don't have work this evening, so I will go to bed early. I promise."

She gave him a stern look. "Very well, but if I find you painting, I will drag you by your ears to bed."

Jean-Luc found himself chuckling. "I've missed this, Madame."

Madame Cordier dropped her hands. "I know . . . I'm sorry, my pet. I wanted things to remain as they were. Of all my tenants, you let me mother you the most. I felt like you saw me as much as your mother as I saw you as my son. I wanted to protect you from all this. You were the one person in Paris I could understand turning a blind eye to everything. I still want to protect you. That's why I've been so cold and distant—I hope you understand."

"Of course, Madame."

She sat down on the edge of Jean-Luc's bed and looked around. "You've been so busy . . . yet I've never seen this room so clean." She sighed. "Children do grow up far too fast."

Jean-Luc glanced around his room. It was still a little messy. The bed was unmade and clothes still lay on the floor, but everything dirty was in a pile shoved in the corner, and his art supplies were organized on the table. He had moved most of his older, unfinished projects to Miró's old studio to make it look as if an artist still lived there, so he had less clutter in the room.

"It's still not very clean," he said.

"Jean-Luc, I don't want you to think it's a bad thing that you couldn't find it in you to kill. It means your heart is stronger than your anger."

"But I put everyone in danger."

"Not that much danger. Perhaps even I blew it out of proportion. If no one else had been able to kill him, then you would have, but Mademoiselle Simone did it for you. And Monsieur Raoul, if what I've heard is true, had the soldier's rifle. It was an unfair test."

"Unfortunately, it was a test I failed. Mademoiselle Simone especially has contempt for me because of it."

"Don't judge her too harshly, Jean-Luc. She was forced to grow up at a very young age. Ever wonder why she lives in a brothel?"

"Yes . . . but I assumed it was none of my business."

"You're such a sweet boy. Her aunt is the madam—her father's estranged sister. Her parents both died when she was very young, and she went to live with her maternal grandmother, a German who had married a Frenchman."

"Which is why she speaks German."

"Exactly. When her grandmother died, the only family she had left was her father's sister, so she went to live with her. She's incredibly bitter and a more recent addition to our little group, but she is a valuable asset, and despite her age, she thinks with a clear and level head. Believe it or not, Monsieur Raoul and your friend Monsieur Alain are more suspicious of you."

"But . . . why?"

"Everyone is frightened of new members, especially after what happened to Jean Moulin last year."

"I remember hearing his name at the meetings. And I think I saw something about him in the newspaper." He could feel the color rising to his cheeks. "But I never really kept up-to-date."

"He was in the Resistance—a brave man. We were all just scattered groups with different agendas until he began working to unite us toward one collective effort. He worked tirelessly, and last year, he was betrayed by one of his own and tortured—" Madame Cordier's voice broke. She cleared her throat and continued, "Tortured to death by the Butcher of Lyon."

"Who?"

"Klaus Barbie—the head of the Gestapo in Lyon. He personally tortured and murdered people he suspected of anti-German activities. He was the one who trapped Jean Moulin—with the help of some collaborating swine. As far as we can tell, Moulin never revealed anything. He knew so much. If he had talked, the Resistance could have been crushed.

"The loss of Moulin was a devastating blow to all of us, particularly for our morale. Everyone is afraid now, knowing that one of our own could turn traitor. Our little group is no different. That is why they are so hard on you."

Jean-Luc nodded. "I want to earn their respect, Madame. I don't expect it to come easily. But seeing that . . . that *boy* so close up, it was hard to see his uniform. All I saw was his mother."

"And again, dearest, it shows you have a big heart, but keep in mind that he would not have hesitated to kill you. Next time, you must kill him. If he was merely a boy sitting at his dinner table, that would be one thing, but he was a soldier. It was his job to kill or arrest you. He is your enemy."

"I . . . understand," said Jean-Luc, yawning.

Madame Cordier clucked her tongue. "You poor boy. Are you certain you don't want me to make your excuses?"

"I'm sure. I must earn my own respect before I can earn theirs."

"I will be glad when this war is over, Jean-Luc. I miss the days when my most important task was making you brioche and keeping my tenants happy." She dabbed the corners of her eyes with her fingertips. Jean-Luc stood up at once and pulled his handkerchief from his pocket. She took it with a slight smile. "Sometimes it seems like it will never end."

Jean-Luc sat down beside her and took her hand. "It will, Madame. And very soon, you will see the day when the Boches are driven from our city forever."

"So certain, so optimistic," Madame Cordier said. "That is why you have always been my favorite boy."

She kissed both of his cheeks. Jean-Luc felt a great sense of relief wash over him. He hadn't even realized how much he had missed Madame Cordier, but there she was again, kissing his cheeks, calling him a good boy, and pretending to be his mother. Suddenly very comfortable and tired, he wished he didn't have to meet Monsieur LeMiel. Giving him the painting would have to wait. The paint was still not dry.

"I'd better get going before the lines get too long," Madame Cordier said. "I already took your ration coupons. Come back here for lunch, understand?"

Jean-Luc chuckled. "Yes, Madame."

With some effort, Jean-Luc stood up, stretched out his back, and walked with Madame Cordier out of the apartment. Once outside, they turned from each other to walk their separate ways down rue Blomet.

Madame Cordier was not the only one who left at dawn to wait in the lines. The street was already teeming with people—mostly women—carrying canvas bags and small children, pleasantly chatting with one another, but each trying to keep a half step ahead of the other so as to be first in line.

"Madame! Madaaaaaame!"

A little boy no older than eight came tearing down the street, screaming at the top of his lungs. Heads were already peeking out of windows, trying to see what the commotion was. People turned and watched the boy as he darted through the crowds, ducking between couples, shoving boys his age aside.

"Madame!"

He rushed past Jean-Luc and crashed right into Madame Cordier. Jean-Luc turned and ran toward his landlady and the boy.

"Madame! Are you all right?" Jean-Luc asked.

"Of course . . . Henri, dear, are you all right?"

The freckled boy panted and gasped for breath, but nodded. "Madame . . . it's . . . hot in . . . Suez," the boy wheezed.

Madame Cordier stiffened. "What?"

"It's hot . . . in . . . Suez," the boy repeated, still doubled over and panting. "The dice . . . are . . . cast. And . . . the arrow . . . will not . . . pierce. That's what . . . Papa said."

"Thank you, Henri."

Henri nodded, then took a few more deep breaths and apologized for bumping into her. Without another word, he ran off again, screaming for "Madame" again until he was out of sight.

"Jean-Luc, do you remember every word he said?"

"Yes, but—"

"Tell Monsieur Gerard. Then I want you to tell Monsieur Maurice and see if we can meet in his basement tonight at dusk."

"Yes, Madame."

Madame Cordier nodded once, then turned and walked away, the Resistance leader once again.

*   *   *

When Jean-Luc arrived at the Louvre, Monsieur LeMiel was waiting for him by the entrance.

"You're late," Monsieur LeMiel grunted. "You finished yet? If it takes you this long, we can't switch very many."

"It's hot in Suez."

Monsieur LeMiel's head snapped in Jean-Luc's direction. In that instant, he looked sober for the first time in years.

"A boy told Madame Cor—Fran—"

"I know who you mean. Get on with it."

"It's hot in Suez. The dice are cast. And the arrow will not pierce."

Monsieur LeMiel dropped his mop and his jaw. The handle of the mop clattered to the floor.

"Are you finished with the painting?"

"Yes, but the paint isn't dry."

"Bring it tomorrow. For now, go find someone who can tell you how to be useful."

"Madame told me to tell Monsieur Maurice after I—"

"Go then!"

"But what does this mean?"

"Later! Go!"

Jean-Luc ran out of the museum and back to the métro station. He was so confused. The entire ride back to Montparnasse he tried to figure out what the three sentences meant.

It's good code, I suppose—but what's going on?

The train reached Pasteur station and Jean-Luc ran up the steps and beelined to Le Café d'Anton. He walked inside with what he hoped was a casual step, struggling to keep his breathing even.

"Bonjour, Jean-Luc," Pierre Anton said when he spotted him. "Come here to eat on your day off?"

"No, Monsieur, I had a question about my schedule." It was a code he and Monsieur Anton had worked out. Whenever Jean-Luc came to discuss Resistance business, he said he had questions about or wanted to rearrange his schedule.

"I see. Come to the kitchen and we'll discuss it."

Jean-Luc followed Monsieur Anton through the kitchen and out the back door, where Jean-Luc whispered the message from Madame Cordier.

"What does it mean, Monsieur?" Jean-Luc asked.

Monsieur Anton dropped his voice so low that Jean-Luc could barely hear him. "It's a call for the Resistance to mobilize and launch the Green and Violet plans."

"The what?"

"I'm not exactly sure what they are, but I can only assume it means to create chaos in any way we can. Do you know what this means?" Monsieur Anton looked up at Jean-Luc, his eyes glistening with tears and filled with both fear and hope. "The Allies are going to invade."

* * *

Jean-Luc sat on a crate in the basement of Le Café d'Anton, his head swimming. Were the Allies really invading? Would they come straight to Paris—or even come at all? How long before the Germans were pushed out? Would de Gaulle be the new leader of France, like some said he already was, or would the Communists, who had been major players in the Resistance, take over?

And what are the Green and Violet plans? Jean-Luc thought as Mademoiselle Simone and Monsieur Raoul emerged from the trapdoor. Monsieur Raoul didn't look at Jean-Luc, and Mademoiselle Simone only gave him a curt nod before taking her place against the wall.

Everyone seemed afraid to speak. It took forever for Madame Cordier, the last of their group, to arrive. For once, she did not have to hold up her hands for silence.

"As many of you already know, we received a message over BBC radio this morning telling us to launch the Green and Violet plans." She glanced sideways at Monsieur Philippe. "Monsieur Philippe and I went against explicit orders in telling you what 'It is hot in Suez' meant. We felt that the mistrust among ourselves was becoming more of a threat than a precaution. However, it was against our better judgment to tell most of you exactly what the Green and Violet plans consisted of.

"Well, the time has come and we must act. These plans call for creating total chaos from within to hinder the Germans in any way we can. They will need to concentrate all of their efforts on defending what they have stolen, and they won't be able to do so if the French unite to make things difficult for them. The Green plan refers to the railroad. We are to derail trains, cut any cables we can, destroy bits of track—anything to disrupt the flow."

"But won't that prevent food from coming in?" Christophe asked. "Rations are scarce as it is, and my wife—"

"I understand your concern, Monsieur Alain, but would you rather your child speak German or French?"

"With all due respect, Madame, I'd rather my child be born and my wife live to raise it."

Compassion and concern, emotions that so seldom crossed "Madame Françoise's" face, flashed in Madame Cordier's eyes. "I know. But the end is so close. Everything we've worked for is at hand. If the Allies succeed in their invasion, it is only a matter of time before they push on to Berlin, and end the war. Then you will not have to raise your baby in a world at war."

Christophe said nothing. Madame Cordier hardened her features and continued. "The Violet plan refers to the long-distance telephone lines—Madame Dominque? Monsieur Louis? Since you work for the telephone company, you will be in charge of telling us where the lines are so we can sabotage them. Nothing local just yet. We don't want to alert the Germans to anything until they are ready to use them."

"They'll notice the cuts and repair them quickly, as always," Monsieur Louis said.

"And we will cut them again," said Mademoiselle Simone. Excitement shone in her face. "It will create mass confusion throughout the country. As they repair one thing, we will destroy another. They can't keep up if they're fighting a battle. Madame Françoise, are they coming directly to Paris?"

Madame Cordier's face fell. "I . . . I'm not sure. There have been no hints in the messages. I imagine de Gaulle would want to free the true capital of France, but—" Her voice croaked and she turned away. Jean-Luc sprang from his seat and rushed to her side.

"Madame?" he said softly.

"Sit down, Jean-Luc," said Monsieur Philippe.

Jean-Luc squared his shoulders and narrowed his eyes. "I will sit when I am sure Madame is all right."

"It's all right, Jean-Luc," Madame Cordier said, wiping her eyes. "Sit. Please."

Enduring glares from the other members, Jean-Luc returned to his crate, but he kept a close eye on Madame Cordier.

"Forgive me, my friends. I am just so happy—and frightened—that this has finally come. I can't lie to you and say that the Allies will come to Paris.

I can't promise you that the Boches won't demand retribution and punish all that they can as severely as they can. But this is what we have worked toward, and we can't let our fears get in the way of our goals." She paused. "Do you have anything to add, Monsieur Philippe?"

Monsieur Philippe cleared his throat. "Other groups, of course, will be working toward the same thing. It will be difficult to tell who is helping and who is collaborating. Be careful."

There was a fair amount to discuss. Christophe and Monsieur Raoul were already talking about how to sabotage railroad tracks on the outskirts of the city. Madame Cordier was saying something about a Blue plan to Monsieur Philippe, though neither disclosed exactly what it was. To Jean-Luc's surprise, Madame Dominique approached him and requested his help in cutting the telephone lines.

"Of course. What do you need me to do?"

"You're an artist, right?" she said. "You need to copy these exactly, filling in a fake name. You will need to forge fake identification papers with it. I need you to pretend to fix the phone lines, cutting the ones I tell you to. Can you finish forging by tomorrow morning?"

"Yes."

"Good. I'll meet you in front of the phone company's office building at ten. And don't worry." She dropped her voice to a whisper. "There is not much chance you will have to kill anyone."

Jean-Luc nodded. "Thank you, Madame Dominique."

"I am doing this for France, Monsieur. In order for you to be useful, you must keep your head. And we will need you."

"Madame Dominique, Mademoiselle Simone," Monsieur Philippe said, holding up the trapdoor. Jean-Luc had not even realized that the meeting had come to an end.

Madame Dominique bid Jean-Luc a quick farewell and followed the scowling Mademoiselle Simone down the trapdoor. It wasn't long before only Monsieur Anton, Madame Cordier, Jean-Luc, and Monsieur Philippe remained.

"Jean-Luc," Madame Cordier said. "I need you to understand that if the Allies invade and come to Paris, you will need to kill. Any hesitation on your part could cost many lives."

"Yes, Madame."

"I'm serious, Jean-Luc. Far too much is at stake for you to be squeamish."

"I understand."

Madame Cordier regarded him for a moment, and then looked away and nodded, her voice cracking again. "Very well. Off you go."

Jean-Luc followed Monsieur Philippe down the trapdoor's steps, struggling not to stumble in the dark. Soon they came upon a heavy door with a hinged piece of wood covering a slit used as a peephole. No light shone through the slit. Slowly, Monsieur Philippe opened the door and motioned for Jean-Luc to step out, then moved to padlock the door.

They were on the edge of a platform to the side of an abandoned métro station. Without a word, Jean-Luc and Monsieur Philippe left the station and started off in opposite directions. Jean-Luc had to fight the urge to break into a run as he made his way back to his studio, the papers from Madame Dominique in his hand. The Allies were coming.

CHAPTER 27

FORGED PAPERS IN HAND, Jean-Luc waited outside the telephone company, adrenaline pumping through his veins. He leaned against the side of the building and waited for Madame Dominique, trying not to grin as he overheard the gossip of passersby.

Paris was abuzz with the news of sabotaged rail lines and cut telephone lines. The efforts his own Resistance group had made surely could not have caused this much of a stir. *There must be more groups out there than I imagined*, Jean-Luc thought. *We'll be free of the Germans before long!*

Parisians worried about power being cut off and discussed how they could prepare for it, but they held their heads a little higher and walked with lighter steps. The Germans were surly, yet they jumped at the slightest sound. They huddled in groups, talking and casting suspicious looks at everyone around them. Jean-Luc tried to avoid eye contact as much as possible. He did not want to draw attention to himself.

"Oh! Good. You must be the repairman." Jean-Luc looked up to see Madame Dominique, looking a bit frazzled and stressed.

"So many lines have been damaged today. It's a nightmare inside. Here." She handed him a set of coveralls and a tool belt. "Follow me. I'll show you where some are that you can fix. Try to keep up."

Madame Dominique didn't give Jean-Luc time to respond. She started down the street, walking at a brisk pace. As Jean-Luc walked next to her, she said out of the corner of her mouth, "Put those on. Cut the wires and then move on. Make sure it's quick. Show your papers if you're questioned." She came to an abrupt halt and pointed to a telephone pole. "See if you can repair the damage up there. Here's a list of some others that were reported damaged." She shoved a scrap of paper into his hand. "I have to get back to work. Good luck."

Without another word, she was gone. Jean-Luc took a look around, then pulled the coveralls over his clothes and fastened the tool belt around his waist. Stuffing the forged papers into the belt, he climbed the telephone pole and looked at the wires for a long while. He didn't know the first thing about electrical work or telephone lines. He hesitated to cut anything right away, for fear of electrocuting himself. There were so many wires in a swirling nest, some with bird droppings dotting the rubber insulation.

"You! What are you doing up there?" called a voice in a thick German accent. Jean-Luc felt the color drain from his face. He looked down to see a soldier pointing his rifle at him.

"Making repairs," Jean-Luc called down to the soldier, hoping his voice was steady. "This line has been cut."

"Let me see your papers," the German said.

Jean-Luc slowly climbed down and handed the papers to the soldier. They were expertly forged, but Jean-Luc's heart still raced. Would the soldier notice that they were new and had no smudges? He had creased them over and over again to make the paper look as worn as possible, but only now did he realize that the paper was so clean.

"You had these ready," the soldier said, eyeing him.

"Yes. You're the third soldier who has asked me for identification this morning. There have been too many sabotaged lines for me to keep up with, and I'm just trying to get my work done."

"Watch your tone." The soldier glared at him. Jean-Luc looked him in the eye.

"You would be irritable, too, if you were constantly interrupted. Go up there and look if you don't believe me. I'm almost finished repairing that one. You can see for yourself that it was cut and is now halfway repaired—I don't know why I bother. I just fixed this one this morning, too. And now it's been cut again."

Jean-Luc regretted the bluff immediately. It was a long shot—too long. The soldier studied him for a long moment.

"Watch your tone," the soldier repeated, shoving the papers back toward Jean-Luc. Jean-Luc took them with sweaty hands and watched as the soldier walked away and disappeared into the crowd.

Jean-Luc swallowed hard and then climbed back up the telephone pole to reexamine the wires. He selected several important-looking wires in the tangle, sliced them through, and then moved on to the next place on Madame Dominique's list.

From atop the telephone poles, Jean-Luc could see people walking in clusters, gossiping about the increased Resistance activity and Marshal Petain's warning not to support the Allies, for fear of German reprisals. He strained his ears, listening for explosions in the distance, though he knew the Allies wouldn't push through Normandy as quickly as he would have liked. There was still no guarantee that they wouldn't bypass Paris in favor of pushing straight on to Germany. Jean-Luc could barely keep his hands from shaking.

Another line cut, he moved on to the next location. Many of the lines on Madame Dominique's list had already been cut, but Jean-Luc was able to cut a fair number. Once he had made it through the list, he returned to Montparnasse to change for work. His head was swimming with ideas of lines swirled into a nest of bold colors, but he fought the urge to paint. He was already running late.

* * *

Celeste Anton greeted him with her usual shake of the head as he entered the café. "You're lucky my husband thought so highly of your father," she said.

"I'm sorry, Madame."

"Don't apologize. Get back there."

Jean-Luc hurried to the kitchen but found that the usual pile of dishes wasn't there waiting for him.

"Not too busy tonight." Jean-Luc jumped at the sound of Nicolas's voice.

"No?" Jean-Luc said.

Nicolas shook his head. "The Boches are all busy and can't take out their whores."

"Good. I hope their mothers beat them," said Georges, one of the cooks. "Collaborating prostitutes are just as bad as the Nazis—no decent French girl would go around with a German."

"When the Allies drive the Germans out of Paris, they'll be punished," Nicolas said. "I've heard rumors. And I hope they're true."

"Like what?" Jean-Luc asked.

"Shave their heads and make them walk naked through the Champs-Élysées," said Nicolas. "Paint swastikas on their faces."

"They should tattoo them on their foreheads," said Georges. "And brand their German-fathered babies."

Georges and Nicolas ranted back and forth, trading ideas and rumors on how best to punish the girls who had coupled with the Germans. Jean-Luc felt sick. He could not justify anything being done to hurt or single out German-fathered children.

He imagined Natasha being marched through the streets, naked, with her beautiful hair shaved.

She deserves it, he told himself.

He pictured her with a swastika tattooed on her forehead, walking past him. He tried imagining her carrying a child fathered by that beast Lorenz, but it inspired no hatred. Even in his imagination, he felt the urge to run up to her, cover her with his coat, and protect her and her child from the vengeful Parisians—precautions and loyalties be damned.

No, she deserves it. She bought into the power. She . . . she . . .

He could not convince himself to stop caring. He clenched his fists and ground his teeth, trying to tune out Nicolas and Georges's ramblings. Relief washed over him as Monsieur Anton appeared in the kitchen.

"Nicolas, up front. Georges, Jean-Luc, back to work."

"Yes, Monsieur."

Nicolas and Georges left Jean-Luc to the small pile of dishes.

Jean-Luc could not get Natasha out of his head. He saw her dancing in every soapy bubble, heard her laughter in every moment of silence. He tried humming loudly to himself to drown out the sound of her voice, but to no avail. Thoughts of her crowded everything else out.

I have to warn her. I have to tell her what they plan to do.

The thought of seeing her again made his insides twist about. How could he look at her and not scoop her in his arms? How could he stand near her and not kiss her? No. He couldn't go near her.

She deserves to be humiliated. She's a soldier's mistress—a collaborationist.

Though he tried again to hate her, Jean-Luc spent the rest of his shift reliving happy memories. The pain in his heart grew with each remembered smile and kiss. He wanted to believe what Madame Cordier and Miró had said, that Natasha had her reasons for pushing him away, but he could not think of any. She knew how seriously he took his painting. There was no reason for her to bring up his artwork in that interview unless it was to reject him.

The evening crept by slowly. Word arrived that the curfew had been extended an extra hour for "good behavior," but it hardly mattered. The soldiers were busy; over the course of the past month, they had been the main clientele at Le Café d'Anton. The café was empty.

"We're closing early," Monsieur Anton announced just as the sun was setting. "There's no one here as it is." He looked at Jean-Luc. "I believe you wanted to discuss your schedule with me after work?"

"Again?" Nicolas rolled his eyes. "You change your schedule more often than anyone I've ever met. I can't believe he accommodates you."

Jean-Luc shrugged. "I'm flexible. I pick up shifts he needs covered."

"Let's go, Nicolas. Finish up," Monsieur Anton said.

Jean-Luc took his time washing dishes. If there was a meeting afterward, he had to make sure he was still working when the last of the other employees left.

By the time Nicolas, Georges, and the other cooks and waiters cleared out, Jean-Luc was still cleaning the sink and putting the dishes away. He finished up as soon as they were gone, then followed Monsieur Anton through the dry storage closet to the basement.

"What was this used for before the Germans invaded?" Jean-Luc asked as he descended the staircase.

"Smuggling. My grandfather dabbled in the black market. When the métro was being built, he had his connections dig the entranceway. Before the Germans invaded, Celeste and I used it as an extra wine cellar—that was when there was plenty of wine and enough sugar and bread to make real brioche."

"Soon," Jean-Luc said. "The Allies are coming."

Monsieur Anton chuckled. "Your optimism amazes me, Jean-Luc. I have my doubts that they'll even come to Paris."

"They have to. Paris is the capital. As a symbol, it's a much more devastating loss for the Nazis."

"I wish I shared your confidence, Jean-Luc."

Monsieur Anton reached the bottom step and pulled the string to click on the lightbulb. He moved the carpet and the table and pulled a key from his pocket to unlock the padlocked trapdoor. Five minutes later, Madame Cordier arrived with a bundle that looked suspiciously like the coveralls and tool belt Jean-Luc had left in his studio. One by one, the other members showed up. Upon her arrival, Madame Dominique ignored Jean-Luc, save for a glance when Madame Cordier called her over and handed her the bundle.

Mademoiselle Simone arrived almost an hour late. Madame Cordier frowned at her, but Mademoiselle Simone was smiling, for once.

"I'm sorry I'm late, but de Gaulle finally spoke on the radio. I copied his speech so you can read it, Madame." She handed Madame Cordier a folded piece of paper.

Madame Cordier unfolded the copied speech and glanced over it once. Tears glistened in her eyes. Jean-Luc moved to stand beside her, but she held her hand up.

"Monsieur Philippe, if you please . . ." Madame Cordier handed Monsieur Philippe the paper.

Taking it, Monsieur Philippe cleared his throat. "The supreme battle has begun," he read. "It is not only the Battle of France, it is France's battle . . ." He read Charles de Gaulle's speech slowly, pausing here and there to prevent his voice from shaking. ". . . For the sons of France, it goes without saying, the obligation is simple and sacred, to fight with all the means at their disposal. They shall destroy the detested enemy, the dishonorable enemy . . ."

As Monsieur Philippe read the speech, Jean-Luc watched Madame Cordier. She smiled through her tears and occasionally looked at Jean-Luc with the kindness she had held back since he joined the Resistance. He wanted to hug her, sharing her joy in the moment.

". . . Behind the clouds, if heavy with our blood and our tears, there is that which will restore the sunlight and our grandeur." Monsieur Philippe wiped his eyes, and the group remained silent for a few moments.

"He didn't mention whether he was coming to Paris," Christophe said.

"Well, he couldn't, could he? Not plainly," Mademoiselle Simone said, still beaming. "They have to come to Paris. France isn't free until Paris is!"

"They could push on to Germany without struggling for Paris," said Madame Dominique.

"No!" cried Mademoiselle Simone, leaping to her feet. "They have to come for Paris. It's *Paris*! It's the capital! Are they going to liberate Vichy and that traitor Petain before the true citizens of France?"

"Calm down, Mademoiselle Simone. We can't be sure of what the armies will do. Monsieur Philippe and I will talk to other leaders and see what they plan to do. In the meantime, de Gaulle has asked that we follow the true government's orders. Right now, their orders are to continue to sabotage but not to take up arms against the Germans until the Allies arrive."

Mademoiselle Simone nodded and sat down. Monsieur Raoul put his arm around her and began to whisper in her ear. For a moment, Jean-Luc saw himself comforting Natasha, stroking her arm the way Monsieur Raoul stroked Mademoiselle Simone's.

Despite the excitement and anticipation, Jean-Luc could no longer think about the Allied invasion. He could think only of Natasha.

CHAPTER 28

NATASHA PACED AROUND the room in the Hotel Meurice. She had been trapped in the suite ever since the invasion of Normandy, permitted to leave only for performances for the past two months. Lorenz had been out most of the time; she was grateful for his absence but hated being confined.

Lorenz's temper and lust had been quick to flare and difficult to extinguish lately. He constantly threatened to send her to Auschwitz, telling her more stories of how the prisoners were treated. He was rough in bed and had ordered her to do things that made her shudder. She couldn't tell him no—especially not after the news of the Allied invasion.

Natasha could have wept. She hated the Germans more than ever before, but France's liberation would spell disaster for her. Lorenz would kill her, send her off to Auschwitz, or drag her with him in his retreat to Germany. If, by some miracle, she was spared and left behind, the people of Paris would take their revenge.

She had heard the jeers of men and women, seen their glares. She knew the Parisians hated her just as much as they hated the occupation. If Paris were liberated, she would never be able to buy bread without being slapped by a stranger, let alone dance before a French audience. The entire city knew whose mistress she was, and everyone hated her for it—even Jean-Luc.

She had seen him several times on the street. She tried not to look, but she couldn't help stealing glances. She thought she saw him look up once, out of the corner of her eye, but when she turned to meet his gaze, he was already gone.

Even dancing did not distract her the way it used to. She felt tired and weak most of the time, and every smell continued to offend her. Her menses had never come last month. As much as she liked to pretend that it was due to stress, she could no longer deny that she was pregnant. She had to call a doctor. If Lorenz knew, he would do the same and likely discard her soon after. She had to be discreet and quick, before she began to show, but she had let opportunity after opportunity pass her by. There was still a chance that this could be Jean-Luc's baby.

She paused in her pacing and went over to the window. She thought she saw Jean-Luc walking by, but it wasn't him.

Of course it's not him. Don't be stupid. You pushed him away, remember? He's not coming for you—not ever.

Natasha gave the curtains a tug and went back to pacing. Jean-Luc's art was so important to him. She had known exactly what would happen if she criticized it.

Lorenz would have killed him, she thought. *Jean-Luc would have been caught forging. I had to say good-bye.*

She slumped down on the sofa and buried her head in her hands. Part of her hoped Lorenz would kill her when he came home, part of her wished the Allies would arrive, and all of her wished that Jean-Luc would charge in, scoop her up in his arms, and whisk her away to Sweden, promising to raise the child as his own, even if it was Lorenz's. The fantasy kept her alive, but it was only a torturous daydream. Jean-Luc would never forgive her.

Footsteps thundered outside the door. Natasha sprang to her feet. Wiping her eyes, she rushed to the bathroom to splash her face with water. If

Lorenz found her crying, he would not be pleased; she was running out of excuses. He was beginning to doubt that she was just worried about him.

Ever since Dietrich von Choltitz had been selected over him to replace Boineburg as the military governor of Paris, Lorenz's temper had flared at the slightest touch. His fury had been much more bearable since the news of the Allied invasion.

Natasha scrubbed her face until she was sure it no longer looked as if she had been crying and then practiced her smile, but Lorenz didn't walk through the door.

It must have been someone walking by.

Natasha wandered from room to room, finally slumping on the bed to stare at the dresser. She longed for her nested dolls. A gift from her father, they had always brought her such comfort. But Kremmler, or whoever had packed her things and brought them to the Hotel Meurice, had not included them. She pulled her suitcase out from under the bed and checked inside for the hundredth time. The dolls were not there.

It was just as well. Within the smallest doll was the Star of David that her mother had worn in secret. Though anti-Semitism was illegal under Stalin, faith of any kind was more than frowned upon; the Party demanded utmost loyalty, not to be surpassed by any god. Natasha's father had been willing to let go, but not her mother. While she had not kept kosher or uttered a word of Hebrew, she had still prayed and observed the holy days when she could, and she had taught her daughter everything she knew.

When Natasha turned thirteen, her mother gave her that Star of David. If Kremmler or anyone else found it, she would be shipped off to the death camps before she could throw herself from a window.

Natasha went over to the window and looked down. Would the fall kill her? Probably not—though she would end up with a broken limb or two. She looked back at the open suitcase on the bed. Then at the dresser. Then at the suitcase again.

If the Allies came, maybe she would have an opportunity to escape. If she were shot in the attempt, at least her death might be quick.

She pulled open the top drawer and grabbed an armful of clothes, pulling a pair of Lorenz's trousers out in the process. She tossed them on the bed and began to roll her own clothes tightly, so as many as possible would fit in the suitcase.

"What is this?"

Natasha spun around. Lorenz towered over her. He reached past her, pulled one of her blouses from the suitcase, and held it up.

"Going somewhere, my love?" His voice was low and dangerous.

"I—no, Heinrich. The news . . . it's not good. I . . . I . . ." Her eye caught the pair of trousers lying among her things. "I was packing for both of us. For Germany. If—if we have to flee."

Lorenz narrowed his eyes. "You doubt German forces?" He grabbed her by the shoulders and shook her. "The Allies will not take France!" He knocked the suitcase aside and stared down at her. Natasha knew the look all too well. Sure enough, he shoved her back onto the bed and seized her with more force than ever before. As usual, Natasha put up no resistance and moaned in the appropriate places, taking extra care not to overplay her part. She imagined Jean-Luc coming to her rescue; it was the only thing she could do to prevent herself from crying.

When Lorenz finished, he did not linger. Instead, he threw her clothes at her. "Get dressed. I have somewhere to be. You will no longer be left alone, in case you decide to be a coward and run."

"I was packing for the both of—"

Lorenz brought his palm clear across her face. "Your lack of faith disgusts me." He dressed without looking at her. "I said to get dressed. I have things to do, and Kremmler or Müller will have to keep an eye on you while I'm gone."

"I have a performance tonight."

"Not anymore." He turned to face her. "There will be no more ballet for you. A Jew should not be onstage. You will be watched at all times. I suggest you use the lavatory now, unless you want one of my men to be your audience."

Natasha touched her cheek with her fingertips. The skin was still hot. She couldn't call a doctor in now, not without Lorenz knowing. What would happen when she started to show?

"Now, Natasha. I won't ask you again."

Natasha gathered up her clothes and dressed, unable to look Lorenz in the face.

Jean-Luc, she thought. *Oh, Jean-Luc, I'm so sorry.*

*   *   *

Lorenz looked down at his palm, flexing his fingers. It was stinging from the slap, but the usual thrill that came with striking an enemy of the Third Reich was coupled with an unfamiliar hollow feeling.

She's a Jew, Lorenz reminded himself. *Worthless, no matter how perfect she looks. Jews are the enemy of Germans.*

He glanced at Natasha. Her cheek was still bright red. She looked as if she had applied too much rouge, like her whore of a friend, and then smeared it down her face.

She already had her skirt on. She always dressed in the same routine. Her undergarments, the left stocking, then the right, sliding them up her leg in one smooth motion. She was so structured, so disciplined in everything she did.

But she was a Jew. And disciplined or not, she had no place on a stage. She had no place anywhere, except perhaps Auschwitz—especially if she doubted the Führer's abilities and strategy. She was lucky he let her live.

He tried to find flaws in her every day, but he never found any. How was he supposed to do his duty when she constantly mocked him with her poise and beauty?

How dare she make a fool of him! Making him believe she was perfect, winding her way around his heart, only to turn out to be a Jew. It was the highest insult—higher than that fool von Choltitz being selected over him as the military governor of Paris. That position should have been his!

She was buttoning up her blouse, not looking at him. Lorenz walked over to her and cracked his palm across her other cheek.

She cried out as she was knocked over to the side. Finally, she looked at him.

"You are moving too slow."

She moved twice as fast, her fingers fumbling with buttons. Lorenz smiled down at her. It was nice to see her obeying orders.

CHAPTER 29

J EAN-LUC HAD NOT been to Monsieur LeMiel's apartment since he had
been a boy, but his feet remembered the way as if it were yesterday.
Monsieur LeMiel opened the door before he could knock, holding a
rolled-up painting in his hand.

"On time, for once," said Monsieur LeMiel. "Did you bring what I
asked?"

Jean-Luc nodded. Bread, a bit of cheese, some turnips, a bottle of artificial wine, and a jar of preserves—all supplied by Monsieur and Madame
Anton.

"What is this about, Monsieur?"

"Not now. You'll see," Monsieur LeMiel whispered. "Follow me."

He started off down the street with a light step. Jean-Luc followed, wiping
the sweat from his brow. It was midafternoon and uncomfortably warm.

"It's hot today, isn't it?" Jean-Luc said.

Monsieur LeMiel grunted.

"It's been over two months. Any word on—"

"No. We're hoping to make headway, but there's tension between us
Gaullists and the Communists."

"You don't think they'd begin anything—"

"Not here, boy!" Monsieur LeMiel hissed.

Jean-Luc knew he should not talk about such things in the open, but so much uncertainty hung in the air that he felt he would explode. If he tried not to think about the Allied army's intentions, thoughts of Natasha instantly pushed their way to the surface. He had been haunted by dreams of her being shaved and tattooed. There were times he could almost hear her crying out to him, begging him to save her.

"By the way," said Monsieur LeMiel, "thought you should know, someone took *The Sleep of Endymion*."

Jean-Luc nodded, torn between excitement that his replica had been accurate enough to be taken and sorrow that someone would steal what they thought was a priceless masterpiece.

"Here we are." Monsieur LeMiel stopped in front of a butcher shop, smoothed the few hairs that remained on his head, and walked inside.

A woman with gray-streaked hair was sitting on the counter, reading a worn book with the cover torn off.

"We have very few pieces of meat left today," she said without looking up. "Our prices are fair but—"The woman glanced up from her book. "Oh!" Her face broke out in a smile and she rushed over to kiss each of Monsieur LeMiel's cheeks. His balding head turned beet red.

"Hello," he said.

"Who is this?"

"Jean-Luc Beauchamp, Madame," Jean-Luc said, taking the woman's hand and kissing it. Monsieur LeMiel rolled his eyes.

The woman laughed. "Madame? Only in dreams, Monsieur. You can call me Babette." She cast Monsieur LeMiel a furtive look. Monsieur LeMiel suddenly seemed a little too interested in a fly buzzing about the room. Babette laughed and shook her head.

Monsieur LeMiel cleared his throat. "Shall we?"

Babette nodded and led the way into the back room and up a narrow staircase to what Jean-Luc could only assume was her apartment over the shop. A frail old man sat upright in an armchair facing the window, a tattered quilt draped over his lap. He glanced at the three of them as they entered the room. His eyes were glazed over, as if he had no idea who or where he was.

"We have visitors, Papa," Babette said.

The old man smiled a toothless grin and resumed looking out the window.

Jean-Luc and Monsieur LeMiel followed Babette to a small bedroom furnished with only a narrow bed and an old wardrobe. Babette closed the door behind them and pulled the shades down on the window. Monsieur LeMiel went over to the wardrobe and lifted one end up, swinging it outward to reveal the door to a crawl space.

"Is this your hiding place for the paintings?" Jean-Luc asked.

Monsieur LeMiel nodded. "Among other things." He opened the door to the crawl space and Babette peeked her head inside.

"Come on out, dears. It's all right."

She stood up again and took a step back. After a moment, the top of a girl's head appeared. The girl's hair was long and dark, and it looked as if it had once been thick but was now dirty, stringy, and matted with sweat. Her body shook as she crept out of the crawl space, clinging to a rag doll. She looked up and squinted in the light, but she smiled as wide as her mouth would allow.

She was terribly pale, as if she had not seen the sun in years. Her face was gaunt, and her arms and legs were thin and frail, but she did not look abused or starved. Once she was used to the light, she looked directly at Jean-Luc.

"I remember you," she whispered.

Recognition came slowly. She looked familiar, but Jean-Luc could not place her until he saw the man who followed her out of the crawl space. He, too, was thin, pale, covered in sweat, and staring at Jean-Luc. Behind his thick beard was a face Jean-Luc knew well.

"Claude? Claude Lévy?" Jean-Luc looked back at the little girl. "Marie?"

Claude's sister, Marie, eyed the package in Jean-Luc's arms. "Is that food? For us?" She looked over at Monsieur LeMiel. He nodded.

Jean-Luc handed her the bundle. Though it wasn't heavy, her thin arms struggled with the weight as she carried it over to her brother. Claude finally took his eyes off Jean-Luc as he and his sister devoured the cheese and half of the bread.

"Save some for later, dears. I have some soup for lunch, but you will be hungry come this evening," Babette said, gently touching Claude's shoulder.

Marie pouted but didn't complain. Babette helped Claude bundle up the remaining bread, the unopened wine, and the turnips, and placed it on top of the wardrobe. Marie began to dance around the room, stretching her legs and humming to herself. Claude stood up and stared at Jean-Luc again.

"I never expected to see you here," he said.

"Christophe said the same thing. He doesn't trust me."

Claude said nothing. He looked over at his sister, who was dancing around Monsieur LeMiel, asking if he had brought her books or puzzles.

Jean-Luc didn't know what to say. Only twenty-two, Claude had been a match for Jean-Luc in boxing just two years before. Now his arms were so thin Jean-Luc doubted Claude could have pushed aside the wardrobe on his own. Claude had been handsome, clean-shaven, and quick to laugh. Now his eyes held fear, and he looked drained of life.

"I brought another painting, Claude," Monsieur LeMiel said as Marie twirled around Babette.

Claude nodded and stared back at Jean-Luc.

"So . . . you've been here all this time?" Jean-Luc asked.

"Two years of sitting in the dark—freezing cold or sweltering heat—not knowing where my parents are, what's going on in the world, or if I'll live to see another day." He looked over at Marie again. "She's the optimistic one. Keeps me going. She was sick this spring. I don't know what I would have done if she had died."

"Do you always stay in the crawl space?"

"For the most part. In the dead of winter, we stay in this room, but we have to stay still, crouched low, because the neighbors ask questions if the shades are down during the day. We stayed a little longer this year because

Marie fell ill, but now it's back to the crawl space. If it gets too hot, Babette leaves the door open a crack and we sit near it to get air. Only on the hottest days can we go into the room. It's too dangerous. One of her neighbors has a German lover and wouldn't hesitate to give us up."

Jean-Luc looked over at Babette, who was urging Marie to calm down. Marie was singing a little louder, hugging the rag doll.

"How old is she now?" Jean-Luc asked.

"What month is it?"

"August."

"She's eleven by now."

"Does she know it?"

Claude shrugged. "She counted days for a long time, but I think she lost track when she was sick."

"Where are your parents?"

"Probably dead," Claude said. "I went to pick up Marie from a friend's house and came home just in time to see soldiers dragging my parents out of the house. I grabbed Marie and ran as fast as I could to Paul LeChoix's house. It was the closest place. Luckily, Sophie was home."

Jean-Luc wanted to give Claude good news, to tell him that the Allies were on their way and Paris would be free again very soon, but as firmly as he believed that, he could not risk getting Claude's hopes up.

"You're different, Jean-Luc."

"Am I?"

Claude nodded. "When I saw you last, you acted as if the Germans had never invaded and were no more than a temporary inconvenience. Your optimism would have been heartening if you weren't oblivious to the laws that did not pertain to you—that infuriated me."

"I'm sorry."

"What changed you?"

"Love."

Claude laughed. Marie's head snapped in his direction, and she gave Jean-Luc the widest smile she could possibly give.

"I shouldn't be surprised," Claude said. "But I am. Love found you at last, did it? Well, that's enough to set a man's head straight while twisting it about in a hundred directions at once. I wish you the best of luck."

Jean-Luc did not have the heart to tell Claude about Natasha. "Thank you."

"Tell me good news, Jean-Luc. Nothing about war, nothing about the Allies or the Germans. Something we would talk about in a café."

"Well, Christophe's wife is expecting a baby . . ."

For hours, Jean-Luc and Claude talked of happier things and remembered happier times. They had a laugh imagining Christophe as a father. They talked about art. Jean-Luc mentioned his job as Matisse's assistant. Claude asked how Jean-Luc had met Natasha, so Jean-Luc gave him an abridged version, doing his best to keep the lump in his throat down. Claude must have read something in his face, for he did not ask any more questions about Natasha. Marie eventually joined them, smiling the whole time.

By the time the sun set, Claude looked a great deal younger and happier.

"Jean-Luc, we have to get going," said Monsieur LeMiel.

Marie looked back at the crawl space door. Claude squeezed her shoulder in reassurance, then he embraced Jean-Luc as a brother.

"I know this may seem odd coming from me, since I'm so much younger, but I'm proud of you."

"Claude . . . I could forge you papers."

Claude shook his head. "They'd arrest me before they looked at my papers." He pointed to his nose. "I look Jewish."

"But—"

Claude held up his hand. "Please. Don't. It's hard enough to go back in there."

Jean-Luc nodded. "Till we meet again."

Marie, whom Jean-Luc had met only a few times before, hugged him around the middle and looked up at him with teary eyes. "Thank you, Jean-Luc."

"For what?"

"For bringing Claude back—making him laugh again. He hasn't since we got here. I missed him."

Jean-Luc ruffled her hair. "Hang in there, all right? And take care of him."

Marie nodded. "I will."

It was difficult to watch Claude and Marie return to the crawl space. Jean-Luc could not imagine how hot and cramped it must be in there. Though Babette left the door open a crack before Monsieur LeMiel moved the wardrobe back, Jean-Luc knew it had to be stuffy and difficult to breathe.

Jean-Luc had never given much thought to the Jews. He had known Claude for years and only discovered Claude was Jewish when the boys they boxed with started to call him "Claude the Jew." Jean-Luc had laughed along with them, but he had never hesitated to invite Claude to a café or to an art gallery. Claude was a gifted artist, a sculptor, and art was Jean-Luc's religion.

He thought about the laws Miró had talked about, the new restrictions on Jews. They had not affected him, so he had not cared.

I should have, he thought. He hoped more than ever that the Allies were on their way.

*   *   *

Jean-Luc couldn't sleep. Maybe it was the heat, maybe it was the thought of Marie and Claude Lévy, or maybe it was the feeling that something was wrong. He had tossed and turned, then painted for a while, then gone back to bed, only to doze and toss and turn some more.

He had no idea how late it was, but he imagined the sun would be up soon.

I need sleep, he thought. Something was about to happen, he could feel it. The anticipation only made it more difficult to fall asleep. He rolled over again and punched his pillow to fluff it up, but he still couldn't get comfortable.

He had just begun to doze when he woke with a start. The sun was up, though just barely, and from outside the open window, he could hear people gossiping in the street.

He threw on a pair of trousers just in time for Madame Cordier to come barging in, looking flustered but happy.

"Oh, good. You are already awake," she said.

"What's going on?"

"The métro and police have gone on strike." She began to pace, looking for something to straighten up, but the room was already fairly neat. "Rumor has it the postal workers are going to strike as well. I have to run, mon chou. I just wanted to make sure you knew. We're going to drive them out soon!"

Madame Cordier flitted out the door, leaving Jean-Luc with a hundred more questions that no one could answer. Would the strikes start enough trouble to draw the Allies to Paris? Would the Allies even make it in time? Or would the Resistance be crushed by the Germans before any sort of reinforcements could arrive? Was it worth the risk? Or was it already too late?

Though it had only been four years, it was difficult to imagine what each day would be like without the German presence plaguing the air. He couldn't wait to walk into a café and hear only French spoken.

But were the rumors Nicolas and Georges had discussed true? Were the people planning on shaving the heads of female collaborators and parading them naked through the streets? Would they do that to Natasha?

She deserves it, he told himself again.

He cursed himself for obsessing over it all. Why did he care so much?

Because I love her.

He could not let anything so humiliating happen to her—especially not at the hands of his own Resistance brothers. He had to warn her. But how? He couldn't approach her on the street or meet her at the opera house. She had rejected him and would not accept him as a visitor.

He would talk to Anya. No matter how angry or jealous she was, Anya loved Natasha like a sister and would never let any harm come to her. She would warn her for him.

Jean-Luc grabbed a shirt off his bed and pulled it over his head as he ran out the door to make the long trek across the city to the Maximovs' apartment. By the time he reached it, he figured, Natasha would be long gone, probably having lunch at a café with Lorenz. Hopefully, Anya would still be there.

*   *   *

The door was smashed in and hanging off the hinges when Jean-Luc arrived at the Maximovs' apartment. He took a tentative step inside, all of his muscles tensing up. There were markings on the walls that looked like fingernail scratches, and brownish stains were splattered on the walls and floor.

There was very little left that would be of use to anyone. In the kitchen, the remains of broken dishes were all over the floor, but the table and all of the chairs were missing. There were a few splinters of wood strewn about, suggesting that someone had smashed the furniture to burn in a window brazier.

The bedroom was no different. Bits of glass from the broken vanity mirror covered the floor. All blankets and clothes were gone. The only items remaining were a few broken picture frames and a tattered hat Natasha had been determined to fix.

Jean-Luc stared at the empty bedroom. "What happened here?" he whispered. No one answered him. He bent down and picked up the hat. Underneath was a set of yellow and red nested dolls. Painted on the bottom in Russian characters was Natasha's name, as she had shown him.

He opened the first doll, then the second, then the third. Inside the fourth was a thin, knotted gold chain with a tiny pendant on the end: a Star of David.

As Jean-Luc pulled the necklace out to examine it, everything clicked into place. Natasha's absolute terror of Germans, the way she avoided questions about her family, her submission to Lorenz. Did the brute know her secret? Was he holding it over her head?

What did it matter? If Natasha was with Lorenz, she was in constant danger. Jean-Luc had to get her away from him. He no longer cared about her insults to his art. Whether she had meant it or said it to push him away, it didn't matter. Only Natasha's safety mattered to him now.

He replaced the necklace, stacked the set of dolls, and ran back toward Montparnasse, clutching them in his fist. He needed help. His Resistance group might not trust him, but Madame Cordier did.

CHAPTER 30

MADAME CORDIER'S VOICE froze Jean-Luc in his tracks as he walked into the apartment building. She was upstairs, somewhere in the hallway, snapping at someone.

"There! His lease agreement. This is his room."

"Watch your tone, Madame."

Lorenz. Jean-Luc would recognize that voice anywhere. Tucking the nested dolls into his pocket, he marched up the stairs and followed the sound of Madame Cordier's voice to Miró's studio.

The door was wide open, and Madame Cordier and Lorenz were standing in the middle of the room, less than a meter apart, glaring at each other. Another soldier stood off to the side, arms crossed over his chest.

"Then where is Miró?" Lorenz asked.

"I have told you a hundred times over, I don't know where he is. I'm not his keeper. He paid this month's rent. He usually leaves at the end of next month, but perhaps he went back to Spain early," said Madame Cordier.

"He has no permission to travel."

Madame Cordier shrugged. "He doesn't need mine when his rent is paid. I haven't seen him for days."

"Where are his paintings?"

Madame Cordier gestured to something behind her that Jean-Luc couldn't see. "Right there."

Lorenz nodded to the other soldier, who grabbed Madame Cordier's wrist and twisted it upward. She cried out in pain.

"Don't toy with me. That rubbish is not Miró's work. Where are you hiding his paintings?"

"Let go of her!" Jean-Luc shouted.

Lorenz turned his head and a bemused smile crossed his face. "The talentless painter. So that's where these worthless things came from." He gave another nod, and the soldier dropped Madame Cordier's wrist. Lorenz took a few steps toward Jean-Luc.

"Where is your room?"

Jean-Luc looked past Lorenz to Madame Cordier, who was gingerly touching her wrist. The other soldier stood with his arms at his side, eyeing her. She didn't appear to be seriously hurt.

Lorenz followed Jean-Luc's gaze.

"You need permission from your landlady?"

Seething, Jean-Luc turned on his heel and led the way to his studio. Jean-Luc walked into the room first, followed by Lorenz, then Madame Cordier and the other soldier. Though the bed was unmade, the room was relatively neat and orderly. There were no clothes on the floor and his art supplies were arranged neatly on the table by the easel. Beside the art supplies was a small meal on Madame Cordier's silver tray. Jean-Luc looked back at her. She granted him a slight smile but frowned again when the other soldier looked at her.

Several of Jean-Luc's paintings were on the floor, leaning against the wall. Lorenz pushed past Jean-Luc and grabbed one of his more recent works.

Jean-Luc ground his teeth behind his closed lips and struggled not to clench his fists. He did not want to provoke Lorenz in front of Madame Cordier. He braced himself for Lorenz to destroy this painting the way he had shredded his *Mademoiselle*.

Instead, Lorenz grinned. He said something in German to the other soldier and handed him the painting. Pacing around the room, Lorenz pointed to several of Jean-Luc's works, and the other soldier gathered them up.

"No!" cried Madame Cordier. "Don't let them take your work, Jean-Luc."

Jean-Luc's heart dropped. *No, Madame. Don't get involved.* He shook his head. "Madame, don't! Let them have it."

The other soldier's eyes flashed. He moved toward Madame Cordier, but Lorenz held up his hand. He laughed.

"Has he been telling you it's his work?" He picked up another small painting and looked it over. "This is clearly a Miró—a new style. Stupid woman. A dead dog has more talent than this boy." He looked at Jean-Luc and shook his head, clucking his tongue. "A liar, too, are we?"

Without warning, Lorenz thrust his fist into Jean-Luc's stomach. Jean-Luc doubled over, winded and struggling to catch his breath.

"Filthy Boches! Stealing art! Stealing cities!" Madame Cordier screamed, tears streaming from her eyes. "Go back to where you came from! I hope the Allies send you back to Germany with your forked tails between your legs!"

Jean-Luc tried to stop her but could only wheeze a protest. "Madame! No!" He coughed again. Madame Cordier stood there, shaking and sobbing. "Monsieur," Jean-Luc said to Lorenz. "I apologize. They are Miró's paintings."

Lorenz laughed again. "Coward. Just as before. A true Frenchman. I'll let you live, I suppose." He said something in German to the other soldier, who led the way out the door. As Lorenz passed Madame Cordier, he gave her another sickening smile. "Thank you for your hospitality, Madame."

Then he pulled his revolver from his belt and fired it into Madame Cordier's chest.

"For your smart mouth," he said. Without another word, he and the other soldier left the apartment building.

Jean-Luc ran to Madame Cordier's side and caught her before she hit the floor. Blood was everywhere. He grabbed a clean shirt from the pile of folded clothes and tried to apply pressure to the wound, but the blood would not stop.

"Stay awake, Madame. Stay with me."

"Jean . . . Jean-Luc," she whispered.

"No, Madame. Save your strength," Jean-Luc said. He could not stop the bleeding. His vision was blurry with tears; all he saw was red.

"Look . . . at me . . . mon chou."

Jean-Luc wiped his eyes and looked at Madame Cordier. She was smiling.

"You're . . . a good man . . . Jean-Luc." She reached up with a blood-smeared hand and touched his cheek. "Children really do . . . grow up . . . too . . . fast."

Her head rolled back. Her eyes closed. Her hand fell to the floor.

Jean-Luc stared at her. Tears rolled down his face.

"Madame?" he said, giving her body a little shake. "Madame?" he said a little louder, shaking her harder.

Jean-Luc opened his mouth, but no sound would come. His face was hot, and he could still feel the touch of her hand on his cheek.

He cradled Madame Cordier in his arms and kissed her cheek. He screwed up his face. "Please come back . . . come back . . . Maman . . ."

But Madame Cordier was gone.

* * *

Jean-Luc was still clinging to Madame Cordier's body when he heard the door to the building open and shut. Someone was knocking on Madame Cordier's apartment door. "Paulette?" More knocking. "Paulette, are you in?"

Monsieur Anton.

Jean-Luc gave Madame Cordier's body one last kiss on the forehead and placed her on the floor. He looked down at his clothes. He was covered in Madame Cordier's blood. Anyone other than Monsieur Anton might have accused Jean-Luc of murdering Madame Cordier.

Looking down from the top of the staircase, he saw that Monsieur Anton was not alone. Madame Anton and Monsieur Philippe were with him.

"Monsieur Anton," he said as he made his way down the stairs. His knees shook, and he held onto the banister to keep himself steady.

The three of them looked up. Madame Anton gasped.

"My God! Jean-Luc, what happened to you?" she cried.

"You won't find her there," said Jean-Luc, nodding toward Madame Cordier's apartment door. "He—Lorenz—that son of a whore—"

His voice cracked and his vision blurred again. He clenched his fists and ground his teeth.

Madame Anton touched his wrist with two fingers.

"Is any of this blood yours?" she asked.

Jean-Luc shook his head.

"Let's get you cleaned up. I'll get some clean clothes from your studio."

"No. Don't go in there. She's—that's where—"

Celeste Anton patted his shoulder. "All right." She turned to her husband. "Should we call the police?"

Monsieur Anton shook his head. "They're on strike. And the soldiers will only accuse Jean-Luc. Monsieur Philippe and I will move the body."

"Before you do that, bring down a set of clothes for Jean-Luc. And a towel."

Monsieur Anton and Monsieur Philippe went upstairs while Madame Anton fished around in her handbag for something. She pulled out a small key and looked up at Jean-Luc with pity.

"I'm so sorry, Jean-Luc."

Jean-Luc said nothing. His hands were still in tight fists.

When Monsieur Anton returned with a change of clothes and a towel for Jean-Luc, he looked older and wearier than ever.

Madame Anton took the clothes from her husband and used the key in her hand to unlock Madame Cordier's door. Jean-Luc hesitated, then followed her inside.

Being in the apartment was more difficult than seeing the corpse. He almost expected Madame Cordier to pop out of the kitchen and tell him to eat something. Celeste Anton took a deep, shuddering breath and wiped her eyes.

"Well," she said, "here we are. I'm sorry it had to be here, but I can't have you walking around the streets like that."

Jean-Luc nodded, but his eyes were fixed on the photographs. There was one of Jean-Luc, leaning over Miró's shoulder the first week he had moved in. Madame Cordier stood in the background, regarding the pair with her usual fondness.

"Come on, Jean-Luc," said Madame Anton, gesturing toward the kitchen. She draped Jean-Luc's clothes over a chair and turned on the taps, checking the water temperature with her wrist. "There. That should be good. I'm afraid you don't have time for a bath. Just change your clothes and clean yourself up. Are you going to be all right?"

Jean-Luc nodded, staring at the running water. "It was Lorenz. I'm going to kill him. I'm going to kill that filthy Boche! He's probably loung-ing around in his suite at the Hotel Meurice while Madame . . ." His voice cracked. "Madame . . ."

"Calm down. Don't do anything just yet or you'll get yourself killed instead. Look at me." Celeste Anton touched Jean-Luc's chin and forced him to meet her eyes. She frowned and asked again, "Are you all right?"

Finally, Jean-Luc relaxed his fists. "Yes."

Celeste Anton sighed. "Well, you will be. Just stay away from the bottle. I'm going upstairs to help Pierre. Don't go anywhere until I come for you. You can't stay here."

"Thank you, Madame," said Jean-Luc.

"You're welcome."

Celeste Anton left Jean-Luc alone in the apartment. Jean-Luc washed the blood off his face and hands, then pulled off his stained shirt and pants. After grabbing the nested dolls from the pocket of his trousers, he threw the bloody clothes into the trash bin. Once he was dressed, he wiped the dolls off with the cleanest bit of towel he could find and stared at them.

Lorenz had murdered Madame Cordier without even knowing she was involved in the Resistance. What would he do to Natasha if he found out she was Jewish?

Jean-Luc had to find her.

Ignoring Madame Anton's order, he ran out of the building, toward the Seine and the Hotel Meurice. If he found Lorenz, he was sure to find Natasha.

*   *   *

Jean-Luc stood just out of sight, watching the entrance to the hotel. It was past midnight. Natasha and Lorenz had entered the building hours ago. He intended to follow them when they came out, wait for a moment when Natasha was alone, and then steal her away. He should have felt tired, but the hate poured through him, keeping him awake and focused.

"You can't do this, Jean-Luc."

Jean-Luc jumped. He had been concentrating so hard on his plan to rescue Natasha that he hadn't heard anyone approach. Madame Anton stood with her hands folded in front of her, her brow creased with worry. Mademoiselle Simone was at her side, looking equally concerned.

"Waiting to kill him will not bring her back, and it will only hurt our cause. You'll start an insurrection before we're ordered to do so," Mademoiselle Simone said.

"I'm not looking to kill—though I'd like to," said Jean-Luc. "I'm looking to save."

"Save?" Mademoiselle Simone put her hands on her hips and cocked her head to one side, ready to lecture.

"Natasha?" asked Madame Anton.

Jean-Luc nodded.

"She is probably sleeping. If you're going to save her, you will need your wits about you and your strength. Mademoiselle Simone's aunt has agreed to allow you to stay with them for a very low rent, plus your tobacco rations."

Jean-Luc shook his head. "I'm fine here."

"Come on, Jean-Luc," said Mademoiselle Simone, tugging on his arm. "You're weary, you're hungry. Madame Fra—that is, Madame Cordier would not have wanted this."

Jean-Luc looked down at Mademoiselle Simone. She did not look annoyed, inconvenienced, or angry. She only looked worried. And she did have a point.

"Natasha is probably sleeping," Madame Anton said again. "Come back in the morning."

Jean-Luc was about to protest, to claim he was not tired, when a yawn betrayed him. He agreed to get a few hours' sleep.

Madame Anton walked with Jean-Luc and Mademoiselle Simone until they were out of sight of the Hotel Meurice, then she left for Montparnasse. Jean-Luc walked with his hands stuffed in his pockets, constantly looking over his shoulder toward the hotel.

Several times throughout the long walk across the city, Mademoiselle Simone opened her mouth as if she were about to say something but then closed it again. When they reached the door to the brothel, she turned to face Jean-Luc and took a deep breath.

"I'm very sorry about Madame Cordier. We all loved her. She made us feel safe, despite what we were doing. And she always spoke fondly of you, even when she was trying not to sound as if she cared too much."

"Thank you."

"Hoo!" called a voice from the window. "Finally brought one back here?"

"Shut it, Cécile. He's a new tenant."

Jean-Luc looked up to see the same woman who had taunted him the last time once again hanging out of the window, wearing only a slip.

"Ignore her," Mademoiselle Simone said. "She's been drunk since the day she turned seventeen."

She opened the door and led Jean-Luc inside. The building was old and in desperate need of some repairs. The wallpaper was peeling away on one wall, and what looked as if it had once been an elaborate and expensive banister for the stairs had at least five posts missing—probably burned up in a brazier. Two young women on a broken couch were unbuttoning a man's shirt. Jean-Luc averted his eyes and stared at his feet instead.

Mademoiselle Simone grabbed his wrist and led him toward the steps. The prostitutes cheered her on, whistling and clapping.

"About time!"

"When you're done splitting her in two, dearie, you come to see me."

Mademoiselle Simone blushed from the roots of her hair but kept her eyes forward. "Skip the third step. It's broken."

Jean-Luc did as he was told and allowed Mademoiselle Simone to lead him upstairs to a tiny room with only one narrow bed and a sink.

"It's not much, but it's a place to sleep."

"Thank you."

"The taps don't work. You'll have to go down the hall. The bathroom is on your left."

Jean-Luc nodded. He stuffed his hands in his pockets and stared out the open window. Mademoiselle Simone sat down on the bed.

"Who is Natasha?" she asked. Her voice was kind—much kinder than he had ever heard from her.

"She is my love."

"And she's with a soldier?"

"Yes."

"Are you sure she wants to be rescued?"

Jean-Luc squared his shoulders. "I know what you're thinking. And she's not a collaborationist." He glared at Mademoiselle Simone.

"Collaborating or not, my question to you is, how can you be sure she doesn't have feelings for this man?"

"She doesn't."

"How can you be sure?"

"She doesn't."

"If you say so." Mademoiselle Simone stood up and walked toward the door. Just before she reached it, she paused.

"Marguerite," she said.

"What?"

"My name is Marguerite."

CHAPTER 31

WHEN MORNING LIGHT crept in through the open window of Jean-Luc's room, he was already wide awake. He jumped out of bed, pulled on his shoes, and made his way down the hall to the bathroom to relieve himself and splash water on his face. There was a few days' worth of stubble on his chin, but he didn't care. He barely acknowledged his reflection in the dirty mirror. Only one thing mattered.

For two days, Jean-Luc had spent every waking moment tailing Lorenz. At first, he hoped to find a moment when he could rush in and steal Natasha away, but Lorenz never left her alone. Everywhere Lorenz went, she went. If he could not be there, he would assign another soldier to guard her—sometimes two or three. Jean-Luc doubted that today would be any different, but he wanted to know where she was at all times, just in case Lorenz tried to hurt her.

No one bothered Jean-Luc on his way out or questioned him as to where he was going. Everyone else was asleep or stumbling off to bed, looking weary and angry at the world. Cécile was passed out on the broken couch, muttering in her sleep about needing real wine.

The streets were nearly empty. It was a few minutes before the end of curfew, but already there were some who wanted to get a jump start on waiting in the ration lines. Birds twittered and wooden-soled shoes clopped on the pavement. Jean-Luc beelined toward the heart of the city to watch the entrance of the Hotel Meurice for any sign of Natasha.

Jean-Luc arrived at his usual vantage point near the entrance to the métro just in time to see Lorenz storming from the hotel, Natasha at his heels. Every time she fell more than two steps behind, he'd pause, put an arm around her waist, and push her up to speed. She looked pale, uncomfortable, and terrified.

She did not look beaten or bruised. She did not flinch at Lorenz's touch, but she tensed when he reached for her. It took every ounce of restraint for Jean-Luc not to run up to Lorenz, punch him in the jaw, and pull Natasha away from him.

Lorenz grabbed Natasha's wrist and pulled her around the corner. Jean-Luc didn't follow. He knew where they were going. Every morning at eight, they ate breakfast at the same café. Jean-Luc had almost been caught the previous morning.

"So that's Natasha?"

Jean-Luc jumped at the sound of Mademoiselle Simone's voice.

Mademoiselle Simone frowned. "You should pay attention to your surroundings, Jean-Luc. Even when you're looking for something else."

"How did you know where I was?"

"I heard you get up this morning. Decided to follow you. You're right. She's miserable with him. So what are you going to do once you rescue her?"

"Kill Lorenz and take her away with me."

"What? Leave France while the Allies push through? Where are you going to go? Germany?"

"I'll figure something out."

"And the Resistance will help you . . . as long as you don't forget to help us. Stay in Paris. We can hide her. There's too much tension. Something's going to—"

As if on cue, someone came tearing through the streets, shouting something about the prefecture of police and the Resistance. Mademoiselle Simone—Jean-Luc was still not used to thinking of her as "Marguerite"— snapped her head to attention and scowled.

"They didn't!"

She took off running toward the prefecture of police, Jean-Luc at her heels. Sure enough, the swastika flag was no longer flying atop the building. In its place was the tricolor flag of France.

Jean-Luc felt immense pride and real fear. If the Allies weren't coming, this was too soon. The Resistance could never stand against the Germans alone. He turned to Mademoiselle Simone.

"Do you know something I don't? Are the Allies coming?"

"I know no more than you do. But maybe Monsieur Philippe does."

Jean-Luc shook his head. "It doesn't matter. The Germans will try to take the building back, and the fighting won't stop there."

"What do we do? We have only four guns. Maybe some other group can—"

"Do you have pickaxes?"

"What?"

"Pickaxes. This is Paris. We have to build the barricades."

*   *   *

Shirt matted with sweat, Jean-Luc worked his muscles sore, men and boys at his side, digging up the streets and piling debris to block off rue Rivoli. Monsieur Raoul, people from other groups, and ordinary disgruntled citizens with no Resistance ties worked alongside him, while Monsieur LeMiel, Monsieur Louis, Monsieur Philippe, and several other members of other groups were armed and keeping a lookout. Little Henri, who turned out to be Monsieur Philippe's son, ran out of a nearby bakery, carrying a glass of water to his father. Monsieur Philippe took the water and pointed over to Jean-Luc.

"See where they're digging up the street? Take whatever you can carry over to the wall."

Eager to please, Henri puffed up his chest. "Yes, Papa."

Monsieur Philippe ruffled his son's hair and then returned to standing watch, his rifle at the ready.

Henri rushed over to Jean-Luc, reached for the biggest rock he could see, lifted it a few centimeters off the ground, then abandoned it for a smaller, lighter piece of the road. He ran over to the barricade and dropped it near an old bed frame, then hurried back over to grab more.

Jean-Luc stood up straight to stretch out his back. He was worried about Natasha. He longed to break away from his group and run toward the Hotel Meurice. Lorenz had to be busy. He couldn't have brought her with him to battle the prefecture of police. Was Jean-Luc missing his only opportunity to free her?

He drove the pickaxe into the cobblestone road and pried yet another stone loose. He was needed here. Only a score or so men and a handful of boys were working to build the barricade. Lorenz had not let harm come to Natasha thus far. For the time being, she was at least somewhat safe.

Jean-Luc caught the glint of metal in the window of a building across the road and squinted in the afternoon sun to see what was up there.

"Get down!" he shouted, grabbing little Henri and covering his body with his own. Bullets ricocheted off the road near Jean-Luc's head. Henri screamed. Monsieur Philippe and the other armed men opened fire on the building.

There were shouts in French and German, cries of pain, and tears of terror from the younger boys. More gunshots came from the other side of the incomplete barricade wall. Monsieur Louis slumped to the ground. Monsieur Raoul rushed to grab the gun and take his place.

Jean-Luc pushed himself off the ground and ran, carrying Henri in his arms, shielding him as best he could from the fire. Hot pain sliced into Jean-Luc as a bullet grazed his leg. He grunted and hobbled forward, shoving Henri through the door of the bakery, then running back to join the men.

He saw the scene as if he were not a part of it. Monsieur Philippe and the other armed men fired at the Germans in the street and at windows, trying to find which one housed the sniper. They kept close to the low, unfinished barricade, calling out to each other. One man from another Resistance group fell. Jean-Luc staggered forward to catch him, but he was already dead.

"It's the second floor, third from the left!" Jean-Luc barely recognized his own voice. It sounded so far away, yet so clear. He felt remarkably calm.

Grabbing the fallen man's rifle, Jean-Luc joined the skirmish, catching several Germans' aim just before they fired and pushing his comrades out of the way just in time. Jean-Luc's aim was poor, but he provided cover as the Parisian men moved about, peeking from behind the barricade, running for more ammunition from the bakery, and tending the wounded.

In what seemed both an eternity and only seconds, the firing ceased. A cheer broke out among the men of the Resistance. Monsieur Philippe gave a cry of victory and began to sing "La Marseillaise" as loudly as he could. The other men chimed in and were joined by the boys emerging from the bakery.

Jean-Luc looked around him. Nine total had fallen, including some ordinary citizens and two of the young boys. Nine sons of nine mothers. He limped around the area, double- and triple-checking that they were, indeed, dead and not simply wounded.

"Jean-Luc," Monsieur Philippe said. "Go into the bakery. My wife is inside. Let her bind up your leg."

Jean-Luc looked at the dark stain on his trousers and suddenly felt the pain of the grazed bullet. He nodded and began to walk away when Monsieur Philippe touched his shoulder.

"Thank you, Jean-Luc . . . for saving my son's life."

Jean-Luc nodded again and went into the bakery. Monsieur Philippe's wife was waiting inside. She was chalk white, but her jaw was set in a way that told Jean-Luc not to question her constitution.

"My husband?" she asked.

"Alive and unharmed, Madame."

Some color returned to her cheeks. She grabbed a clean towel and handed it to Jean-Luc, telling him to apply pressure to the wound while she boiled water to clean it.

Jean-Luc grunted when Monsieur Philippe's wife placed the boiling hot rag against the open wound. Fresh blood trickled down his leg. She bound up his wound with a clean strip of cloth, tying it tight.

"There. You should be fine, but you look pale," she said. "Rest up. I have three sons to feed, so I can't give you any food, but I can give you a place to sleep for a few hours."

"No thank you, Madame."

Monsieur Philippe's wife put her hands on her hips. "Monsieur, I was a nurse at fifteen in the Great War, and I am a mother of three boys. I have my ways of getting you to do what's good for you. I will box your ears if I have to."

Jean-Luc had to laugh. There she was, a gaunt woman with a scowl on her face, reminding him so much of Madame Cordier that he could have cried.

"I am needed, Madame."

Jean-Luc stood up, thanked Monsieur Philippe's wife again, ruffled little Henri's hair, and then limped back to the barricade.

"I'm surprised she didn't order you to bed rest," said Monsieur Philippe as he and Monsieur Raoul looked over their ammunition.

"She tried to."

"You *should* get some rest. You look awful."

"I can't. I have a responsibility here." Jean-Luc picked up his pickaxe and continued to dig up the street.

As Monsieur Philippe went inside to reassure his wife, Monsieur Raoul approached Jean-Luc and said, "Marguerite tells me you are looking to rescue a lover."

"Yes."

"Why are you still here?"

"I will find her when I can. For now, I can do nothing for her. There is plenty I can do here."

Monsieur Raoul picked up his own axe and resumed work. After a few minutes, he paused.

"I was wrong about you, Jean-Luc. I hope you can forgive me."

Jean-Luc looked Monsieur Raoul in the eye. "Of course. But the Germans will not stay away for long. We can't use that much ammunition every time, so we need better defenses. We have to finish the barricade."

CHAPTER 32

JEAN-LUC WORKED JUST AS HARD as before, focusing all of his thoughts on Natasha and pouring all of his frustrations into his task. He worked until his muscles ached, pausing only for water and for Monsieur Philippe's wife to redress his wound. Once again, he refused to take a nap.

As the barricade's construction progressed, Jean-Luc's priorities shifted. He wondered where Natasha was and how he could find her. He considered the possibility that Lorenz might be battling the prefecture of police and that he was now missing his opportunity to save Natasha.

There was a shout. Jean-Luc tensed, ready to grab the rifle he had left at the barricade wall, but another shout identified the newcomer: Christophe.

He, too, had been wounded in a skirmish. Dried blood was caked around a scrap of cloth tied around his arm. Whoever had dressed his wound did not have the skill of Monsieur Philippe's wife.

Monsieur Raoul and Jean-Luc rushed to meet him.

"Ammunition," Christophe panted. "We need it. Further down rue Rivoli."

"Can we spare any?" Jean-Luc asked Monsieur Raoul.

Monsieur Raoul shook his head. "I doubt it. I don't think we would last another two attacks on what we have."

Christophe's expression didn't falter, but his shoulders slumped a little. Jean-Luc touched his friend's shoulder. "Come on. Let's get you inside. Your wound needs redressing."

Christophe shook his head. "I don't have time."

"If you don't get your wound looked at, you won't be much use to anyone." Jean-Luc said. He guided Christophe into the bakery. "Monsieur Raoul, could you please check with Monsieur Philippe about the ammunition?"

Monsieur Raoul nodded as if Jean-Luc's order had come from a commanding officer. Christophe chuckled. "I take it you've proven us wrong?"

"Something like that."

"I owe you an apology."

Jean-Luc shook his head. "You don't owe me anything." He pushed open the door to the bakery. Monsieur Philippe's wife pounced on Christophe's arm the instant he walked in, clucking her tongue at the slipshod dressing.

"You could get an infection from this," she said. "Sit down."

Jean-Luc left to find Monsieur Philippe and Monsieur Raoul. They were in a deep discussion with members of the French Forces of the Interior. As Monsieur Raoul suspected, they could not spare any ammunition.

"He comes from another barricade," Jean-Luc said. "Can you think of a place where he can get what he needs?"

"We have some supplies," said a man with an FFI armband. "Houses are all over the city. If he goes to one wearing an armband, they'll give him what he needs."

"We could use more ammunition here, too," said Monsieur Philippe.

"I'll go," said Jean-Luc.

"No," said Monsieur Philippe. "We need you here."

"You have enough men here to fortify the barricade. One less won't matter."

Monsieur Philippe stared at him for a long moment, then nodded. Jean-Luc's heart raced as the FFI man revealed the location of several houses that stored ammunition and homemade explosives.

"Here." The FFI man tied a Cross of Lorraine armband around Jean-Luc's bicep. "Wear it with pride."

Jean-Luc nodded. He would fulfill his duties to the Resistance, but seeking Lorenz and Natasha all the while.

I will not sleep until she is safe.

* * *

Gunshots rang out yet again. Civilians ducked down behind debris or their own bicycles to take cover from the snipers in the windows. Jean-Luc stood flat against the side of a building, cradling a grocery bag of ammunition. A young woman threw herself against the building beside Jean-Luc, panting. Jean-Luc positioned his body to give her more cover.

"I might've known you'd do something like that," she said.

Jean-Luc looked at the young woman's face and blinked. It was Mademoiselle Simone, carrying a grocery bag of her own, undoubtedly filled with ammunition and highly explosive Molotov cocktails.

"Where are you going?" he asked.

"The Hôtel de Ville. The Resistance has taken the building. The Germans won't let them keep it for long. You?"

"Rue Sainte-Antoine."

"André is there."

"Who?"

"Monsieur Raoul. I saw him yesterday, and he said he was going to help with the barricade there." She peeked around Jean-Luc to look at the skirmish they had hidden from. "You're not going to get through that. Come with me—past the Place de Grève."

There was a pause in the gunfire. Jean-Luc hesitated.

Mademoiselle Simone snapped her fingers in front of his face. "Are you awake? When was the last time you slept?"

Jean-Luc thought about the question for a moment. He couldn't remember.

"I'm fine. Let's go."

Jean-Luc had barely noticed the chaos of the last few days. His feet carried him toward a barricade to distribute what he could, but his heart, his mind, and his eyes were searching for Natasha.

He usually took the routes that brought him closer to German soldiers. He pretended to be just another commuter going to work or getting rations. Although the streets were empty throughout most of the day and the supply of food was growing even more scarce, the lines were still long every morning. Instead of bread, Jean-Luc's rations were bullets and bottles of Molotov cocktails, packed with rags squashed between the bottles to prevent them from moving around. Aside from light dozing while standing, waiting for ammunition to be packed up, he hadn't slept.

"Do you really need the cocktails?" Mademoiselle Simone asked. "The barricades aren't nearly as important as the city hall."

Jean-Luc shook his head. "They need it at the barricade."

She nodded. "I hope I can make it in time. I wouldn't be surprised if they lost the city hall before I even got there."

"You don't sound optimistic. The prefecture of police still holds."

Mademoiselle Simone looked at Jean-Luc. For the first time since he met her, she looked weary and frightened. "It's mostly people my age, but with more to lose."

Jean-Luc felt torn. Teenagers. And it was likely that very few of them had the experience and skill of Mademoiselle Simone. They would need all the ammunition they could get, but the ammunition he carried was not his to distribute. He had been instructed to take everything to the barricade at rue Sainte-Antoine. It was still under construction and needed every bullet. The barricades were essential. They provided a maze for the German tanks to navigate through, slowing them down and blocking their paths.

As they neared the Place de Grève, they heard a low rumble and a shout from across the square. Jean-Luc's heart leapt to his throat.

Tanks rolled into the square and opened fire on the building. With every shot, a deep vibration resounded in Jean-Luc's chest. The Hôtel de Ville could not withstand a tank attack. Shots were fired from the windows at the soldiers walking behind the tanks.

Mademoiselle Simone pulled a bottle from her grocery bag, then shoved the bag into Jean-Luc's arms. "Take it all to the barricade," she said. "Block the tanks!"

She charged into the crossfire, right toward the lead tank. She smashed the bottle against the turret, then ran back across the square, where Jean-Luc waited with her bag of ammunition.

Halfway across the square, she slumped to the ground.

"No!" Jean-Luc cried. He started to run to her, but the fighting only intensified as the tank she had assaulted burst into flames. Seconds later, it exploded. The other tanks turned and rolled out of the square, leaving a few soldiers firing on the building as they retreated.

Jean-Luc stared at Mademoiselle Simone's body in the middle of the square, watching, praying for any sign of movement. She was still. The bags of ammunition felt heavy in his arms.

Marguerite's body, he corrected himself.

Fighting the urge to run to her, Jean-Luc forced his eyes away. He continued past the Place de Grève and toward the barricade at rue Sainte-Antoine. He could do nothing for Marguerite, but he could make sure that as few Parisians as possible shared her fate.

* * *

His comrades had made decent progress on the barricade's construction. Bed frames, signs, and the dug-up remains of the road were piled up almost to a man's full height. Jean-Luc whistled to let them know he was approaching. A man's head appeared over the top and shouted out to the rest of the men there.

"It's Jean-Luc! He's brought ammunition!"

The voice belonged to Monsieur Raoul. He ran out to greet Jean-Luc, with two teenage boys at his heels. The boys relieved Jean-Luc of his grocery bags and ran back behind the barricade. Monsieur Raoul slapped him on the back.

"You made it! It took you longer than usual. I wondered if you—what's wrong?"

Jean-Luc regarded Monsieur Raoul with a heavy heart. "André, I'm sorry."

Monsieur Raoul let out an uncomfortable laugh. "Marguerite told you my name, did she? Don't be sorry that—that you were late." He was pale and beginning to shake.

"I'm sorry, André. She's dead. She saved the Hôtel de Ville by blowing up a tank, then a bullet cut her down."

Monsieur Raoul stared into Jean-Luc's eyes.

"I'm so sorry," Jean-Luc whispered.

Monsieur Raoul gave a strangled cry and collapsed where he stood, pounding the dug-up street, moaning unintelligible things into the ground. Jean-Luc bent and urged him to stand up.

"No, no, no, no . . ." Monsieur Raoul croaked, gripping his hair.

Jean-Luc squeezed Monsieur Raoul's shoulder. "Come on. We'll get behind the barricade and find a place for you to rest." He hoisted Monsieur Raoul up and led the way back to the barricade.

He pictured Marguerite's death over and over in his mind. Each time, she changed until she no longer looked like Marguerite, but Natasha. *Where is she? Is she still alive? Has Lorenz discovered her secret?*

Jean-Luc brought Monsieur Raoul over to a shaded corner and allowed him to sit down. "Someone get this man water," he ordered. "And something to eat."

"Was he wounded?" one of the teenage boys asked.

Jean-Luc shook his head. "Just look after him. Don't leave him alone." He pulled the pistol that Monsieur Philippe had given him from his trousers and reloaded it from the handful of bullets in his pocket.

"If you can give me any information on the whereabouts of an Oberst and his lover—a beautiful woman, thin, fair, a Russian dancer—I would appreciate it," Jean-Luc said to the teenager.

The boy shook his head. He pointed over to a man standing beside the barricade. "Maybe—"

"Thank you." Jean-Luc could wait no longer.

Natasha, Natasha, Natasha . . .

He ran back toward the heart of the city, keeping close to buildings for cover. When he had to cross a boulevard, he'd dash out into the open, fire a few shots at nothing and no one in particular for cover, then run to the other side of the road. He asked anyone he met along the way if they had seen Lorenz and Natasha. A few remembered seeing the pair around the city before the insurrection, but no one had seen them for days.

He had no idea where his feet were carrying him. He tore through the city on instinct. Unless a barricade was fighting Germans, he stayed at each one just long enough to take a drink of water and ask whether anyone knew anything about Natasha.

For days he wandered around the heart of the city, circling the area surrounding the Hotel Meurice. At night he would keep watch, unable to sleep, despite the urgings of his Resistance comrades.

"You have to sleep, Jean-Luc," said Michel, a member of the FFI who worked in the café Lorenz and Natasha had frequented. They were at one of the barricades on rue Rivoli.

"I have to find her," Jean-Luc said. He took a long drink of water. The early morning was hazy but warm. The afternoon was going to be uncomfortably hot. He was so tired he felt drunk, but he could not rest any more than absolutely necessary until he found her.

Michel said, "I have some news for you."

Jean-Luc's head snapped up. Michel looked at him and frowned. "Before I tell you, I want you to get some sleep."

Jean-Luc threw the cup to the ground and grabbed Michel by his collar. "Where is she?"

"Look at yourself, Jean-Luc! You can't help anybody like—"

"Where is she?" Jean-Luc shouted, lifting Michel up to his toes and shaking him.

"My daughter saw a car pull up to the Hotel Majestic yesterday afternoon. She said a German soldier dragged a woman who fits Natasha's description inside."

"Thank you, Michel!" Jean-Luc lowered Michel to the ground and embraced him quickly. Without another word, Jean-Luc was off again, the buildings streaming past him in a blur.

Natasha. Natasha. Natasha . . .

The word thundered in his ears with every step, drowning out gunshots, the rumble of jeeps, the clatter of tanks, and the shouts of joy and relief.

"The Allies! The Allies have arrived!"

CHAPTER 33

THE HOTEL MAJESTIC was a death trap. American and British troops had already joined the fight, taking over command and trying to order the Resistance away from the crossfire.

Jean-Luc pulled out his pistol, taking cover in an alley between two apartment buildings across the street. He waited for a bit, then started to run out into the open, but someone grabbed his shirt and pulled him back. An Allied soldier said something in English. Jean-Luc shook his head and shrugged his shoulders. The soldier pointed to the hotel and mimed firing his rifle, then jerked his head behind him to indicate that Jean-Luc should stay back. Jean-Luc looked up at the hotel. Stone was chipped from the side of the building, and windows all over were shattered. Germans were firing from windows; a few of the dead were draped over the railing of the second-floor balcony. Jean-Luc gripped his revolver. Natasha was in there.

As soon as the Allied soldier let go of his shirt, Jean-Luc dashed into the open. The soldier shouted something; Jean-Luc ignored it. He felt detached from his body, as if he were watching himself in a film, silently giving himself commands on where to move, when to run, and when to stop. His head was clear, his senses alert.

Dust rose from the road whenever bullets ricocheted off the street. Jean-Luc had to sidestep and leap over several bodies of fallen soldiers. More than once, he heard a high-pitched hiss close to his ear.

Across rue Dumont d'Urville, he hurled himself into the doorway of an adjacent building, running smack into another group of Allied soldiers. One of them pulled him against the wall.

"You crazy bastard!" He had a heavy American accent, but his French was flawless. "Running out into the open like that. You want to get killed?"

Jean-Luc said nothing. The soldier pulled a grenade out and tossed it through a shattered window. Jean-Luc watched in a panic as fire burst through the window, licking up toward the sky. What if Natasha had been in that room?

The American soldier pulled the pin out of another one. Jean-Luc snatched it from his grasp and tossed it through one of the lower-level windows—a place he was sure Lorenz would never put Natasha.

The grenade detonated and the American soldier said something in English. Jean-Luc tore past him and leaped through the same window in which he had tossed the grenade. Flames from burning draperies singed his hair and burned his arms, but he didn't care.

The room had been an office. The carpet, the furniture, and the bodies of the German soldiers that had been in the room were on fire, but there was a clear path to an open door and the hallway beyond. Jean-Luc checked the ammunition in his pistol. Only five shots left. Then he'd have to rely on his boot knife.

I will have to make sure I don't miss, he thought.

He peeked out the door and slipped into the empty hallway.

*   *   *

A blast from somewhere close by rattled the lamps in the room. Natasha screamed and covered her ears. Tears poured down her cheeks as she crouched behind the couch, away from the windows, rocking back and forth.

"Stop it, stop it, please stop it," she sobbed.

When Lorenz had been called to the Hotel Majestic to help defend it, he had dragged her along with him, shoved her in this room, and disappeared, leaving her alone for the first time in weeks. The door was unlocked, but it didn't matter. They both knew that if she left the room she would be shot, one way or another.

The first three days, Lorenz had returned to the room each night long enough to give her meager portions of food, have his way with her, and sleep for a few hours. The past two days he had failed to bring food, but he never missed an opportunity to bed her.

As terrified as she now was, she was thankful for the insurrection. It had made Lorenz so busy that he hadn't noticed that her abdomen was firm and beginning to swell.

Machine guns went off and the window shattered. Natasha screamed again, cowering lower to the floor and closer to the couch, shielding her belly as best she could. Her stomach gurgled and she belched up a foul taste.

I know. I'm frightened, too. Hush now, Jean-Luc . . .

She often had silent conversations with her baby. They kept her going. In her heart, she knew it was a boy, and she had named him Jean-Luc. She would never know if it was really a boy or not. Lorenz would never allow her to come full-term.

It's better that you don't come into this world, Natasha thought as she sobbed into the upholstery.

Footsteps thundered out in the hall, then faded. Natasha stayed as low to the floor as she could.

I'm sorry, Jean-Luc.

*   *   *

His mind racing, Jean-Luc climbed the stairs two, sometimes three, at a time. Would Lorenz keep her near him? Or would he keep her safe? Jean-Luc wanted to believe he'd keep her safe, but he had seen what the man was capable of. How much did Lorenz know about Natasha?

The door to the hallway of each level yanked at his heart. Was she there? Which floor was she on, which room was she in? The vague plan in his head was to start at the top and work his way down. Somehow, that didn't feel quite right, but he didn't know what else to do.

As he flew past the door of the next floor, it creaked open and the voices in the hallway became clear. Jean-Luc turned to climb the next few steps and waited there, concentrating on keeping his breath quiet and his feet absolutely still. He peeked around the steps to see Lorenz standing in the doorway.

Jean-Luc's pulse quickened. He had a clear shot at Lorenz's head. Slowly, he took aim, ready to have revenge for Natasha, Paul, and Madame Cordier.

He hesitated. *Shoot him*, he told himself.

"Lorenz!" someone said from within the hallway. Lorenz turned back to the door, scowling.

Even though Lorenz's head was now partially covered by the door, Jean-Luc could kill him. His aim was not the best, but Lorenz was in such close range that it was doubtful even an amateur shooter like Jean-Luc would miss.

Still, Jean-Luc hesitated, letting every swear word he had ever known stream through his mind. Whoever Lorenz was talking to would, in turn, open fire on Jean-Luc and probably kill him, leaving no one to save Natasha. Too many risks were involved.

The man Lorenz was speaking to stepped into the stairwell and began screaming in German, gesturing back toward the hallway. He lightly slapped Lorenz's cheek and went down the stairs. Lorenz followed.

Jean-Luc crept back down the steps and watched Lorenz and the other soldier, voices in his head battling for control. The voices sounded eerily like Madame Cordier.

Two shots. Kill them.

But what if you miss? You have to save her.

You won't miss. They're close.

Find her! You're here for rescue, not for revenge!

Jean-Luc caught the door before it could latch shut. He peered though the crack, checking the hallway. It was empty. As he stepped out of the stairwell, the entire building shook from a tank shell. Somewhere down the hall, a woman screamed.

Jean-Luc ran, following the sound. He stopped at the end of the hall and looked around. Two doors faced him, one on either side of him; the scream could have come from either. If he chose the wrong one and found soldiers, he would be killed on the spot, but he couldn't stay in the open hallway.

Gathering his courage, Jean-Luc tested one of the doors. It was unlocked. Gun at the ready, he entered the room.

The window was shattered and glass was everywhere. A lone sniper lay on the floor in a pool of blood beside the window. There were more gunshots. Jean-Luc threw himself to the floor and heard the woman screaming again. She was in the room next door.

Jean-Luc couldn't be sure it was Natasha, but he had to find out. As soon as the fire quieted, he pushed himself up and followed the screaming. He threw the door open and felt as if his heart would burst.

Natasha was curled into a fetal position, her face buried in the side of a couch. She shook from head to toe, sobbing.

"Natasha."

Jean-Luc barely croaked the word. He hurried to her side and touched her shoulder. Her head snapped around. She looked terrified. Then, as recognition sank in, she stared at him in disbelief.

"Jean-Luc?" Her eyes filled with tears. "Oh, Jean-Luc!" She threw her arms around his neck and sobbed into his shoulder.

Jean-Luc pulled back. He dropped his gun, cupped her face, and kissed her. The feel of her lips, the taste of her mouth, and the way she fit into his arms brought forth a surge of energy. He broke away.

"Are you all right? Can you walk?"

"Yes. Am I dreaming?"

"No."

"Am I dead?"

"No," Jean-Luc said. As he helped Natasha stand, her blouse lifted, exposing her abdomen.

"Natasha, are you . . . are you going to have a baby?"

Fear flooded her face. Jean-Luc had not seen her look at him like that since they first met. She nodded.

A thousand emotions and questions crashed over Jean-Luc all at once, but they were all drowned out by the more powerful happiness. Whether the child was his or not, he would raise it with Natasha. He was going to be a Papa!

Jean-Luc lifted Natasha up in the air and spun her around. When he set her down again, he kissed her. "Our baby is so lucky," he said. "Born into a free Paris."

Natasha buried her face in his chest. "I wanted you to come. I hoped and wished and I . . . I . . . oh, Jean-Luc, I'm so sorry. I didn't—"

"Shh . . ." Jean-Luc kissed her forehead and pulled her to him. "I know. It's all right. I came to get you out of here. You're going to be my wife."

"I love you," she said.

He kissed her again, deeply. In that one moment, Jean-Luc knew that everything would be right in the world. The war would end. The Allies would prevail. Paris would be free again. And he and Natasha—and their baby—would be together, always.

A gun fired. Natasha's head jerked back. Something warm and wet splattered on Jean-Luc's face as Natasha fell limp in Jean-Luc's arms.

Jean-Luc opened his eyes. Natasha's head lay to one side, blood pouring out of the bullet hole in her right temple. Jean-Luc tried to cry out, but no sound escaped. He looked up at the doorway and saw Lorenz standing there, his pistol still raised. Lorenz's eyes were wide and his face was pale. He stared at Natasha's body and made no move to shoot Jean-Luc.

Jean-Luc stared at him. His own gun lay at his feet.

Lorenz shook his head and the color returned to his face.

"Dreckige Jude."

He looked at Jean-Luc and grinned, moving his gun a little to his right to take aim. More gunshots sounded, and Lorenz's body convulsed. He fell before he could squeeze the trigger.

Allied soldiers charged into the room, their weapons at the ready, shouting at Jean-Luc in English. Jean-Luc did not flinch. He held tight to Natasha's body, looking at the strange faces around him. He recognized the French-speaking soldier from whom he had snatched the grenade. He said nothing.

The French-speaking American said something in English to the other soldiers, then approached Jean-Luc.

"She's dead, friend. Let her go."

Jean-Luc eased Natasha's body to the floor, still unable to speak. He wiped his brow and looked at his hand. It was covered in blood—her blood. He gave a strangled cry and crouched over her body, tears falling down his cheeks and onto hers.

"Come on. This place isn't safe yet." The French-speaking American tugged at his arm. Jean-Luc jerked his arm away. The American spoke to the others in English. It took three soldiers to pull Jean-Luc to his feet and away from Natasha.

His ears began to ring, muffling out every voice, except those in his head.

Only you can decide what is important to you . . .
Love is the most important thing of all . . .
You're brilliant, Jean-Luc. Everyone will love your work . . .
I hope my performance has enabled them to overlook the
      horrendous scenery . . .
He's too soft for what we do . . .
It wouldn't surprise me if you gave in to blackmail . . .
You want to be a good painter? Cut out your tongue!
Love must be fought for . . .
You're a good man, Jean-Luc . . .
I love you . . .

Jean-Luc let out a long wail and drew the knife from his boot. A few of the soldiers around him pointed their guns at him and started asking him questions, but he couldn't even understand the one who spoke French. The room waved and swayed around Jean-Luc, and he staggered to keep his balance, though it seemed the more he struggled to stand, the more the room spun around him.

Natasha was dead. He had told her she would be his wife. He had promised her. And now she was dead.

"Monsieur, please. Sit down." The voice of the French-speaking soldier finally reached him. Jean-Luc looked around at the soldiers and, for the first time, realized that he was still alive.

Everything he had wanted no longer seemed possible. She was his love, his life, everything in the world that had truly mattered to him—above painting, above art, above any cause or way of life. How could he ever face another day? How could he laugh again? Paint again? She had wanted him to be a good painter.

Matisse's words echoed in his brain.

You want to be a good painter? Cut out your tongue!

Jean-Luc stared at Natasha's body. For her. He would do this for her—his last words would be to her.

Tears spilling from his eyes, Jean-Luc kissed the knife, pointed it toward Natasha, and then, in one swift motion, sliced off his own tongue.

The soldiers around him jumped and shouted, but Jean-Luc heard nothing. He felt the blood draining from his mouth. He struggled to stay on his feet, but the room spun out of control as darkness closed in. He took two steps toward Natasha's body and the darkness fell upon him completely. He fell beside her, his arm sprawled across her waist.

CHAPTER 34

CHEERS ERUPTED ACROSS the city. "La Marseillaise" resounded from every window and echoed off every lamppost, every barricade, every building.

Jean-Luc could see Charles de Gaulle standing in front of thousands of Parisians, welcomed home as a hero. As de Gaulle greeted the crowd, there was an odd sound, like a radio being turned on. Men spoke all at once, but their voices were not part of the roar of the crowd. They were closer.

Static. Groans. More words. Someone, somewhere, was tuning a radio.

"Here it is! Shh!"

De Gaulle spoke. His voice was fuzzy.

"These are minutes which go beyond our poor lives. Paris! An outraged Paris! A broken Paris! A martyred Paris! But . . . a liberated Paris! Liberated by itself, liberated by its people with the help of the armies of France, with the support and the help of all of France, of the fighting France, of the only France, the real France, the eternal France!"

The crowd cheered. Someone gave a loud shrill whistle.

*   *   *

Jean-Luc awoke.

He opened his eyes and immediately slammed them shut again. His entire face felt swollen, and his jaw throbbed with pain. His mouth was numb. Slowly, he eased his eyes open again.

He was in a room that he didn't recognize, lying on what must have been a luxurious bed before it had been caught in crossfire. Furniture was overturned and bullet holes covered the walls. Allied soldiers—mostly Free French Forces—were gathered around a radio in the corner of the room, smoking cigarettes and trying to listen to de Gaulle's speech. A few American soldiers stood among them. Jean-Luc recognized the French-speaking one who had helped pull him off Natasha's body. He was muttering in English to the other Americans—Jean-Luc assumed he was translating the speech.

Natasha.

The pain spread from Jean-Luc's face to his heart. Paris was free, but Natasha was not with him to celebrate. He had failed her, and his punishment was living without her.

". . . We have nothing else to want than to show ourselves, up to the end, worthy of France. Vive la France!"

The soldiers cheered and clapped along with the radio as de Gaulle finished his speech. Outside the broken window, Jean-Luc could hear the distant roar of hundreds of citizens. Silent tears slipped down his cheeks, some of pride, some of despair.

One of the soldiers turned and saw Jean-Luc lying with his eyes open, looking around the room. "He's awake," he said.

"You all right?" another asked. He had an armband with a red cross on it, marking him as an army medic.

"I told you, he's a crazy bastard," the French-speaking American soldier said. "Paris is lucky to have men like him." He held out an open cigarette case. "Smoke?"

"Don't give him that now. He just cut out his damn tongue," the medic said.

"From what those Resistance fellows told me, sounds like the man deserves a real smoke."

Jean-Luc shook his head. He tried to thank the soldier but only managed a strange moan—a moan that sent a dizzying wave of pain through his head. He saw spots.

"Easy there, friend," the medic said, handing Jean-Luc a cup of water. Jean-Luc drank with difficulty, spilling water everywhere. His mouth stung, and the metallic taste of blood slid down his throat with the water, but the dizziness subsided.

"Jean-Luc," said a voice from the doorway. "His name is Jean-Luc."

A French soldier walked in, followed by Monsieur LeMiel and a bandaged Monsieur Philippe.

Monsieur LeMiel looked at Jean-Luc and grunted, "All right there, my boy?"

Jean-Luc nodded.

"Is this your son?" the medic asked.

Monsieur LeMiel looked at the soldier, then back at Jean-Luc and smiled. "I'm not that lucky, Monsieur. He's a friend."

"We're going to get him over to the hospital as soon as we can. For now, he has to stay put."

Monsieur LeMiel sat on the edge of the bed. "These men told me about Natasha. I'm sorry, Jean-Luc."

Jean-Luc turned his head away.

Don't say her name.

"Your father was devastated when he lost your mother. But he had you to take care of, so he lived on—barely, but he lived on. Too many people have died already. Don't waste away like he did, dying slowly, while everyone he loved watched him go."

But I have no one. No father, no mother, no children—no one to leave behind, Jean-Luc thought.

"I remember when François Cordier died," Monsieur Philippe said. "I was only a boy then—maybe seven or eight. My mother and I went over to see Paulette every day. She had lost everything, including her unborn child. It took a week of coaxing before we could convince her to get out of bed."

He touched Jean-Luc's shoulder. "She would have wanted you to live on, Jean-Luc, making the best of every day."

Jean-Luc said nothing. He could not bring himself to meet Monsieur Philippe's or Monsieur LeMiel's eyes.

"When you get out of the hospital, stop by my house. I have something for you."

Without another word, Monsieur LeMiel and Monsieur Philippe left. The medic turned to Jean-Luc.

"You should get some more rest. You still have some morphine in you. When that wears off, I doubt you'll be able to sleep at all."

*   *   *

When Jean-Luc left the hospital days later, the tricolor flag was hanging from nearly every window. There were still ration lines every morning, but little by little, more food was available. There were rumors of meat being reintroduced into the Parisian diet—meager portions, but meat nonetheless. Jean-Luc could only imagine. Aside from having absolutely no appetite, he had difficulty eating without his tongue. He could barely stomach the broth the nurses had forced him to eat, clucking their tongues in a way that made him ache for Madame Cordier.

He dragged his feet to Monsieur LeMiel's apartment. He dared not return to his old studio; he had no desire to see whatever bloodstains remained on the floor.

Though far from back to normal, Paris was decidedly different. Jeeps rumbling by inspired waves and smiles. Rations were somehow less of an inconvenience, and the inability to speak French was easier to forgive. The barricades still stood, with flowers and letters placed against them to honor the men and women who had fallen in the fight to liberate the city, and the French flag was finally flying atop La Tour Eiffel.

Jean-Luc's pride was weighed down by loss. He wished he, too, had fallen at the barricade. Absently, he reached into his pocket to grip the nested dolls he had found in the Maximovs' ransacked apartment.

It took him twice as long as it should have to reach Monsieur LeMiel's apartment. The door opened almost immediately after he knocked, but it was not Monsieur LeMiel who answered.

"Jean-Luc!" Marie Lévy threw her arms around Jean-Luc's waist. "Babette says we don't have to go back into the crawl space anymore. Isn't that wonderful? Are you feeling better? Monsieur LeMiel said you were in the hospital. Did your tongue grow back?"

Despite himself, Jean-Luc smiled. He shook his head.

"Will it ever grow back?"

Jean-Luc shook his head again.

"Can I see?"

"Marie, don't pester him," came Claude's voice from behind her. "Come on in, Jean-Luc. It's a little crowded right now, but Babette has made some lunch."

Marie took Jean-Luc's hand and dragged him inside, leading him toward the tiny kitchen where Monsieur LeMiel sat at the table and Babette stood at the countertop, cutting up half a loaf of bread.

"Hello, Jean-Luc," she said as Marie led him in.

Monsieur LeMiel grunted and stood up to greet Jean-Luc. "You made it. Good. I have something for you—"

"Lunch first, Jacques. The poor boy must be starving," Babette said.

Jean-Luc had no desire to eat. He tried to gesture that he did not want anything, but Marie dragged him over to the table.

"Sit by me, Jean-Luc. Babette said I can have the place by the window."

Unable to refuse little Marie's beaming face, he took the chair next to her. It was a painfully slow process for him to eat solid food, so lunch dragged on. Babette tried to eat as slowly as possible, idly chatting about the remarkable change in everyone's attitude over the past few days.

"Everyone is just so much more pleasant. Rations are still tight, but people are so much less snippy when they're waiting in line. The Boches were wearing on everyone's patience."

Marie kept leaning toward the window, looking out into the world with a bright smile on her face. She waved to anyone who looked up as they passed by and asked at least six times if she could play outside after they finished eating. For the first five minutes, whenever Jean-Luc lifted food to his mouth, she stared at him intently, trying to catch a peek of his missing tongue.

"Marie, dearest, eat your lunch. Don't stare," Babette said.

Marie concentrated on her meal for all of ten seconds before she began stealing glances at Jean-Luc again. Jean-Luc paused, swallowed what he had in his mouth, turned to Marie, and opened his mouth.

"Ew!" Marie turned her head away.

"Jean-Luc!" Babette said.

Claude and Monsieur LeMiel snickered.

Claude, in contrast to his sister, tended to lean away from the window and flinched whenever anyone shifted their chair. If sunlight fell on his skin, he jerked his arm away, and every time Marie waved at people in the street, he'd hiss at her to stop.

Marie stuck her tongue out at him. "I'm going to wave to whomever I please. There are no Germans here to take me away."

"Marie, don't be rude," Babette said. "Claude, let her have her fun."

Jean-Luc could not suppress a smile. Marie grinned back at him, then went back to waving at people outside the window.

"Vive la France!" she shouted down to passersby. Claude paled and jumped. Voices echoed her words and she beamed. Jean-Luc had never been so impressed. Marie had lost so much—her parents, her home, four years of her life—and yet she embraced her tomorrows with a smile. The innocence in her eyes was gone, but it was replaced with hope. Jean-Luc could just imagine Madame Cordier pinching the little girl's cheeks and telling Jean-Luc to learn from her.

Children really do grow up too fast . . .

Monsieur LeMiel remained as silent as Jean-Luc. He, too, ate slowly, trying to match Jean-Luc's pace, but he was not successful. Jean-Luc finished eating long after everyone else.

"Well, now. Marie? Claude? Will you help me clear the table while Jacques and Jean-Luc have a little chat?" Babette said.

"Come on, my boy. You heard her." Monsieur LeMiel stood and motioned for Jean-Luc to follow him into the bedroom. Furniture had been moved around to make room for an easel—Jean-Luc's easel—to be set up near the window. Jean-Luc's brushes, palette, and tubes of paint were lying in a box beside the stool, and leaning against the window was Madame Cordier's silver tray.

"I went to your old studio and grabbed whatever I thought would be of use to you. Some of your clothes are in the top drawer of the dresser, as well as some of Babette's father's old things. You're welcome to sleep here on the floor for a few days . . . unless you want to go back to your studio."

Jean-Luc shook his head, keeping his eyes fixed on the tray.

"I thought as much. Stay until you get yourself back on your feet. But I'm warning you now, I won't let you drink yourself to death the way I let your father. He was my best friend, and I owe him that much."

Jean-Luc nodded. Tears were beginning to sting his eyes again.

Monsieur LeMiel cleared his throat. "Well, I'll just leave you to your thoughts." He left the room, closing the door behind him.

Jean-Luc walked over to the window and looked down through the glass at the people walking by. A group of men were marching women with shaved heads and swastikas painted on their foreheads down the street. People passing by jeered and spat on the collaborators. Some went so far as to tear bits of their clothing off. Jean-Luc looked away. There were trials and executions being held for all sorts of collaborators. Jean-Luc had mixed feelings about the whole mess. On the one hand, collaborators had helped the Nazis exploit Paris and her citizens. They had made it easy for the Boches. They had catered to them and welcomed them, instead of ignoring and alienating them. On the other hand, Jean-Luc thought of Natasha and her secret. He couldn't help but wonder who else had secrets they were trying to protect.

His eyes fell upon the easel. A blank canvas had been placed upon it—a gift from Monsieur LeMiel. Jean-Luc sat down on the stool and rummaged through the box of art supplies. Each paintbrush was like a long-forgotten friend. His world was so different now.

He stared at the blank canvas for a long while, thinking of Natasha and the life they would never know together. Tears dripped down his cheeks and fell onto his lap. He reached up to rub his face. There was a few days' worth of stubble, but Jean-Luc had no desire to shave. He had no desire to do anything.

He looked over at Madame Cordier's tray. Taking a deep breath, he mixed some colors, let his mind take a step away from his body, and began to paint.

CHAPTER 35

A HUNDRED RUMORS CIRCULATED throughout Saint Paul de Vence regarding the silent painter. Some said he had been a spy who had cut out his own tongue to ensure he would never talk if he were caught. Others said a German had cut it out for saying the wrong thing at the wrong time. The stories were endless. Jean-Luc was amused by them all.

He did well, selling his paintings to tourists and Frenchmen alike, though the prestige he had craved had taken a back burner to a calm and peaceful life. Paris brought too many memories to the surface too quickly, so after a year of mourning, he had left the city and moved to the Riviera to pick up the pieces of his life.

The village of Saint Paul de Vence had a quiet beauty, and Jean-Luc felt at peace the moment he set foot in his new studio. He had few visitors at first—most of the townspeople were a little wary of the man with no tongue and paint-stained clothes. He quickly became the one the children dared each other to approach, the one whose apartment windows they challenged each other to peek through.

Jean-Luc suspected that was how people discovered he had been in the Resistance. He kept the armband he had worn during the Liberation of Paris on display above a painting of his he had christened *Soldiers Around a Radio*.

From that point forward, he was invited to dinner. Young boys would gather around him as he painted outside, sometimes asking questions that he would only answer with an amused smile. It was almost a rite of passage to see Jean-Luc's missing tongue.

Jean-Luc sat at his easel just outside his apartment building. It was a pleasant April afternoon, the first truly warm day of spring. Children shouted greetings to him as they ran past, chasing each other and laughing. Jean-Luc smiled at them and waved, then returned to his painting.

A shadow fell across the canvas. Jean-Luc paused for a moment, then traced the outline of the shoulder and neck with a long, heavy brush-stroke.

The owner of the shadow laughed. "It's been too long, Jean-Luc."

Jean-Luc had not heard Miró's voice in six years, but he would have recognized it anywhere. He carefully placed his brush and palette down, and then stood up to embrace his mentor.

"Look at you," Miró said. "I hardly recognized you."

Jean-Luc rubbed his full beard in response. He could feel a little dried paint clumped on the hairs, and he knew he smelled like turpentine. His clothes were spotted all over with yellow—souvenir splotches from his last painting—and a fresh smear of red on his lap announced his current project.

"I heard a story," Miró said, "that you were caught by the Nazis and one of their collaborating women fell in love with you. Torn between her loyalty to the Germans and her love for you, she set you free but first cut your tongue out so you couldn't tell anyone who had helped you."

Jean-Luc laughed. He, too, had heard that tale.

"Will you ever tell the world what really happened?"

Jean-Luc only smiled.

Miró peered behind Jean-Luc to get a good look at the canvas propped up on the easel.

"What do you have in mind for this one?"

Jean-Luc glanced at his painting, then turned back to Miró. He smiled through pursed lips.

Miró laughed. "The mysterious silent painter, indeed."

Jean-Luc gestured toward his apartment and tilted his head, inviting Miró inside.

"Thank you," Miró said. Leaving his easel where it stood, Jean-Luc led the way.

The studio was spotless. Though Jean-Luc's clothing was covered in paint, not a drop littered the studio floor. The bed was neatly made, and all his art supplies were arranged in boxes on a table near a large window that led out to a small balcony. There was no mirror.

Several paintings were hung on the walls, all bearing Jean-Luc's signature. The armband of the Resistance hung above the bed. Madame Cordier's silver tray lay on the nightstand. Resting on it was a set of nested dolls, all taken out and set side-by-side. A Star of David on a thin gold chain was on display in front of them.

Against the wall opposite the bed, near the stove and the sink, were a smaller table and two chairs. Jean-Luc walked over to the stove and held up a percolator.

"Yes. Thank you."

While Jean-Luc brewed the coffee, Miró studied the paintings. Jean-Luc watched him from the corner of his eye, awaiting his reaction. The paintings told of torment and passion, but in each work, one little piece faded to softer tones—intentionally drawing attention, pulling an observer in. There, the painting gave off a sense of peace. In *Soldiers Around a Radio*, a halo of serenity hovered just above the radio, though none of the soldiers seemed to notice it.

Miró lifted his chin and cocked his head slightly back and to the right. He dropped his left shoulder and pursed his lips, examining the painting. Jean-Luc could not help but notice that the amount of wrinkles seemed to have doubled over the last six years.

Miró studied Jean-Luc's work until well after the coffee was ready. Jean-Luc set the cups on the table and waited, his heart thudding in his chest. Finally, Miró looked back at him.

"Well done."

Jean-Luc stood there for a moment, waiting for the usual stream of criticism, but Miró said nothing more. Jean-Luc glanced over at the nested dolls on his nightstand and smiled. As usual, the painted faces smiled back.

Miró followed his gaze.

"I heard about Natasha and Madame Cordier. I'm so sorry, Jean-Luc." Jean-Luc nodded and looked at the dolls again. He gestured to Miró to sit down and offered him milk and sugar with his coffee.

Jean-Luc brought out a slate and a piece of chalk to help him say what motions and looks could not, but it was hardly needed. Jean-Luc had long since perfected his gestures and now communicated well through his eyes.

Miró chatted about his family back in Spain, about artists he had met and heard of. He brought news, both good and bad, of their mutual friends and the old Rue Blomet Group. He talked of his completed *Constellations* and how happy he was with the results.

After nearly an hour of talking, the coffee long since finished, Miró suddenly stopped and laughed. "I think, Jean-Luc, this is the first time I have ever been able to speak for more than thirty seconds without being interrupted."

Jean-Luc smiled. The two friends were silent for a long while before Jean-Luc's eyes sparked and he leapt to his feet. He gestured toward the balcony and the chairs, then wrote on his slate: "Sunset. Be out in a moment."

"Making an old man move chairs by himself," Miró chided. Jean-Luc shrugged, then went over to the closet and rummaged through the shelves. When he joined Miró on the balcony, he presented a wine glass and displayed the bottle he was about to open: a 1902 Bordeaux.

"You have excellent taste in wine, Jean-Luc."

Jean-Luc smiled. He poured the wine and sat down with Miró to watch the brilliant sunset. The view from his balcony amazed him. Sunrise, sunset, afternoon, and late at night, it always inspired him and made him think of Natasha.

"Well," Miró said, "you will be happy to know that I received a call a few weeks ago. The paintings of mine that a certain German officer stole from my old studio have been discovered and have been returned to Paris. They are now on display at a gallery in Montparnasse. That is why I came to France. There is only one problem." Miró looked over at Jean-Luc. "I left no paintings in Paris. I had to correct the misunderstanding." He smiled. "The gallery now headlines the returned works of Jean-Luc Beauchamp. From what I understand, many paintings have been sold. I volunteered to notify you that they await your arrival in Paris. A visit, I think, would do some good."

Recognition. Being featured at a Parisian gallery. Natasha would have been so proud.

Miró raised his glass. "To you, Jean-Luc, and your art."

Jean-Luc tapped glasses with Miró.

To Natasha, he thought, and took a sip.

Jean-Luc and Miró sat in silence until well after the sun had set and the stars began to appear.

"They are beautiful, aren't they?" Miró said.

Jean-Luc nodded. As he looked up into the clear night sky, he could almost hear Madame Cordier's voice.

The ones we love who pass on are up there, in the stars, doing what they love best . . .

Jean-Luc smiled to himself, thinking that Monsieur Cordier could finally do what he loved best, now that his wife had joined him.

Natasha, too, was up there, waiting. Jean-Luc knew she wanted him to live a long and happy life, so for her, he would—but he would never love another. If he stared hard enough, he could almost see her, dancing and dressing her hair by the light of the stars, waiting for the day they would find each other again.